SF MASTERWORKS

Limbo

BERNARD WOLFE

Copyright © Bernard Wolfe 1952
Introduction copyright © Harlan Ellison® 2014
Introduction copyright © David Pringle 1985
All rights reserved

The right of Bernard Wolfe to be identified as the author of this work,
and Harlan Ellison and David Pringle to be identified as authors of the
introductions, has been asserted by them in accordance with the
Copyright, Designs and Patents Act 1988.

This edition first published in Great Britain in 2016
by Gollancz
An imprint of the Orion Publishing Group
Carmelite House, 50 Victoria Embankment, London EC4Y 0DZ
An Hachette UK Company

1 3 5 7 9 10 8 6 4 2

A CIP catalogue record for this book is available
from the British Library

ISBN 978 1 473 21247 3

Printed in Great Britain by
Clays Ltd, St Ives plc

MIX
Paper from
responsible sources
FSC
www.fsc.org
FSC® C104740

www.gollancz.co.uk
www.orionbooks.co.uk

To the Boss

'To my mind, Bernard Wolfe remains one of the most remarkable original writers of the 20th century'

Harlan Ellison®

'Shrewd, and sometimes profound, comments on Western civilisation'
Observer

'Deep, strange, and wonderful, *LIMBO* represents a straight arrow pointing from the cautionary dystopias of Orwell and Huxley to the postwar absurdist mode of *CATCH-22*, Pynchon, and Philip K. Dick'
Jonathan Lethem

'As to the books of Bernard Wolfe, his extraordinary imagination, his range of styles and genres, should alone qualify him for a conspicuous role in 20th century American literature'
Thomas Berger

CONTENTS

INTRODUCTION TO BERNARD WOLFE
by Harlan Ellison®

Here's how it began for you, how you came to realize Bernard Wolfe is one of the finest writers this country has ever produced, how you came to share the years with him.

In 1952, you were still in high school and very impressed with Salinger, Hemingway and Shirley Jackson, taking inordinate pride in having read *Moby-Dick* in its entirety, even the sections describing the riggings of the Pequod. Then, one day, quite by accident, while looking for a new book of science fiction you'd somehow missed in your voracious reading, you came across something called *Limbo* by someone named Bernard Wolfe. And you bought it, or borrowed it, or perhaps even shoplifted it, because even at that tender age you sensed the secret – books held it all – and reading books was more important than being well-liked or being able to shag flies in center field.

And you read it; and your reading was difficult because every once in a while you'd realize that you hadn't been breathing, that this Wolfe person was so good at what he was doing you had forgotten to take care of even the unconscious business of systole-diastole. And when you finished reading that big novel, you sat back and savored the heat this Wolfe had put into you. *Yes*, this was what reading was all about! You had to have more, had to have periodic transfusions from this man's supply of imagination.

One year earlier, 1951, just making a buck freelancing, Wolfe dipped merely a toe into the digest-sized-magazine (sf genre) with a remarkable novelette – "Self Portrait" in *Galaxy* magazine, and with rare good sense, foresight of literary "ghetto" imprisonment limitations (like Vonnegut, years later), scampered for dear life and a reputation in "the Mainstream."

Yet despite Wolfe's fleetness of foot, the rapid eye-movements of perceptive readers caught the slamming of the door, and having been dazzled by "Self Portrait" they began asking, "Who the hell was *that?*" They found out in 1952, when Wolfe's first novel, *Limbo*, was published by Random House; and for the first time insular fans who had been cringing with talented dilettantes such as Herman Wouk sliding into the genre to proffer insipid semi-sf works like *The Lomokome Papers*, now had a mainstream author of stature they could revere. Preceding by almost twenty years "straight writers" like Hersey, Drury, Ira Levin, Fowles, Knebel, Burdick, Henry Sutton, Michael Crichton and a host of others who've found riches in the sf/fantasy idiom, Bernard Wolfe had written a stunning, long novel of a future society in purest sf terms, so filled with original ideas and the wonders of extrapolation that not even the most snobbish sf fan could put it down.

They did not know that six years earlier, in 1946, Bernard Wolfe had done a brilliant "autobiography" with jazz great Mezz Mezzrow, called *Really the Blues*. Nor did they suspect that in the years to come he would write the definitive novel about Broadway after dark, *The Late Risers*, or a stylistically fresh and intellectually demanding novel about the assassination of Trotsky in Mexico, *The Great Prince Died*, or that he would become one of the finest practitioners of the long short story with his collections *Come On Out, Daddy* and *Move Up, Dress Up, Drink Up, Burn Up*. All they knew was that he had written one novel and one novelette in their little arena and he was sensational.

In point of fact, the things science fiction fans *never* knew about Bernard Wolfe would fill several volumes, considerably more interesting than many sf novels. Of all the wild and memorable human beings who've written something, *any*thing on which the "sf" label has been slapped, Bernard Wolfe is surely one of the most incredible. Every writer worth his pencil case can self-aggrandize on the dust jacket of a book that he's been a "short order cook, cab driver, tuna fisherman, day laborer, amateur photographer, wrestler, horse trainer, dynamometer operator" or any one of a thousand other nitwit jobs that indicate the writer couldn't hold a job very long.

But how many writers can boast that they were personal bodyguards of Leon Trotsky prior to his assassination (or prove how good they were at the job by the fact that it wasn't till they *left* the position that the killing took place)? How many have been Night City Editor of Paramount News-Fawcett Publications, specializing in technical and scientific reporting? How many have been editor of *Mechanix Illustrated*? How many appeared in *The American Mercury*, *Commentary*, *Les Temps Modernes* (the French existentialist journal whose first director was Jean-Paul Sartre), *Pageant*, *True*, *Esquire* and, with such alarming regularity, *Playboy*? How many have worked in collaboration with Tony Curtis and Hugh Hefner on a film named *Playboy* (and finally, after months of hassling and *tsuriss*, thrown it up as a bad idea, conceived by madmen, programmed to self-destruct, impossible to bring to rational fruition)? How many were actually Billy Rose's ghostwriter for his famous gossip column *Pitching Horseshoes*? How many writers faced the Depression by learning to write and composing (at one point with an assist from Henry Miller) eleven pornographic novels in eleven months (memorialized in his great semi-autobiographical novel *Confessions of a Not Altogether Shy Pornographer*)? How many have ever had the *San Francisco Chronicle* hysterically grope for a pigeonhole to clutch up some singular appellation of "Wolfe" in their own frustrated style and finally could helplessly only come up with "… Wolfe writes in a mixture of the styles of Joyce and Runyon …"?

Bernard Wolfe was not a "science fiction writer." I am not a "science fiction writer." We both have used the tropes of that genre to create memorable fiction. To my mind, Bernard Wolfe remains one of the most remarkable original writers of the 20th century.

Sherman Oaks, CA
December 2014

Excerpts of this Introduction originally appeared in *Again, Dangerous Visions*, edited by Harlan Ellison®, (Garden City, NY, Doubleday, 1972) Copyright © 1972 by Harlan Ellison®; renewed 2000 by Harlan Ellison®. All rights reserved. Excerpts of this Introduction originally appeared in the *Los Angeles Times* (September 23, 1974) Copyright © 1974 by Harlan Ellison®; renewed 2002 by Harlan Ellison®. Harlan Ellison® is a ® registered trademark of The Kilimanjaro Corporation. All rights reserved.

INTRODUCTION TO *LIMBO*
by David Pringle

If *Brave New World* and *Nineteen Eighty-Four* are the two great dystopian visions in modern British fiction, then Bernard Wolfe's *Limbo* has some claim to being their closest American equivalent. Yet, curiously, it has failed to exercise that claim, either in the popular imagination or in the literary-critical consensus. I think it is a masterpiece, although I must admit that it has been a sadly neglected one. Perhaps its central image—of a near-future society in which men cut off their own limbs to prevent themselves from waging war—is too disturbing, too crazed, to make for ready acceptance. It is easier to imagine us succumbing to the 'feelies' and *soma*, or indeed to the everlasting boot in the face, than it is to project ourselves into Wolfe's limbless, lobotomized world of 1990.

But what a grand cornucopia of a book *Limbo* is! It is big (413 pages in the Ace paperback edition), blackly humorous, and full of a passionate concern for the problems of its day—particularly the problems of war, institutionalized violence, and humanity's potential for self-destruction. It is a novel which goes gloriously over the top, replete with puns, philosophical asides, satire on the American way of life, comments on drugs and sex and nuclear war, doodles and typographical jokes, medical and psychoanalytical jargon—a veritable *Tristram Shandy* of the atom-bomb age. In an afterword the author pays tribute to Norbert Wiener, Max Weber, Dostoevsky, Freud and, surprisingly, the sf writer A.E. van Vogt. 'I am writing,' he continues, 'about the overtone and undertow of *now*—in the guise of 1990 because it would take decades for a year like 1950 to be milked of its implications.'

Bernard Wolfe (born 1915) earned a B.A. in psychology from Yale University, and for a short time he worked as a bodyguard to Leon

Trotsky in Mexico, though he was not present when Trotsky was eventually assassinated. His first book, *Really The Blues*, was about jazz music, and he went on to write a variety of novels and non-fiction works. Evidently a man of parts. Except for a few short stories, *Limbo* remains his only venture into science fiction, yet it gives ample proof that he understood the form better than most. 'The overtone and undertow of *now*' is precisely the subject matter of all the most serious sf.

The plot concerns the travels and travails of Dr Martine, a neurosurgeon who in the year 1972 fled from a limited nuclear war to the haven of a forgotten island in the Indian Ocean. He has spent eighteen years there, performing lobotomies on the more antisocial of the simple natives (this is a humane continuation of the natives' ancient practice of *mandunga*, or crude brain surgery). In 1990 Martine sets out to rediscover the world. He finds a partially destroyed North America in which the ideology of 'Immob' holds sway. In this grotesque post-bomb society men have their arms and legs removed and replaced with computerized prosthetics, in the belief that self-mutilation will prevent the recurrence of world war. It is a faulty equivalent of the islanders' *mandunga*, the lobotomy which cuts away aggressive urges. Martine is horrified to discover that much of the inspiration for 'Immob' comes from a diary which he himself wrote and lost in that fateful year of 1972. He is the unwitting prophet of this nightmarish state; his jokes of eighteen years ago have been taken all too seriously. In any case it has all been in vain, for things are falling apart and a new war is about to begin. The story ends with Martine fleeing to his peaceful island as the bombs fall once more on the cities of America. It sounds grim and fatalistic, but in fact the novel is enormously funny and invigorating, and in the end holds out a kind of hope. Rich with ideas, all-embracing in its references, it is a book which uses the science and psychology of 1950 to grapple with the largest issues of our century. It is time that *Limbo* was recognized for what it is: the most ambitious work of science fiction, and one of the most successful, ever to come out of America.

© David Pringle, 1985

Since all the characters in this book are real, any resemblance between them and imaginary persons is entirely accidental.

Raymond Queneau

ACKNOWLEDGEMENTS

The quotation on page 53 is from *Cybernetics*, by Norbert Weiner (The Technology Press and John Wiley & Sons Inc.), copyright 1948 by The Massachusetts Institute of Technology.

The quotation on page 104 is from *The Selected Writings of Henri Michaux*, published by New Directions. Translation by Richard Ellmann.

The quotations from Norbert Wiener on pp.187–190 are from *The Human Use of Human Beings* (Houghton Mifflin Co.), copyright 1950 by Norbert Weiner.

The quotation on pp. 188–189 from John McDonald is from *Strategy in Poker, Business and War* (W. W. Norton & Co.), copyright 1950 by John McDonald and Robert Osborne.

The chart on page 397 is from *The Battle of the Conscience*, by Edmund Bergler (Washington Institute of Medicine), copyright 1948 by Edmund Bergler.

The quotation on pp. 410–411 is from Thomas Mann's introduction to *The Short Novels of Dostoevsky*, copyright 1945 by The Dial Press.

. . . Verily I say unto you, Except ye be converted, and become as little children, ye shall not enter into the kingdom of heaven.

Whosoever therefore shall humble himself as this little child, the same is greatest in the kingdom of heaven . . .

Wherefore if thy hand or thy foot offend thee, cut them off, and cast them from thee: it is better for thee to enter into life halt or maimed, rather than having two hands or two feet to be cast into everlasting fire.

St Matthew, 18

Bah! Let's make all sorts of faces.

Rimbaud (who became as a little child,
and had his foot cut off, and died).

Part One

TAPIOCA ISLAND

chapter one

"Much prognosis today," the old man panted.
The climb up the mountain was hard for him, several
times he had to lean against the trunk of a raffia palm and
try to catch his breath. With each halt he went through the
same ritual of malaise. Removed from his head the green-
visored tennis cap (found in a well-preserved Dutch sporting-
goods shop in Johannesburg). Unwrapped from his emaciated
middle a delicately figured silk paisley scarf (from the intact
shelves of an excellent London haberdashery in Durban).
Mopped brow with loincloth. Then reached down to massage
his feet through the cricket sneakers (souvenir of the Cape
Town country club, rescued from a locker which had belonged to the last naval attaché stationed at the British
consulate there).

He knew he was not supposed to tax himself ("Without
much care," Dr. Martine had told him bluntly, "prognosis
unfavorable") but he would not take time out for a real rest,
much less turn back. From his knobby shoulders hung the
only native garment he could boast at the moment, a loose
chieftain's robe made of pounded bark and decorated with
neat alternating rows of stylized parakeets and cacao flowers;
he hitched it to his knees as he picked his way through
the brush, arthritic ballet.

The jungle was noisy today, fidgety as an insomniac (he
had been suffering from insomnia lately, Dr. Martine had

8

been treating him for it), fronds rasped against each other, trees creaked, mynah birds shrilled nasal obscenities at the sun, marmosets jibbered in falsetto. He disapproved of this order of sounds, they were symptomatic of hyperthyroidism, hypertension, hypertonus. He frowned upon such tension, in Nature as in himself. Better to be like the slow loris, heavy-lidded, tapioca-muscled. Lately, though, he had been very tense.

Each time he interrupted his climb toward the Mandunga Circle he looked down in the direction of the village. Silly, of course, there was no chance of his being followed. As for the villagers, nobody was allowed to approach the Circle except the troubled ones and those who had business with them; and as for strangers, well, none had been seen on the island in his lifetime. Ever. None except Dr. Martine. Still, he kept looking back over his shoulder.

His intelligent deep-amber face, shining with sweat under a thatch of crinkly white hair, was fixed in a scowl now, muscles coagulated in ridges—welts left by some whip of woe. It felt as though he were wearing some sort of mask, he was not used to worry or the crampings of worry and the knots around his mouth and in his forehead quivered. Insomnia, bunched-up muscles, tremors, worry—it almost looked, he thought, as if he had developed some of the signs of the troubled ones. Unpleasant notion. He wished he had a bowl of tapioca, it relaxed the bowels.

"Mandunji most mild people," he said half-aloud in English, remembering with irony a remark Dr. Martine had once made. "With us musculature rejects tonus like eye of owl rejects light. We sag very much, bristle never." Immediately he corrected himself: "*Are. The* musculature rejects tonus like *the* eye of *the* owl." It annoyed Dr. Martine to hear his language spoken without the silly, unnecessary words he called articles and verbs and so on.

A tarsier peered down at him from a branch and hiccupped dementedly.

A moment later, puffing hard, he had reached a small clearing on the crest of the mountain, bare except for a scattering of yuka and cassava plants. Memorable spot. Here was the center of the Mandunga Circle, here, eighteen and a half years ago, he had first set eyes on Dr. Martine. Looking down over the carpet of pinnate leaves thrown up by the raffias, he could see the saw-tooth cliffs on the perimeter of the island—island which by some miracle, Martine liked to say, had never been charted on any map by any cartographer—and the glinting waters of the Indian Ocean beyond. The sky was without a trace of cloud, a flawless impermeable blue—"as dazzling," Martine sometimes said of it, "as a baboon's ass."

It was on just such a day eighteen years ago, as the sun was heaving up over Sumatra and Borneo (Martine insisted there were such places to the east: called them the islands of Oceania), that the doctor had been tossed out of the sky onto the mountain top. What more ominous bundles was that cobalt vacuum preparing to sprinkle over the island today?

"Tomorrow sunny and continued warm," he said to himself, still in the doctor's language. "Prognosis for weather, anyway, favorable." Added, "*The* prognosis. For *the* weather. *Is.*"

Shading his eyes with a bony hand, he began to search the ocean for ships. It would be suicide, he knew, for mariners not familiar with these waters to attempt a landing anywhere on the island's coast because of the treacherous reefs and the razor-backed cliffs which jutted out into the surf. Nevertheless, he looked. Ships could carry planes. It was possible these days for strangers to come by air as well as by sea. Dr. Martine had come by air.

Was that a vessel he saw, that speck on the horizon beyond which lay Mauritius and Réunion and Madagascar (places he had glimpsed only from thirty thousand feet up, on scavenging trips in Martine's plane)? Out there in the direction of the forgotten trade routes which had once slashed this untonused old ocean? Way off to the west there, where if you traveled long enough you came at last to Africa, whose toppled cities were filled with fabulous paisley scarves and tennis caps, cummerbunds and opera hats and cricket sneakers, even crates of penicillin and electroencephalographs, and no people? The speck seemed to be moving, he could not be sure.

"No," the old man said. "Otherwise, Doctor, prognosis not favorable."

His features settled in a deeper frown, it felt like a hand grabbing his face. He re-entered the jungle to begin the descent on the far side of the summit, a galago dashed hysterically across the path.

In a few moments he reached the landmark, a tall column of scaly rock almost entirely overrun with creepers and ferns. Squatting in the thicket, he called out as loudly as he could, "Peace to all! Peace and long life. Open up, here is Ubu."

It was not English he spoke now but the throaty, resonant, richly voweled tongue of the Mandunji.

Facing him was a boulder which bulged out from the base of the rock, hidden from sight by a tangle of briers. It swung inward, briers and all. Stooping, Ubu stepped into the cavern.

"Peace to all," he repeated. His hands went up in the ceremonial greeting, fingers extended and palms up as though a tray were resting on them, to indicate that their owner came without weapons and therefore in friendship and good will.

"Peace, Ubu," the tall teak-complexioned young man at the gate answered sleepily. He yawned, a cosmic gape. Then he remembered the rest of the salutation and awkwardly stuck his hands out in turn. They were not empty; in one was a brush dripping red berry juice and in the other a sheet of pounded bark partially covered with rows of painted mynah birds and manioc plants. Apparently he had been working on this decorative drawing when Ubu arrived. "I . . . do not mean . . . to offend," he said slowly, searching for the words. It was dawning on him, Ubu could see, that he had committed a serious breach of etiquette by not emptying his hands before holding them out. "My thought is far away . . . I was making a design and. . . ."

Ubu smiled and patted him on the shoulder. At the same time he leaned forward to examine the scar on the young man's shaved head, a ribbon of pink tissue which ran in an unwavering line from the forehead past both ears to the nape of the neck. It was the welt that was always made when the dome of a troubled one's skull was sliced off with a Mandunga saw and then neatly pasted back in place.

"It heals nicely," Ubu said, pointing to the scar.

"It has stopped itching," the boy said.

"No more trouble there?"

The boy looked puzzled. "I do not remember the trouble people speak of," he said. "Dr. Martine says I used to fight much . . . and there was much tonus in my muscles . . . I do not remember. Mostly I like to sit and draw birds and trees. I want to sleep all the time."

"You are much improved, Notoa. I noticed just now that when you said, 'Peace' it was not just a thing to say, you meant it. The reports I hear from Dr. Martine are very good."

"People say I used to fight," Notoa said, looking down at the floor. "When I hear about it I feel ashamed. I do not know what used to make me hit my relatives."

11

"You were troubled."

Notoa regarded his hands with wonder. "It is very hard now even to make a fist, when I try it is a great effort and it does not feel right. Dr. Martine says the electric charge in my tensor muscles is down many points, he showed me on the measuring machine. Most of the time I am very sleepy."

"Only the troubled are afraid of sleep." Ubu patted the youngster again. "Speaking of Dr. Martine, where is he?"

Notoa yawned again. "In surgery. Moaga was brought this afternoon."

"Yes, I forgot." Ubu nodded and started down the corridor. Notoa swung the slab of rock to, and abruptly the rustling, crackling, croaking, twittering, twanging, twitching, ranting, jeering sounds of the jungle were cut off. In the sudden hush Ubu became aware of the throttled hum from the fans Dr. Martine had installed in camouflaged shafts overhead to pump a steady flow of fresh, filtered, dehumidified and aseptic air into the great underground hollow. The doctor liked to put his motors everywhere: on fishing boats, on the chisels and adzes used in hollowing out logs to make canoes, on stones for grinding maize, even on the saws for cutting skulls off. Such machines were not necessary, of course, they only took a man away from his natural work and made his mind and hands idle. One thing only was bad about this mechanization, it upset the routine. Because there were so many machines to do the work the young men now had much time to talk and study with the doctor and the old habits of work began to slip. The old habits made for a great steadiness, a looking in one fixed direction along a straight line. . . .

As he passed the row of cubicles, Ubu peered through the oneway glass on each door at the patient inside. Most of these Mandungabas were recent operatees, with tentlike bandages still on their heads, but some of them had had their dressings removed and were beginning to sprout new crops of hair over their scars. Ubu studied their faces as he went along, looking for signs of the tautness which had been a chronic torment for all of them before Mandunga. He knew what to watch for: narrowed eyes, tight rigid lips, corrugated foreheads, a hunched stiffness in the shoulder muscles—flexings of those who live in a world of perpetual feints and pounces.

No, there was no telltale strain in these once troubled people. If anything, their features and bodies seemed to have relaxed to the point of falling apart: heads lolling, mouths

12

loose and hanging open, arms and legs flung like sacks of maize on the pallets. Well, a sleepy man does not break his uncle's nose.

Beyond the cubicles was the large animal-experimentation chamber in which the tarsiers, marmosets, pottos, lemurs and chimpanzees huddled listlessly in their cages, most of them also wearing head bandages; beyond that, the laboratory in which most of the doctor's encephalographs and other power-driven apparatus were kept; and finally, in the farthest corner of the hollow, the operating room. The window in this door was of ordinary two-way glass, Ubu could see that Dr. Martine was just slicing through the last portion of Moaga's cranium with his automatic rotary saw.

What a sick one was this poor Moaga, Moaga the troublemaker, the sullen, the never-speaking, the vilifier of neighbors and husband-slasher. The riot had been drained from her body now, she lay stretched out on the operating table like a mound of tapioca (it would be nice to have some now), so completely anesthetized by rotabunga (would be nice to have some of that too) that although her eyes were wide open they could see nothing. She was naked and Ubu could see the tangle of wires that led from her arms, her legs, her chest, her eyelids, from all the orifices of her bronze body, to the measuring machines scattered around the room. He knew that in a few minutes, when Mandunga took place, the indicating needles on those machines would sink from the level of distress to the level of ease and Moaga's sickness would be over, she would stay away from ganja ("marijuana," in the doctor's peculiar language) and eat more tapioca, take more rotabunga. Done with electric trepans and chrome-steel scalpels and sutures, or with an old-fashioned chisel driven by an old-fashioned rock, the result was always the same magic: the troubled one came out of it no longer troubled, only a little sleepy. When, of course, he did not die. It was true, fewer patients died since the doctor had introduced trepans and asepsis and anatomy and penicillin.

Dr. Martine inserted a thin metal instrument into the incision and pried; in a moment the skull gave and began to come away. An assistant was standing by with gloved hands held out, in spite of the surgical mask Ubu recognized him as Martine's son Rambo. The boy took the bony cup, holding it like a bowl in the ritual of the tapioca feast, and immediately submerged it in a large tray containing the usual saline bath.

13

Despite the dozens of times Ubu had watched this ceremony, despite the hundreds of times he had performed it
(at least the ancient rock-and-chisel version of it) himself in
the old days, before Martine, he still felt a certain thrill at
the sight of the brain's crumpled convolutions—"those intellectual intestines, that hive of anarchy," the doctor called
them.

Suddenly Ubu thought of the black dot he had seen on
the horizon: had it really been moving? Involuntarily his
shoulders hunched and he sucked his lips in until they were
thin and bloodless.

"You are lucky, Moaga," he said, reverting to English.
"Soon no more worries, prognosis good. But for some worries, no scalpel, prognosis very bad. . . ." This time he did
not add the articles and verbs and so on.

chapter two

PULSE NORMAL, respiration normal: the rubber bladders
through which she breathed clenched and unclenched in
perfect rhythm, two pneumatic fists. Rambo trundled a large
Monel metal cabinet over to the table, through its glass
front a bank of electronic tubes glowed. Everything was in
order.

From the machine, which contained an array of slender
steel probes attached by coiled wires to the electronic circuits within, Martine selected a needle and brought it close
to the exposed brain. He applied the point carefully to an
area on the cortex, signaled his readiness with a nod, Rambo
twisted one of the control dials on the machine's operating
panel. Moaga's left leg shot up and twitched in an absent-
minded entrechat. Another contact made the shoulders
writhe, another doubled the hands into fists and sent them
paddling in the air, a fourth set the teeth to grinding.

Now the doctor began the multiple stimulation tests, applying four, then six, then eight and ten needles simultaneously to various cortical centers; with the final flow of current
Moaga's face grew contorted, its muscles worked in spasms
and her abdomen arched away from the table and began to
heave. In spite of himself Martine felt his own abdominal
muscles contracting, he always had this sympathetic response
to the mock intercourse induced by a few expertly distributed
amperes. "I got rhythm," he said to himself.

He looked around the chamber. All his assistants were at

their posts, watching their measuring dials and recording at each stage Moaga's variations in temperature, muscle tonus, skin moisture, blood pressure, pulse rate, intestinal peristalsis, pupil dilation and eyelid blinking, lacrimation, vaginal contractions. Measure for measure. A measure operation. "Measure's in the cold, cold ground," he said under his mask. He was annoyed with himself for indulging in such nonsense but he knew he couldn't stop it, luckily he was light of hand, sly of hand, sleight of hand, his fingers were so agile and dedicated that they did their job even under an avalanche of bad jokes from their massa in the cold cold groan.

Rambo wheeled away the machine and brought up a table, on it was a row of hypodermic needles filled with liquid. Strychnine. The next step was neuronography, strychniniza-tion, the firing of certain key areas of the cerebrum with this potent excitant in order to trace the pathways from the brain's jellied rind to the hidden cerebellum, the thalamus, the hypothalamus. He made the injections expertly—but tensely: he was always tense with hypodermic needles—while his assistants jotted their scrupulous notations about the pursing of the lips, the fluttering in the cloaca, the squirmings of the pelvis.

While the strychnine bulleted through the brain's maze and the indicators jumped, he looked down at Moaga's face, down into the wide-open eyes which saw little and said much. Babbling eyes, ranting eyes. As always, the rotabunga drugs had induced a completely comatose state in which the eyes remained open; for almost nineteen years he had been performing Mandunga here in the cave and never once had he been able to turn his attention entirely from those open soapboxing eyes. What was it he always thought he saw in them? Icy accusation, glaciers of accusation.

Once the routine experiments were out of the way it did not take long for the actual surgery. First he put in place the fine surgical threads which marked the upstart areas on the patient's frontal lobes, then he speedily made incisions along them and added several deft undercuts with the scalpel to free the spongy masses at the desired depth, then he removed these masses with a suction cup and quickly tied off the blood vessels. He reached down into Moaga's throat and made her cough: no leakage from the sliced veins, everything in order.

Rambo returned with the Monel cabinet. The ten electric needles were applied to the same spots as before: the

15

woman's pelvic area remained inert, the vaginal indicators did not move. While Martine doused the exposed area with penicillin Rambo brought the skull and very soon it was back in place, the flaps of skin knitted together with stitches and silver clips.

Martine nodded and stepped back, beginning to strip off his rubber gloves. "Done it again," he said to himself. "Goddamned Siamese twins. I've cut out the aggression, I've cut out the orgasm, can't seem to separate the two. Sorry, Moaga. The pig-sticker did his best."

Masseur in the cold cold groin. . . .

Martine looked up at the door and saw Ubu's face through the window. His eyes widened with pleasure, then hardened. He yanked his mask off and came out looking angry.

"Peace to—" Ubu began, in English.

"What the hell are you doing here?"

"I bring news."

"Couldn't it have waited?"

"No. We must have talk together."

"Well. . . . What's it all about?"

"Another fishing boat. The men went as far as Cargados Island, they were following a big school of swordfish. They bring a bad report."

"The queer-limbs again?"

"Yes, the queer-limbs. Yes, forty, fifty. And a large ship, most peculiar shape."

"They were white?"

"White like the others, speak English like the others. They called to the fishermen but our boys pretended they did not understand and went away."

Martine raised his hand and rubbed his eyes wearily. He thought: I know why he's telling me this in English. This is the most terrifying thing that's ever happened to him, he's got to push it away from him, by talking about it in a remote language he hopes to make the whole thing remote. He always switches to English when we talk about orgasm, too.

"So," Martine said. "This makes the seventh time they've been seen in, let's see, five weeks or so. Each time they come a little closer."

"More news," Ubu said. "Over an hour ago I stopped at the clearing and looked out at the sea. I am not all sure but I thought I saw something moving far away to the west, where the water ends."

16

"Sounds to me as though they've got some base of operations around the Mozambique waters. They seem to be covering the whole area pretty systematically, they're obviously looking for something, Christ knows what."

"Maybe—for you?"

Martine stared at the chief in astonishment. "That's crazy, old man, in over eighteen years they've forgotten all about me."

The door of the operating room swung open and Rambo came out, wheeling Moaga. Ubu watched as the bed rolled down the corridor, then he said hesitantly, "You think of something to do?"

Martine laughed; these gentle people were good for everything but crisis. Then he put his arm around his friend's shoulders and began to walk with him down the corridor. "Not exactly, but I'm not going to go up to them with my hands held out and say, 'Peace to all.' A guy can get himself very dead that way."

"You suggest we hide then?"

"No good, they'd find the village and know we were around somewhere. We've got to face them, I guess, but it's not easy to work out a way of dealing with them. All we know so far is that these people, creatures, monsters, whatever they are, are exactly like us—except that where their arms and legs ought to be they've got tubular appliances that you can see through and that flicker as though they were filled with fireflies. And they speak English, American."

"That bothers you?"

"As much as anything," Martine admitted. For eighteen and a half years, he had to confess to himself, he hadn't thought too much about his home and the people there, hadn't even been much concerned to know whether there *were* any people left there. He'd had so little interest in the past that when his plane cracked up he'd saved all the machinery and surgical equipment and energy capsules but hadn't hesitated to destroy the radio and video. "I wish," he said, "I'd kept the short-wave radio from my plane."

"You are good with machines," Ubu suggested. "Perhaps you could build such a radio."

Martine laughed again, shaking his head. "It's a little late for that," he said. He reached out and squeezed Ubu's arm affectionately. "That's the trouble with you, dear Ubu, with all the Mandunji—you've become such congenital pacifists that when a threat finally does show up, your

17

minds just go blank. One pugnacious bum with a slingshot could take over the village and dispose of the lot of you."

It was perfectly true: six hundred years of doggedly good will had left these people without any will at all, you just had to say boo and they all but fell to the ground in a hebephrenic huddle. The village had been in a state of frozen panic for weeks, Ubu hadn't been able to sleep, his whole metabolism was on the blink.

"Do not make fun," Ubu said. "I have a great worry."

"Calm yourself, old man. There is nothing to be done."

"I have a worry not only for the village. Since these queer-limbs came, I have stayed awake many nights thinking—he will go, the doctor will go."

"Suppose that happened?" Martine said. "Would it be such a calamity?"

"You must not leave us."

"Nonsense." Martine took Ubu's arm and steered him over to the row of cubicles which housed the convalescents. "These Mandungabas," he said, "used to be pretty scrappy characters. They spent a lot of time in hiding, making themselves spears and bolos and stilettos and poison darts that are forbidden by village law. They refused their doses of rotabunga and smoked ganja and went into trance and raided their neighbors' yam gardens at night. They made effigies of their mothers-in-law and other people they didn't like and stuck pins in them, a form of magic which is strictly taboo. They had a terrible thirst to be different from the others, to stand out, to be raised above the mass, while our normal citizens are so leery of distinguishing themselves in any way they have to be brow-beaten into taking any kind of office, including your own. They poured so much aggressive energy into their sexuality that their mates were often seriously maimed and disfigured, sometimes even killed. All in all, a pretty edgy, stand-offish and blood-thirsty lot. Well, it certainly looks as though they've become very meek and mild citizens—except for the ones who have relapses or develop other infirmities, you and the elders don't like to think about *them*. So I guess you'd say they're improved."

"Prognosis good," Ubu said happily. "Is."

"From the point of view of the village, sure. But how does it look from the point of view of the man? Prognosis one big yawn."

"A man," Ubu said, "is well to the extent that his village is well."

18

"A moot point. Come on in here for a minute." He led the way into one of the cubicles. There was no one on the pallet. "This is Notoa's room," he explained. "Before he was assigned for Mandunga, you remember, he gave his wife quite a thrashing—her eyes were black for days after. But he seemed to love his wife as passionately as he hated her, made love to her much more often and for much longer periods of time than our more normal men do with their wives. Well, Notoa doesn't want to beat his wife any more, that's true, but he doesn't want to caress her either, he's bored with her. When she came to visit him yesterday she obediently lay down on his pallet so that he could take his pleasure of her but he simply ignored her, sat in a corner munching on his nails and drawing parakeets and dozing off from time to time."

"Love which is tabooed by the village," Ubu said, "cannot be enjoyed. True love is gentle and with much quiet and no tonus, not wild."

"When I cut out the aggression much of the sexuality goes too, they're Siamese twins. Maybe love is only for the wild."

"Those who enjoy such love are sick."

"Tell that to Notoa's wife," Martine said. He remembered his last conversation with the woman: she hadn't had an orgasm since Notoa's operation, she was scared out of her wits that she might *never* be satisfied any more, she knew that often happened to the wives of Mandungabas. "She's getting very tense."

"Then she is sick also. Perhaps Mandunga—"

"Absolutely not!"

Ubu was disturbed by the doctor's sudden forcefulness. "Dear friend, is there something wrong?"

"We've had this out before. So long as a woman is not an active physical danger to anybody I will not attack her orgasm with a knife, even if you think its's worse than an epileptic fit."

"It is a sickness," the old man said stubbornly. "We have many normal women in our village. Why do they not have this wildness?"

"For a very good reason—because you define a normal woman as one who does *not* have this wildness. It's a joke, Ubu. Do you know why we always speak of these matters in my language, English? I'll tell you why, it's because you have no words for such things in Mandunji. Oh, I know, I know, for you this orgasm business, especially in a woman, is a collapse, a pathological letting-go, the same thing has been believed by many tribes. But I have told you over and over that it is a sickness only if the community *says* it is a sickness. In the West, where I came from, it was something that everybody wanted and was encouraged to want, even women. Perhaps one woman out of ten fully achieved it and perhaps only four men out of ten, but the sickness was *not* to have it. According to the doctors, anyway, the better doctors. The priests were a little mixed up about the subject."

"It cannot be a good thing," Ubu said. "The women who work to have it build up too much tension."

"Orgasm is the body's best way of discharging its tension. Maybe a seesaw is better than a coffin. But look, I'd forgotten what I wanted to show you. . . ."

In the corner was a stack of sheets of pounded bark, and nearby several pieces of statuary carved out of mahogany. Martine picked up the sheets and held them out, one by one, for the old man to see.

"Ah!" Ubu's face lit up. "Notoa is making many pretty things. Good! Very good!"

"Not so good," Martine said. "Look at them."

"I see, I see. The boy always had much talent, but before he drew nightmares and daydreams and visions and such troubled things from inside, he lived too much inside himself. Your scalpel has given Notoa back to his people!"

"Sure. But maybe I've taken him away from himself."

"A man only finds himself when he belongs to his village."

"Notoa has found nothing," Martine said emphatically. "He's only gone to sleep. Look: who else in the village would have the plain inventive audacity to carve a man with a canoe for a nose—cassava leaves sprouting from his ears— the fanged head of a cobra springing out where the genitals should be—malevolent lynx eyes bulging from each finger in place of the usual nails! Notoa made such a statue, I have it in my hut. Now look at the trash he's turning out—rows of cute little symmetrical raffia trees, all combed and curried, well-groomed parakeets flying about, one in each corner, and stupid manicured rays of gold pouring from a stupid manicured orange slice of a sun! No, Ubu. Notoa the man has been excommunicated, thanks to my scalpel. In his place, wielding the artist's tools, is—the village. Notoa's changed from a madman into a spokesman, and Notoa the Spokesman turns out only vast sunny mediocrities, all symmetry and slop. This stuff is, balls, insipid."

"You are saying strange things," Ubu said patiently. "Now

that he expresses himself as other artists do, the whole village can understand and take joy in his work. It is a cure."

"Listen to me," Martine said. "If you tell me, better that the social life should be good and peaceful than that the individual devil be nourished, I'll readily agree—granted there has to be a choice. But first, let's make sure the village *is* really happy, not just drugged. And don't, for heaven's sake, don't pretend to me that the pretty-pretty paintings and statues that come out of people who see through the eyes of the village instead of their own unique bedeviled ones are automatically, ipso facto, good."

"If there are no more people with a taste for disease," Ubu said softly, "then will disease have any, uh, what you call esthetic value?"

"Fortunately," Martine said, "that situation will never come about. The meekest, most self-effacing people will always, from time to time, spew up wild-eyed self-assertive individuals with riot in their souls. And these deviants will always make up an amuck fringe-world ringing you subdued ones in. Which is probably a good thing for the normal ones, Ubu. The sleepwalkers should occasionally hear a spine-chilling bellow from the blowtops on the outskirts, just to keep them from falling asleep entirely. If disease isn't an esthetic good of and by itself, neither is stupor."

"Mandunga will in the end do away with this fringe. All will be quiet."

"That's what I'm afraid of. It drains off the most vital blood from the much-needed lunatic fringe. That's the reason I've always insisted, all these years, that I wouldn't operate on anybody, no matter how off-center he was, unless he had definitely, *physically,* harmed another person or tried to."

"Always, when you talk this way, I think to myself—he must come from a place of much tonus."

"That's very true," Martine said. "My people couldn't sit still, that was always their trouble."

He went to the door, opened it, and motioned to Ubu to follow him.

"All right!" he said. "For the sake of the village: no more bolos, broken ribs, black eyes, pins in effigies, tonus, bohemians, or cobras where the genitals should be. But seriously, we're in bad trouble, we must have some sort of plan. Let's go to my office and talk. . . ."

They passed through the animal lab; marmosets and spider

monkeys, pottos and slow lorises raised their bandaged heads and regarded the two men with indifference. At the far end of the room they passed through an archway and entered Martine's office-library. They sat down on matted-straw chairs.

Martine waved his hand at the bound volumes which lined the walls, hundreds of them, the case histories and experimental records accumulated in eighteen and a half years of Mandunga. "If the queer-limbs come," he said, "they must not get their hands on all this. Whether they come as friends or as enemies."

"What bad could they do with it?"

"Such knowledge can be misused, it's happened before."

"You have something to propose?"

"If you had asked me that earlier," Martine said seriously, "I would have proposed something very concrete. Instead of destroying the contraband spears and poison darts and bolos made by the troubled ones, cache them away and keep them sharp. And instead of cutting the bloodthirstiness out of the troubled ones, keep them in fighting trim."

"Ah," Ubu said, shaking his head, "you are making fun again."

"Not at all. Obviously, these violent ones are the only Mandunji ready to fight for the village. That lunatic fringe might have made a first-rate rampart. . . ."

"This is not meeting the problem."

"Right," Martine said gloomily. "But mumbling peace-to-all and holding empty hands out isn't meeting it either." He sat up in his chair and waved his index finger at the chief. "Look here," he said, "suppose we took all those hacked-up monkeys out there and set them loose in the jungle? Why, their unlobotomized brethren, who still have the pathways of lust and attack open in their corticalthalamic areas, would tear them to ribbons in a minute. . . . Hell, I don't know what to propose, really. . . ."

They sat without talking, the old man with a look of bewilderment on his face, the doctor stroking his chin and staring at the volumes in his bookshelves.

Sound of running in the corridor; a young villager burst into the room panting and covered with sweat. His hands were trembling as they went out in greeting. "The elders sent me," he said, in between shuddering breaths. "The queer-limbs, the glass-limbs have landed!"

"Not glass," Martine said irritably. "I've told you over and over. Plastic, probably. Some kind of plastic."

22

Ubu stood up, pulling his robe around him. "How did it happen?"

"A ship came near the shore," the boy said. "Then from the ship a second ship, a smaller one, rose up in the air with wings flying around and around very fast and floated over the village."

"Helicopter," Martine muttered.

"Then it went back to the large ship and picked up many men and brought them in to land at a clearing. All men with funny arms and legs. Now they are cutting their way through the jungle with flames and saws."

Martine sighed and rose to his feet. "All right," he said. "If they mean us harm we can do nothing, but if they don't then we must play a game."

"A game?" Ubu was puzzled.

"Yes. First, these strangers mustn't find out that so many of the villagers know English. Only a few, including you, Ubu, must let on that they know the language. You be spokesman, you like the role. You can easily explain how you know the language by saying that long before the war—the *third* war, in case there've been others since then—you were over on the African mainland, say in Johannesburg, as a student."

"What shall I say?"

"Tell them nothing about the village, nothing. And try to find out everything you can about why they've come here. Oh, and one other thing—" Here Martine hesitated, made a face.

"Tell me," Ubu said eagerly.

"If it seems in order, try tactfully to inquire about their arms and legs. Ah—no, on second thought, maybe you'd better not. I've got a feeling. . . . Maybe you'd better skip the whole thing."

"What will you be doing, Martine?"

"I'll be hiding in my hut. Under no circumstances breathe a word about a white man living in the village."

"Yes," said Ubu. "Anything else?"

"All the Mandungabas must be kept out of sight. If it does happen that these men notice the Mandunga marks on somebody, explain them this way: say they are harmless decorations, like tattoos. You know what a tattoo is, you've seen the one on my arm."

"Let us pray it works."

"Yes," Martine said as they walked down the corridor to

the entrance. "And if it doesn't let's regret all those lunatics we whittled into pacifists. A little spare tonus might come in handy in the next hour or so."

chapter three

THE FIRST ones came by land. Deep in the jungle there was a low woosh and rumble like the surge of surf far away, strangled bassoons, it grew louder and soon there was added to it a soprano effect, shrill metallic yelps such as might be made by steel teeth eating into bark and wood pulp. Wisps of smoke began to curl out of the foliage; the villagers stood motionless around the maize grinder, watching.

The smoke grew denser, billowing black clouds spurted from the trees. Suddenly a ten-foot-wide wall of fire appeared on the edge of the jungle, the villagers sighed in terror, trees were crashing and bushes and vines went up in puffs of intense white flame. In a moment, as though by the flick of a switch, the sheet of fire was gone and behind it everyone could see that a ten-foot tunnel had been blasted open in the vegetation.

In the pathway stood the strangers.

Martine lay on the wooden floor of his haphazard attic, Ooda beside him. Through a slit in the thatching he studied the first white men he had seen in over eighteen years. It was true, it was all true. They were wearing shorts and T-shirts with large blue "M's" on their fronts, their limbs were exposed. Instead of arms and legs they had transparent extensions whose smooth surfaces shone in the sun. Each of these limbs was a tangle of metallic rods and coils, scattered all through each one were tiny bulbs which lit up and faded as the limb moved, sending off spatters of icy blue light. The strangers advanced a short distance into the open, arms and legs flashing as though, yes, as though they contained swarms of fireflies. And now something else: with each movement a very faint staccato sequence of clicks and clacks, an almost inaudible susurring, as of twigs snapping.

All of these men had four artificial limbs, always four, but the ones in front, the ones who had cleared the path through the jungle, were wearing specialized instruments in place of their right arms. Some had what looked like flame-throwers, long tubes terminating in funnel-shaped nozzles which were still smoking, a moment ago they had been spitting out fifty-foot tongues of fire (the bassoons); others

24

had long many-jointed claws on the ends of which were mounted high-speed rotary saws (the sopranos). Some twenty of these men emerged from the thicket. When they stopped, those in the lead pulled the tools from their arm stumps, picked up regular plastic arms which were hanging from their belts and snapped them into place in the empty sockets.

They stood in a group, surveying the village and the natives assembled in dead silence behind Ubu. They made no further move. Except for the blasting and cutting tools now dangling from their waists they seemed to have nothing even remotely resembling a weapon with them. They talked quietly among themselves, looking up to the sky from time to time as though expecting something there.

In a few seconds another group, aerialists, came into sight some forty or fifty feet over the tops of the raffia trees. Each was self-propelled: two counter-rotating rotors attached to an elongated right arm made each man a human helicopter.

The airborne ones landed as a unit and quickly substituted regular arms for the helicopter ones. Then they closed ranks with the others and the whole group began to move toward the center of the village where Ubu stood waiting, the elders arranged in an anxious half-moon behind him. The strangers walked with the ease and assurance of normal men, even more, even a little cockily, their legs taking firm, brisk steps and their arms swinging gracefully at their sides. At the head of the party strode a well-built, good-looking man in his late thirties, close-cropped moustache, rather taller than the others and with an indefinable air of authority about him. The face under his crew-cut blond hair was firm and powerful in spite of its ruddy youthfulness, there was strength in it, but he was smiling now.

"Oh, bad," Ooda whispered. "Bad, bad, bad."

"Shhh," Martine said, squinting to get a clearer look at the leader's face. "Be patient, monkey. Maybe it's not as bad as you think."

"They are all like you, Martine. Only for the arms and legs."

"That's a big only."

That handsome, genial, youngish face interested him. In fact, the whole shape of the head interested him. The skull was impressively broad, that was one thing. "Brachycephalic," he whispered. His free hand automatically curled, as though taking hold of something.

The big man came to a halt several feet from Ubu, flanked by two of his comrades; the others remained tactfully behind him. At a nod from the leader his two companions turned to Ubu.

"Wamba domuji kuana ashatu?" one said.

Ubu's eyes opened wide, he said nothing.

"Bwa zamzam, bwa riri?" the second man said.

Ubu was still silent.

"Try again," the leader said in English. "Maybe you'll hit on something."

"Fakshi tumpar, oo ah?" the first man said.

Through his terror Ubu finally got the point: these men were not simply making peculiar noises, they were translators. He understood what he had to do and raised his hands in the palms-up gesture. "Peace to all," he said in English. "Long life. May *the* war stay on *the* other side of *the* river." He felt it was only polite that on such an occasion he should use the full greeting rather than one of its abbreviated forms.

The leader was startled. "I'll be damned," he said. "No. Don't tell me you speak English?"

"Oh, yes," Ubu said. It made him feel good to be able to please the stranger. "I have studied English, I know many words. Prognosis, electronic, bohemian, cobra, rampart."

Now he remembered that he was supposed to explain his knowledge of English and he hurried on to tell the story: Johannesburg, school, long time ago, and so on.

"That's interesting," the stranger said. He held out his hands as he had seen Ubu do. "Peace," he said. "My name is Theo."

"Mine Ubu. Is."

"I'm very glad to know you, Mr. Ubu." The stranger was studying the old man's face, politely but with interest. "Tell me, Mr. Ubu, are your people in any way related to a tribe called the Bantus? There's something in your faces. . . . Your island isn't indicated on any of our maps, we haven't been able to find a reference to it anywhere."

"There is some of Bantu in us. Likewise Malay. Likewise Arab. Many things. We are the Mandunji."

"Mandunji? That's a new one on me."

"Few people on the outside know of us, we make no trouble."

"Where did you get your name?"

"Easy to explain. In our language *Mandunji* means literally, *those whose heads are without devils.* You see, we have also a word *Mandunga,* it is a verb meaning *to chase the devils from the head,* it refers to some of our old ceremonies, our name comes from the same root. Among us

26

there are also some people called *Mandungabas,* this means *those from whose heads the devils have been chased.* However." The thought occurred to him that he might be talking too much, he felt Martine's eyes on him. "To make a free translation, perhaps in English one would say *Mandunji* means simply *the sane ones, the normal.* Among us it is considered a very good idea to be normal, we have a great respect for it."

"Fascinating, fascinating," Theo said enthusiastically. "My people too have great respect for the normal, and they also hope that war will stay on the other side of the river, all rivers. We have a lot in common."

"Your people?" Ubu said courteously. "By what name are they known?"

"We are Inland Strippers. We come from a place called the Inland Strip."

"It is a big island?"

Theo laughed, not at all offensively. "Big as hell," he said. "Used to be called America. You've heard of it?"

"Oh, indeed. Many times, when I attended school."

"Well, the Inland Strip is the only part of America that's inhabited now. You see, there are many fewer people there now, since the Third. . . . Oh, excuse me, I mean the third war, that's the way we refer to it. You know about the war?"

"Ah, rumph, yes, some men came in a ship many years ago and told us of the terrible events. EMSIAC, hydrogen bombs, radiological dust, supersonic ships, I remember many things. They said Johannesburg was an ash heap."

The old man stopped in confusion: his muscles were stiff with tension, it was such a horrible effort to lie. Especially to a person as pleasant and friendly as this Theo. He longed to put away all the subterfuges and talk frankly with the good man, tell him everything. But, aside from other deterrents, Martine was listening.

"Yes," Theo said soberly. "For a short time during the war I served in Africa. I saw with my own eyes what happened to Johannesburg. Johannesburg and many other cities."

He noticed that Ubu was staring at his body.

"Oh?" he said. "You haven't heard about Immob?"

"Immob?"

"Yes. That's what's behind these arms and legs."

"Is it that you and your friends were injured in, in the Third? In some hydrogen explosions?" Ubu said sympathetically.

"No, no, nothing like that. Immob has to do with a very

27

great effort to keep the war, the steamroller of war, on the other side of the river. Forever."

Theo was obviously pleased with himself for having found exactly the right formulation for his thought. He moved several steps closer to Ubu. "Mr. Ubu, I'd like to tell you why we are here. We come in friendship, with no desire to upset the life of your village. You see, my comrades here are all athletes. You know what athletes are?"

"I remember from school," Ubu said uncertainly. "Running and lifting weights and walking on the hands. Things like that."

"Exactly. Men who engage in sports must train, practice, and that's what we are now doing—we're on a training cruise, and we stop here and there on our travels to see new sights and meet different peoples. We'd like very much to know your island better, especially since it's not charted on any of our maps, we'd like to collect some data on your flora and your fauna, too—for example, my hobby is butterfly collecting. Our intention is to establish a base at the other end of the island, where we won't be a bother to you, and make some surveys."

"You will stay long?"

"I myself must leave in a few weeks, but the rest of the party will stay for some months. They'll be making some more expeditions around."

"Good. We shall talk much and tell each other many things."

"That'll be just wonderful. We'd like to know all about your people, and it may interest you to hear about the Immobs. We'll be friends."

"You come in peace, Mr. Theo," Ubu said, "and you are welcomed in peace. I shall send to you a present of some sweet cassava, it is what you call tapioca, I believe. Relieves intestinal tonus, very excellent for the bowels."

"Thank you," Theo said. "Perhaps you would like some pistachio ice cream."

The two men looked at each other with mutual respect. They ceremoniously extended their hands toward one another again, Theo's flickering. Then the white man turned and, accompanied by his friends, retreated across the clearing, disappeared into the newly cut pathway.

Ubu stood for some time, looking thoughtfully at the mouth of the tunnel; some of the bushes and plants were still smoldering from the searing fire of the flame-throwers. Then he faced about and went to Martine's house.

28

The doctor was standing in the doorway, staring at the hole in the jungle down which the strangers had vanished. Brachycephalic as hell, skull at least as broad as it was long, cranial proportions at least 10:10, he was thinking. And Immob? What, for God's sake, was Immob? Nonsense syllable. But his pulse had never before been sent racing at 120, at least 120, by a nonsense syllable.

"You heard?" the old man asked.

"Most of it."

"You feared for no reason."

"Maybe."

"But this Mr. Theo is such a nice, friendly man! There is no harm in him, he would not trouble a spider."

"The guy certainly spoke well enough, but that whole line about training cruises and flora and fauna—it sounds fishy to me."

"You see fish everywhere, Doctor, it is the characteristic of tonicity."

Martine turned his head—Ooda, standing in the shadow inside, quiet and anxious. He reached out, drew her close to him. "I see something else: a great fire-shooting arm and a great sharp-toothed hand. These could be very nasty weapons. Worse than a slingshot. Or a steamroller."

"What suspicious is there in all this? It seems to me very simple: all the men from your country are in love with machines, they make all kinds of machines, very good, these arms and legs are just more of the toy machines they like to make."

"You once saw what such toys can do. Or don't you remember what Johannesburg and Durban and Cape Town looked like after my people got through playing with them?"

"No connection," Ubu insisted. "Mr. Theo says his country wants only to keep the war on the other side of the river. However. If they want to collect some plants and insects, why not?"

"Let them go swishing their butterfly nets all over the place," Martine said absent-mindedly. "Maybe they're all harmless as rabbits. In any case, their coming here complicates matters a good deal."

"I do not follow."

"I mean just this: under no circumstance can they learn about my work here. I absolutely insist on that. All Mandunga ceremonies must be suspended completely. All us devil-chasers are out of work, Ubu, let's face it."

"Suspended?" Ubu said dully.

"More: the cave must be sealed up, with all the records and research data. All the experimental animals must be destroyed—if we turned those four-footed pacifists loose in the jungle our visitors would certainly come upon them and wonder at their scars and strange behavior. Besides, you can't keep all the Mandungabas under cover indefinitely and Theo's men would soon see a connection between their scars and the scars on the animals. Remember: you must all act as though Mandunga does not exist and never existed. Or Martine, either."

"You, you, you," Ubu echoed. "Always you say you, not we. What of yourself?"

"I was thinking about that," Martine said. "Obviously I can't stay here."

He felt Ooda's shoulders stiffen, he held his arm tighter around her.

"Why not, Martine? We could hide you, maybe in the cave."

"For months? I'd go nuts with boredom. Besides, these are smart, observant people, if there were a white man on the island they'd find out about it one way or another. Especially since our people aren't good liars. You yourself were ready to blab the works just a few minutes ago, weren't you, when you were talking to the nice man? No, I've got to disppear, there's no other way."

Before Ubu could say anything, before Ooda could find words for the fear that was spilling into her eyes, Rambo came across the clearing and approached his parents' hut.

"You sent for me, Father?"

"Yes," Martine said. "I have a job for you. I want you to go to the camp of these strangers."

The boy's alert eyes widened, but he said nothing.

"You will carry a basket of sweet cassava, tell them it is the present Ubu promised. No doubt they'll be very polite, ask you to stay and eat or drink. Accept, and in the course of the conversation, without showing any unusual curiosity, ask them certain things about their country which I must know. Do you think you can do that, Rambo?"

"Yes."

Martine began to enumerate, item by item, the things he wanted to find out, going into careful detail about those matters which could not mean very much to the boy: passports, routes of travel, currency, clothes, and so on. When he was through the boy nodded, promised to report as soon as he returned, and left.

Ubu hardly heard the exchange between Martine and Rambo. "Disappear where, dear friend?" the old man said now with some agitation. "Komoro? Madagascar? If these strangers can find you here, they can find you anywhere in the archipelago."

"I know that," Martine said. "I've thought the whole thing out. I can disappear only in one place—where all the other people look like me."

"Martine. . . ."

"I've got to go to America, or whatever's left of it. Incognito, of course. You should understand that: all the normal Mandunji live with each other all their lives incognito."

"You must not go," Ubu said in a trembling voice. "They think you dead, do not change their minds. Besides, you cannot leave us, your friends. . . ."

"Maybe you're friends of another one of my incognitos." But there were tears in the old man's eyes. "Don't go dramatic on me, Ubu," Martine said gently. "That's another thing about low tonus, it makes you sentimental as hell, your emotions get as flabby as your muscles. It's just that I'm curious about what's been happening back there, now that I've seen these soft-spoken monsters. I want to examine *their* flora and fauna."

"If you go you—you will not come back," Ubu said. "You will forget us. How shall we live without you now?"

"This is my home. I'll come back, count on it."

Ubu was silent for a long time. Martine could feel Ooda's body quaking in his arm as though she had a chill. Finally the old chief said in a low voice, "When shall you leave, Martine?"

Martine held Ooda tight. "The sooner the better," he said. "Tonight, if it's possible."

chapter four

THEY LAY on the slabs of foam rubber (salvaged from the seats of a cocktail lounge in Pretoria), their bodies just touching. After a while she reached out and lit another cigarette of ganja.

The moonlight streaming in through the aperture in the far wall, spray of pearl dust, cut across their bodies just above the knees; he studied the juxtaposed shanks. Hers

31

was a tawny brown, brown of chestnuts and dried tobacco leaf, sprinkled with bronzing; his, for all the years of exposure to a brutal sun, remained a white man's leg, low in melanin, chalky, cheeky. Smug leg. Arrogant. Wore its bleach like a white badge of asepsis, a halo. The white man's burden was first of all whiteness.

Her body was still trembling, he could feel it. With her, agitation always took a motoric turn. She had it bad this time.

And so, finally, after centuries of sahibism, these two legs, hatched and stained in opposite hemispheres, one in the leafy suburbs of Salt Lake City, the other in a jungle some hundreds of miles southeast of Antananarive, now lying side by side on a mattress of foam rubber in the middle of the Indian Ocean. One filled with the messianic blood of Mormons, the other with a pacifist Bantu-Arab-Malay brew called Mandunji. A coupling to shatter a Kipling. . . .

She made a hissing sound as she pulled the smoke into her lungs, inhaling kinesthetic ease, trying to.

. . . . Meet. He had never genuinely *met* anybody before, he thought with surprise. Nobody back home, certainly: not his father or mother, not his friends and fellow students—had he ever really known Helder, his "closest" friend, after all those years of living with him?—not his ex-wife Irene; oh, Irene least of all. They were all strangers, he and they had just made stereotyped sounds at each other and that passed for intimacy. But here, lying next to him, brown and intense and cringing now in misery, was the one being in the world whom he could claim to know a little. The introductions had somehow been made: the light-years that gape between any two skins, no matter what color, had somehow been spanned, superegos had crawled toward each other, glands had gushed, two sets of psychic feelers had prowled and locked, vibrations had been stirred up between their parasympathetic nervous systems—whatever wizardry of sense or essence had turned the trick, they had met, on levels deeper than words.

"Have you been happy with me?" he said.

She took another puff on the cigarette and passed it to him. He sipped as she had taught him; held the smoke as long as he could, then let it out in dabs which he immediately sucked up again and swallowed. He felt the tingling in his viscera, in his toes, in his fingers, the stuff was as penetrating in its way as diathermy.

32

"I mean really happy," he said. "All the way. So you feel there is nothing more."

. . . . Two wondrous weeds grew on the Isle of the Mandunji, one full of emotional helium, the other an emotional steamroller. Hemp, the sharpener of sense and whetter of appetite, the spreader of glow, and rotabunga, the blunter of feeling and carrier of coma. One to leaven, the other to lull. Mutually negating flora, gift of the ambivalent gods. It was a real clue to the Mandunji personality that, having stumbled upon a garden of such pharmacological riches, it quick outlawed ganja and made rota an official beverage. But Nature went on planting its contraries, not only in the weeds of every jungle, but in the creatures of every village. That was the trouble, really, there were liberal dosages of both ganja and rota in all human clay. Every man was, at least incipiently, a bit of a blowtop and a bit of a somnambule, squirming simultaneously toward Eros and Thanatos, the berserk and the vegetative. Rule: every blob of protoplasm teems with ambivalence, yearns at one and the same time to freeze and to blow up. A community committed to stupor might decree all excitants to be illegal, drive them underground and force-feed their devotees with sedatives and anesthetics, but riot will out. In a sense these two loggerheadstrong plants were only symbols of the two linked psychic poles: the Dionysian, the blowtop, the oceanic, headed for abandon and the ultimate in sensation and all-engulfing consciousness; and the Apollonian, bedded down in mildness and limit and order and even-tempered restraint and a certain programmatic heavy-liddedness. Despite all pharmaceutical totems and taboos the twain would always and everywhere meet, in every jungle, in every village, in every cell of every body—every neurone, every muscle strand, every synapse. More Siamese twins. . . .

He handed the cigarette back to her. He had to deliver a lecture tonight, he had just this moment decided on it, it would be tricky, he would need his wits about him.

"Well?" he said. "Have you?"

"Happy?"

He understood the sullen question in her voice. Many times, in the early days, he had asked her the same thing, and always her answer had been: "The word has no meaning for me. It is a sound, like water running. When my people mean it goes well they say it is peaceful, quiet—is that what you mean? No, it has not been peaceful."

"I am not talking about peace," he said. "You were not meant for peace, you did not have peace before I came."

"No, but I was alone. I did not live near others. There was no one close enough to hurt me. When I felt a hurt it came from inside, not from another. . . . Now the hurt comes from you. You are near but many times I feel alone. . . ."

"I want to know: in your life with me, do you use yourself up? All of you? You feel that what is in you comes out, you like the feeling? Do you yawn?"

She took a long drag on the cigarette, held her breath. "No," she said, sulky, as she exhaled. "I do not yawn."

"Is it good not to be sleepy?"

"This is how I would have it, not the regular way. With you it is very low one moment, very high the next, always the going up or down. I would not like it to be the same always. Although when we are low—when you go away from me and into yourself—it is sometimes very bad. It does not bother me too much." He felt her body begin to tremble again, worse than before. "Now we are down far, to the bottom. I feel a hurt that will make me crazy."

"No. No."

He put his arms around her and drew her to him. She tried to fight down the sobs, he stroked her shoulder. Her body was lithe and compact, she was thirty-six now but with no suggestion of flabbiness or sag in her flesh. Not skimpy, breasts full and firm, hips gently swelling, a roundness in the thighs; still, unlike the more typical women of the village, she had a slender and hard-packed quality. Concentration. A blowtorch blazed inside, consuming all excess tissue and tempering what remained, whereas the complacent ones, the sleepy ones, often ran to fat. Definitely somatotonic physique, with a touch of the cerebrotonic. Very much like himself, although he was more clearly the cerebrontonic with a touch of the somatotonic. If the mixtures were slightly different (he lived more in the nerves, she in the muscles), the ingredients were the same. They were birds of a mottled feather. A taboo feather.

"Monkey," he said, "while I'm away you must not smoke any more. It could be serious."

"No more bed," she said. "No more talk. No more ganja. I am to stop living when you go. And you always go. Somewhere, where I am not to follow."

"You must be careful. You know that you have a need to be very active when you are feeling bad, that in itself is dangerous in the village. When you smoke the need is greater."

"That is my business."

"Mine too. When I'm here I can protect you but there are many who don't like you, even fear you, as they fear all who are different. Many were sent for Mandunga only because they smoked, before I came."

"When you go, the knives go," she said bitterly. "I do not fear the cave."

"If you are found smoking it will go badly with you, even without Mandunga. They will find ways to hurt you. The mild ones often make the best torturers."

"What is the use to save myself? You will not come back."

"Why shouldn't I? There's nothing there to keep me."

"Something will keep you. Another woman with her orgasms, something."

He could not help laughing. "Jealousy too? You know the normal ones consider themselves above that sort of thing, it's much too violent an emotion."

"Jealousy. Another word you taught me. Another hurt."

"That's so, isn't it? I guess my real contribution to your life was a vocabulary of distress. But not only that. Also a vocabulary of joy."

"Jealousy. Happy, unhappy. Orgasm. All the up-and-down things."

"But remember." He propped himself up on one elbow and tried to see her face in the dark. "Listen and remember this: you were up-and-down before I came. All I gave you was a language to describe the swings of the seesaw. You can blame me for the words, not the seesaw. And to be on a seesaw is not the worst thing."

"You make it the worst. You lift me up very high and then you go away. Always you are going away a little. Even in bed. . . . Ah, sometimes I hate you. All this talk. I could scratch your eyes out."

"Fine Mandunji sentiment. People have lost all of Region Nine, and a good part of the thalamus too, for less." He began to run his fingers down the fine warm curve of her back, down to the compact haunches. "I'm sorry, monkey. I haven't always been good to you. Sometimes . . . . There are many things that trouble me, now with these queer-limbs—"

He stopped: sound of footsteps outside.

"Father?"

It was Rambo. He slipped into his shorts and went out.

35

"I did as you said."

Martine nodded.

"Many things were happening in their camp. Some were using long poles and jumping over trees with them. Others were leaping in the air, twenty and thirty feet, and turning many somersaults each time. Others were picking up whole trees they had cut down and throwing them as though they were only spears. All this they were doing for Mr. Theo, he told each one of his mistakes and how he could do better."

"How did they act toward you?"

"Very friendly, we talked and I learned some words. They call themselves amps, from amputee. The arms and legs they wear are pros, that is short for pro, uh, prosthetics. In their country most of the younger men are amps and almost all wear the pros but there are quite a few men of your age, men over forty, who are not amps. There are different kinds of amps, it depends on how many arms and legs are gone—uni-amps, duo-amps, tri-amps, quadro-amps. Then they also have the word Immob—"

"Good, good." He was annoyed by the nonsensical word, made an impatient gesture to cut Rambo short. "What else?"

Rambo went on to give a full report, running in sequence through the items his father had outlined. Martine listened attentively: some of the information was astonishing, nearly all of it was good. The trip was not only feasible, it promised to be a cinch.

"One thing more," Rambo said. "I do not know the meaning of it. When I was going to the camp I heard noises from the jungle."

"What sort of noises?"

"I could not identify them so I left the path and went to look. I was very careful, no one saw me. The thing I found was strange. They have made their camp down at the low end of the island, near a place where there are many rocks and boulders and high walls of stone. Many of the queer-limbs were at this place, some had instruments in place of their arms, high-speed drills and scoops and other things for digging and breaking stone. These men chipped out little pieces of stone and others took them to some machines, they poured chemicals over them and examined them under special lights and things like that. After a while I left and went on to the camp."

"This begins to make sense," Martine said. "Oh, a whole lot of sense."

36

"What does it mean, Father?"

"They say they're interested on in sightseeing and in collecting flora and fauna, but the first day they begin to examine rocks. A much more meaningful hobby. . . . You did well, Rambo. This news only proves what I've thought right along: I must go." He looked at the boy. "You know I'm going away?"

"Yes," Rambo said soberly.

"How do you know?"

"Ubu has arranged a special feast in the eating room, they are all there now."

Martine looked across the clearing toward the large communal mess at the other end of the village: it seemed more brightly lit than usual, people were going in and out with baskets on their heads.

"They are eating some peculiar stuff," Rambo said. "Very cold and sticky. Theo sent it in return for the cassava."

"It must be the ice cream he promised. What color is it?"

"Green. With little solid pieces in it."

"Pistachio ice cream!" Martine said. "Very, very good for the bowels." He thought hard for a moment. Then, in a whisper: "Two more things I want you to do, Rambo. In back of the machine shop, in the shed, I have some valises packed and some baskets of food. Get a couple of the boys to help you and carry everything down to the boat—I'm taking the blue-and-white power catamaran. Then visit all the students and assistants and nurses, take them aside and tell them one by one to slip away in an hour's time and go to the lecture room in the cave. Only the young ones, understand, only those who have worked with me, no others. You will come yourself, of course, I want you to hear."

"All right, Father."

Martine watched the boy disappear around the side of the hut, then went back inside. As soon as he rejoined Ooda he reached out and touched her thigh: her first response was to move away. He caught hold of her leg and pulled her back toward him, desire began to stir in him as he increased the pressure. The miracle of flesh: pliant on the outside, steel inside; one learned that at the breast. A surface of giving wrapped around a core of denial (if you wanted to take it that way: it could also be taken as a simple, neutral, structural fact). She lay back without moving, yielding to his superior strength but implying that she would defeat him by another stratagem—indifference.

37

"Passivity?" he said. "Oh, no. It doesn't become you. You're not *that* normal."

The more he caressed her, the more he sensed the tension in her body as she strained to keep from reacting. His mind, not fully involved yet, still partly a bystander, went racing on. It could be put in cytoarchitectonic terms, of course. One cluster of linkages in the cerebral mantle and the corresponding thalamic areas was firing the erogenous zones and impelling her with neuronic pitchforks to spread her legs and beg for release from the ache within. But superimposed on that libidinous network was a contrary one, aggressive, temporarily activated by anger and grief over his leaving, working to outwit the want. Result: a simultaneous excitement and freezing. Out of which came a lust-in-loathing, a need-and-nausea. Sex and aggression in a bear hug. But did anybody ever reach except in recoil? Wasn't it old Freud who had had the courage to suggest that there is a fringe of distaste around every human desire, even under the best of circumstances? That—putting it another way—it is the prohibition which lends enchantment to the desire, totem must be flecked with taboo? After Freud (if it had needed him) it was impossible to look at any emotion without seeing its opposite crouching just behind it, he had made it starkly clear that the tenderest love comes with an inflexible spine of hate.

This was the twoness which the Mandunji couldn't stand. These pacifists required a love which would hold up without a spine, impossible. The calm ones, they had driven the undersides of their emotions so far down that with them had gone the emotions themselves. That was the danger in trying to outlaw doubleness, try to be monolithic and you turn into a monolith. Maybe, after all, the depth and inensity of feeling came, not from the strength of this unilinear urge or that unilinear urge, but from the strength of the conflict between urges—the surfacing of opposite drives simultaneously, a cortical-thalamic *No* befuddling every *Yes*. Undeniable: the river rages most at the point where it is dammed up most, a trickle never becomes a flood until it meets an obstacle. Trouble with the calm ones: since they shunned tensions—the emotional dams—their lives consisted of trickles, no gushes. . . .

Without warning, no putting up of storm signals, there was some kind of rumpus in her. She had been arching away from him, steeling herself against the erotic propaganda of his hands; to let her desire break through her disdain the moment he crooked a finger would be more of a defeat than she could stand, it would make her a mechanism which could be turned on and off at his whim. (Sometimes he sang a song: "*Love is like a faucet, it turns off and on.*") He was asserting himself brutally with his insistence on leaving her, the supreme rejection, one big dramatic one to dwarf the long procession of little ones; the blow had sent her reeling, what she needed now to restore her own bruised sense of worth was an equally brutal assertion of her own. It was not good to be nothing but a faucet. So she would not rise to the sensuous bait; it must be established that she was not an automaton tied to his urges. Who was he to say when she should turn off her venom and turn on her warmth—did he give her the right to tell him when to trot off in wander-lust and when to stay put in devotion, was she even con-sulted? This emotional tyranny made her taut with misery, and when she felt her body quicken under the reconnais-sance of his hands, some mutineer in her conspiring with his hands, that only made it worse.

"You devil, devil," she said.

She jerked into a sitting position, swiveled, began to pum-mel him. On the legs, on the shoulders, on the rib-cage—her fists avoiding the genitals and the eyes and other parts of the face; even as a berserker she chose her targets care-fully. Her muscles chortled, her nerves chirped, this was what she had needed all evening. The good feel of his obstinate flesh giving under her knuckles. The retreat of his stubborn bone and cartilage. The stinging impact of skin against skin. This was *her* will on parade. Good, good, good.

He lay with his body tensed against the attack, it hurt but he did not try to stop it. He knew that she had never felt so much torment before and he had no pain-killers for her. Besides, within this hate there was a firm skeleton of love, he knew that too. There were times when to love meant to be a punching-bag for the one you loved. Especially if it was your taste to love a somatotone.

All of a sudden her belligerence caved away in an un-accountable landslide: one, two, it was gone. The rigid cyl-inder of her body collapsed and she was all concave and receptive, a bowl of yearning. Her arms went imperiously around him. "Martine," she whispered. "Ah, yes, I want you."

For the first time tonight she was speaking to him in Mandunji. It was their language of intimacy, they fell into it automatically when they were closest. The first night he had made love to her, months after he came to the island, at the

39

height of it he had found himself whispering to her in his faltering Mandunji, wildly, in a gust of feeling. It had given him a strange, triumphant glow. He had thought: I am speaking to her in her language, I am reaching her, for the first time I am reaching a woman. (For him, he now speculated ironically, the breaking through to a woman really meant learning a foreign language!) After that they had fallen into an easy pattern of talk, English for the day-to-day things, Mandunji for the times of the night when there was nothing but a jabbering schizoid jungle and they were burrowed in it, holding on tight to each other in their pooled loneliness. . . .

"As I want you."

All ease. All soft and giving way. The one and the other locked, limp, riding on the softness. No effort, no fight, soft waves and no need to go against the waves. Rippling, ride with the crests, bobbing, being bobbed, some metronomic "It" having its liquid undulant way with the world, everything in synchronization, perfect, the one in phase with the other, a coming and going, the meeting and the gliding away and the meeting again, minuet of the one and the other, opposites linked, bobbing together, being bobbed, being done, everything being done, a magnet pushing and pulling, periodicity of two and one, without effort the halves seeking and shunning, the swayings and shrinkings dictated by the source of all waves, the activating "It" in the center and the ripples spreading in circles out from it and on the ripples outward softly riding, everything arranged, the gentle thrust and the gentle tug, the twoness and the oneness, nothing to do, a yielding to the crests, the surges, the prearranged rises and falls, peace of being moved, ease of going along with the movements, trance of being rocked in the cradle of the Mover, the swings subtly growing faster, taking on momentum, energizing of the lazy movements, the waves beginning to surge, the trance being shredded, strain, a tightening, limpness gone, lulling gone, alertness coiling upwards in an expanding spiral, wider and wider arcs of awareness, swinging with the stronger waves, the quickening surges, stirrings within, bobbing, jogging, jouncing, awareness bulging up in the center, the center no longer outside but inside at the core of awareness, surge becoming a rush becoming a torrent, the surge not outside but inside, at the center, seething, geyser welling up inside at the center with every wave and awareness clamped over it, fighting it down, stuffed, swelling, ballooning, drift giving way to drive now, the

Mover not far away but invading awareness now, becoming awareness, the done-to becoming the doer with faster and faster tug and stronger and stronger thrust, "It" becoming "I," outside becoming inside, the magnet inside, the metronome inside, the waves inside, the swayings and shrinkings inside, the cradle inside, surge become self, "I" become the center and doing and commanding and domineering the softness and forcing the way, the effort pounding, inside the pressure battering and awareness full only of the pressure, ready to burst with the pressure, the other (feeling what? a yielding? a fighting?) caught up like a leaf on the battering waves thrust out by the Mover the Doer the "I," lost on the sea churned by the Arranger the Self the All-Aware, and now, trickling now, creeping now, surging now, seething, now, at last, the heave, the hoist, the shudder, finally the spurt of the geyser at the center exploding the clamp sending the skin of awareness flying in shreds, "I flooding into the sea becoming the sea becoming the waves becoming everything becoming nothing, and ah, ah, swimming now, drowning now, in the other, deep in the center of the other (feeling what? a doing, a being done to? a giving, a taking?), stirrings, quakes, pulsings, spasms, throbs, a clutching, a surge, waves surging up to mingle with his own, willed by his own, dictated by his own, echoes of his own, the waves and the echoing waves meeting now and the sea all a swirling and seething and for a moment the one and the other (feeling what?) drowning in it, in each other, the two immersed in one, in the melting and the softness and the ease. . . .

A long time later: "Martine, Martine. Stay with me. With you I am used, I use myself. All that there is in me."

"It will be that way again. I will come back."

Something teasing him, for all the elation: tonight, as on too many nights before this, his love-making had been burdened, he sensed, with vague sidetracking irrelevancies—a rush of rhetorical shadows, soggy metaphors, bumbling poetry, on the outskirts of awareness. Head stuffed with lame images from a hundred bad novels, preventing total immersion in the flood of feeling: a smokescreen of words. And it was too good, too complete with Ooda to be damped with literature. Besides, there was something jarring, mockingly offkey, about the images, they were not only inadequate, in some taunting way they were grotesquely wrong—

He raised his head from her shoulder.

41

"I want you to know. In my country a long time ago I had a wife. It was bad. She was like the normal ones here in the village, even worse—the normal ones here are not supposed to feel anything and they do not pretend to feel. It was a game. I knew all the time that she pretended but I never told her that I knew, I pretended that I had been fooled by her. That was my part of the game. Very often it happened this way in my country, and not only in my country. Here they say you are not normal, but you are very lucky to be as you are and not to know about this."

He took her hand and held it cupped against his cheek. "Listen. We have done everything together, you and I. Night after night. It was never like this for me before, you are more woman than I have ever known. What days I have left, I wish to spend with you. Oh, I will come back." He slipped his arms around her and held her tight. "When I come back," he said, "I will not go away from you again. Even a little. I will try. I do not want to be so troubled and turned in on myself, but there is something—and lately. . . ." He got up, pulled on his shorts and a shirt.

"Now?" she said. "You are going now?"

"No, no. I have a headache, there are no pills here. I will go to the cave to get some." He leaned over and kissed her. "Try to eat something," he said. "There is some tapioca on the table."

chapter five

How, REALLY, do you go about saying good-bye? With a lingering toodle-oo? With a kick of the heels and a soft-shoe shuffle? It was over eighteen years since he'd gone anywhere, he'd forgotten how the thing was done.

Leaning against the edge of the desk, looking down at the rows of intent faces, he went on talking about facts, history, matters of the record; all very objective and impersonal. When you can't say an intimate thing you can always lecture: a technique for using words to insulate yourself against your audience.

There were, he mechanically reminded his listeners, two important dates in Mandunji history. The first, as nearly as one could guess from the old stories told around the evening fires, was in the fourteenth century, that was when the founding fathers, fleeing from the wars in Africa and Madagascar, had accidentally come upon this remote button of land and decided to settle here. With them, of course, they brought a recently developed ceremony named Mandunga. The second date could be given a little more exactly: October 19, 1972, at 7:21 in the morning. That was when he, Martine, in flight from the EMSIAC wars, had caught sight of this island—again, entirely by accident—and brought his plane down. With him he had all the tools for a recently developed ceremony called lobotomy. Mandunga and lobotomy met, looked at each other, and saw with a start that they were twins.

"Those are the two dates," he said. "In the six hundred-odd years between them, nothing happened. It was not because people were too busy to preciptate big events and promote memorable excitements and create red-letter days that would remain in the tribal mind. They were just too sleepy. Sleepy people do not make history, they just yawn. For the Mandunji, the gap between the fourteenth century and the twentieth century is one long yawn."

Many of the faces out in front lit up and dimpled: there were quite a few titters, even some outright laughs. Immediately Martine's mood began to brighten. These were sober people, the Mandunji, to them the bellylaughable was as remote as the blowtoppish and for very much the same reason; in the old days his observation would have been taken for a simple neutral statement of fact, as though he had remarked that water is wet or a lemur hairy—what was so hilarious about a datum? Somehow, without meaning to, he had managed to create among these young people (if he could take the credit for it) an atmosphere of irreverence in which it was possible to look at a solemn fact a bit slantwise and see in it a pint of pigeon's milk, a pratfall. These kids had somehow learned to back off from themselves and their parents a bit, had discovered the sidelines, and suddenly they had spied the slapstick in the sobrieties—a touch of mirth had entered their lives. And, just as suddenly, Martine had stopped living on the sidelines: he had company. The full implication of this change struck him now, and he began to warm up to his subject.

Since 1972, he went on, things had gotten a bit livelier—a certain dynamism had filtered into the village. This was due first of all to the machine, all the machines which had been salvaged from the deserted African cities and made to run the traditional tools of the village. Where it had taken a dozen men a dozen days to grind a certain quantity of maize, now one man could do the same job in a few hours.

As a result the young people were freed for a good part of the day, or for whole days at a time, to do other things. What they had chosen to do, most of them, was to study and work in the labs. Liberated from the deadening routine of manual labor, they had gravitated toward the cave.

And the result? Quite a few of them were now half-doctors, and good ones; others were more than competent laboratory technicians, machinists, chemists, pharmacologists, electronics engineers of a sort, even statisticians; still others were anesthetists, nurses, and so on. So that was one way in which movement had crept into the village: the young people had started to become things that nobody had ever been before in the tribe's history, they were learning what it felt like to be unprecedented, to live with an aura of newness. It was possible, they were discovering, for a man to be defined by something other than the old routines, to define himself somewhat by choice, from within. And as they had begun to make themselves into something new, a ferment of newness had seeped from them into the life of the village.

There was change in the village, dramatic change. It could be defined first of all in medical terms. They all knew the statistics of the past fifteen years or so: infant mortality cut down almost to zero, deaths in childbirth practically eliminated, most infectious diseases wiped out or under control, no epidemics of malaria or anything else for almost a decade, no deaths from snake bites, gangrene, perforated appendixes and peritonitis, no more hookworm or elephantiasis, no villagers left crippled because of unbalanced diet or inept bonesetting. This medical care by itself had broken up long-standing "facts" and made them turn into their opposites.

The elders, understandably, were made a little dizzy by this stirring; they were used only to a soothing sameness, to things reproducing themselves with no surprises century after century. But the younger people had begun to feel a sense of excitement, of things happening—tomorrow might be different from today, the future promised to be an adventure instead of a dreary perpetuation of the past. Because question marks began to appear up ahead, because the invasion of change had abruptly cracked the shell of determinism encasing the village, the young people began to wake up from the long, traditional sleep. Life had, within one generation, squirmed out of the clamp of repetition and routine and opened itself up to the possibility of the miraculous, one began to feel alert and anticipatory.

And so, a paradox. Because they had mastered the machine in the cave, the future began to crackle with question marks. Therefore, a quickening sense of anticipation. But whenever there was anticipation of the new, uncertainty about the shape and feel of tomorrow, there was also anxiety. *Anxious* anticipation: that was the mood of the young ones, they were joining history. But the organ of anxious anticipation was—the prefrontal lobe: exactly what the cave was intended to annihilate. The Mandunga cave was the breeding ground of its sworn enemy; the young lobotomists were sprouting bigger and bigger lobes of their own. . . .

But it was important to ask a question: Why this great shift? It had not been done *to* or *for* the village by outside forces or agencies. The young people had done it themselves, first by changing themselves and then by imposing their new selves on the old, rigid mold of the village. So they felt that they were the movers in this communal jolt, this return to the making of history, not the moved; and that accounted for much of their excitement. They were developing a sense of power and a taste for it—a sense which, they must recognize, was strictly taboo in the mores of the village.

"Always in the past," Martine said, "the Mandunji were so appalled by energy that they could not tolerate any display of it. Whenever they saw an active man, they assumed that the energy activating him was the energy of belligerence, and therefore a threat. If a man energetically attacked trees and snakes and weeds and rocks and rivers, they felt, how could one be sure that he would not some day shift his targets and just as energetically attack his fellow-villagers? That is why, for six hundred years, your ancestors invented no new ways of chopping and hollowing trees, of fishing, of maize grinding; they established certain lazy routines of dealing with Nature and then they followed these routines forever after, in a kind of comforting daze, content to feel more done-to than doing. What was suspect to them was the very impulse to self-assertion and the triumph of will; what was reassuring was the drowning of all sense of the self in routine. Therefore: a life-in-the-mass, of dull incognito. Therefore: no new technics, no experimentation, no science, no medicine. Everything you have learned in the cave they abhorred as sheer willfulness and the push of ego—that which makes war. I need only add: it also makes poetry. And painting—painting which is more than just insipid design, which has the bold stamp of personality on it."

He stopped and rubbed his temples with his fingers,

blinking hard. He felt overheated, the thoughts were racing, maybe he'd had more ganja than he'd thought.

"Here is the point," he said, wondering whether, after all, he knew what the damned slippery point was, whether there was any. "In a village where everything is habit and repetition, no man can feel that he is in control of anything, the outside world or himself. He is not a doer but a thing done to, a victim. Even his body is a victim: of germs, of hookworms, of all the other dangerous things in Nature which are not stamped out or subdued. Of snakes, of sharks, of poisonous berries, of perforated appendixes, of gangrene, of rickets, of beriberi. Also, of backbreaking labor from sunup to sundown, because it would take too much will to invent laborsaving devices.

"All right," he said more forcefully. "You young people sitting in this cave, you are the first ones in the history of your village to shake off some of the sense of menace and taste the sense of power. The first for whom the world is not entirely a steamroller—" He frowned; hadn't meant to say that. "The very first. You have begun to acquire some control over your bodies—with pills, with drugs, with microscopes and splints—and simultaneously over the physical world in which your bodies are planted—with the tools I have just mentioned, and also with machines and other equipment. All of that became possible only because you had the audacity to break away from routine and make yourselves into something new. As a result, the human body in our village is healthier than it has ever been before. But we have learned that diseases are not only of the body, they are also of the mind. So we must now ask: How healthy is the human mind on our island? What about Mandunga?

"About Mandunga, one big point. It is a wrong thing and a bad thing to make fun of the old people. They may begin to look ridiculous, with their solemn ceremonies and their set ways, but there are very strong reasons for their attachment to certain archaic forms and attitudes. You will find those reasons in the harrowing past of your tribe. You all know the story. . . ."

They did, indeed, know the story. They had heard it many times from Martine's lips. The story began at an undetermined time, on some undetermined plateau in north-central Africa. Here, barricaded from the outside by a ring of mountains, lived the X's, pastoral, vegetarians, without the spears and knives of the hunter and the warrior. One day they were discovered and overrun by a band of fierce young men, offshoots of the Bantu tribes far to the east: lean and hungry young men, bristling with arms, without women— they had been banished from their own villages because they had been discovered plotting to kill their fathers and take over the households of women monopolized by their fathers. The X-men were enslaved, the X-women expropriated.

Thus began the X-Bantus. Life was easy on the plateau, the warriors from the east relaxed and forgot about meat eating and turned their hunter's spears into spades. Then came another throng of strangers: burnoosed and sword-brandishing Arabs, fleeing from the terrible wars of extermination in the deserts far to the north. Lean and hungry, armed to the teeth, without women, and so on. Thus began the X-Bantu-Arabs.

Peace again—until scouting parties reported more bands of wild men swooping down from the north. By now a heritage of guilt lay heavy on the tribe, the guilt of two ravishings followed by a sort of yielding to and blending with those ravished: a very common thing, as witness the Americans and their Negro slaves. So, thought the guilty pastoral descendants of rapists, if the plateau had been overrun twice, could it not happen a third time? In panic the chiefs gathered and reached a decision: they must become nomads and tiptoe southward to a haven beyond the reach of war and the fugitives from war.

They ran away. For many years they wandered wretchedly. Many died. Through the Sudan and Kenya they wandered— as Martine reconstructed it from the old stories—into Tanganyika, then west to the Congo, then east again through the Rhodesias. So, finally, to Mozambique and the placid blue waters of the Mozambique Channel. They settled here in a lush coastal area, far from the scrapes and skirmishes of other peoples, and time passed. Then a violent war broke out between two tribes to the north. Suddenly the combatants had a bright idea: why should they go on eliminating each other when they might pool their warriors and jointly attack these timid, defenseless people huddled on the coast hardly daring to breathe? Better to kill strangers, interlopers—neighbors of long standing should not spill each other's blood, and so on.

The X-Bantu-Arabs were attacked, many were killed. The survivors piled into their boats and paddled furiously to sea, not knowing what was ahead, knowing only that once more they had to run from something behind. The whole continent of Africa seemed like a sharp-toothed trap that was continually snapping shut on them.

They reached the shores of Madagascar. Rich country, everything went smoothly, life became one long sunny romp, not too bad even for the slaves. Until the ferocious Malays put in their boats and swarmed ashore: they'd come a long way, bellies caved in, few women but many flashing scimitars, the old story. Heads hacked off, rape, enslavement. Then things were quiet for a few generations, and the population grew so rapidly that a second village was established. But soon bad blood began to develop between the two villages: each chief claimed that the other was plotting to murder him and take over his village. The slaves in both villages were put to work making more spears and bolos.

Working side by side during the day, lying side by side in their huts at night, the terrified slaves talked over what was happening and tried to evaluate it in terms of their past experiences. They had much to talk about: in each slave's veins ran the guilt-laden blood of three ravagers. And as a result of their secret musings and nocturnal communications, a radical idea began to take root in the guilty minds of the slaves: what their forefathers had been running from for centuries could not be escaped geographically, the trouble was in the head. Those who make spears and think of war have devils in their heads, they are insane. Internal geography had to be considered. And if the trouble had finally been traced to its pathological source, it was clear what had to be done by way of therapy.

Some night between 1450 and 1500, very late, the same thing happened in both villages. A group of men, faces hidden by masks with tusks and fangs and tiger tails on them, bodies slashed with brilliant paints, crept up to each chief's hut, overpowered the guards, gagged the chief and stole away with him into the jungle. In the morning both chiefs were found on the bank of a small pool halfway between the two villages. They were bound together with braided vines, hands interlocked, and between them was the body of a freshly killed owl, symbol of peace and fraternity.

The chiefs were not dead but they were unconscious, and their heads were swathed with bandages of bark. From the forehead of each a circle of bone had been chiseled, a portion of the brain scooped out, and the bone carefully wedged back in place. They were the first Mandungabas. No way of telling whether they lived, and whether the removal of their prefrontal demons prompted them to call their war off; those who might have told the story were no longer on the scene. By this time all the slaves who could manage it were far out to sea in the hardy boats of their Malayan masters, with as many of their masters' women and children as they had been able to carry off.

They headed east, of course, southeast, rather, because to the north and west lay Africa and their memories of Africa were not good. Again they had no idea where they were going, whether they would ever find land again or simply sail to the water's edge and slip off the rim of the world, but they were happy that Madagascar was behind them. This time luck was with them: after some hundreds of miles they sighted a small, thickly overgrown island, lying far away from all the sea routes, which turned out to be entirely uninhabited. It was hard to land because of the reefs and cliffs, two boats were broken to bits and most of their passengers drowned, but the rest of them made it.

Very soon they were settled. When their nerves had stopped vibrating they began to squat around their evening fire and talk about their miraculous adventures. Mostly they talked about the great discovery they had made: that there these devils could be cut out with a chisel and a rock. (They called it a "discovery," although they never knew the results of their first devil-chasing experiment: but who is empiric in his myth-spinning, who concocts his reveries in a test tube?) Back on Madagascar they had decided to call this new ceremony Mandunga, "to chase the devils from the head." These X-Bantu-Arab-Malays now realized that they needed a name for themselves, and since they were people who had no wish whatsoever to fight they saw that it was logical to call themselves the Mandunji, "those whose heads are without devils." It was a definition designed to appease the guilt which everybody felt, everybody without exception—because, to be perfectly honest about it, no human head is entirely without devils. From it came the mild incognito personality of every tribesman.

They immediately decreed the therapy of the chisel for any villager who showed a taste for violence, and settled down to sleep for six hundred years. . . .

"You all know the story," Martine said. "Anatomically speaking, the founders of Mandunga showed a good deal of

49

sense. Somehow men have always known that those bumps of anticipation and anxiety, the frontal lobes, are the seat of most human troubles: from them come art, imagination, conscience, curiosity, egoness, migraine and tension. And more than once, when confronted with behavior which frightens them—because it reminds them unbearably of their unacknowledged selves—men have hit upon the Mandunga method of dealing with it. In many parts of the world archeologists have dug up very old human skulls with holes bored in them, and this must be the explanation. It is, in short, a very common form of magic. In the twentieth century my own people discovered it and named it lobotomy."

He reached up and unrolled two large sheets of pounded bark which were attached to the edge of the blackboard: both of them diagrams of the brain, showing it in top, side and bottom views and various cross sections. Studying them, he felt a rush of dizziness again, as though his own brain had broken loose from its moorings and started to whir around and around inside its pan, exactly the same swimming sensation he had experienced earlier in the evening when, hidden in his attic, he had stared down at the big blond head of Theo and heard the nonsensical references to Immob.

Funny: he had only heard the word spoken once or twice, but he had a clear visual image of it—i, m, m, o, b, he was quite sure it had to be spelled that way.

He took hold of the desk to steady himself, a voice inside reassured him senselessly, "Brachycephalics are very common," in a moment it was over and he turned back to his audience.

"I don't have to tell you about my people," he said. "You know my story too. . . ."

Back in the 1960's Martine had been a medical student in New York, preparing to be a neurosurgeon. By that time insanity had become so frequent among his people—very anticipatory, very anxious, his people—that it was a major health problem, as much as cancer: things had gotten so bad that one out of every fifteen Americans could expect to be a psychotic patient in a mental institution at some time in his life. The situation was all the more upsetting because there were not nearly enough psychiatric doctors, and those who were practicing did not know enough about the diseases of the mind to do much good: there were ways

50

to deal with some of the milder neuroses but the psychoses were very stubborn and hard to treat. Martine himself, when he finished his medical studies at the age of 20—by that time college preparations for the technical professions had been greatly accelerated, and, besides, he had skipped some grades in public school—had been so startled by this situation that he had been tempted to go into psychiatry, but other pressures on him had been too great.

How did his people react to this growing threat? In their characteristic way: they turned to the machine for help.

Nothing more natural. His people had been remarkably good with machines, but in the course of their fantastic technological development something peculiar had happened. To oversimplify: the Americans had built themselves remarkable machines to overcome the steamroller of their environment—and then, somehow, the machine had reared up, gotten out of control, and become a new steamroller. People, cowed by the machines that had grown bigger than themselves, could no longer think except in mechanical terms. It was common knowledge, for example, that when a clock stops ticking or a simple electronic calculator develops tremors, it can often be fixed by jiggling it or giving it a kick—the jolt meshes the teeth of the cogs again, or untangles the short circuits. So, when faced with human beings breaking down in various psychotic dysfunctions, the first thing people thought of was—give the machine a jolt, shake up its gears and circuits a bit.

This they accomplished at first with a technique called shock treatment. They built electric shock machines, they induced narcotic shock with shots of insulin and metrazol. For a decade or two this was more or less the routine in mental hospitals. And a little later, after the middle of the century, the new fad became lobotomy and related brain operations. Here the principle was essentially the same, mechanical: now the troublemaking cogs and circuits were snipped out of the machine or at least cut off from it.

This form of Mandunga was the major psychiatric therapy when Martine was a medical student. There was, of course, an acute shortage of lobotomists, and since he had shown promise as a neurosurgeon he was selected to become a practitioner in the new field. He worked very hard at his studies, but as the time approached when he was to join a hospital staff and begin operating on human brains he began to feel uneasy about it. This uneasiness came from an idea that was growing in him until it became an obsession: before you irrevocably remove a portion of the brain you must be very sure that you know everything about that brain, but what medical science actually did know was next to nothing.

How could you be sure that, in allegedly cutting away some devils from the brain, you were not at the same time cutting away some guardian angels? You could only be sure of that if you knew what every single cell of the brain did, and how it was entwined with all the other cells. But there were 10,000 million cells in the brain. Neurologists knew a tiny bit about a measly few dozen of them, maybe; and about all the possible interweavings between these 10,000 million cells, about the way they act in concert, they were almost entirely in the dark. How, then, could you know what your scalpel was doing when you slid it into the gray matter of someone's brain? You could dismiss this question and go ahead with your surgery only if you looked upon people, not as unique organisms with unique personalities—unique neuronic tangles, if you liked—but as machines. Machines are expendable and replaceable. One machine is very much like another.

This had been his dilemma: he was a lobotomist who didn't dare to go near a human lobe. He solved the problem, at least temporarily, by dodging hospital duty: went into a laboratory where they were conducting brain-surgery experiments on the higher mammals. Here he worked out some new surgical techniques and performed several unusual experiments which won him quite a reputation; his papers were published in many technical journals, he was invited to lecture before learned bodies, and so on.

But, although he was helping to acquire important new knowledge about the brain, there remained the terrible doubt that this knowledge would ever be solid enough to warrant applying it to human beings via the scalpel. For one thing, he remembered what a very wise neurologist had written in 1946: "most of our present understanding of mind would remain as valid and useful if, for all we knew, the cranium were stuffed with cotton wadding." For another, he was haunted by the words of Norbert Wiener, the mathematician.

He had told his students all about this unusual man— the man who during World War II had developed the science of cybernetics, the science of building machines to duplicate and improve on the functions of the animal; the man who understood more about machines and their meaning in American life than any other. Wiener had seen the horror of the mechanistic approach to the troubles of the mind. He had written this about lobotomy:

"Now, there is no normal process except death which completely clears the brain from all past impressions (among which are the sources of mental trouble); and after death, it is impossible to set it going again. Of all normal processes, sleep comes the nearest to a nonpathological clearing. . . . However, sleep does not clear away the deeper memories, nor indeed is a sufficiently malignant state of worry compatible with an adequate sleep. We are thus often forced to resort to more violent types of intervention in the memory cycle. The more violent of these involve a surgical intervention into the brain, leaving behind it permament damage, mutilation, and the abridgment of the powers of the victim; as the mammalian central nervous system seems to possess no powers whatsoever of regeneration. The principal type of surgical intervention which has been practiced is known as prefrontal lobotomy, and consists in the removal or isolation of a portion of the prefrontal lobe of the cortex. It has recently (1948) been having a certain vogue, probably not unconnected with the fact that it makes the custodial care of many patients easier. Let me remark in passing that killing them makes their custodial care still easier. However, prefrontal lobotomy does seem to have a genuine effect on malignant worry, not by bringing the patient nearer to a solution of his problems, but by damaging or destroying the capacity for maintained worry, known in the terminology of another profession as the *conscience*. More generally it appears to limit all aspects of the circulating memory, the ability to keep in mind a situation not actually presented. . . ."

There were, in short, many negative sides to lobotomy. Why, then, did the lobotomists feel free to proceed with their knives, quite as though these negative sides did not exist or were irrelevant? In thinking this over, Martine had been forced more and more to consider the motives of the brain surgeons and of the society which sponsored them. The lobotomists could not be acting purely out of altruistic desire to help the worried. No, they did not know enough to be sure that they were curing or alleviating anybody's worry. So this was not entirely science; it was magic as well. Any ceremony performed in the absence of reasonable knowledge as to cause and effect is magic. And in magic the need of the victim is less important than the need of the victimizer—medicine man, witch doctor, lobotomist, or whatever.

What, Martine had had to ask himself, was the need of the lobotomist, and of the whole society backing him up? Was it not the need of an anticipatory and anxious people, harried by the fear of being led away from statistically average behavior by their own errant prefrontal lobes (60 to 70 per cent of these people had one or more headaches a week, every year they consumed an average of twenty-four sleeping pills per person), to remove themsleves momentarily from this threat by punishing those whose "headaches" had, in a sense, run away with them? To show that they were not endangered by this malignancy but, on the contrary, were in control of it? Was this not a therapy designed to comfort, not the one in fifteen who went mad, but the fourteen who were left behind in panic? Just as, among the X-Bantu-Arab-Malays, Mandunga was created out of a sense of overwhelming guilt—a diversionary maneuver?

While Martine was asking himself such questions, the Third World War broke out. The completely mechanized war, the war of machines turned into steamrollers, the war of EMSIACS. He was almost happy when he was drafted and sent off with a flying hospital unit: it meant he could forget about lobotomy for a while. And then, after two years of war, he had landed on the Mandunji island.

At first he was horrified by Mandunga and would have nothing to do with it. But time after time he saw that, because of the primitive way in which the ceremony was performed, the patient died. The elders, of course, attributed these deaths to the stubbornness of the devils in the head, but Martine knew differently: they were due to lack of asepsis, gangrene, blood clots, hemorrhaging, a clumsy removal of too large cortical masses, and so on. Could he stand by and let this continue? With or without him, the ceremony would go on; if he participated, at least the patients would not die or be left permanently crippled—crippled, that is, beyond the minimum considered normal among the Mandunji.

Of course, to anybody with a streak of the messianic in him, the temptation of the cave—the chance to carry out a wild mass experiment in reshaping human clay, with no moral responsibility for the experiment—was almost irresistible. That had to be considered too. He had considered it many times, in private. But this part of his story he had *not* passed on to his students. . . .

"You know my story too. So we can turn to the real

question: How healthy is the human mind on our island?"
He waved his hand at the diagrams of the brain which
hung behind him. "There it is," he said mockingly. "The object of our affections, in the ugly flesh. In it are all the
secrets—"

There was a patter of feet in the corridor. A boy rushed
into the room, eyes wide with fright. "Queer-limbs in the
Circle!" he panted. "On top of the mountain, in the clearing—jumping over trees, playing games in the air!"

"I'll go and see," Martine said. "The rest of you stay here."

He signaled to Rambo to come with him. The boy rose
from his seat and followed his father out of the lecture hall.

chapter six

HIDDEN IN A clump of raffias on a ridge, they watched the
amps, some ten or twelve of them, hopping about in the
clearing below. The strangers, all of them wearing short-
sleeved sweat shirts with large blue "M's" pasted over their
chests, were playing a Bunyanesque form of leapfrog: each
man took off from a crouching position, sailed over the back
of the next man effortlessly as a kite, and came to earth
again at least fifty feet beyond, shouting exuberantly.

"All right, fellows." It was Theo's voice. "That's enough
horsing around. Let's do some dexterities and discernments."

It was easy to follow the vaulting bodies, as they rose and
fell the tubes in their limbs blinked agitated semaphores; the
clearing looked like an enormous telephone switchboard
gone berserk. And there was more illumination than that.
The amps seemed to be carrying powerful searchlights—
no, Martine saw now that the index finger on each amp's
right hand was itself a searchlight, from its tip projected a
beam of light.

"Come on, you guys," Theo said. "This isn't getting us
anywhere. Your jumping's fine—it's your d-and-d's that are
ragged."

Shouts of protest from the playful athletes: "Follow the
leader! Let's play follow the leader!"

The last suggestion seemed to appeal to everybody. "Great
idea!" "Follow the leader!" "Come on, Theo, you be leader!"
A dozen index fingers pointed at Theo, his bulging-skulled
head was bathed in light.

"All right, men," he said humorously. "All right. This is no way for humanists to pass the time, but I guess you deserve a little relaxation."

The beams of light were still on him. He bent his legs. "Here goes!" he called, and took off from the ground. Up he rocketed, thirty feet or more, caught hold of a raffia branch and whirled around it, the tubes in his limbs leaving trails like miniature comets. Then he let go and dropped, his body twisting so fast that it could be seen only as a twinkling blur. There were whistles, shouts of approval.

Now the athletes followed suit: one by one they jumped, pinwheeled, spun back to earth.

Theo laughed. "What a bunch of duds," he said. "Not one of you made it. Haven't you noticed anything about my sweat shirt?"

The lights flashed on him again. He turned around slowly, the young men gasped in surprise: the "M" that had been on his chest was now on his back.

"Let that be a lesson to you," he said. "That shows you what you can do when you really concentrate on your dexterities—as I was dropping from the tree I slipped my arms out of my sleeves, twisted my shirt around, and put it on again backwards. You'd better do some woodshedding on your discernments too—if you'd been a little more discerning you would have noticed it. . . . All right, you humanists! Back to camp for some shut-eye—let's go!"

He jumped for a high-hanging branch again, described one loop around it, then let go and sailed almost fifty feet to another tree, then to another. One by one the athletes— whooping: "Yippee!" "Wah-hoo-wah-hoo-wah-hoo!"—took off after him.

The lights flickered through the trees. When they had disappeared into the jungle, Martine patted Rambo on the shoulder.

"We can go back now," he said. "I guess they're gone for the night."

On their way to the cave Rambo said, "They do not act like metallurgists."

"No, they don't." Martine began to laugh. "Funny— some pessimists used to say man would wind up back in the trees, swinging from the branches. But nobody ever thought it would happen *this* way. In the name of humanism."

"What does the big 'M' mean?"

"I don't know. But I don't think it stands for Man."

Martine pointed again at the cytoarchitectonic maps.

"There it is!" he said. "Huddled like a turtle under its mantle, wrinkled, hunched, clamming up. Sometimes it will babble away a mile a minute—you've all heard it screeching on the encephalograph—but the moment you ask it a simple question about how well it's doing, it falls into a sulk and won't talk. That's its secret, it intends to keep mum about it, our old brain does. It's too brainy to be a chatterbox. Examine it well, all of you. Under those wrinkles are all the secrets, and all the answers—to war, orgasm, amuckism, art. But it's very hard to pry loose any of its secrets and answers. Oh, it's a taciturn old onion, the brain is."

He was feeling a little flushed and giddy again, thoughts darting out in all directions at once, fizzing pinwheels, he had to calm down. Ganja had a tendency to make you too baggy-cephalic, raggy-cephalic, brachycephalic. . . .

"Very well," he said. "Now, we have been opening up skulls in this cave for eighteen years. You all know how many brains we have had exposed bfeore our eyes to study and operate on, how many hundreds of thousands of pages of data we have collected on those brains. I'm pretty sure that here in this cave we have learned and recorded more about the human brain and its workings than is known anywhere else in the world. Much, much more. Look at the evidence."

He pointed again to the two diagrams. The one on the left was entitled "Post-Brodmann Cytoarchitectonic Map of the Human Brain (1970)," the one on the right, "Mandunga Cytoarchitectonic Map of the Human Brain (1990)." Both of them had areas outlined and numbered all over the cortical surfaces and in the cerebellum, the thalamus, the hypothalamus, the hypophysis, and other interior parts: in addition, special enlargements traced the paths of certain interconnections between individual cells of the various parts—between hypothalamus and hypophysis, between thalamus and prefrontal lobes of the cortex, and so on.

"These two diagrams tell the story," he said. "The first shows how much the neurologists in my world had found out by 1970, the year the Third World War began, following the work of Brodmann and other pioneers. The second shows how we in the cave have added to and corrected this picture. The difference is fantastic. We have discovered things those neurologists hardly dreamed about. But—" He pointed a finger at his hushed listeners, in a sort of pedagogical bluster which he was very far from feeling. He was not sure of anything at this point, he was groping, fumbling, but he had an urge to say something not too negative. "—remember this. Of all the billions of possible brain connections we have tracked down only a few thousand, the simplest of the couplings. The puny knowledge we have wrested from the brain would be just as valid if the cranium were stuffed with cotton wadding—it's still almost literally true. We try to cut away some tonus, we also cut away the alertness, imagination, memory, sense of self. We excise much of the orgasm, the sexuality. We go after the tensions that come from great emotional ambivalence, we often kill the emotionality altogether—we attack anxiety and wind up smothering anticipation. We don't know what we are doing, we don't know. It is ceremonial magic. We must confess: the therapy is more for ourselves, for the village, than for the patient."

Of course, a simple answer could be made to this line of reasoning: the brain which emerged from such therapeutics was the brain considered healthy in this village. The village defined a healthy mind as precisely one which inhibited imagination and alertness and egoness, which shunned any intense emotionality, did not produce much tonicity or orgasm or sexuality.

A simple answer indeed; much too simple. Because there were no grounds other than wishful thinking for the belief that the brain defined as normal locally was, ipso facto, the ideally healthy brain. Other villages defined the normal brain very differently, and each one believed that its norm was synonymous with health. They could not all be right. At least, some had to be more right than others. Or less wrong.

Is deviation from the locally approved norms always and everywhere to be taken as disease? Is it possible that in some communities the norms are defined too narrowly and severely, thus placing the onus of sickness on what are often nonpathological individual variations? Couldn't many of these variations, stemming from unique subjective powers, enrich the life of a village, give it a stimulating complexity, if the village were tolerant enough to see them as differences rather than diseases? Doesn't the rigidity and narrowness of a village's norms often drive a deviant from difference into disease?

"What do I think?" Martine said. "I must study more too, much more. But I have arrived at a certain credo. *Primum non nocere*: Above all, do no harm. I think that it is vicious

58

and evil for one man to do damage to another, or even to wish to very intensely. But I think that flabbiness can be a vice and an evil too. Sleep destroys human beings as much as war. Sleep is self-imposed damage, and I think it is evil for a man to do damage to himself as well. . . ."

His voice faltered, died away. Why, suddenly, did he have the sickening feeling that, behind the mask of the Olympian lecturer, he was really talking about himself? That, maybe, he had been sleeping, curled like a foetus, for well over eighteen years in this cave? Sleep—sleep was a steamroller too. Immobilization—self-immobilization, that was the worst steamroller of all. . . .

"And if it is wrong to do damage to another, what if Mandunga should turn out to be a damage? In the months ahead, you can find out for yourselves: add up all the data in our thousands of case histories and make a statistical summary. And keep this last question in mind: If Mandunga *is* a damaging, what are we to say of those who inflict it on others? Are they not carrying on, under the slogan of pacifism, a war of their own, a surgical-magical war? Then are these pacifists not the subtlest kind of aggressors? I leave it to your statisticians to give us the answer."

A long time ago, Martine said, a poet had asked a very pointed question: "Are there other lives?" And he had answered the question for himself: "It seemed to me that to every creature several *other* lives were due." Could it be that here, in their own village, other lives, lives that were not bland incognitos, were both possible and due? The same poet, sensing that what a village calls out from a man may not be his whole or even his best potential, had thundered a warning: "Don't be a victim." Martine's credo was a slight elaboration of that: Don't be a victim—of the outside *or* of yourself—and don't victimize anybody else.

He had to leave now, for a while. In his absence, he wished them peace—with alertness. He wished them long life, and the energy to live it hard and fully.

He hoped that the war would stay on the other side of the river. But he hoped that some of the ego push which war stirs up in men and puts to terrible use, some of the greed for experience and zest for the new, would come to *their* side of the river. Some of the cerebrotone and somatotone tension of war, without war.

If that happened, there might be a third date in Mandunji history. That would be something to anticipate—perhaps without too much anxiety.

Rambo went first down the narrow winding path, carrying the searchlight. No sign of the queer-limbs about. It was a long climb, but finally they came to the little dock alongside which dozens of fishing boats were tied up—in an inlet whose mouth was almost entirely hidden from outside view by a thick overhang of branches and vines. The trim blue-and-white catamaran with its gawky pontoons, the biggest of the vessels, rode peacefully in the moonlight; Rambo stopped when he reached it, and a moment later Martine joined him on the dock.

"Did you understand my lecture?" Martine asked.

"Some, I did not know all the words. I shall understand more, I shall study."

"Good." The moonlight filtered down into the basin, he could see Rambo's bronzed, solemn face. "Don't study just the serious things. Try to understand the jokes too."

The boy nodded; his eyes sparkled too much, he was near tears.

"I want to tell you something, son. The poet I mentioned in my talk, he was a Frenchman, his name was R,i,m,-b,a,u,d, pronounced Rambo. You were named after him."

The boy was startled. "Why? Was he a man to imitate?"

"No. No, it was not that." Martine spoke slowly, he wanted to get this very straight, it was important to make Rambo understand but first *he* had to understand. "He was not a man to imitate. But, you see, when he was only two years older than you he decided that he could have other and better lives than Europe would allow him, he thought Europe was dead and finished and he ran away to Africa. And when I came to the island a hundred years later I was running away from the West too, from its wars, and I felt that what I had left behind was hopeless too. So I thought a lot about Rimbaud. And a little later, when you were born, I decided to name you after him, it was just a romantic gesture against my past."

"But what was good about this man?"

"His life was not good. You see, when you have to spend your whole life attacking and running away from something, you are no better off than those who spend their whole lives uncritically defending that thing. A man who is driven to flee from a village is no more free than those who are driven to stay and support it's ways. One is as compulsive as the other, and so long as you are pushed by compulsions you are not free. Some 'It' is riding you, the 'I' is not in control and that's the big thing. . . . But if this man could not be

free in his life, he sometimes through his agony saw
things, important things that others did not see so clearly.
Although he was all his life a victim of his compulsions,
he saw that the worst thing was to be a victim. And to be
asleep. . . . It is a good name to have. His book is in my
hut, take the time to read it."

"I shall, Father." Then: "Is—is some 'It' riding you now?"

"Maybe so." Martine put his arms around the boy and
kissed him on both cheeks. "You are intelligent and alive," he
said. "It is a good feeling to look at you and to know you
are my son. If I leave nothing behind me in the world but
you, I will be satisfied."

He climbed down into the catamaran and started the
motor. It coughed a couple of times, then began to hum
smoothly.

"Your mother is suffering very much," he said. "It would
only give her more pain if I went back to see her again. Say
good-bye to her for me, Rambo—and take care of her, she
has no one else."

"I shall do my best."

"Tell her there will be no more going away. I will not
come back until I am sure of that."

The boy's eyes were very wet now, pools of bewilderment
and hurt.

"You've got to understand!" Martine said, more loudly
than he had intended. "I have to go, I have to, for more
reasons than I know myself. Maybe it doesn't have much
to do with these damned queer-limbs at all—maybe it's just
that I've been living here incognito all these years, feel that
I have, and now the time has come to go looking for my
real self. Something like that. Something's been stirring in
me ever since these damned queer-limbs first showed up—
even before. . . . But I will do everything to come back. So
long as I am alive, I will try to come back. If I don't, you
will know that I am dead—but that until I died I kept trying."

He cast off the rope. Rambo leaned over, tears were
running down his cheeks, he said excitedly, with a quaver in
his voice, "I do not know what you are going to look for out
there, Father. But may you find it."

"Thanks, son. I hope I find it too. Whatever it is." He
waved, the boat began to move.

from dr. martine's notebook
(mark ii)

MAY 30, 1990
Diego Suarez, Madagascar
Three days to get here. Sea calm as tapioca all the way.

Town's a junk yard, just about as I remember it from my last trip (not long before my plane fell apart: 1947?). Deserted except for a few old Afrikanders—they run a small airstrip, a rickety dock, and a fleabag called, in a splash of anachronism, the Royal Dutch Inn.

No curiosity about me. They swallowed my story without batting an eyelash. I'm Dr. Lazarus, parasitologist, been studying tropical diseases in the area, going home now to report my findings. Pleased with that—nifty incognito.

The catamaran will be safe here, they'll look after it until I pick it up. Paid them a year's rent and maintenance fees in advance. Reaction to my old greenbacks: Royal Dutch glee.

Boat for Mozambique due in five days.

Growing a beard to go with my moustache.

MAY 30, 1990
Mozambique, Mozambique
Pretty much the same setup here: airstrip, few warehouses, dock, flophouse-hotel, handful of inward-turned old Afrikanders. There's one ancient tub, apparently, that shuttles between here and Durban. Scheduled to pull in about four days from now, it's pretty erratic in its movements.

Place hasn't changed much. Flowers, vines, creepers sprout on everything: the branch office of Lloyds' of London, an old automobile pump, a first-aid kit, an equestrian statue of General Smuts, a tarnished silver box containing a pessary.

Walked along the waterfront this morning, dodging the craters. Few blocks from the hotel: a Cadillac convertible ('69 model) covered, inundated from radiator to rear bumper, with bougainvillaea.

Awake all night thinking about Ooda.

JUNE 5, 1990
Durban, Union of South Africa

Another coastal whistle-stop. Everything the same here, except the old folks are Belgians. Still not a sign of a plastic leg. Another wait of a few days, for the prewar freighter that limps between here and Cape Town.

My greenbacks received with great enthusiasm here too. Glad I thought to pick some up during my scavenging days: must have somewhere between 400 and 500 million in old American bills back in the cave, plus about half that amount in other currencies, plus Christ knows how much in bullion. Mother always told me to lay aside a little something for a rainy day.

Seems I can catch either a plane or a ship at Cape Town. Guess it's the ship for me. Slower, give me time to get my beard under way.

Rambo certainly got the straight dope about passports: people seem to have forgotten there ever was such a precious hunk of paper. From the looks of things anybody can hop onto any kind of ship and go anywhere in the world, with no questions asked. Hurrah for the Brotherhood of Man.

What about this business of destiny? Thinking of my mother a minute ago reminded me of it.

Of course, everybody has moments of grandiosity in which he likes to think that he's something special—that some special force is hovering over him, taking charge of his affairs and seeing to it that he glides through his charmed life. Destiny, in that sense, is just one more word for the "It" which people, panicky over being responsible for themselves, dream of in flurries of nostalgia for the blessed passive state: a self-propelled Womb-Cradle which carries the quiescent "I" down the greased tracks of Kismet and Karma to some benign End.

Still—wasn't there some kind of putty-nosed destiny that steered me to the Mandunji?

If my end doesn't clinch the thing, consider my beginnings. Here I can call upon my mother as witness. As she reconstructed it for me many times, she was already over three months pregnant when my father was summoned from Salt Lake City (where he was connected with the medical school at the University, as professor of radiological medicine) to Alamogordo. At first he was to stay there for just a month or so, planning some of the medical tests to be used in the first experimental atom-bomb explosion. But it stretched

63

into two months, then three, then four, and finally it looked as though he would have to stay right through the explosion and for some time after. Since he didn't want mother to be by herself he sent for her and she was installed in a cottage in Los Alamos.

Came the morning of July 16, 1945. Mother was in the parlor, knitting baby socks. There was a tremendous flash of light in the skies outside, the windows clattered, soon a wild wind rushed through the room. My mother blinked, swallowed hard, gave a deep sigh, and almost immediately went into labor. I was born an hour later, almost two months before my time.

Was there some Fate that arranged for me to make my debut under the Sign of the Mushroom? Whisked me from July 16, 1945 (Los Alamos), to October 19, 1972 (the Mandunji cave)—from the Sign of the Mushroom to the Sign of the Scalpel?

Destiny? Or what the surrealists used to call *l'humeur noir*? (Rough translation: "a crepe-hung gag.")

Crazy thought: maybe my mother's still alive? No, no, that would be too much *l'humeur noir*. . . .

JUNE 7, 1990
Durban
Something bothering me: why have I started to keep a notebook again? It's an asinine schoolboy's trick, haven't done it since the war, 1972.

Seems that in big moments I'm moved to eloquence. Strange, considering that I never did put much stock in words—always twitted politicos like Helder because they gabbed so much, spouted such a mucky sloganizing lingo— as though words were anything but dust in the eyes, lures, decoys.

Do I consider *my* words so remarkable? At least markable? Is the diary a mealy-mouthed way of trying to make a mark, of telling the world: Mark my words? Maybe I ought to label my notebooks the way cyberneticists used to label the successive versions of a guided missile or a robot brain: Mark I, Mark II, Mark III. . . .

Last time it was more understandable, in a way. I was a lot younger and I'd been off to the EMSIAC wars for well over a year, operating day and night. It was really getting me down (Helder seemed to take it better than I did), and at odd moments I would huddle up in my bunk in the barracks plane and make jottings in my notebook just to hold on to whatever shreds of sanity I had left.

Wonder what happened to that old journal of mine? I beat it in such a hurry that I didn't stop to round up the odds and ends.

Still, why fool with a notebook? You could say it's just a diversion, way of passing the time, but the motive is more devious than that: some furtive itch for immortality or whatever. (For that matter, why "go along" with Mandunga? Same itch?) Back in the war, though, I wasn't conscious of writing my notes for anybody's eyes but mine. Nor am I now.

Correction: just looked back to yesterday's entries and saw that when I mentioned my father I added a parenthetical phrase identifying him as a professor of radiological medicine, etc. I could hardly have slipped in this biographical tidbit for my own eyes, I know damned well the old man was professor of radiological medicine. For whose eyes, then?

My God, maybe I have some megalomaniacal myth about being a man of destiny after all. Maybe I've hung on to some tattered idea that my life is somehow significant and star-ridden—that I'm fated to have an impact on the world, heaven help us. (Through Mandunga, if nothing else offers itself?) The Western ego has a hell of a tough time shaking off its sense of mission. . . .

Just thought of General Smuts back in Mozambique, lying on his side without arms, knees still clutching his legless horse, covered with banyan creepers and lichens. Immediately restored my sense of balance. . . .

JUNE 9, 1990
Durban
Still waiting for that lackadaisical freighter.

Went poking around the outskirts of town today, on the other side of the bomb craters. Came across a little neighborhood library in pretty fair condition. Just inside the door, hunched under a desk, a human skeleton, female, about forty-five I'd say, quite brachycephalic (wish I could forget that word). Most likely she'd tried to hide when the bombers came over but the radiological dust got her: tortoise-shell eyeglasses still hugging the skull (once a librarian, always a librarian), a rubber stamp with the date "August 23, 1972" still between the bones of the thumb and index finger of the right hand. Over in the corner a pile of books, the wooden shelves had rotted away and they'd all tumbled to the floor. One book lying off to the side covered with red

ants, brushed it off and picked it up. French edition of Dostoevsky's *Notes from Underground*, which I read several times
over when I was a medical student in New York and
hanging around the Village a lot. (Time I was rooming with
Helder.) As I remember, the story is devoted to the theme
that twice-two-equals-four is an evil proposition. Theme
that's been carved in my hide. (Helder hated the book,
wouldn't read it; but he was the one who suggested the
tattoo.)

Case of Notoa: psychiatric teaser, and it's important. Not
just because it would be nice to have good books and
paintings around—that's relatively unimportant, people can
live without the esthetic frills. No, what's crucial about the
sick artist is that he merely dramatizes the plight of the
average person in the community. With *everybody* the
problem is to wrest energy away from the masochistic
compulsions (the "It" inside) and make it available to the
"I" for creative work. Mandunga begs the whole question,
just goes after every sign of energy with a knife.

JUNE 15, 1990
Cape Town, Union of South Africa
Made it, finally. Things are a little livelier around here,
town's still a mess but a section of the waterfront's been
restored. Handful of Americans around waiting for the liner
(due in next week from Dakar), including a few young
quadro-amps: they strut around the place like cocks of the
walk, everybody kowtows to them.

Observe with relief that, just as Rambo reported, the non-
amp older men dress very much as they did twenty years
ago. My elegant prewar tweeds and flannels will do very
nicely, seems nobody pays much attention to non-amps
anyhow.

Having my meals brought up to my room. Don't want to
meet any of my fellow countrymen out here, they might get
too interested in my story.

Beard coming along splendidly: beginning to look like
General Smuts.

JUNE 22, 1990
Cape Town
Sleeping and eating, eating and sleeping. Mind's been a
blank for a week. Dreamed last night that I was back home
with Irene, I was tied down to the bed and she had one of

66

my scalpels in her hand and was cutting off my limbs one by one, me yelling bloody murder. "Oh, stop complaining," she kept saying. "Didn't your precious Rimbaud say, 'One must be absolutely modern'?" Woke up in a sweat. With a silly phrase knocking around in my head: "There's too damned much tapioca in the hypodermic needle."

Liner's arriving in the morning. Hallelujah.

JUNE 23, 1990
Aboard S.S. Norbert Wiener

That's what the liner's called, all right. Breezed up the gangplank, bought my passage from the purser, installed in nifty outside stateroom, nobody said boo.

Weird sort of ship. Must be a larger version of the one the Olympic team's cruising in: like a long box lying on its side, open at both ends, the bottom side missing (the one that would be in the water). Cross section:

Topside has several layers, decks with staterooms, cargo space, etc.; supporting it are two thin vertical slabs which rest in the water, between them open space. Run by an atomic power plant, of course. Jerry, my steward, tells me the vessel is developed from an experimental ship Gar Wood built back in the forties.

Real break having Jerry for my steward: nice kid, about nineteen, red-haired, very amiable and very naïve. Uni-amp. No suspicions about my story—parasitologist, staying in my cabin because of a touch of malaria, haven't been back home for many years.

"Guess I'm sort of out of touch with things," I said when he brought my lunch. "As you see, I'm not an amp."

"Oh, lots of the older men aren't," he said. "It's not the older men who fight the wars."

Gather from Jerry's remarks that there are two major powers in the world: the Inland Strip, which is the focal point of whatever little clusters of communities have been

67

rebuilt in the Western Hemisphere, and the East Union, which is based in what used to be Russia and takes in whatever centers have sprung up in the Asiatic, Near Eastern and European areas. Together they make up the civilized world: everything's sweetness and light between them, one big happy family.

"How big is the Inland Strip now?" I asked.

"Population's up to thirty-four million," Jerry said. "Of course, it's still peanuts compared to what the States were. I guess you'd remember the States, wouldn't you? They've really shrunk some."

"They weren't sanforized," I said.

His face was blank and I didn't press the point.

JUNE 24, 1990
Aboard the Wiener

Just my luck. (Or destiny?) Was looking out the porthole a few minutes ago, daydreaming, when who should stroll by on deck but Theo.

Theo! Of course he *did* tell Ubu he had to leave in about a month—guess he flew to Cape Town and boarded the ship yesterday.

Think I'll stick close to my cabin—something about this guy bothers me, I'd just as soon avoid him.

It's not just that he's so strikingly brachycephalic. He's also got a hell of an ugly jagged scar running all the way down from his crown to his neck, I hadn't seen that on the island. It jumps right out at you when you see him from the rear, because of his crew cut the whole thing's visible.

Haven't seen a male passenger under forty with all his own limbs. Another thing, there's some kind of hierarchy of status involved, it hits you immediately in people's attitudes. Seems to depend on how many limbs are gone. I notice, for example, that the captain and first mate of the ship have four artificial limbs, the second-rank officers have three or two, and most of the deck hands and stewards only have one. And those with fewer artificial limbs treat those who have three or four with great deference. Quite a few women on board, none of them amps.

But, to judge from what I see through the porthole, Brother Theo is really kingpin around here. Everybody butters up to him, even the captain and the other quadros.

Who in the name of sweet Jesus is he? Why, every time I catch sight of him, do my fingers begin to twitch?

JUNE 26, 1990
Aboard the Wiener

This morning I noticed Jerry's tie-clasp. Large button with the design of a triskelion, circle with several legs fanning out from the focal point, running legs: miniature prosthetics, transparent, inside them luminous pinpoints representing tubes and gold elements duplicating the moving parts.

"Nice," I said. "Where'd you get it?"

"My mother gave it to me. Birthday present."

That reminded me of my own speculations about birthdays; they seem to keep coming back. "Tell me something," I said. "Do you think the day you're born on is pretty much a matter of accident? Or do you think it's all part of a scheme?"

"How do you mean?"

"Well, what about people who get born on special days, real red-letter days? Such people often think it was arranged that way—that they were somehow *picked* for the honor. For example, I know of a fellow who played with such ideas about himself. He was born on July 16, 1945."

"Huh!" Jerry said. "Alamagordo Day. Who doesn't know somebody who was born on *that* day?"

I didn't know what to answer. Did he mean that there'd been a mass labor precipitated around the country on the Day of the Mushroom, that women had given birth all over the place? I'd never heard that before, it irked me a bit, made my distinction seem a commonplace.

"I've got a pretty special birthday myself," Jerry added.

"What is it?"

"I was born October 19, 1972."

I choked on the toast, quickly got over it with a couple gulps of coffee. Why, he might have popped on the scene at the very moment the bombs were cascading down over our encampment; maybe even the moment I was taking off in the surgery plane.

"What's so special about that?"

"Heck," Jerry said, "a lot of people will tell you that Immob really got started that day, that's all. That's all that's special about it."

"Oh, sure," I said. "I see what you mean. For a moment I didn't make the connection."

When he left me my head was spinning. Wish to hell I *could* make the connection. Something else must have taken place on the day I gave up, something big. Talk about destiny—looks like my career is cluttered with red-letter days. And red-letter nonsense syllables.

Immob. Is it a word or a hiccup?

Part Two

TO THE INLAND STRIP

---

chapter seven

VOICES OUTSIDE the porthole. Martine put his pen down and flexed his cramped fingers, he'd gotten out of the habit of writing, it was tiring.

Slowly, without concentrating on it, he became aware that one of the voices coming from the promenade deck was Theo's. He switched off the desk's softly glowing glass top, turned out the luminous plastic ceiling too; then he went to the porthole and opened the curtains a slit.

Balmy: in the moonlight the subtropical Atlantic was like melted quartz. Several of the V.I.P.'s were sitting around a large umbrella-topped table near the railing, drinking lemonade and chatting. They were all quadros—should they be called plus-fours or minus-fours?—among them the ship's captain, a few of his officers, and some of the more distinguished-looking passengers. All of them, including Theo, their guest of honor, were in evening clothes: white dinner jacket with sleeves shortened to expose the arms, striped black trousers ending well above the knees to show the legs. Logical costume—no extremities to keep warm.

"So it was a nice trip?" the captain said.

"Perfect," Theo said. "Did me a world of good. I always seem to relax more on a boat than in a plane, that's why I decided not to fly home."

"Did you put in at any interesting places?"

"Well, we just lazed around the Indian Ocean mostly, visited islands here and there. On one of the islands there was a pretty unusual tribe called the Mandunji. I caught some butterflies there that were honeys. Then I flew up to

Lake Victoria to see how the Dredging Project is coming along. Got in some fine skiing on Kilimanjaro."

"Sort of a pleasure jaunt," the second mate said.

"The Olympic team was aboard, it was really a training cruise for them. I just went along for the ride."

"That was a real break for them, having you around to give them some pointers," the first mate said.

"Well, my athletic days are over, you know. Last time I competed in the Olympics, let's see, that was six years ago. I'd already slowed up pretty badly."

"Slowed up, my eye. That year, if I remember, you broke seven world's records."

"Sure," one of the passengers said. "I remember the exact figures. High jump, thirty-nine feet something. Pole vault, sixty-three feet something. Broad jump, eighty-seven. Shot put, three hundred and—"

"Don't give me too much credit for all that," Theo said. "Don't forget, 1984, that was the year our pros got really good."

"You had good pros, all right," the first mate said, "but you still had to co-ordinate your pros. Why, the sports writers still refer to you as the greatest neuro-loco co-ordinator who ever took part in the Games."

"Meadow dressing," Theo said. "You want to take a look at some of those boys I left out on the training yacht."

"What about the East Union team? They've been talking pretty big lately."

"They always shoot their mouths off before the Games, but look at the record. They're good, all right, but just not good enough, it's a question of technological know-how and technique and in those departments they can't hold a candle to us. We're a cinch to win every event, just as we always have."

Martine pulled the curtains shut and switched on the lumi-ceiling again. He wandered around the room absent-mindedly, did a waltz step, scratched his left armpit, sang a few lines from an old Mandunji chant, a pentatonic work song that went,

> Knots are very hard to cut with an adze.
> They blunt the edges of the adze.
> How hard I am working to cut these knots.

Then he sat down at the desk, opened his notebook to the last entry and began to write rapidly:

72

They're very cybernetics-minded, these amps. Also, they seem to be very much interested in metallurgy. (Jerry, for instance, is studying the subject in some university, hopes to get a civil service job as a cybernetics metallurgist.) Which makes sense: you can't build machines without metals, cybernetics is after all only the science of duplicating in the metal what exists less perfectly—because more ambiguously—in the flesh. All right. But there's a mystery here: why is this Theo so damned cagey about his interest in metals? Why does he have to dress up a mining expedition around the islands of the Indian Ocean as an Olympic training cruise plus a little innocent tourism? Why does he keep mum about the rock digging and the ore assaying? And he doesn't only lie to the Mandunji about it, he lies to his friends and fellow amps as well. . . . Like to find out more about this fellow. When we hit Florida tomorrow I may be, by a most peculiar turn of events, the only person in the Western Hemisphere who knows that when Theo says sports he means digging, when he says botany he means digging, when he says zoology he means digging. . . .

Once again he put the lights out and went to the porthole.

". . . . tell the truth, though," Theo was saying, "events like weight-lifting and jumping and shot-putting always left me cold. They're tests of strength, not skill."

"I don't follow you," the first mate said.

"Well, take the high jump. What gets a man up thirty-nine feet and down again? Can he take the credit for the leap? No, sir. The real credit goes to the engineers who built his pros, the cyberneticists. What's being demonstrated, mostly, is the efficiency of the elements in the pro: the solenoids, the atomic-energy plant, the servo-mechanisms, the oleo-strut shock absorbers."

"Which events *do* you like?" the captain asked.

"The dexterities, most of all. The dexterities and the discernments."

"I think I see what you mean," the ship's doctor said. "The d-and-d's test the cortex controlling the pros."

"That's it exactly."

"You've got a point," a passenger said. "Since we're all supposed to be humanists—"

"That's what I'm getting at," Theo said enthusiastically. "Immob is the first real humanism in the history of human

73

thought. The d-and-d's show the potentialities of the human brain and point the way to the superior brain of the future."

"According to your way of thinking," the captain said, "a lot of the standard events ought to be dropped from the Olympics entirely."

"I'm sure they will be," Theo said. "When Immob really comes of age, I foresee that athletics as we know them, in the old strength-testing sense, will disappear."

"I'd hate to see the old events go entirely," the first mate said. "I think we'd lose something. We ought to feel a *little* proud of our cyberneticists and the machines they make."

"Certainly, but from an Immob perspective. If the EMSIAC war taught us anything, it was that all our machines are monsters unless we have a firm mastery over them. In this transitional period, I think, we're sometimes in danger of forgetting that our pros, marvels though they are, aren't one straw as astonishing as the brains of the cyberneticists who designed and built them and the brains of the amps who operate them. See what I mean? The human being must always be central, not the products and objects of his skill and energy. Wiener used to say that over and over. That's the whole spirit of Immob."

Theo stood up and raised one plastic hand. With a series of lightning-quick movements he lifted the collar of his shirt, unbuttoned it, undid the tie and slipped it off. "Here," he said, "I'll show you what I mean."

Still holding the tie, he reached over to the table and took from it two small saucers.

"Think back," he said. "Remember how awkward your real hands used to be? For example, most people with real hands don't co-ordinate well enough to juggle anything at all, even two small saucers, and when it comes to tying a bow tie, well, they're often all thumbs. Now watch this."

Using only one hand, he began to toss the saucers above his head, one at a time. After each heave, in the split second between the release of one and the catching of the other, the hand flew up to the neck, fluttered there, then came down again just in time to meet the descending saucer. The observer's eye could follow the gross, overall movements—arm raised, hand working at neck; arm down, hand poised to catch saucer—but the detailed twitchings of the digits went much too fast to be seen as anything but a blur. Still, the thing was getting done: while the saucers rose and fell in perfect rhythm, the collar was buttoned, the tie was placed around the neckband, its ends were crossed, one end was tucked under and through to form a knot, the two halves of the bow were pulled out on each side to tighten the knot, the loops were adjusted in length and straightened, the collar was pulled down.

Theo put the saucers down, moved over closer to the umbrella (a luminous one), and turned so that his back was to Martine. "It took me almost seven months to learn that one," he said with a modest laugh.

His friends began to applaud. Martine ignored them: he was staring again at the long, zigzagging scar which ran down that broad-beamed skull, worm of a scar, white and lumpy.

Shit, what was he trying to remember?

He stood in the darkness for a moment, holding his hands up as though he had just sterilized them and were waiting for the rubber gloves: he felt a formicative creeping in the fingertips.

A peculiar thought came to him: My hands are blushing.

He turned the light on and examined them, they were glistening with sweat.

He knew that with him strong emotional states always tried to find some kinesthetic expression through the hands. Naturally, when he was trying hard to grasp something his supremely trained organs of grasp were mobilized in the effort. In this respect his cortex must be very much like that of a watchmaker or an embroiderer or a sculptor.

Still, he wasn't prepared for this: a 10:10 brachycephalic, a cranial scar, and immediately his hands were drenched and the fingers poised in a tense curled position and visibly tremulous. It didn't make sense, this pseudo-Parkinsonianism. It was as though his hands contained their own self-reverberating memory loops.

Then "in a flash" he saw what this digital positioning meant. He had been side-stepping its meaning for a month now, ever since Theo had first appeared in the village and his fingers had automatically hooked on thin air, but now he saw it. The fingers had fallen into the operative set, one hand was holding an invisible scalpel and the other a suction cup or suture clamp, something like that.

That, of course, didn't account for the trembling or the sweating. Theo's deep, soft, musical laugh drifted in through the curtains; Martine went back still again and looked out. Theo had turned around, his pleasant face, creased now with laughter, was bathed in the bright glow of the umbrella.

Martine's hands went up to his forehead, the palms pushing hard against his eyeballs. He felt weak, he thought that he might fall. He stood still for a time, afraid that if he opened his eyes and tried to take a step his legs would buckle. When he did finally move, his feet felt heavy, they dragged, it was like walking through water, but he managed to make it to the desk. He took up his pen and wrote in his notebook, over and over again: "October 19, 1972, October 19, 1972." Then he buried his head in his arms and, sickeningly, remembered.

October 19, 1972. He could reconstruct it pretty accurately. It had started the night before, October 18. He'd been without sleep, except for cat naps at odd moments, for close to four days, operating almost continually. The flying hospital unit was stationed for the moment in Central Africa: Belgian Congo, somewhere northwest of Stanleyville. Up north there'd been a head-on collision between one of the biggest American air fleets and an equally big Russian one; for three days a tremendous dogfight had been going on in the skies all the way from Morocco to the Libyan Desert, with thousands of planes being blown to bits and practically all the inhabited areas beneath being pulverized.

That was how the war went in those days: the fleets would cruise about, each under orders from its own EMSIAC, then they'd meet and open up on each other. The idea was to knock enemy planes out and bomb any installations on the ground that seemed to be used by the enemy or might be of potential use to him. Naturally, the casualties were terrific. Whenever possible, helicopters would go in and try to rescue the downed airmen, and if they were wounded but still alive they'd be given emergency treatment and flown to the nearest mobile hospital unit. So Martine's outfit got most of the casualties from North Africa. The brain-surgery cases, of course, were routed over to Martine and Helder and their crew: the skull-duggery boys. They kept at it until the instruments were about falling out of their hands.

Toward evening on October 18, they brought Babyface in. He was as bad a mess as Martine had ever seen, bad as you can get without being a corpse. The head injury was serious enough: the whole cranium had been ripped open by a fragment of shrapnel from the eyebrows down past the ears. To complicate things, both of the kid's legs had been snapped off neatly above the knees—that had happened, apparently, in a crackup somewhere around Tunis, when he was already unconscious from the cranial wounds.

It was a miracle that he was alive, he'd lost a lot of blood. But those helicopter rescue squads were good, they'd snatched him off the ground, pumped a lot of plasma and whole blood into him plus some cortisone and ACTH derivatives, doused him with penicillin and anti-bleeding chemicals, and shipped him down south by emergency jet plane to be fixed up good as new. He was still unconscious when they brought him in: respiration ragged, pulse awfully spotty. Martine didn't give him a chance.

While the kid was being prepared for surgery, purely as a matter of routine, Martine did the usual thing—went through his papers to check his identification, medical record, blood type, etc. He was stunned by what he found.

Babyface had a pretty remarkable background for a twenty-year-old, and not just medically: he was, for one thing, America's most famous ace of World War III. From the clippings in his wallet Martine learned that, single-handed, he had eliminated more enemy cities than any other five airmen put together, he had to his credit the destruction of Chungking, Warsaw, Paris, Johannesburg, and several other great cosmopolitan centers.

Martine kept trying to think as he read the clippings: How does it feel to know you erased Paris? Funny: he was a good-looking, raw-boned youngster, as nearly as you could judge from the scorched and blood-caked face, indistinguishable from millions of other American kids, and still when you looked at him you knew that he had certainly killed several million people with a few flicks of the wrist. By this time they were using H-bombs by the crate, including the delayed-action type which goes on spewing radioactivity over a wide area for a long time. And, when wind conditions were good, these were supplemented with radiological-warfare dust, RW dust. So that one efficient airman could knock out a whole cosmopolitan population pretty thoroughly.

But that wasn't Babyface's only claim to fame. Among his papers there was also a card which indicated that he'd been a leading member of Tri-P, the pacifist movement called the Peace Pledge Program which had been so active before the war. Helder, when he had roomed with Martine in New York, had been one of the organizers of Tri-P, he'd always been after the other students to join.

That was surprising about Babyface. Obviously, in some

idealistic spurt during his student days just two or three years before, he'd been revolted enough by the idea of war to have joined this movement which was sweeping the youth and to have signed its pledge "never to participate in any war whatsoever under any circumstances whatsoever." Even more, he'd been so much in earnest about the thing that he'd made quite a name for himself as a campaigner for peace at all costs—there were some clippings about that, too. Three years later, how many millions of notches did he have carved on his bombsight?

Martine couldn't resist showing the clippings to Helder. A look of horror came into Helder's eyes, he went over and studied the kid's face more carefully. "My God," he said shakily. "Sure, it's Teddy Gorman. I've spoken from the same platform with him a hundred times. I didn't recognize him on account of the blood."

"Take a good look," Martine said. "Observe the life cycle of the pacifist."

They were both out on their feet but even so Martine felt like baiting Helder, and Helder felt like arguing about it; he was never one to look an irony full in the face without blinking.

"What's it prove?" he said.

"Nothing much. Just that people are glad to be pacifists—in between wars."

Martine was thinking, too, about the movement initiated by students before World War II, the movement around the Oxford Peace Pledge. It was before his time but he'd read about it, matter of fact Tri-P was pretty much a revival of the Oxford idea.

"This is no reflection on the philosophy of pacifism," Helder insisted. "It only shows that up to now pacifist movements have been inefficient, tactically and programmatically."

"Sure," Martine said, "and for a very good reason. Look at this baby-faced mass murderer. Like all good pacifists, he was ready to sign the peace-at-any-price pledge at the drop of a slogan. And, two years later, to sprinkle H-bombs around at the drop of a slightly different slogan. Doesn't that suggest there's a certain gap between slogans—yours, anyhow—and motives? That people are a bit more complex and ambivalent than you merchants of good will recognize?"

"People are fundamentally simple—at the core of any man is the simplest thing of all, a great fund of good will.

We just have to find the words that will reach that simple core and activate it."

"Onward and upward!" Martine said. "If you'll excuse a wisecrack at such a time, maybe you should change that idea of progress to *unword* and upward. Your words only get people to agree not to fight when there isn't any fighting to be done."

"I'll grant you that we've got to do some serious thinking about how to extend the emotional appeal of our program," Helder said. "We're in a difficult transitional period."

From up forward came the clear steely rat-a-tat of the EMSIAC receiver.

"While you're at it," Martine said, "think about how to extend the emotional appeal of your program to you and me. I'd like to point out that at this precise transitional moment the two of us are not especially active in advancing the brotherhood of man. As I get the picture, we're somewhere in the Belgian Congo, on orders of EMSIAC, patching up soldiers' skulls because that's what EMSIAC wants us to do."

"Our movement isn't finished. Transitions are always hard to ride out. After this war we'll find a way to counter the propaganda of the war-makers."

Martine had to laugh at the flamboyance of the remark. Just two days before, word had reached their unit to the effect that the entire Eastern seaboard back home, from the Massachusetts coast down to Baltimore, had been pretty systematically laid waste in a mass H-bomb attack. Way over twenty million people had been killed or wounded, in spite of extensive civilian evacuation (delayed-action radioactivity and RW dust no doubt accounted for many of the casualties), and this followed on the heels of a similar attack on the West Coast, which had been reduced to a mass of rubble from San Diego to above Puget Sound. Already the population back home had been cut down by much more than a third, and the end wasn't yet in sight. Who could tell? Very possibly Martine's family and friends, and Helder's too, were now distributed in dainty shreds over some vast radioactive landscape, atomized at last into tranquillity.

"Noble words," Martine said. "Let's hope the war-makers leave a few people around for you to propagandize."

He handed Babyface's wallet to an assistant. Then he couldn't help adding, "The hitch is, it's hard to tell just who these war-makers of yours are any more. By the looks of things these days, just about everybody makes war. Or do you see some stout-hearted pacifist standing up to EMSIAC and telling it off?"

By this time the kid was ready for surgery; they both took some energy pills, then Helder got to work on the stumps and Martine went at the head.

For over three hours Martine's hands were probing around inside that mashed skull. He tried some daring techniques—he thought it was hopeless anyhow, what was there to lose?—experimental procedures that he'd never attempted before on anything but laboratory animals. His crew men stood around in amazement, it was one of his better efforts, a real virtuoso bit of protoplasmic tailoring. Several times the respiration bags went limp and the pulse disappeared, but with oxygen, digitalis and a dozen other things they managed to bring him back each time.

While his fingers maneuvered around in the head, Martine's mind was racing. The side of him that worked for EMSIAC did its job, and brilliantly. The other side hadn't yet been spotted and given its marching orders by EMSIAC, and it was thinking: Why in hell bother? Why not just let him die? Why not let them all die?

It wasn't enough to say that Babyface had been sloganized into doing what he'd done; you still had to consider his susceptibility to slogans. Because even Babyface was more than a morally neutral robot, he didn't simply carry out EMSIAC's instructions, before he carried them out he had to acquiesce to carrying them out. What Martine wanted to know was, where could this acquiescence be tracked down in this pacifist-homicidal brain—if somebody would only tell him, he would go after it immediately with his scalpel. He wanted to know what incisions to make in order to produce a brain which would say no to EMSIAC. As soon as this thought hit him, sweat began to roll down from his forehead. It wasn't only the heat or the exhaustion. No, his next thought was: *I* don't say no to EMSIAC either, I just abstractly, therapeutically, approve of the idea. . . .

The next minute—by this time he was fitting the tantalum plate which the lab technicians had prepared into Babyface's skull—he snapped back a little, saw a partial answer to his questions. Somewhere in this lacerated cortex, in some associational cluster he wasn't skillful enough to locate, was also a set of pathways which were loaded with idealism and good will and devotion to noble causes like Tri-P. This side of the brain didn't bulk very large against the more deeply rooted aggressions: the fondle networks are always

80

dwarfed by the fight networks: the pacifism only came into play during lulls, standstills and interregnums, when nobody had any use for the aggression. The surgical problem, then, was one of liberating the pacifist networks so that they couldn't be immediately blocked off by the violent ones the moment some EMSIAC sounded the bugle call.

As soon as he put it to himself that way he saw that it was not a surgical problem: nobody could ever know enough about these contraries in the brain to amputate the one without crippling the other. Maybe the truth was that you couldn't cut the ambivalence out of a human organism without hacking up every single cell in it, one by one. So knives were out. He couldn't do anything but sew Babyface up again and set him loose to prowl for more Parises. He wasn't God, he was only a patcher. You had to be a Helder to think you were God. . . .

That night he couldn't sleep; his eyes wouldn't close, although they smarted from exhaustion. For three or four miserable hours he sat huddled in his bunk, listening to EMSIAC clacking up front, listening to Helder snore away just above him. For a while he tried to read, a passage from Wiener, a few lines from Rimbaud. Then he opened his diary and began making notes.

He wrote for a long time, putting down all the ideas that had tumbled through his head when he'd been operating on Babyface, trying to escape that infernal snore. The jottings were pretty wild and bitter—among other things there was some sort of imaginary dialogue with Babyface that rambled on interminably.

From time to time he stopped writing and thought idly about his folks, such as they were: his father, who was dead: his mother, from whom he'd always held himself aloof, whom he hadn't seen for years: Irene, who'd divorced him right after he'd gone into the service, after months of estrangement; Tom, the son he'd never even seen—born just after the divorce, when Martine was already on overseas duty with the medical corps. He couldn't tell whether any of them were still alive, of course, although there hadn't been any reports so far about mass bombings up around Utah.

All of a sudden, though, he realized that he didn't much care. It made very little difference whether he ever saw them again or not, all personal relations had come to seem a bit indecent and irrelevant these past few years. The only one he cared about seeing was his son, he was interested in him. As for the rest of them, relatives, friends, neighbors, they all seemed suddenly to be just as insane as the whole civilization that had brought everybody to this point of mutual extermination. All the people he knew and had cared about (including himself: see his life with Irene) seemed to him now, in retrospect, to be little EMSIACS, little war-makers, little robot brains; the big EMSIAC had just put them all together, pooled their little wars and made a hell of a big war out of them. . . .

Somewhere way after two in the morning he put down his notebook. He was dizzy, he rubbed his temples and whispered to himself, "No. I don't want any more. Fuck it. I'm through."

What happened right after that was hard to remember. EMSIAC was clattering away imperviously, Helder was snoring hideously. He slipped the notebook under his pillow and went outside, thinking that he needed some air. Then he walked over to the surgery plane—it was a long distance off, they were carefully dispersed—and found there was nobody in it.

He climbed inside the plane and poked around for a few minutes. Just for something to do he checked to see how many atomic-energy capsules there were—many dozens, enough to run all the motors in the plane for two or three hundred years. He eased into the cockpit and energized the starter, just for the heck of it.

The next moment, without anything in his mind, he took off. Automatically, since everything that nauseated him lay to the north and west, he turned south and east.

Not a minute too soon. Talk about the hand of destiny. He looked at his watch and saw that it was 3:29. Then he became aware of EMSIAC clicking away in the communications room. The click was mixed with another, more ominous sound: the hoarse foghorn blast that was the signal for a red-flash emergency. He realized that the blast had been going on for minutes, it just hadn't registered.

He set the controls on automatic flight and hurried back to look at the tape. With uncomprehending eyes he stared at the little ribboned announcement of catastrophe:

Hospital Unit X-234-BL . . . attention . . . red flash alert . . . squadron of enemy bombers cruising toward your position approaching north northwest . . . expect attack 3:31 . . . do not try to take off . . . assume defensive positions . . . all anti-aircraft personnel to

Martine dashed back to the cockpit and peered out through the Plexiglas bubble. Sure enough, at about 3:33, great blinding flashes began to shimmy up from the encampment area, then seething white mushrooms of cloud. He couldn't see the bombers, the smart thing for him was to get the hell out of there even though there was some awful fascination in the scene.

Minutes later, with a jolt in his belly, he realized something. The mushrooms weren't receding any more. He had set the auto-flight for southeast and steep climb, the mushrooms should be dropping away and back as he watched. They weren't any more. They were coming closer, getting bigger. The plane wasn't climbing away, it had circled and was heading back in toward the camp.

He jumped. A metallic gutty voice bellowed out at him from the rear of the ship, twanging and hollow: *"Surgery plane 17-M, Hospital Unit X-234-BL. You are on unauthorized flight. We are returning you to base. Report to your commanding officer immediately upon landing for court-martial. You are on unauthorized flight. We are returning—"*

It was EMSIAC's voice, the electrovox voice which was activated only in the most extreme emergencies. The dreaded voice which never came through except to bark instructions involving the most urgent disciplinary procedures.

Martine understood now. The automatic pilot was not steering the plane. EMSIAC had taken over command of the flight and was whisking the craft back to its base despite the upstart wishes of its occupant. If the plane touched ground again it meant death for Martine. Even if he was lucky enough to survive the bombing attack, he would be shot for his desertion. The articles of war were perfectly clear about unauthorized flights.

He was insane with rage. They didn't give him a chance. They couldn't be bothered to find out whether this unauthorized flight indicated desertion or—oh, shit, absent-mindedness, vertigo, nausea, a cramp in the fingers from too much writing in notebooks, a shudder in the eardrums from too much snoring in the bunk above, a feeling of being smothered, a need to get out in the open and breathe, a need to sleep, anything. They didn't inquire as to his intentions. They didn't ask whether he'd intended to go away or just get a breath of fresh air. Unauthorized flight meant desertion meant court-martial meant a dozen slugs in the bread basket. They didn't even stop to consider that, no matter how he had happened to get into the air, now he *was* in it and down below everybody was going up in a boil of radioactive dust and it was more important to save him and the ship than to yell discipline and send him back to be vaporized too. They didn't care, the fucks. Whoever "they" were. The "they" that was the "It" that was EMSIAC.

In a blind panic he ran back to the communications room and began to pound the EMSIAC casing wildly with his fists.

"—*for court-martial,*" the voice droned. "*You are on unauthorized flight. We are returning you to base. Report—*"

There was a fireman's axe hanging on the corridor wall just outside. He noticed it now. He ran into the hall and yanked it away from its supports. Back in the communications room he began to hack at the EMSIAC container savagely, screaming with each blow.

"*Resistance is useless,*" the voice boomed. "*Do not try to resist. Do not touch the* EMSIAC *box. We are returning you—*"

Finally the casing gave way and the blade of the axe sank into the innards of the mechanism. Glass flew as he chopped through the banks of electronic tubes.

"*Do not touch the* EMSIAC *box. Resistance is useless. Do not tryeeeeeeeeeee—*"

There was a rattle, a violent hum, some incredible smothered grumble. He chopped, he hacked, sweat poured down his face. He was still screaming like a stuck pig.

Now in abrupt choked sound, an eerie gurgle. The hum grew and grew, became a crazy reverberating roar—

and stopped.

Just like that.

Dead silence.

He kept on swinging the axe, kept on until he had chopped through all the cables and tangles of multicolored wires. As he sliced through the last of them the plane gave a violent lurch, then shot up at a sharp angle, sending him sprawling on the floor.

Good, good. He had cut EMSIAC's connection with the automatic pilot. The plane was on its own now, resuming the course he had set for it.

He lifted his hand wearily, gasping, and looked at his watch. It was exactly 3:39.

He seemed to hear a metallic hum deep in his rumbling stomach. The hum turned into a snore turned into a clanging whistling screeching electrovox which said, "*Do not go berserk, it is unauthorized, stop screaming, it is unauthorized.*"

High-tailing off into the emptiness southeast, thinking that no doubt Babyface and his tantalum plate, Helder, his fountain pen, his notebook, his Wiener, his Rimbaud were back there now in a boiling mutuality, blended in an ooze of brotherhood.

Fleeing from the wars in Africa, his plane catapulting unerringly and all unknowing toward a speck of an island far off in the Indian Ocean—island that miraculously had never been charted on any map by any cartographer—where a handful of serious dark-skinned men were busy eating tapioca and chasing the devils from each other's heads. It had taken the Mandunji at least four centuries to flee the wars in Africa and get to the island, it was to take his plane at the very most four hours. . . .

He remembered it all now, almost all. When he could control the shake in his fingers he tried to write it all down as he remembered it. He wrote:

October 19, 1972.

Did it finally. I, my unrobotized side, said no.

I said no to "It."

I said NO.

I said

86

October 19, 1972. Jerry's birthday? Hell, no. Mine. Day I became a hobo in a jet. Day I was born, started to get born. . . .

But what was I getting born *as?*

No name for it yet, after eighteen years. Hard to recognize it, it's been smothered with incognitos.

Hard to write. Head was like a yoyo, eyes filled with swirling fog, but after resting for a minute he was able to focus on the notebook again and make his final entry for the day:

Mystery of Theo solved. I might have known—if that scarred brachycephalic head made my fingers curl and tremble so it was because they'd once been inside it. Of course. Got a good look at his face a few minutes ago and remembered, finally. To be sure, he's older, there's a suggestion of jowls and a touch of gray at the temples and the moustache threw me off too, but essentially it's still Babyface, the eraser of cities. Under the Theo there's the old Teddy: humanist with a tantalum skull.

My God, my God, *what's happened to his arms?*

chapter eight

MIAMI WAS part shambles, part ghost town. Through Jerry's high-powered binoculars Martine could see that the town had suffered a relatively light and haphazard bombing, not a merciless earth-scorching one: while many of the flimsier buildings had been razed, others, maybe because they had been built to stand off hurricane winds, had only been gouged and nipped at and made to buckle at the joints, not demolished.

He scanned the implausible vista from end to end. Here and there along the ragged skyline, jutting up senselessly from the rubble like an oversight, he could make out a lopsided villa, an upended hot-dog stand, the corkscrewed framework of a beach-front luxury hotel, a sagging night club with a fragment of neon tubing on its façade to remind the seagulls that its name had once been LA TROPI something or other—the rest of the letters were missing.

Martine rubbed his eyes and looked again. The thing he had seen was still there, it was moving: it was a giraffe and

87

it seemed to be nibbling at the neon letters on top of the night club.

The place was not quite deserted. Now he became aware of other movements in and around the debris—an undeniable camel here, an indisputable llama there, what could only be an okapi sprinting improbably down the avenue just beyond. Chewing its cud idiotically alongside a tiled swimming pool, a yak. Further on, standing guard outside a tilted real-estate office, a zebra.

Flashes of violent color. Flamingos, pink and preenful, were waddling on erector-set legs along the pock-marked pavements, poking their aristocratic beaks into the piles of—what?—one could only guess—sandals and sun-lotion bottles, contraceptives and cash registers.

Needing some point of orientation in the jumble, Martine began to search for the skyscraper hotel in which, right after his internship, he had spent a month's honeymoon—month (for Irene) of pouting, tearful unacknowledged frigidity, and much histrionic love-making in between by way of camouflage. Farcical month of pretending to himself and to Irene that a sham Eros was both the genuine article and superior to the genuine article—the thankless assignment handed to all inwardly fuming and martyr-complexed husbands by their glacial wives. There it was, on the beach down to the left, walls caved in and girders warped but still standing: THE BREEZEWAYS. By counting the cross pieces, memorials to vanished floors, he was even able to locate the corner suite in which the month-long charade of eroticism had been played out. (*I love a charade, the beat of the gums. . . .*) Something stirred on the steel beam: a spider monkey doing handsprings. . . .

Jerry came in to get the lunch tray.

"This is crazy," Martine said. "It looks like a menagerie out there. I just saw a giraffe."

"They're all over the place," Jerry said. "The circus was stationed at its winter quarters near here when the attack came, and most of the animals escaped. Later on, when we opened up the port again, we shot all the dangerous ones, but there wasn't any reason to bother about the others."

"I see Miami hasn't been rebuilt much."

"Question just never came up, I guess. The new cities in the Strip are more than enough for the people we have."

"Hasn't anything been done to the coasts at all?" Martine asked.

"Not much, outside of getting a few docks back in shape and laying out a few airfields."

"What about seaside resorts and all that? We used to be a nation of bathers and sun worshippers—is that all gone?"

"Pretty much—they don't have water sports in the Olympics any more, for instance. We've got plenty of sports and hobbies to keep us busy where we are."

"Like what?"

"Well," Jerry said, combing through his shock of red hair for the answer, "there're all kinds of evening classes for adults in the various schools. In Yoga breathing, panic control, auto-suggestion, moral equivalents, neuro-loco co-ordination, dianetics, semantics, and all that. Besides, for the younger amps there's Olympic training, we have special clubs for that, just the training in the d-and-d's takes up a lot of time. Oh, there are lots of things."

Something "clicked" in Martine's mind: a universal snared a particular. From Jerry he had gleaned all sort of information—about ways and means of transportation, the biggest cities in the Strip, hotel accommodations to be had—and he knew that the biggest city of all, the one he had made up his mind to visit himself, was called New Jamestown. Now Jerry had mentioned something called "moral equivalents," and abruptly his cortical nets began to put two and two together. William James, a philosopher and psychologist back in the nineteenth century, founder of pragmatism, had written an essay called *The Moral Equivalent of War*—Martine remembered it well from his college days. Was it possible that New Jamestown was named after him, not the historic Virginia settlement? If so, old James might be wishing that he could eat his words.

"That giraffe out there," Martine said, "could use a little coaching in semantics. He thinks words were meant to be eaten. He seemed to be eating words off old neon signs."

"The glass'll do terrible things to his stomach," Jerry said seriously. . . .

Martine waited until he saw Theo go down the gangplank, let another hour pass, then shook hands warmly with Jerry and went off in a cocoon-shaped transparent-shelled bus to the airport. The plane was a triple-deck jet, with room for a hundred people on each deck; it took off from a vertical position, resting on its tail, the seats swiveling so that the passengers were always upright regardless of the angle of flight.

Two men preceded Martine up through the entry hatch

89

and took seats directly in front of him. They were obviously foreigners: the heavy-shouldered, swarthy one looked like some sort of East European, something of the Balkans in him, something of the Slavic; the other, a short dumpy man with an Oriental cast to his features, seemed to be a Eurasian. Both were duo-amps, only their legs were artificial. The other passengers kept looking over in their direction and whispering, the airline personnel scraped and bowed. East Union bigwigs, Martine gathered; names were Vishinu and Dai.

When the craft ramped off from Miami Beach Martine pressed his forehead against the window and took a last look at the wrecked town. Directly below, munching on the grass around the remains of an orange-juice stand—VITALIZE WITH VITAMINS said the faded letters on the roof—was a herd of docile buffalo: in the end as in the beginning. Down Lincoln Road, at a point where a stuccoed beefburger basilica poked up through the ruins, a mother kangaroo was loping along, self-propelled pogo stick. From her pouch a baby kangaroo peered out at the sun-kissed havoc on both sides, wide-eyed and interested in everything, like a tourist in a boardwalk wheelchair.

Tampa was a sprawling junk heap; ditto Tallahassee; ditto Mobile, New Orleans, Houston and San Antonio. The sequence of mauled cities was so monotonous, so unrelieved, that after a while Martine hardly bothered to look down: one's senses were easily stunned, the cortex could encompass the fact of an individual's annihilation but not that of a hemisphere's.

Somewhere between the Panhandle and the Rockies the plane began to go down. He looked out and spied New Jamestown; he was electrified. He had been briefed on what not to expect; he remembered that even before the war most basic industry had gone underground, and Jerry had explained that when the rebuilding began these underground installations were kept and new cities were laid out over and around them. So he was not surprised to see no belching smokestacks and open hearths, none of the fume and grit of manufactures. But he was not prepared for the sheer geometric beauty of this glass-and-concrete diorama: it was as though the reverie of some city-planning visionary had been peeled from a drawing board, blown up and pasted life-size over the countryside.

He gawked. Spacious parkways fanned out from one enormous central hub, which seemed to contain all the commercial and institutional buildings; and in easy concentric arcs between these spokes, along tree-dotted and garden-lined streets and boulevards, great meandering stretches of streamlined skyscraper apartments, interspersed with sprinklings of smaller individual family living units. No neocolonial or neo-gothic horrors, no aping of the squat cubism of a vanished frontier or the gingerbread of an equally vanished, or at least irrelevant, European mother culture. A whole cosmopolis designed from scratch as a *machine à vivre*, without umbilicals or the pretense of umbilicals. And the old puritanical taboo on the spectrum, on chromatic playfulness, had at last been broken through: everywhere pleasant pastel shades and some richer still, lemony and carroty colors, colors of lobster and copper and absinthe, of plum, xanthite, the crocus, cinnamon. Apparently the H-bomb had in one great continental sizzle accomplished what the reformers and uplifters had never been able to: with a spurt of social-engineering efficiency it had cleared the slums from America overnight. It took Martine's breath away.

Oh, there was something seriously wrong with all this, of course, it wasn't really to his taste. It was all too hygienic and prissy, a bit too meticulously scrubbed behind the ears, too well-groomed, too goddamned aseptic. Wielding their compasses and T-squares, the planners had throttled the landscape with geometry, forced Nature's essential anarchy too severely into the perfections of circle and right angle, imposed the discipline of symmetry on what would be more reassuring with a touch of primordial chanciness, of riot and accident. So beautifully balanced mathematically, the city was, in another sense, unbalanced—all rota and no ganja. Still, it was a belated leap several centuries long. And besides, for those who cared to be reminded of Nature's penchant for the disheveled and the unkempt, there were, far off in the sunny haze to the west, the delectably disordered mountains: swooping, soaring, all random zigs and zags like a fever chart, the spatter of snow over their peaks unplanned as dandruff. It would do. There were compensations. From ten thousand feet up (the plane was losing altitude rapidly now, plummeting down for an upright tailpoint landing), squinting through puffs of cumulus, he could be uncritical enough—his evaluative centers momentarily hoodwinked by the flood of perceptions—to feel a twinge of pride in such a sculpture, the pride of one manual worker in another's superb handiwork. . . .

The two men in front of Martine were looking down at

91

New Jamestown now and talking in a precise, clipped English which bore traces of some polyglot cosmopolitan accent.

"Nice," said the short one. "Laid out very good."

"Façade is not unimposing," the other man said. "But underneath, phuh, you will see, all the old garbage. Same old exploiting mentality, Anglo-Saxons stick the noses up, Negroes segregated, the class struggle in a different form."

"Understood. I meant only the laying-out."

"Not so good as in New Tolstoygrad. Or New Singapore. Even New Saigon or New Pyongyang or, yes, New Surabaya."

"Naturally."

The stewardess, a provocative bit with swashbuckling bosoms, imminent strip tease in her swaying walk, came down the aisle and stopped opposite the two men. Her attiude was at once deferential and come-onish. She was wearing an extremely low-cut blouse; when she leaned over to talk with the taller man, who was in the near seat, her breasts were half-exposed.

"Excuse me," she said, husky voice full of the promise of prompt and unreluctant intimacies. "Are you gentlemen being met at the airport or would you care to use the copter shuttle service into town?"

"The transportation is entirely arranged," the heavy-set man said stiffly. The tips of her breasts brushed against his shoulder; he pulled away from the chesty overture. "We are to be met by a limousine of the Olympics Arrangements Committee."

The girl knew that she was dealing with dignitaries; she was all eyes, haunches and mammary glands.

"You—you're Brother Vishinu, aren't you?"

"Yes. And," the man added, "we need no advice on how to get around New Jamestown, thank you very much. I have been here many times before."

The girl looked hurt and angry as she moved down to Martine's seat. The Eurasian said softly, "They become worse and worse, the women. Absolutely without shame."

"With the fists out, like prizefighters," Brother Vishinu said loudly and distinctly. "Everywhere it is like that, but here they are the worst, they were with fists to begin with. It is all garbage, phuh."

The girl's face was flushed, she hardly noticed Martine as she rattled off the routine question.

"I'd like the copter service, I think," he said. "I want to go to the Gandhiji Hotel."

"Gate Three," she said mechanically. "The copter there will take you directly to the Gandhiji roof."

"Thank you." He wanted to add, "And here's a friendly tip: a real woman doesn't have to be a tout for herself," but he contented himself with thinking it. Was this the female that had come out of all the decades of much publicized and much denounced "momism," coyness dethroned by clamorousness? That was all very well, but when the old trappings of modesty were ripped off something still more suspect came into sight: a too blatant boasting about one's erotic prowess. Case of protesting too much. Because the rock-bottom truism about feminine sexuality (as indeed about male sexuality) remained: genuine potency and warmth requires no gusty salesmanship, no hullaballoo and hoopla—it's simply there, all phony modesty aside, and it will be sensed and savored and sought out by those whose emotional antennae are attuned to its subtle wave lengths. No sign-posts needed. Toss out the pudibund air, the downcast eye and easy blush; take all the "equal rights" and suffrage and sexual parity; still, why the showiness, the exaggerated undulation of the hips, the cosmetic over-eroticizing of the lips—the Hollywood flimflam that had always been taken by the gullible for real eroticism? It was a giveaway: torch on the surface, icicle underneath. There was about this girl the quality of an infant who had cleverly picked up certain gestures and mannerisms from her elders without knowing what they meant, the smell of the perpetual clitoridean type mired forever in the adolescent preliminaries to real sex, pelvis locked and erotic depths anesthetized. Shades of Irene. . . .

He had to smile at his upsurge of pique, the moment he was reminded of Irene he recaptured a touch of his old martyred feeling. No doubt he was feeling a bit put out because this girl, although she wore her superficial heat like a sandwich board, hadn't deigned to notice him. But personal feelings aside, he was curious to know whether this aggressive girl was typical of the new Inland Strip woman. If so, it might conceivably be that a real sexual revolution had taken place, at least that an old one had at last been completed. Such women, among other things, might have acquired such a taste for the upper hand that they would insist on it in bed too—it had happened before, shades of Irene. Which could lead to some positional alterations. He would have to make some cautious inquiries, as part of his research. Excuse me, madame, I don't mean to intrude but I have come to inquire about a position. . . .

He had wondered if the girl's obvious play for the two men hadn't been prompted by the fact that they were dignitaries; but no. Across from Martine was a young quadro-amp with the face of a petulant boy scout; when she approached him her wiles were just as lavish and blunt as they had been with the East Union duos. Obviously there was something erotically enticing about an amp, Martine simply was not in the running. Except that with these amps the running seemed to be in the wrong direction: a furious skedaddle, not a chase.

"Are you being met at the airport, sir?" she said, bending so low that her breasts were not only in the boy's line of vision but almost in his line of mastication.

"I am not," he said curtly, looking out the window.

"The copter might be crowded. Tell you what, I've got my car parked at the port. . . . I'd be glad to give you a lift."

There was murderous hostility in the amp's voice as he said, "Get this straight—I don't care to be given a 'lift,' by you or anybody else. I'm not a cripple."

So these amps hadn't managed to keep all wars on the other side of the river; the war between the sexes was very much with them. In some pretty spectacular forms. Phuh, garbage, etc.

As the plane backed down into the airport Martine, filled with anticipation and more than a little anxious, looked out. Several cigar-shaped objects in the sky some distance off, in the direction of New Jamestown: dirigibles, with signs on their sides that flashed on and off. Too far away to make out the letters.

chapter nine

THERE WAS A reservations desk in the roof-top solarium of the Gandhiji, for the convenience of those who arrived by copter. Martine had no trouble getting a room.

"Do you intend to stay long, Dr. Lazarus?" the clerk asked.

"Hard to say. I'm a parasitologist, I study parasites. When a new one turns up somewhere they send for me."

The clerk looked concerned.

"Don't worry," Martine added. "I'm not at the Gandhiji on business. It looks like you run a nice, clean place here."

"Oh, you won't find any parasites *here*, Doctor," the young man said emphatically. "The Gandhiji caters to a very exclusive clientele."

"Parasites are extremely democratic," Martine said. "They have much less class prejudice than people. A cat can only look at a king but a bedbug can dine on him for weeks. Henry the Eighth—"

The clerk's face was polite, interested, sober, clerkish. . . .

It was early, hardly more than dinner time, he was looking forward with excitement to his first glimpse of the city's street life, once he'd cleaned up and changed into some fresh clothes. But after showering he found that a numbing weariness had seeped through his body; the trip had been much more exhausting than he'd suspected, especially the last tropospheric leg of it.

Lethargy. He lay back in his shorts (excellent raw-silk ones from Switzerland, with the distinguished label of the House of Espuma-Rumpf inside the waistband) and let his thoughts wander. Somewhere in the sugar-candy city a clock boomed the hour: seven strokes.

Seven. On the Mandunji island it was way past midnight, everybody snoozing. But if there were any insomniacs still awake (Ooda?—smoking?—Rambo?—reading?) very few of them would be aware of the time as "past midnight." On the island, sunup to sundown was reckoned as day and the stretch of darkness as night, and no finer calibrations were needed. So long as you did the same thing all day long, shucked and ground maize or pulled in fishing nets, what reason was there to chop the day up? That had become necessary only for the young ones who had embraced the machine.

The moment the machine appeared in a community the clock appeared too, it was inevitable. And the machine had launched a real class struggle among the Mandunji: between the inert old with their lulling rhythm of day and night (calendar-oriented: each indivisible day like the day before) and the anticipatory young with their tense and jerky rhythms of hours and minute and seconds (clock-oriented: each striated day unlike the day before). Of course, mechanization had not yet swamped life on the island, men had not yet been made adjuncts of the machine. When that happened, when the Industrial Revolution was completed, life for all but the managers became a nightmare of metronomic monotony, a series of Pavlovian twitches—witness the Ford plant and Taylorism.

He slipped on a robe and went out on the balcony.

Directly to his left and two stories below, in another tier of sundecks, a young quadro-amp was stretched out on a couch, reading.

As Martine watched, a pretty and buxom girl came out, wearing high heels but dressed only in a brassiere and a pair of skimpy, clinging panties. She stood at the side of the couch for a time, looking down at the boy and tapping her foot, but he wouldn't raise his eyes. Then with a determined movement she pulled the book from his gleaming hands and dropped it on the floor, sank down beside him and stretched out so that her almost nude body was pressed against the whole length of his.

He made no movement. After a time she curled her arms around his shoulders and squirmed about until she was lying on top of him, her lips pressed ardently into his neck. She began to whisper something to him; she freed one hand, with a deft twist unplugged his left arm and put it on the floor.

For the first time the amp showed some sign of life. An expression of peevish rage on his face, he placed his remaining hand on the girl's back and with one powerful heave—Martine could hear the clicking—sent her sprawling across the floor. Then, his face frozen again, he retrieved his arm and plugged it back in, picked up the book and went back to his reading. The girl sat on the floor, rubbing her shins and glaring at him.

The girls seemed to be getting pretty forward, all right. Forward, upward, topward. Maybe position *had* become everything in life, at least in love. The girls seemed to have become positively disarming, preferred their lovers handsome but without hands—all this would take some looking into. But—the more the girls panted, the more the boys pouted.

What could the amp's book be: *War and Peace?* . . .

He leaned on the balustrade, looking down at the glittering Christmas tree of a city some fifty floors below. There were skyscrapers on every side, bright ones, peppermint sticks. Why? Why this devotion to the imperishable up-and-down, this anachronistic hunching and cramping? Strange, now that an atomic can-opener had pried the horizons open again and there was more elbow room on the continent than anybody had felt since Columbus and Cortez. Maybe all this, too, was dictated by a time-sense which was like a traffic cop, presiding over the instincts with a stop watch.

Clearly, when the ethos of a people was dominated by a fidgety awareness of the goose stepping minutes, the "play" minutes had to be carefully tagged so as not to become jumbled with the "work" minutes. There was only so much energy available to each organism: the bulk of it was permanently trapped in the "culture" networks, against which the frailer "instinct" networks struggled in vain—the top-sergeant frontal lobes saw to that. When schedules permitted a bit of a sensate romp it could only be fleeting, momentary, and then the instincts were not really unleashed, the dog collars remained on them. One was allowed, at best, a quick pause for breath between sobrieties. But if play couldn't encrouch on work, work butted in on play: men often made love as though it were an assignment, a job to be done, another bit of robot routine. A metronome in every cortex. An old medical book statistic (Kinsey?): three-quarters of American men reached the climax in less than two minutes, the bulk of them in less than thirty seconds; Johnny-Come-Earlys! Time must have no stop! Music, the art whose medium was time, through moods of resignation (metronomic regularity) or revolt (syncopation).

The instincts, in short, were verticalized: hasty soarings, even hastier plunges back to earth. The instincts on a high-speed elevator. And any symbol which stressed the verticals would be far more impregnated with meaning for such a people than one which proliferated horizontally, hugged the earth and bowed to gravity, meandered in the lateral stretches, shunned compression and thrusting rigidity in favor of bohemian flow—smacked of the feminine rather than the masculine. Not by accident that the instinctual, the emotional, had always been equated with the feminine. . . . And this instinctual verticality came all the more easily to a puritanical people who feared and mistrusted their bodies and could acknowledge them only in hasty surrenders—who shuttled between the ups of the "lofty" spirit and the deeps of the "lowly" flesh. Calvin had begun to preach his metronomic morality in Geneva only when Geneva had become a city of watchmakers. . . .

Wasn't jazz, too, part of this time-saddled picture? In its syncopated play with time, what was jazz but a toying with the idea of disrupting schedule and smashing the metronome—a toying, a nihilistic charade, but never the complete breakthrough? The trumpets and clarinets kept promising to desert the thumping four-four rhythm section and fly off anarchically into timeless, chaotic, unmetronomic space: that was the thrill in improvisation. But the promise was never fulfilled, any more than it was in Notoa's paintings. Jazz, with its abrupt orgasmic spasms and its split-second frenzies,

97

was nothing but emotional verticality transmuted into sound, and what seemed like joy in it was really anguish. The soloist made a pretense of evading the clock-ridden musical community in a brief blast of willful subjectivity—then sank back again into the harmonic and rhythmic traps of the community. . . .

Yes, what dictated motives was echoed in motifs. People with verticality in their instincts would cotton to verticality in their architecture, their sculpture, their playthings, their music. They would build trylons at their fairs, parachute drops and loop-the-loops in their Coney Islands; they would invent the airplane and jazz. And after a disaster, in a state of shock, they would perhaps draw inland too, close to the mountains and away from the sea—the sea is all a sideways flowing, ease and extension that knows no boundaries; the mountain is crammed and effortless upness, monument to tonus. And so: skyscraper equates with jazz equates with mountain equates with metronome equates with metronomic instincts: Eros punching the time clock. When would all this be plotted on the cytoarchitectonic map, when would the overzealous metronome be located in the cortical-thalamic networks so that something might be done to—?

A dirigible floated into sight over the skyscrapers and wheeled slowly around the hub of the city. The electric signs on its sides flashed on and off, Martine studied the words in astonishment:

> *Dodge the steamroller!*
> *Dodge the steamroller!*
> *Dodge the steamroller!*

Just that, over and over; nothing more. Gibberish. Why not, with equal logic, dodge the cyclotron? The player piano? The giraffe?

Still there was something tantalizing about the slogan. It had some slippery aura (error: horror) of meaning. The word "steamroller" set up reverberations—some unco-operative net of neurones shuddered. He remembered his farewell lecture in the cave: Why had he kept on using the silly word and being upste by it?

He turned from the epigrammatic dirigible and wandered inside again. He sang,

> *Knots are very hard to cut with an adze.*
> *They blunt the edges of the adze. . . .*

He stopped at the bureau and examined his face in the mirror, murmuring irrelevantly, "Dodge the skyscraper." Beard coming along nicely, he had trimmed it down into a neat Van Dyke.

What was it Abraham Lincoln had said about the human face? Something like this: Every man past forty is responsible for his own face. He was forty-five now. Was he ready to take responsibility for that bewhiskered oblong casing him from the mirror? Well, take the eyes (blue as a baboon's butt). They were a little wary and too bright, pulling back into their sockets as though to avoid being dazzled too easily: not too good but not too bad. Or take the lips. They were full, suggesting that their owner might be a bit of a voluptuary; but they dissolved in ambiguous shadows at the corners, suggesting that for all his plunges into the sensual he wondered if, finally, sensuality itself wasn't something of a joke, a dodge, a diversion, loaded with ironies as every human ardor eventually was, because the human being couldn't quite bring off the animalistic: he looked too ridiculous on all fours. Lips that poked fun at themselves, ends negating middles. But the real tug-of-war was between the eyes and the lips. The eyes hovered editorially over the lips, making their own sardonic comments on every smacking and nuzzling and guzzling—they were Peeping Toms on every lust which transpired below, through their windows the prefrontal lobes peered out, interpreting and labeling the whole gamut of greeds the mouth was slave to. Not entirely good, not entirely bad either, maybe. . . .

But there was something else in the too intent blue eyes that wasn't so good, something more chesty than cheeky. Some of the brightness came, not from leeriness and irreverence, but from a sense of dedication, mission. It was the gleam of the messianic.

But at least there was mischief in the face to dilute the missionary. A good old American trait too. Only it seemed out of place in this new America. If his first quick impressions were correct, nobody bellylaughed around here any more. These people had suddenly become as dour as certain Middle Europeans of the old days. . . . All that had been in Lincoln's face, certainly: terrible naked melancholy, sure, but mingled with it an ineradicable mischief. No mischief in these amps. Every time he'd tried a joke on somebody, Jerry, the desk clerk, it had fallen flat on its face. Queer: back among the Mandunji the kids were beginning to learn how to chuckle, here they had suddenly dropped into a grinless and gagless sobriety. . . .

There was a thin volume lying on the night table, he noticed it for the first time. He picked it up and examined the dust jacket: BASIC IMMOB TEXT NUMBER TWO, said the type across the top, and all around the borders ran a design of triskelions filled with running prosthetics. The book was a handsomely designed edition of William James's *The Moral Equivalent of War,* and appended to it was a long essay by Mahatma Gandhi on the philosophy of nonviolence and passive resistance. He flicked the pages. Across the bottom of each page were printed three words in boldface caps: **DODGE THE STEAMROLLER!**

Martine reached for his notebook and slipped it into the jacket of the James-Gandhi volume. He placed it on the night table, the original book he put away in the drawer.

Over the bed there were several knobs fixed to a large wall panel—switches, as he could see from the labels, for the radio loud-speaker and the television screen which were fitted into the opposite wall. He turned on the radio and played with the tuning dial until he found some music.

Program of jazz recordings; he recognized the tune being played as Louis Armstrong's "Four Or Five Times." After that came other Hot Five classics of the twenties, "Didn't He Ramble," "Wish I Could Shimmy Like My Sister Kate," "Jelly Roll," "Beale Street Blues." An all-Satchmo program! Maybe New Orleans had come back still another time to a world it had never made but somehow inseparably belonged to. . . .

When the disk-jockey program was over he fiddled with the television until he got a clear image on the six-foot-square, full-color screen. A young quadro-amp was giving a lecture to the young Immobs of the Olympic athletic clubs. On a large table before him were all parts of a disassembled pro leg, he was explaining the structure and function of each.

"With the Games coming up," the lecturer said, "all of us ought to brush up on the design of our pros—you can't appreciate the Games at all, fellows, unless you understand something about pro engineering. Now, kids, what say we take a look at the insides of this doodad. . . ."

Number One: the element he was holding now, he explained, was the socket. This was fitted permanently into the stump by cineplastic surgery, connected up with all the muscles and nerves of the stump. Designed so that any kind of limb could be snapped into it and immediately be hooked in with the musculature and the neural system. . . . Number

Two: the atomic-energy capsule, the power source of the mechanism. The movements of the limb were guided and controlled by neural impulses relayed from the brain through the central nervous system, but they were powered by this built-in plant. Which made the artificial limb infinitely stronger than a real one. . . . Number Three: this gadget, consisting of a wire coil and a metal rod which moved in and out of its electrical field, was a solenoid. Translated electrical into mechanical energy. Equipped with a system of levers and linkages which did the work of the original muscles and tendons but with much more power and control. There was a solenoid for each muscular unit of the original leg: one in the thigh, one in the calf, one for each of the toes. In the arm, of course, the setup got a lot more complicated. . . . Number Four: all these tiny objects were thyratron vacuum tubes and transistors. Hundreds of them in each limb, laid out in relays they converted neural impulses into electrical ones to operate the solenoids. . . . Number Five: the oleo-strut shock absorber, in which compressed air, oil and springs were combined to cushion the impact of a fall. . . . Number Six: the gyroscopes, which controlled balance. . . . Number Seven: the strain gauges. Attached to pads on the fingertips, they duplicated the sense of touch by converting pressure into neural impulses. . . . Number Eight: the thermo-couples, which converted temperature stimuli into neural impulses. . . . Number Nine: the cooling system. . . .

"Efficiency!" the lecturer said. "That's the point. With real limbs, the maximum amount of work the human organism can put out over a sustained period of time, say for an hour or so, isn't much more than one-sixth of a horsepower. But with these self-powered jobs you can sustain indefinitely a level of work amounting to dozens or even hundreds of horsepower. Because the power doesn't come from your body, it comes from the energy capsules. All your body does is direct that power. Man, in other words, finally K.O.'s the machine by incorporating the machine into himself! At last we've got the answer to EMSIAC—the machine that incorporated *man* into *it*. Isn't that something, kids. . . ?"

An announcer came on.

"Ladies and gentlemen," he said, "there's great news for all Inlanders tonight. Brother Theo is back! Yes, he returned to his office in the presidential mansion just a half-hour ago, after weeks of cruising with the Olympic team and taking a much-needed rest from affairs of state. We have the privilege now of bringing you some film sequences of this training cruise which Brother Theo just turned over to us. Don't go 'way now—our boys are in great shape, you're about to witness some amazing action shots. . . ."

The film began on board the training yacht, a glossy miniature of the *S.S. Wiener*. The boys were indeed in fine shape. They played leapfrog over thirty-foot ventilation stacks. Hurling javelins, they hit the bulls-eye on targets being towed two hundred feet behind the ship. They catapulted into the air from a standing position and did twelve or fifteen flips before landing. They balanced themselves on tight ropes with one finger, each gymnast juggling balls and rings with his free hand and both legs. Using only one hand, a man lifted a dozen others on a rope. . . . They were spry, they were bulletlike, they cavorted three-dimensionally, almost as though they had broken out of the sphere of gravitation and inertia and were roving free-orbit and weightless through outer space. It was a neuro-loco vision of space drained of determinism—space no longer a menacing outerness which trapped and isolated a man, an abyss, but suddenly an infinitude of freedom and promise on all sides, waiting for the cybernetic rape.

Next came the d-and-d's, the dexterities and discernments. A group of trainees were sitting on deck, some of them operating typewriters at high speed with their toes, some doing knot tricks with lengths of string. Theo, stop watch in hand, came up to one of the boys doing discernments and handed him a deck of cards.

"There are seventy-three cards here," Theo said. He took the cards back, held them behind him for a moment, then returned them. "Now tell me how many cards there are." The boy weighed the cards, he looked puzzled. "The pack's heavier now," he said, "but not by a full number of cards. By something more than six cards, less than seven. I'd say there were, let's see, seventy-nine and about one-fifteenth cards here."

"Not bad," Theo said. "I added six cards to the deck but on one of them I pasted a postage stamp, a three-cent one. You ought to practice with stamps of different sizes, they'll get your perceptions real sharp."

Another boy performed a dexterity with a pack of cards: he shuffled the deck with one hand while Theo clocked him.

"Time's good, Hank, two-point-nine," he said. "And you shuffled them right, the original order's exactly reversed. But you've got to watch the action of that index finger, you bent one card just a bit in the corner."

Theo held the damaged card up, the camera moved in for a close-up. The picture on the card's face seemed to be a stylized drawing of a steamroller.

The scene now shifted from the ship to land: a large group of people sitting around straw mats feasting. Martine stared. It was the communal mess hall of the Mandunji village, Ubu and the elders were sitting cross-legged with Theo and his friends, the rest of the villagers were in the background.

"This is an interesting shot," the announcer's voice said. "I've got a note here from Brother Theo about it—these are the natives of an island off Madagascar, they're throwing a big tapioca feed for our boys, yes, folks, I said tapioca. . . ."

Theo was talking. Ubu listened, shoveled gobs of cereal into his mouth, listened, gobbled, a warm and trusting smile on his face. Then Theo stopped and Ubu began to speak volubly, filled his mouth, swallowed, babbled. No voices, they hadn't been recorded on the sound track.

Martine studied the familiar faces all around. Off to one side, Notoa: he yawned, scratched his head, a look of puzzled concentration came over his face. Further on, Moaga, a large bandana wrapped around her head, the hair hadn't grown back yet; animated as a cabbage.

In the far corner—Ooda. Hunched up, not eating, face frozen. Crumpled in her hand, something white—a piece of paper? Next to her Rambo, holding her hand, patting it. . . .

Theo was the center of attraction in the scene. His presence was electric, for his own associates and for most of the villagers. He breathed galvanic authority as others emanate hesitation.

This was the last thought in Martine's mind as he closed his eyes and began to doze off. The man, he reflected sleepily, was a magical-mystical figure to the Inlanders, a mass-dream walking—on electronic legs. Wherever he showed up people automatically began to salaam, kowtow, genuflect, woo and curry flavor, favor, what they were compulsively after was a curry-flavored favor. He was a spellbinder by the sheer numbing weight of his presence, a hypnotic catalyst before whom people became will-less and malleable: an "It" to crush the mass "I". . . . Man to be watched. Why, why did he tell such nonsensical lies?

At this point Martine was asleep. Very soon he found himself out in blue space, now he was watching, not the

training yacht as it rollicked around the Indian Ocean, but—
a giraffe.

Far up in the tropospheric blue, on top of a needle of a
skyscraper whose base was lost in mist, was a brilliant neon
sign which spelled out the words, DODGE THE STEAMROLLER!
The giraffe, Martine noted uneasily, was stretching its snout
up to the sign and nibbling delicately on the last word. It
had already chewed off most of the exclamation point, it was
about ready to begin on the final "R" and Martine was in a
sweat.

"Don't eat those words," he called out, aware as he spoke
that what he was going to say was a bad non sequitur.
"They're not your words, why eat them? They'll do terrible
things to your stomach." When the giraffe went right on he
spoke more loudly, almost shouting: "That's the code word,
you'll get a code in the node, don't you understand?"

The giraffe whinnied, maybe it was heehawing, and
turned its head to look at Martine. "You've always got to eat
your code words," it said, voice gruff, phlegmy, touch of
some East European accent. "Accents of panic? Wounded
babies? *There* are some code words for you. But you simply
won't see what unites us, tragically, and separates us. Be
stubborn."

"I know that poem too," Martine called. "This is no time to
be giving me poetry readings."

"Phuh, it's as good a time as any." And the giraffe assumed a mock-solemn platform manner and began to recite:

> "My giraffe-violin has by nature a low and significant
>   sighing sound, tunnel-fashion,
> an air of being downtrodden and stuffed with itself,
>   like that of the gluttonous big fish of the deep,
> but with, at bottom, an air of sense and of hope all
>   the same,
> of having flown, of an arrow, which will never yield.
> Raging, engulfing me in its lamentations, in a heap of
>   nasal thunders,
> I suddenly snatch from it almost by surprise
> such piercing, searing accents of panic or of wounded
>   babies,
> that I myself, then, turn upon it, uneasy, seized by
>   remorse, by despair,
> and by I know not what, which unites us, tragically,
>   and separates us.

"Henri Michaud, very good poet," the giraffe said. "But be stubborn, if you want to. Deny the remorse, turn on me. Who do you think is the wounded baby, gangster? All garbage."

The giraffe licked its chops daintily, arched its neck still higher, and went on munching, scrunching.

The mist began to clear away below. Looking down, Martine could make out little figures bustling around the giraffe's feet—men with flame-throwers and whirring saws extending from their arms. At their head was Theo, authoritative as ever. Most of the men were swarming up stepladders to reach the giraffe's bony knees. Now Theo began to climb a ladder, his uptilted balloon, respiration bladder of a babyface getting larger with each step. His hands grew out until they were twenty feet and more from his body, they were scalpels, they were scissors, they were hypodermic needles, they were snapping lobster claws. Martine's stomach contracted as the face swelled and the claw-hands clacked.

"Dr. Smuts, I presume?" Theo said with an ingratiating smile. "Understand, it's not only because of the steamroller. It's not just that. The beast has too much verticality, that's all there is to it. Down with all verticals, as the good doctor says! We've got to cut him down to sighs, that's the thing. Reconcile him to the horizon. Give him lots of more latitude, right?"

In a moment the saws and claws began to cut into the animal's skinny forelegs, just above the knees. It was sheer agony to Martine, he felt the searing pain in his arms, just above the elbows, white flames licking into his biceps, it was his arms they were hacking off, he was the giraffe.

"Lay off!" he bellowed. "Listen! My work's too important, please believe me, I must keep my hands. Haven't you seen my cytoarchitectonic map, gentlemen? I've got the sure cure for tension. Besides, listen, there's Ooda. . . ."

He was entirely ready now to stop chewing up the neon sign (if only he could!), the slivers of glass were making mincemeat of his gums and tongue, but the saws kept tearing at his flesh. Numbed by the pain, his neck drooping listlessly over the top of the skyscraper, petrified, he felt the thin bones of his upper legs cracking and crumbling as the metallic teeth bore in. Any moment now his legs, paws, arms would give like peanut brittle and he would fall muzzle first into the abyss not the promise, finished for all time with knives and forceps and the things men hold in their hands when they work not play. Hypodermic needles too. A strangled, sobbing, agonized trumpet began to bleat off in the distance, Satchmo, sure enough, blowing his guts out on a chorus of "Four Or Five Times" while something, a steeple clock, a metronome, hammered out deafening tocks that made the atmosphere quake.

"Down the length and up the breadth!" Theo shouted happily as he clipped and sawed. "That's the long and the short of it! Down with skyscraper, up with horizon! Down mountain, up sea! Down the ups and up the downs! Off with his damned arrogant verticality! Unhand the bastard, the Smuts, he'll find it very disarming! This's sure to stump him!"

Louis was singing now, blues-crooning, "*Poppa, how hahd Ah is wuhkin' to cut dese knots, oh babe. . . .*" Then the matchstick legs were breaking off, the metronome was smashing in his ears, he felt his front supports going and he saw the blood spurting from the absurd little toothpick stumps that were left, his body was teetering, he was just about to drop downward, just then Louis' throaty voice changed into another voice, harsher, stiffer, more gravelly, it wasn't singing any more, it was lecturing, the accent had something in it of the Balkan and something of the Slavic. . . .

"To all good Immobs I say this," Vishinu began. "Brother Theo is a bad Immob. He lies. What good did it do this man to cut off his arms? He still keeps his tongue and with this tongue he tells imperialist lies and makes trouble. When he says he is skiing on Kilimanjaro it is garbage. When he says he is only coaching the athletes it is garbage. His athletes are also very good, trained metallurgists. He is snooping all over for columbium, not butterflies, he wants for his imperialist masters a monopoly of all the columbium in the world. This is a very dirty way for a vol-amp to act. . . ."

Cataclasm; he crawled out of the debris of sleep. Then two things happened simultaneously.

First, a thought that was like a blow. All this amputeeism of Immob, it was voluntary. Vol-amp: that meant, voluntary amputee. Somehow Martine knew that, knew it with finality. All these amps were vol-amps, he knew that too. *It was voluntary!* What good did it do Theo to cut off his arms, Vishinu asked. In that question was the answer to another question: What had happened to Theo's arms? He had cut them off, voluntarily. All this amputeeism was voluntary, and voluntary amputeeism was somehow the essence of Immob. And he must have realized it over a month ago, when he lay hidden under the roof of his hut and, sick with anxious anticipation, listened to Theo speaking with Ubu; Theo's

106

words had made it clear enough then that these men *willingly, eagerly, cut their own arms and legs off.* But he hadn't wanted to face the fact that it was voluntary—all the while anticipating it—from that moment on he had slammed a mental door shut on it and refused to let it out. Maybe that was why he hadn't allowed himself to recognize Babyface: if he had, he would have had to consider why his arms were gone. He had been curious about everything else, had asked all sorts of questions, but none about *how, exactly, these amps got that way*—secretly he'd known, he didn't want to be told. When he'd sent Rambo to the strangers' camp that night, he'd instructed the kid on all sorts of questions he might pop but not a single one about the amputeeism. When Rambo had mentioned Immob, he'd changed the subject. Whenever Jerry the steward had showed signs of bringing it up, he'd changed the subject fast. Until this moment he had refused to think about it, even to acknowledge that there was anything to think about. He had avoided the word "Immob" even in his thoughts, because somehow or other it seemed to imply a voluntary side to this amputeeism. *It was voluntary.* That was the horror. But some even more shriveling and obscure horror lay in the fact that he couldn't bring himself to face it, his memory bank had tried to go into a deep freeze from the moment Theo showed up, every meager recollection he'd dug up since he'd had to fight for tooth and nail. . . .

And in the split second when he realized all this, he also realized something else. He hadn't dreamed Vishinu's voice. It was in the room, it had filtered into his dream from this room, it was there with him now.

He sat up in bed. There was Vishinu on the television screen, big as life, poker-faced, massive, being interviewed by an announcer who was on the thin edge of hysteria.

"Brother Vishinu, why, surely you don't mean to imply—"

"I imply nothing," Vishinu said bluntly. "I say it plain. This cruise was not for purposes of athletics, the athletics were only for cover-up, it was a clever imperialist maneuver."

"But Brother Vishinu, how could you possibly know?—I mean, such information, if it is information—"

"You want to say, such information could only come from spies and spies are outlawed by us Immobs. Phuh, spying is not needed. We have friends in various places, they communicate with us. No doubt your own officials have their correspondents equally."

The announcer made an effort to regain his bland public

personality. "Thank you, Brother Vishinu!" he said with false, faltering heartiness. "Ladies and gentlemen, you have just heard Brother Vishinu in a surprise interview and quite a surprise it was, ha, ha. . . . This interview was arranged at Brother Vishinu's own request, he said he had something of importance to say to all Inland Strippers, no doubt you all found his remarks as, uh, provoking as we did here in the studio. And now—"

A uni-amp page boy came into the studio and held out a slip of paper. The announcer read the note, then raised startled eyes to the camera.

"Here's an exciting development, ladies and gentlemen!" he said tensely. "Word has just come from the capital that Brother Theo heard Brother Vishinu's remarks and wishes to reply to them. Hold tight, now—take it away, L.A.!"

The screen was in darkness for a second, then Theo flashed on. He was sitting at a desk, on the wall behind him there hung a large silken scroll with the words, DODGE THE STEAMROLLER!

"I've just been back in the capital a couple of hours," he said. "Naturally, I was just as shocked as all of you by Brother Vishinu's words. I cannot and will not question his sincerity, of course, but I most definitely want to question his facts. Brother Vishinu is badly misinformed, and that can make trouble. It was mostly misinformation that led the East and the West to go to war with each other in the old days. Even today, under Immob, it can do lots of mischief between Immob peoples and nations. So lets get the facts straight by all means.

"What are the facts? Well, the facts about columbium aren't too good, we all know that. We need this awfully rare metal for practically all the vital parts of our pros and there just isn't very much of the stuff around. So we can understand Brother Vishinu's concern about this precious material—we're concerned too. But why should this concern lead to mutual suspicion? After all, it's a problem facing the whole Immob world, and we ought to approach it as one world. Through international conferences the Himalayas and the North Pole have been designated as East Union territory, and the Andes and the South Pole as Inland Strip territory. Fair enough, isn't it? Then where the heck is all this imperialism and monopoly? What's imperialistic about divvying things up fifty-fifty?"

Theo was sitting up straight now, talking earnestly. It was incredible: his voice trembled, it had a real ring of sincerity—either he was a consummate actor (this babyface?) or it was all a hopeless muddle. . . .

"A few more facts. There was no ulterior purpose for my cruise. To put it baldly, I was dog-tired, pooped. When the Olympic team was kind enough to invite me along on its trip I was delighted—maybe you know that the Games have always been my first love. And all we did on this trip was what you saw in my films a little earlier—trained, got some sun, visited various places and met various people, and collected quite a few odd plants and animals for our museums and zoos and botanical gardens. Brother Vishinu's correspondents no doubt meant well, but their reports weren't very accurate. All I can say is that it behooves Immobs, above all, to make sure their information is, ah, first-hand." He smiled at the joke, then reached into his drawer. "Here, folks, is the columbium we imperialists came back with." He held an object up: a tremendous iridescent butterfly, floated in a slab of transparent plastic.

"As for the talk about monopoly, cartels, and all that—well, let me put it this way. I was surprised to hear Brother Vishinu use such antiquated words. In the old days, of course, such phrases used to fly about all the time: his forefathers were constantly accusing ours of Wall Street imperialist plots, ours were forever accusing his of Comintern-Cominform-Soviet imperialist plots. And every so often the accusations would break out into open warfare. Well, communities bound together by Immob don't talk about each other that way. There's no room for talk of greed, plots, bad will, and all that rotten old junk. Our only competition is a fraternal one, symbolized by the Games."

The tremolo again: he looked as though he were about to bawl.

"Soon the Games will be with us again. Let's go forward in the happy unity they represent and forget this momentary misunderstanding between brothers. . . ."

"It's a lie, Babyface," Martine said drowsily. "A goddamned lowdown dirty unmitigated monstrous cerebrotonic-somatotonic bitch of a lie. You weren't butterfly hunting. You were digging."

"Immob": he was quite sure now that the nonsensical word had something to do with immobilization, with the idea of immobilization, with some thoroughly obscene and improbable absurdity involving the idea of immobilization; quite sure, too, without knowing why, that hidden somewhere in that idea was some incredibly ghastly joke. Code word. Thoroughly inedible.

He switched off the television and turned over on his stomach, closed his eyes, saw Ooda's face, saw her high full breasts. His fingers curled around the pillow, he remembered from somewhere the phrase, "a soft merchandise." Then he slept.

Part Three

THE IMMOBS

---

chapter ten

THE SUN, amuck, splashed through the open window. A frisky breeze spilled over his face. He had bolted out of sleep with such a sense of exhilaration that he felt light-headed; now he lay still, in a room all sheen and soft ferment. Marvelous to feel surge of tone through muscles again, the sudden clamor of appetites. Nerve strands bursting with hosannas, opening their yaps and beginning to crow; his—

He sat up and began to laugh. To pinpoint himself in time and space, he had forced his mind to focus on the scene—the Inland Strip—and then the date—July Fourth, 1990. It was Independence Day! At least what used to be called Independence Day.

Well, he'd already had a king-size Independence Day in his life. His own personal Declaration of Independence had been signed with a flourish just about eighteen years ago. Darting supersonically out of the jaws of the EMSIAC trap, he'd been stunned to find that the world, until then shriveled in death convulsions, had suddenly flared open again with hope and possibility. The same sense of remove from all external compulsion, no doubt, was responsible for his giddy mood now. Of course there were atrocities waiting for him all up and down the Strip—but ghastly though the spectacle might be, he would be less than aghast. It would have nothing to do with him. Or—

Dancing under the icy needles of the shower, gasping, he found himself weighing another possibility. True enough, he would observe the cyberneticized fauna of the Strip much as an interplanetary tourist might explore the craters of the moon. Still, there might be a deeper source for his euphoria than detachment. It might be that this Fourth of July marked the second subjective Declaration of Independence in his life.

111

Because, it had to be confessed, despite his stand-offishness he had been sucked pretty deeply into the emotional orbit of his hosts, engulfed by their projects, commmitted to their ends. (Or: was it that some obscure—messianic—end of his own had been involved?) Maybe he had merely exchanged one EMSIAC for another. Maybe he was now snapping out of the second long cataleptic trance of his life, an eighteen-year snooze of acquiescence disguised as moral neutrality ("they started this lobotomy") and simple humanitarianism ("might as well teach them anatomy and asepsis"). Maybe he'd gotten involved, willy-nilly. And maybe that was why, the moment an excuse presented itself, he'd felt such a strong compulsion to run away from the island—a compulsion he hadn't been able to explain adequately to Ubu or Ooda or Rambo, for all his glibness.

His Bond Street—Champs Élysées duds were so impeccable that when he emerged from the elevator and began to pick his way through the crowded lobby nobody seemed to suspect the psychic loincloth underneath. Nobody even noticed him. With one exception: an extraordinarily beautiful girl with jet black hair and marvelously full lips and an aura of lolligag and mash about her. Dressed in a pink-and-blue diagonally striped dirndl and a low-cut off-the-shoulders peasant blouse, she sat in an armchair facing the elevator doors, busying herself with a sketch pad in her lap; when Martine passed she raised her eyes and studied him coolly for a long moment, then quite unhurriedly went back to her work.

In all his life he had never seen a less coy or more calculating look on a woman's face. Her eyes had not only undressed him but had then gone on, in an access of bookkeeper's thoroughness, to measure each portion of his anatomy and record the more or less vital statistics in some amatory card-index. And he, of course, had replied in kind: measure for measure. At once intrigued and disconcerted by the semaphore of come-on passing between them, he slackened his pace so that he might keep her in sight a moment longer. Sure enough, she raised her eyes and stared again, boldly and unequivocally. He began to address himself urgently: no, no, foreign entanglements were out.

Stopping at the newsstand to buy a paper, he glanced over his shoulder. A real stunner, with some tantalizing suggestion of the Oriental—Mongolian? Indonesian? Malayan?—in her exotic, slightly tilted eyes and the rich rose-olive tint of her skin. The fact probably was—he tried half-heartedly to console himself with the thought—that this girl, with her jutting Eros and propositioning eyes, was just as cold and ersatz as he'd decided most of the women hereabouts were. Profile of the Immob female: first-rate frustrate irate ingrate castrate. Shades of Irene, etc.

He went into the hotel restaurant, ate a big breakfast, and over his coffee began to examine his paper. Pictures of both Vishinu and Theo were plastered over the front page. BRANDS INLAND ATHLETES "IMPERALIST" AGENTS, one streamer announced, while directly underneath another read: THEO: VISHINU CHARGE "SEMANTIC MISUNDERSTANDING."

"He'll eat his words," Martine whispered mechanically.

His eye wandered to the masthead of the paper. Just above the name, NEW JAMESTOWN DAILY HERALD, was the tastefully executed slogan: DODGE THE STEAMROLLER!

Staring at the smears of egg yolk left on his plate, Martine felt his throat muscles tightening. They were clamped so rigidly that it was hard for him to swallow when he sipped his coffee.

"Steamroller": word to stick in the craw. Why on earth did he find this nonsensical admonition staring him in the face again and for no reason at all think of the equally non-sensical phrase, "He'll eat those words"? Why did his lips go dry and his gullet contract? He pushed his chair back and went out without looking at the paper again.

When he re-entered the lobby he found himself face to face with the dark-haired girl: she had shifted to a seat directly in front of the restaurant door. He headed for the barber shop to get his hair trimmed. Twenty minutes later, when he came out, she was still sitting in the lobby, still sketching. Now she was in a chair which commanded a view of the barber-shop entrance.

He was tempted to sneak up behind her and get a look at what she was drawing, but he decided it would be a waste of time unless he was prepared to follow up with some kind of pass. And Dr. Lazarus was not a bird of that kind of passage. Mustn't be. Well, he probably wasn't missing much anyhow.

He pushed through the rotary door, gloomed unexpectedly by the whimwhams, went out into the sparkling sunlight.

There were amps everywhere on the boulevards, all of them young, most of them in their twenties. Very few men with all their limbs intact were under forty, and those who were seemed to be wearing the scarlet letter of some enormous turpitude: they invariably had a hunched, hunted, defensive look about them which suggested that they were in ill repute and knew it, felt the disdain which bellowed at them from all eyes as they skulked along. These untruncated heretics were obviously the troubled ones—slackers? Immob's 4-F's?—around here.

First observation: a man with his own legs had no footing here; if past forty he was a dotard, if in his twenties or thirties a pariah. And it was equally striking that those who had the maximum number of artificial limbs also had what, for lack of a better word, might be called the best standing: the quadros were gazed at worshipfully and with palpitating greed by all the women, from tremulous teen-agers to maudlin-eyed matrons. From the way these amps lazed around, from their air of having infinite time on their Plexiglas (or whatever) hands, it was a fair guess that the quadros, as well as many of the tris and even the duos, had few workaday affairs to occupy them: they were the leisure class.

Once this idea occurred to Martine he found evidence to substantiate it on all sides. Those who did the menial jobs—tossing flapjacks in restaurant windows, clerking behind store counters, running elevators, driving busses and taxis—were non-amps; most of them, in fact, were women, and more than a few were Negroes.

So it was clear: there was a ladder of status with a carefully measured quota of eliteness doled out to those perched on each rung. All of which, to be sure, had been true of Martine's people for as far back as he could remember, but in pre-Immob times the marks of social standing had been different ones. There had been many standard indicators of one's degree of Jonesness, from the conspicuousness of one's consumption and the whiteness of one's collar to the telltale shape of one's proboscis and the generation in which one's ancestors got up off their emaciated and much-booted European rusty-dusties and took it on the westward lam. Now everything was simplified, there seemed to be just one spectacular badge of status: the number of plastic arms and legs displayed. Conspicuous consumption had apparently given way to conspicuous mortification of the peripheral flesh (a good old American practice), conspicuous maimery. (Where to locate the maimery glands in the human anatomy?)

And before long Martine observed something else. These sidewalk charades of sahibism and pariahdom unfolded in an atmosphere drenched with slogans. There were slogans everywhere, assaulting the eyes and eardrums: they blared from loud-speakers, they were lettered on buildings, on store fronts, on newspaper vans, on women's scarves and bandanas and dresses, on lapel pins and scatter jewelry, on banners strung across the boulevards like the electioneering signs Martine remembered from the old days. These Immobs were the sloganizingest people since the invention of the catch-word, which no doubt occurred simultaneously with the in-vention of the word. And what slogans they had spewed up!

HE WHO HAS ARMS IS ARMED, one slogan proclaimed.

WAR IS ON ITS LAST LEGS, shrilled another.

MAKE DISARMAMENT LAST, a third advised.

As a prosthetic footnote to that idea, the public was also advised that DISARMAMENT MUST BE TOTAL AND PER-MANENT.

TWO LEGS SHORTER, A HEAD TALLER, one sign said pro-vocatively.

ARMS OR THE MAN, was the flat statement on another.

PACIFISM MEANS PASSIVITY, boomed the speaker in front of a radio shop.

NO DEMOBILIZATION WITHOUT IMMOBILIZATION, Martine read from the inscription on a girl's blouse, directly over her breasts.

That one startled him, it seemed to be the clue to some-thing. Now that he allowed himself to think about it (and why, why, hadn't he thought about it until now: it had been a full month since he'd first heard Theo speak the evocative syllables?) he realized that the word "Immob" had overtones too: Immob, immobilization, there was certainly a con-nection. . . .

And everywhere, leering down from roof tops and yapping up from inlaid sidewalks, the schizoid motif: DODGE THE STEAMROLLER! It was far from unpleasantly hot but he found himself sweating profusely. By the time he sighted the park, a huge circular patch of greenery at the hub of the city, his shirt was soaked through around the shoulders and he felt rivulets trickling down his armpits.

In the center of the park was a statue, a fifty-foot-tall marble enormity perched on a great slab of concrete. The bold geometer's lines of this stone mammoth were strongly reminiscent to Martine, they seemed the caricatured end-product of the massive-monumental-modern style, the car-toony gigantism, which for so long had been the keynote of both American advertising and display and Soviet propa-ganda.

Martine was standing alongside the statue now. It was a

many-times-life-size replica of a machine: a steamroller, un-mistakably a steamroller. Stretched out supinely in front of it, his legs crushed by the great cylindrical roller right to the hips, right to the gentials, was the oversized body of a man. An agonized expression contorted the face, the neck muscles stood out like guy wires, the arms were flung beseechingly into space, almost like—except for the nails: the steamroller took the place of the nails—those of Christ on the Cross. Cut into the base of the statue were the exasperating, belly-tightening, throat-shrinking words: DODGE THE STEAMROL-LER! . . . .

And somebody was shouting the words. "Dodge the steamroller! Oh, yes! Fine idea! But how can we minorities dodge anything so long as we're denied our full amp rights?"

It was a beefy red-faced woman in a severe tweed suit; she was standing on a platform to one side of the statue, addressing a small crowd through a microphone. Above her was a banner reading, LEAGUE FOR THE EMANCIPATION OF IMMOB WOMEN: EQUAL AMP RIGHTS FOR ALL!

"We minorities," the haranguer continued, "have to get together in a united front and fight this thing through! Women, Negroes, all the victims of discrimination. Unless we go to real extremes we'll never get rid of our ex-tremities. . . . Now it's a real pleasure to introduce our guest speaker—Brother Bethune of the N.A.A.C.P.—he's going to say a few words about the Negro problem. Brother Bethune!"

A tall, lathy colored man came up the steps and took his place at the microphone. "We're in this united front with the League all the way," he boomed. "We of the National Associ-ation for the Amputation of Colored People know what it means to be denied all human rights. If all the locked-out minority groups can get together like so many fingers to form a mighty, invincible fist, we will smash through the wall of discrimination and gain our full amp rights, the great good fight will be won. . . ."

So democracy had *not* quite triumphed: it remained a set of old saws even after surgery had come along with its new saws—

"Doc!"

He was so absorbed in his thoughts—rather, in his utter, appalling lack of them—that at first the voice which came from behind him did not register. But it was insistent.

"Hi! Dr. Lazarus!"

Of course: *he* was Dr. Lazarus, parasitologist extraodinary, plagued now by a most extraordinary parasite of a word which had bored into his brain and wriggled there. He turned and saw a mono-amp coming toward him, unruly red hair blazing in the sun, stack of books under one arm.

"Jerry!" Martine said. "How in hell did you get here?"

They shook hands and the boy explained. So many passengers had left the S.S. *Wiener* at Miami that the skipper had decided to cancel the seaboard leg of the cruise and proceed to dry dock for some long overdue repairs; many of the stewards had received extended vacations; Jerry had hopped a plane last night and here he was, with three months in which to attend lectures and bone up for his civil service exams.

"It's a real break," Jerry said. "This means I'll be here for the Olympic Games. I would have given my, well, the nose off my face to see the Games."

"I thought you were going to say—you would have given your right arm."

"I started to," Jerry said sheepishly. "Some of those old-fashioned sayings still come up now and then, no matter how much linguistic reconditioning a guy has. It's awful hard to erase old words from the brain."

"Yes. Words aren't amputated as easily as arms or legs." Hardly aware of what he was saying Martine added: "Maybe the only way you can really get rid of bothersome old words is to eat them. . . . Look, tell you what, if you're going somewhere I'll walk along with you for a while. I'm just getting some air."

"You planning to go to the Games?" Jerry asked as they cut across the park.

"If I'm here. Unless they're called off or postponed because of that business last night."

"You mean Vishinu's speech? Aw, not a chance. Those Union guys have been talking like that, only not so rough, for years now, my pop says. It doesn't mean anything much."

"It used to mean a lot in the old days."

"That was before Immob," Jerry said. "Immob really unites people."

"Vishinu didn't sound very united to me."

"When Vishinu talks that way, beating his gums about imperialism and monopoly and all that, why, it's just a verbal hangover from the time of wars and armies and all. It's like my almost saying I'd give my right arm for something."

117

They had crossed the park now and were standing on the curbstone of a broad avenue, waiting for the light to change.

"How do you find things around here?" Jerry asked. "I guess the old place must've changed a lot since your day."

Plus ça change, plus c'est la maim chose. Plus ça change, plus c'est les mêmes shows.

"Yes, it's changed."

As they started across the street Martine took hold of the boy's arm and began to talk intently. "Listen, Jerry, I've been away for so long, I'd like to put a few kindergarten questions to you."

"Shoot, Doc."

"Well, suppose I were one of the African tribesmen I've been living with—say the chief of the tribe, a fellow named Ubu—"

"I like names like that, Hannah, Asa, Otto, they're the same backwards or forwards."

Martine suddenly remembered, for the first time in three decades, a palindrome that had once been told him by an elder of the Mormon Tabernacle: "Lewd did I live & evil I did dwel."

"That's right," Martine said. "Palindromically speaking, it's much more symmetrical to be called Ubu than, say, God. No balance there, backwards that's doG. Well, just imagine that I'm this chief named Ubu. He's never seen an amp or even heard of Immob, then one day you show up with your pro. First off he wants to know: How did you lose your leg?"

"I'd set him straight fast, Doc. I *didn't* lose it."

"I know, but how would you explain it so that it makes sense to a complete outsider like him?"

Jerry looked a little bewildered. "That's a cinch," he said. "I'd just tell him what I went down to the Immob registration office like anybody else, on my sixteenth birthday, and passed all my entrance exams. One week later my turn came and I reported for surgery."

"And what about the pro?"

"Well, when the stump was all healed I went back and had another operation. This time they inserted the permanent socket, tied in with the muscles and nerves of the stump. And when I recovered from *that* I went down to the Neuro-Loco Center and had my pro fitted. Then I went through nine months of tough neuro-loco training, passed my co-ordination tests, and got my certificate as a first-degree amp. Nothing to it."

"That's the how of it, all right. But Ubu might want to

118

know something else: Why? People who don't know anything about Immob might be a bit taken aback by the idea of anybody *volunteering* to have a leg cut off." Martine shuddered: it was the first time he'd said the word aloud.

"Uh, I suppose so. Primitive people, you mean. Well, I'd just point out to this guy that demobilization doesn't mean a thing without immobilization. There's no pacifism without passivity. I'd put it to him that way."

"Not bad—but you'd have to enlarge on that a little."

"O.K., I'd explain that disarmament can't amount to much unless, well, a man is really disarmed. Arms are what men fight with, and legs are what take them to the battlefield, right?"

"I see. But suppose Ubu said it was a contradiction to remove a man's arms and legs and then fix him up with even better artificial ones?"

"Oh, come on, Doc. Even Ubu couldn't be that naïve."

"Naïve?"

"All thumbs in the brain. Muscle-bound between the ears. Listen, remember that clenched-fist emblem the communists used to have? Well, in the old animalistic days they, everybody, used to be slaves of the clenched fist—a real hand always wants to make a fist and slug somebody, and it can't be stopped. But the pro, it's detachable, see? The minute it starts to make a fist, zip, one yank and it's off. The brain's in charge, not the hand—that's the whole idea of humanism."

"Pretty neat."

"Sure. Through amputeeism you make a man into a perfect pacifist. All right. You going to leave him flat on his back? A pacifist's got to get around to have any effect, otherwise all his charisma is wasted."

"We can't waste any charisma, God knows. Now. What would you tell Ubu about—about the steamroller?"

"Oh, it's got to be dodged," Jerry said gravely. "That's the main thing."

"Right," Martine said, his stomach fluttering.

Blur of color flitting among the pedestrians across the street, pinks and blues in a provocative ripple of skirt. Martine caught it out of the corner of his eye but just as he was about to turn his head and look, something happened.

They were crossing the street, they were almost at the curb. Suddenly Jerry's artificial limb erupted with a series of loud explosions as he was beginning to mount the curbstone. Instead of accomplishing the movement naturally and

119

gracefully he halted in the middle of it, poised on his real leg, and the pro snapped upward with such force that the bent knee hit him squarely on the chin. The boy was thrown so badly off balance that he would have fallen if Martine had not reached out hurriedly and grabbed him by the elbow.

The streets were crowded, quite a few people had seen the incident. Martine noticed something strange: everybody in the immediate neighborhood was looking at Jerry and grinning. It was the first time since his arrival that Martine had found any hint of a comic sense among these people.

"Goddamn," Jerry said furiously. "Oh, balls. I'll never learn."

"What happened?"

"I didn't co-ordinate right."

"How come? I thought you went through a pretty exhaustive training program."

"Sure, only some cortexes take to this advanced co-ordination better than others. Even in the best of cases it takes an awful lot of progressive exercising, along with drug-induced hypnosis, various kinds of auto-suggestion, and so on. You see, if the neural directions your brain sends down are the tiniest bit out of line, what you intended to be a crook of the finger might turn out to be a hefty right to somebody's jaw, and what you meant as a wriggle of your big toe might be a spine-crushing kick in somebody's ass."

"That being the case," Martine said, "it's a lucky thing everybody with pros is a pacifist."

"That's no lie. What happened just now, I slipped back into pre-amp co-ordination and sent out the kind of impulse you would to step up on a curb with a real leg."

"Very interesting—your kinesthetic centers went nostalgic on you."

"Maybe, but according to the neuro-loco guys it's a lot tougher to be a mono than a duo or a tri than a quadro. That's because with the mono and the tri the neuro setup of the body isn't symmetrical. On one side there's an artificial limb and on the other a real one and the brain has to keep on sending out two entirely different sets of impulses at the same time."

"Lopsided," Martine said. "Like being God on the one hand and Dog on the other."

"It's a bitch," Jerry said.

"Why not take off both legs or both arms at the same time and keep your symmetry?"

"Heck, that's out, this step-by-step induction is a kind of initiation. They want you to learn your co-ordination the hard way and then they give you the symmetry, kind of as a reward."

"Years ago," Martine said, "secret societies like the Masons had a system like that. They had different degrees of membership and you had to get into it gradually. It took a lot of work."

"So does this," Jerry said. "I can't tell you too much about the neuro end of it, though. Metallurgy's more up my alley."

"Metallurgy," Martine said. "That reminds me. What about this metal called columbium?"

"Well, you can't build pros without it. The reason it's so important is because it's the only metal whose alloys will stand up under real terrific temperatures."

"Is it really so rare?"

"You're darn tooting it is. During the fifties everybody began to make a lot of high-powered jet fighters and bombers and they discovered that columbium was the only metal whose alloys would hold up in a jet engine's combustion chambers. Well, between the Second and the Third the aeronautical engineers cooked up certain things that would pinchhit for columbium in jet engines. But in an atomic power plant, which gets a hell of a lot hotter than a jet engine, there's simply no substitute for columbium. It's a funny thing, we're so advanced technologically that we can work out substitutes for damned near everything under the sun, including arms and legs, but we can't find anything at all to replace the almost nonexistent metal that's needed for our substitute arms and legs. Looks like Nature played a big joke on us cyberneticists."

"Yes," Martine said, "it was very unkind of her to give us so many arms and legs, so much chromium and steel to make saws with which to cut these arms and legs off, and so little columbium to build bigger and better arms and legs. But where is this stuff found?"

"Most of the deposits, such as they are, are located in out-of-the-way places. The main ones have all been divvied up between us and the East Union, of course. Now we're getting the idea that more deposits may be found at the poles, so the Strip has been assigned the Antarctic regions and the Union has the North Pole. The trouble is, we haven't had a chance yet to explore the poles very thoroughly. Boy oh boy, that's something I'd really like to get into when I pass my civil service exams. That is, if I couldn't get into the Lake Victoria Dredging Project, but *everybody* puts in for that. Next to Victoria, I'd like best to do my Moral Equivalents in polar exploration."

Lake Victoria? Dredging? Martine frowned. "If all the possible sources of columbium have been divided equitably, why all this tension?"

"Oh, lots of reasons. For example, there's a suspicion that some deposits may exist along the southeast coast of Africa and maybe on some of the more mountainous islands of the Madagascar group. Do they go with the South Pole? Then there's an outside chance some will turn up on the edges of the Humboldt Glacier in north-western Greenland. Does that go with the North Pole? Besides, since we haven't had a chance to do much systematic looking yet, neither one of us knows for sure whether the other didn't get the better pole."

"As far as columbium goes, the Strip and the Union would seem to be poles apart."

"Only because of the semantic hangover," Jerry said earnestly. "Poles are apart only in the old vocabulary. Immob supplies the Hyphen."

They were now approaching a haberdashery establishment which seemed to specialize in garments for amps. On display in the window, draped on amp dummies, were fine tweed and gabardine suits, slacks and sports jackets, all of them with truncated sleeves and legs. To the rear of the window was a long placard along the top of which were drawn rows of miniature steamrollers, interspersed with triskelions, in a pattern of decorative waves; this sign carried the company's slogan: SHOW OFF YOUR PROS TO BEST ADVANTAGE—WEAR BROOKS BROTHERS CUSTOM-MADE SHORTIES. Reflections of passing pedestrians paraded across the window; among them a pink-and-blue dress swirled momentarily, then disappeared into the crowd again.

"About the Olympics," Martine said. "I'm especially interested in the dexterities and discernments."

"They're keen," Jerry said.

"Theo's really good at them, isn't he?"

"He's the greatest."

"The d-and-d's must be hard to master."

"Don't let anybody tell you different. The sensory parts of the cortex were never intended to register such fine impressions as the neuro system of the pro can transmit and the kinesthetic parts weren't built to send out such delicate impulses as the amplifiers can receive and act on. That poses

122

a real challenge to the brain; it's got to catch up with the machines it runs."

"Sounds like these pros can be something of a headache."

"Oh, you're not kidding," Jerry said soberly. "Sometimes I get terrible migraines."

"Maybe the brain just can't catch up with the pros."

"It will, the headaches are just growing pains. There was an article in *Reader's Compress* just the other week pointing out that, according to some research they've been doing up in the Neuro-Loco Center, the brains of many Immobs are already larger and heavier in certain areas than those of non-amps, and that eventually Immob will lead to an entirely new kind of brain, once we get through this transitional period. Of course, I don't remember the technical details very well, all that's pretty much over my head."

Martine laughed at the phrase but Jerry's face remained serious.

"I gather that the East Unionists don't show up very well against us in the Olympics," Martine said.

"No, they just haven't got the engineers or metallurgists or neurologists or cyberneticists to stand up to ours. Wait'll the Games, you'll see, we'll beat the shorties off them."

On the next block, across the boulevard, was a pale green skyscraper. When they reached the corner Jerry stopped and jerked his thumb in the direction of this building.

"That's where I'm heading," he said. "That's the M.E. University."

"M.E.? Mechanical Engineering?"

"Oh no, M.E. stands for Moral Equivalents. Say—" He looked at Martine with sudden enthusiasm. "Look, Doc, why don't you come in with me and visit around in some of the classrooms? The summer session's on right now and we're having pre-exam reviews today."

"I don't know," Martine said cautiously. "I'd be rather out of place, wouldn't I?"

"Not a chance, we have loads of visitors all the time, nobody'll even notice you. The last few weeks especially, we've had these East Union artists and other tourists wandering all over the place."

"Artists from the East Union?"

"It's part of the cultural exchange program between the Strip and the Union. When the Games are held in New Jamestown a lot of Unioneers come over here and when they're held in New Tolstoygrad a lot of our people go over there. Haven't you seen all these foreign-looking people around town with their sketch pads and everything?"

"Yes—yes, I guess so. I just didn't know who they were."

"Well, that's it. What do you say, want to come in with me?"

"If you're perfectly sure—"

"Sure I'm sure. Tell you what, I'll sit with you in the different classrooms and if there's anything you don't understand I'll tip you off."

"O.K. I warn you, though, I may need a lot of tipping off. Most of this brain-building stuff is way over *my* head."

At the top of the stairs Martine turned and saw the girl in the dirndl skirt and peasant blouse crossing the street. She came up the pathway that wound through the University lawn, seated herself on a bench near the entrance, opened her sketch pad flat on her knees and began to draw. On the stone back rest of the bench was a representation, in bas-relief, of a steamroller. The pattern of her full-cut skirt, Martine now noticed, consisted of diagonal rows of tiny steamrollers, some of them pink, some of them blue.

chapter eleven

ON THE demonstration table Martine saw a foot-long machine built in the shape of an insect. The glossy black plastic body was segmented into head, thorax and abdomen, beady eyes projected from stalks mounted on the frontal hood of the carapace, delicate feelers probed the anterior air, rows of bony articulated legs jutted from both sides like fractured oars drooping from a Roman galley.

It was moving. Slowly, with loathsome arthropod doggedness, it crawled across the table. Several feet above, suspended by wires from the ceiling, was a circular track rather like those used in toy railroads; gliding along this track was a floodlight whose rays were focused by a reflector on the robot below. As the light moved the mechanical monster followed suit, its ciliated toothpick legs groping with stiff centipede rhythms across the platform.

The lecturer behind the table was a scholarly-looking young man, a quadro.

"You all know Jo-Jo the Moth-Bedbug, I think," he said, patting the robot insect on the back. "Let's review what we've learned about him. Jo-Jo, of course, is a tropism machine, a machine with one simple fixed purpose built into it. What is this purpose? To respond to light either positively, by moving toward it—in which case Jo-Jo is a moth—or negatively, by moving away—in which case he's a bedbug. Jo-Jo has a communication and control system inside him, complete with feedback mechanisms which, through his photo-electric-cell eyes, keep him in touch with a constantly changing environment—a sort of primitive nervous system, with wires and transistors taking the place of neural strands and synapses. Jo-Jo's feedback mechanisms are designed to make him responsive to certain changes in the intensity and position of the light source. But if these changes become too extreme he has a nervous breakdown."

The lecturer played with some switches behind the table. The traveling bulb immediately picked up speed and began to flash dazzlingly. The insect stopped in metallic consternation, it stood stock still and began to quiver. At first the tremors were tiny, then the oscillations grew in scope until the whole organism was racked with huge shudders. The lecture hall rocked with laughter: any breakdown of any mechanism, apparently, was an occasion for great merriment to the Immobs.

"The feedback's too intense and rapid," the lecturer said. "Jo-Jo's drowning in tonus that can't find any outlet in action."

Now the speaker pressed a button and the room was plunged into darkness. In a moment a movie was projected on a large screen hanging over the blackboard: a man dressed in hospital pajamas was sitting at a table on which there was a glass of milk. The man began to reach for the glass; as his hand went out it began to oscillate, in little swings at first, then in wider and wider sweeps. Concentrating, a look of sweaty despair on his face, the man could not manage to get hold of the glass and lift it.

"Intention tremor," the lecturer resumed, "frequently occurs with certain types of injury to the cerebellum. This man's trouble is exactly the same as Jo-Jo's, motion-picture studies prove both oscillations are of the same order. Result of overloading the feedbacks in both cases: breakdown, accumulation of tonus, purposeless flutters."

The movie ended and the lights came on again.

What, the speaker asked with a smile, did this little demonstration prove? Simply that there is no unbridgeable gap between the animal and the machine: they are both tangles of communications and controls, c-and-c systems. Man is a multiple-purpose machine, while Jo-Jo is a single-purpose machine. But clog the feedbacks and both of them begin to dance at random, the same tremulous jogging dance.

Jo-Jo, of course, was only a crude cybernetic toy, there were now many infinitely more complex machines which demonstrated that all c-and-c systems follow the same basic laws. But the moth-bedbug was the very first such machine ever invented by man in his struggle to bring the animal and the mechanical together, hyphenate the great incompatibles. All honor, then, to the man who, back in the forties, had played a leading role in building the first moth-bedbug—Norbert Wiener.

Wiener. Professor Norbert Wiener. A name to remember and to cherish. Back in the days of the Second, at the Massachusetts Institute of Technology, this mathematical genius had called together colleagues from many fields and with them created an entirely new science required by the times: cybernetics. He had invented the name himself, from the Greek κυβερνήτης, meaning "steersman," and forged the first definition, "the science of control and communication in the animal and the machine." Most remarkable of all, he had had the vision to see that, once engineers knew enough about c-and-c systems, it would be possible—more: it would be necessary—to build machines which would duplicate, and then improve upon, even the most complex parts and functions of the animal.

The greatest human function to usurp, to duplicate, ultimately to perfect, was that of thought itself—for if the brain could perfect itself in an electronic model, it could then imitate this model and thus become perfect itself. Wiener realized that the most important machine to develop was the calculating machine, the reasoning machine, the so-called robot brain. He argued that the *machina ratiocinatrix* was the next daring leap which the scientific imagination had to take, it followed inevitably from Leibniz's *calculus ratiocinator*: for once you had perfected a mathematical logic you needed a perfect machine to employ that logic.

And so the first cyberneticists set to work building the thought machine. Their first efforts were pretty primitive—the M.I.T. Differential Analyzer, Harvard's IBM Automatic Sequence-Controlled Calculator, Bell Laboratories' General Purpose Relay Calculator, the Kalin-Burkhard Logical-Truth Calculator, Moore School's ENIAC (the Electronic Numerical Integrator and Computer). But in twenty short years they perfected EMSIAC (the Electronic Military Strategy Integrator

126

and Computer). And ultimately all the marvelous electronic brains had been developed which now ran the robot factories in the Immob world and thus freed man at last from the drudgery of inhuman labor so that he could concentrate on perfecting his own brain, to bring it closer to the perfection of the reasoning machine.

Wiener had gone still further. With his intuitive genius he had somehow dimly sensed the Immob future which cybernetics would eventually usher in. So he had concerned himself from the beginning with duplicating other parts and functions of the human animal—in the machines called prosthetics.

"The loss of a segment of limb," Wiener had written in 1948, "implies not only the loss of the purely passive support of the missing segment or its value as mechanical extension of the stump, and the loss of the contractile power of its muscles, but implies as well the loss of all cutaneous and kinesthetic sensations originating in it. The first two losses are what the artificial-limb maker now tries to replace. The third has so far been beyond his scope. . . . The present artificial limb removes some of the paralysis caused by the amputation, but leaves the ataxia. With the use of proper receptors, much of this ataxia should disappear as well. . . . I have made an attempt to report these considerations to the proper authorities, but up to now I have not been able to accomplish much."

Of course he had not been able to accomplish much, the lecturer went on. His had been a brutalized war-bent society, all too ready to spend billions developing the A-bomb but quite reluctant to allocate even a penny to work out adequate prosthetics for those maimed in its periodic wars. It had remained for Immob to perfect artificial limbs superior to natural ones.

"What'd you think of him?" Jerry asked as they walked down the corridor.

"I had a sort of negative tropism to him—guess I'm not prepared to see the light yet."

The next lecturer was a philosopher. Remembering the philosophers he had known during his own student days, Martine rather expected that, as against the cyberneticist's hammer-blow style, this man would be on the wispy and wishy-washy side. After all, the ephemera of metaphysics provided a much leaner diet for a man than the reassuringly tangible entities of physics and neurophysics. Because philosophers dealt in ideas with fuzzy rather than machined edges, in concepts which oozed out of pigeonholes and ran stickily together, they would only be putting themselves out of business if, following the cyberneticists' logic, they tried to establish in the gray matter equivalents of the unerring networks of caged vacuums—if such a venture could succeed, metaphysics would be reduced to an exercise in hooking up electronic circuits.

But Martine was dead wrong about this Immob philosopher. The young quadro plunged headlong into his subject as though he were regarding reality through the physicist's electron microscope rather than the metaphysicist's muzzy smog.

Where, he wanted to know, did the philosophy of Immob start? With William James—more concretely, with the immortal *The Moral Equivalent of War* which James wrote, incredibly enough, in 1910. Here, at least in embryo, was to be found the core of the whole Immob concept—the idea that the heroic, derring-do energies of youth must neither be bottled up nor drained off by war, but must be given adequate outlets in peaceful, constructive projects which capture the young imagination.

Wherever Immob operated—in the East Union orbit as well as the Strip orbit—one could see Moral Equivalents which pitted man against the elements rather than against his fellow-men. At this very moment brigades of mono-amp youths, serving for two-year periods without pay, were seeding and dispersing clouds to control rainfall, throwing up mighty dams to stem and divert rivers, exploring Lake Victoria's depths: man against water. Others were working on projects in which mountains were literally moved and valleys filled in with atomic explosives: man against earth. Still others were helping to build and test rocket ships which eventually would break away from the earth and, free orbit, catapult into space toward the moon and the nearby planets: man against the air and the ether and the exasperating clutch of gravity. And there were those who were risking their lives every day to test new types of personal armor and noninflammable suits which one day would allow human beings to bore through to the infernal center of the earth or land on the boiling surfaces of other planets and come away unscathed: man against fire.

And the result? As men through mutual effort conquered and humbled the universe, they speedily lost the feeling of alienation from their environment and came, through mastery of Nature, to feel at one with it. And this in turn caused men to feel less alienated from each other: masters can mingle freely and exuberantly, while slaves can only skirt each other and cower in lonely skin-encapsulated terror. So the anguish of being a puny creature engulfed in an infinitude of threat was done for: the problem which had so haunted a certain antiquated pre-Immob school of philosophy called existentialism that it had defined the emotions of man—supposedly cowed and alienated for good—as those of nausea, anxiety, dread, fear and trembling, the sickness unto death. The morbid emotions of alienated man were finished, in their place were mutuality and joyousness. Man was now regaining that sense of the oceanic, of mystic, majestic connectedness with Nature and his fellows, which the old Freud had found to be so shriveled in his neurotic civilization that he had questioned whether there was such a thing.

Every man was now coming to feel that the universe was close to him, wandering more deeply into his grasp all the time, meek, diffident, tamed, bursting with unsuspected intimacies. The universe was a mere extension of himself. Freud had long ago pointed out that in the beginning of life the infant does not distinguish between selfness and otherness, but this is a megalomaniacal myth and it is a rude, often shattering shock to the young one when reality intrudes on autarchic pleasure and it learns painfully that the world is less oyster than octopus. Everyone suffered this shock of Itness at the beginning of life, and the neurotic fears which resulted no doubt explained a good deal of the war-making energies which grown people unleashed against each other.

Immob had found the way to heal this infantile wound. A mature kind of megalomania was now becoming possible. Now the universe was truly, literally, becoming an appendage of man's ego. What the child lost in self-esteem, Immob restored on a higher plane. Omnipotence was rapidly becoming mankind's everyday experience, infantile myth was yielding to cybernetic might. Thanks to the boundless heroism generated by Moral Equivalents, men were coming to terms with the once nauseatingly distant and indifferent universe and recapturing the exhilarating sense of the oceanic. And such men do not fight with each other, they embrace. Moral Equivalents were a strategy to restore human megalomania by smashing the "Its," the steamrollers.

"I couldn't follow him on that last point," Jerry said. "He's too deep for me."

"Me too," Martine said. "He seems to have a theme song: *How Deep Is the Oceanic?* I wonder, though, if Vishinu hears him singing."

"Oh, sure he does. Why, at this very moment there are lecturers in universities all over the East Union who are saying exactly what this guy just said, word for word. Matter of fact, that last prof wrote a textbook on his subject, *Community and the Sense of the Oceanic* I think it's called, that's used as an advanced M.E. text in the Union same as here."

"Do they really teach exactly the same things over there?"

"Well, some of their philosophers like to sound off more on Tolstoy and Kropotkin and Pavlov than William James. Then their cyberneticists are a little sore about Wiener having been an American, they claim they had their own Wieners a long time ago and one bird even argues that he's got documents to prove the Russians invented the first artificial leg. But mostly it's the same."

"Maybe," Martine suggested, "Vishinu feels unoceanic toward Theo because he thinks Theo's a bit too oceanic about the Indian Ocean. That may be why everybody's at sea today. Where do we go next?"

"Elementary Semantics."

Alfred Korzybski, the next lecturer explained, had been a mathematician and expert on military logistics who had served as a Russian intelligence officer during the First. He had been filled with revulsion by the devastation which followed in the wake of the Versailles peace treaty. What was wrong with his moribund society, he had decided, was simply that it remained bound by Aristotelian logic—logic of the childhood of the human race. He had invented General Semantics to bring about an anti-Aristotelian wrench in human thinking.

Here, in capsule form, was Korzybski's idea. No doubt it represented a great advance over the old atomistic and particularist thinking about man to say that he is an integral unit, and that consequently he cannot be studied as a grab bag of separate parts. Hyphens had been inserted between his various parts by modern psychologists and philosophers, the emphasis had shifted from part to Gestalt, man had come to be defined as a mass of patterns and connectives and interactions. That was all to the good. But, Korzybski emphasized, one had to go much further before a science of human nature became possible. For man is not simply a functional unit, a bundle of hyphenated complexities which are themselves hyphenated—(mind-body)-(instinct-thought)-(conscious-unconscious) - (id-ego-superego) - (cortex-thalamus)—he is such a unit in a surround.

The human skin is an artificial boundary: the world wanders into it and the self wanders out of it, traffic is two-way and constant. Therefore the proper approach to a science of human nature, the only possible one, was to define the object of study as man-as-a-whole-in-his-environment. The unit under observation is whole-man-wholly-surrounded. The moment the hyphenation was completed and man was defined that way it became necessary, of course, to determine what the human surround consisted of.

Korzybski defined the human surround. Above all, he said, it is a neuro-semantic and neuro-linguistic environment which emanates from man and then envelops him, a sheath of self-generated signs and symbols. For as man generates words, verbalisms, articulated images and tokens to represent objective facts, he projects them into the world about him and institutionalizes them. After millennia of such semantic spewing by the human race, every child is born into a world saturated with man's verbal projections.

Precisely here, Korzybski said, was where the difficulty lay. The environment which man spins about himself does not represent objective facts; the words and symbols which make it up are increasingly at variance with reality. Sheath of signs and symbols? No. Rather, a smoke screen.

Why should this be? Well, there has always been an Aristotelian flaw in man, at least during his protracted childhood. From the beginning of human time there has been a certain gap between what exists and the representations which people developed for what exists. The reason was that man always took his words for the realities, the Aristotelian error. The sounds which become words were first produced by man in consternation—a series of oh's and ah's—precisely because he was bewildered by the ferment and dazzle of the world around him. But he never guessed that when these sounds hardened into words the words were not reflections of the real so much as they were muddied, groping, subjectively distorted substitutes for it—particularly since the world changed at a geometrically accelerating pace while words remained fixed. It did not occur to him that although he is in touch with the dynamic real world, both inner and outer, on a silent level, when he begins to verbalize, his static symbolic sounds wander very, very far from that silent level of things-as-they-really-are-and-are-sensed.

Behind the Aristotelian frame of mind there had always been a belief in the magical power of the word. This has always been a delusion of primitives, children and neurotics, the megalomaniacal fiction that what the mouth produces molds and marshals the world outside. The classical Greek veneration for the Olympian mind—Aristotle's assumption that simply by turning in on itself the human mind could fathom the real nature of things and then find verbalisms to convey that knowledge—was only a more sophisticated version of the same magical trust in words. This notion, because it made shaky men feel important, ruled human thinking for long centuries. As a result, thought remained entirely anti-pragmatic and anti-referential, there was no checking with the silent levels.

"What is the way out?" the speaker demanded. "To clear away the verbal trash choking the feedbacks and preventing mature megalomania. To understand that the word is not the object, eloquence is not photography, sound does not equate with substance. The map is not the territory. *The map is not the territory.* This was Korzybski's inspired slogan."

How did this slogan fare under Immob?

"With Immob, with the capture of the oceanic sense, the primitive neurotic childhood of the human race is ended. For neurosis, primitivism and childishness consist in a cleavage between 'I' and 'It.' Immob makes possible a sort of cosmic hyphenation, which is the cure for neurosis—hyphenation of man within himself, of man and man, of man and his whole environment, of will and idea, word and thing, map and territory. Between the idea and the reality no longer falls the alienating shadow lamented by T. S. Eliot, a poet of the Aristotelian world in its death agonies. On the silent levels we can drill our way into reality with our bore-arms, sear our way into the truth with our flame-arms, indulge quite literally in epic flights of the imagination with our heli-arms, dispense with ethereal verbiage because increasingly we can roam at will, physically, through the real ether. Alienation is thus yielding to a universal integration, and our language reflects it. The multiverse is becoming a universe. The Age of the Hyphen has begun. . . .

"Now it is a distinct pleasure for me to introduce a guest lecturer from the Institute for Political Semantics."

Several assistants wheeled a large cratelike box into the

room. The end turned toward the class was draped with a black cloth.

Another sober, intent-looking young quadro stepped briskly up to the lecture platform and began to address the audience.

"Most of you are acquainted with the Hallucinator," he said, pointing toward the box. "Perhaps you remember that it was invented in the first half of the century by one of the greatest Immob pathbreakers, Professor Adelbert Ames of the old Institue for Associated Research. Perhaps you know, too, that when Professor Ames presented his celebrated demonstrations in 1947, at the Princeton Bicentennial Symposium on Man and his Physical Environment, the death-blow to Aristotleian man was delivered."

The lecturer walked over to the box and pulled the drape from its near end, exposing a small round aperture. By craning his neck Martine managed to bring this opening into his line of vision. Inside, clearly outlined in white against the thick gloom of the cubicle, was the figure of a large man, obviously a quadro fitted with pros, bending over a hillock and boring into it with some sort of special-purpose arm.

"Those of you who are sitting directly in front of the Hallucinator," the speaker continued, "can see what is inside. At least you *think* you can see what is inside. Will someone in the class be good enough to describe what his eye registers?"

There was a volunteer in the third row. "It's a man boring into a pile of something with a special pro," he said.

"Good. Now, in the context of semantic events of the last twenty-four hours, does this 'spectacle' suggest anything more concrete to you?"

"Well, what Brother Vishinu accused Brother Theo of last night. The first thing that comes to mind is that this represents Brother Theo digging for columbium during his cruise with the Olympic Team."

"Excellent. But the question is: Is this stimulus really what it seems to be in its momentary neuro-semantic setting? Let's see."

The large box was mounted on a platform that swiveled readily to the touch. Now the speaker gave the box a half-turn, stopping it when its rear end was facing the class. There was an aperture at this end too, and through it Martine could make out a jumble of sticks, strings, irregularly shaped slabs and slivers of metal and plastic, twisted lengths of wire, seashells, bits of tin foil—a spatter of disconnected objects suspended in space, all painted white to stand out

133

against the black walls of the box. When these fragments were seen from the angle of the front aperture—only the edge of a plastic slab visible, only the cross-section view of a piece of lumber, only the upright arm of a right-angled strip of metal, and so on—they seemed to be joined to each other rather than scattered without pattern in space, and joined in such a way as to form the outlines of a man drilling. Only when you circled around the assembly and got a look at it backstage could you see that your eye had been hoodwinked by purposely misleading appearances.

"The Hallucinator is faster than the eye," the lecturer said. "You see: what looked like a man named Theo drilling in some African rock for some metal called columbium is—a hodgepodge of sticks and stones, pieces and particles. These components are not assembled in reality. It is the human eye which is tricked into doing the assembly job, when it looks from a certain angle. It was the discovery of this trickery which led to modern, nonrepresentational art. Early in this century artists, out of a nausea with appearances, all hoodwinking surfaces, set out to explode them simply by changing the customary angle of vision. They wanted to show that the most meaningful assemblies, reeking with bourgeois neatness, break up into meaningless spatters when seen from another vantage point or from several vantage points simultaneously. From which it must follow that any arbitrary meaning assigned to this or that spatter must originate behind the eyeball. The same principle, exactly, is behind the Bates system for correcting bad vision, a system which Aldous Huxley had the farsightedness to endorse and campaign for: The mind dictates what the eye sees."

Now, perhaps, the speaker suggested, his listeners could appreciate how important it was to avoid semantic backsliding, to keep up one's linguistic reconditioning. For every semantic carry-over plugged up the feedbacks and thus generated hallucinations, dictated the eye's vision from within so that it was blind to what lay without. And last night there had been a most interesting example of such backsliding—the word "imperialism" had been salvaged from the semantic junk heap.

In pre-Immob times, as everybody knew, both Russia and America had been hopelessly bogged down in Aristotelian hallucination. Each was devoted to a set of semantic symbols which had no connection with reality whatsoever. Western culture had been filled with resounding nonsense syllables like "individualism," "initiative," "enterprise," "laissez-faire democracy," "the twenty-one points," "the four freedoms," and so on; Eastern culture had likewise had its share of vibrant shibboleths babbled without regard for meaning or pertinence—"classless society," "dialectical materialism," "collectivism," "socialism," "anti-imperialism," "proletarian democracy," "withering away of the state," and so on. Even worse, these were all fighting words.

But under the schizoid eloquence which blanketed both societies something most dynamic had been happening on the silent levels. The march toward the managerial society. Yes, Russia and America, each from its own direction, had been approaching the same goal—a society in which the technicians, the management engineers, the efficiency experts, the executives and personnel directors, fully equipped with batteries of robot brains, would be in control of the state apparatus, which in turn would preside fully over the activities of its citizens.

And as the managerial revolution proceeded, both countries began to proliferate the kind of mass culture it required, a culture welded together into a tight, quickly mobilized monolithic unit whose nerve centers were the lightning-quick mass media, radio, television, movies, great daily newspapers and picture magazines, comic books, progaganda books—media through which gushed a constant torrent of slogans and catchwords. But, alas, these slogans and catchwords were hopelessly dated. Trapped by the traditional laggard sounds of their respective cultures, great floods of hallucinating verbiage, the Aristotelians of East and West glared at each other and made strange antiquated noises—it was as though the sound track of a film lagged minutes behind the action. Their feedbacks were jammed. Politics and diplomacy had degenerated into mere oscillation.

In 1970 Russia and America simultaneously came to a hallucinated decision: they, and not merely their vocabularies, were such diametric opposites that they could not exist side by side on the same planet. So the Third, the global EMSIAC war proved only one thing: that the cybernetic-managerial revolution had been carried to its logical end and now Russia and America were absolutely and irrevocably alike. In fact, it was precisely in preparation for the global showdown of the EMSIAC war—a war predicated on the assumption that the two had nothing in common—that they had come to be mirror images of each other. For each was now the monster that Wiener had warned was coming:

the totally bureaucratized war machine in which man was turned into a lacky by his own machines. And each was presided over by the super-bureaucrat of them all, the perfect electronic brain sired by the imperfect human brain. Years after the war, when survivors came to study and compare the military-strategy calculators which both societies had invented and then subjected themselves to, they found that they were absolutely alike—and understandably, for both had been designed to cope with the same sets of mathematico-military problems. The vacuum tube, that manager of managers, could say with greater justice than did the old pacifist Eugene Debs: I am a citizen of the world.

Obviously, before the industrial revolutions there was no democracy possible. In the absence of a leveling machine civilization to tell them otherwise, men of different races and cultures could look at each other and be struck by how different they were—different in stature, complexion, language, shape of nose, texture of hair, and so on. But once the machine was introduced, first in the West and then in the East, these superficial differences tended to get lost in the mechanized shuffle: after all, a swart Kirghiz and a tilt-nosed Irishman working on lathes on opposite sides of the world had something in common. Lathes are no respecters of national differences. The machine was, in a sense, a great leveler, a forger of interpersonal Hyphens: it tended to iron out the disparities between gestures and languages and attitudes. But what the machine started along these leveling lines it took the vacuum tube to complete. For only when the robot brain was developed did it become clear that all men on earth had a tremendous thing in common: the human brain, which is the same the world over because all c-and-c systems are alike. When a managerial society, Eastern or Western, strove to project into the electronic world a perfect model of the imperfect human brain, it came out everywhere the same—see EMSIAC.

Such were the silent realities of the mechanized twentieth century, which the queazy, machine-shy intellectuals completely overlooked. But prior to Immob neither Russia nor America could shake off its Aristotelian blinders sufficiently to see them. Their feedbacks were crippled. Each power berated the other as a greedy "imperialist" plotter, clinging to a word which was as irrevocably dead as the nineteenth century. To judge by the pejorative rhetoric which choked the atmosphere, the Third was simply a war between the capitalist imperialism of the West and the Soviet imperialism of the East. (The real imperialism involved here was only a semantic one: each side wanted to impose its vocabulary on the other.) But in all this rhetorical skirmishing nobody ever stopped to consider *why* it should be that in both East and West some vital expansionist drive, which semantically backward folk could only call imperialism, stubbornly kept asserting itself. Obviously the answer could not be economic, because economically the struggle was ruinous for both sides. No: both sides of the world were hungrily opening their arms in an effort to embrace the world because inside both, at the very heart of both, the machine-grown-rational was thrashing desperately about, trying, in spite of its blind human environment, to fulfill its democratic all-leveling destiny by making its managerial scope universal. The Eastern and Western *machinae ratiocinatrices* were simply trying to embrace.

Instead of facilitating this cybernetic brotherhood, men interfered with it by hurling themselves against each other, pitting EMSIAC against EMSIAC: the Third was a war of mutual annihilation between twins. Their feet planted in the dazzling electronic-atomic realities of the twentieth century, their heads were still in the archaic clouds of nineteenth-century semantics. They could not see that they were all c-and-c systems with similar imperfections, similar strivings. They harped on the differences—in their philosophies, their noses.

"Last night," the speaker said, "Brother Vishinu revived some of the antiquated noises from bygone centuries. Even now, this semantic smoke screen can only conceal the simple silent-level reality—the blood relationship, the neuro-cortical relationship, of the two peoples. Which only points up, once again, a grim truth. When a culture is overrun with reality-screening words, all of its members will be steamrollered by those words. Brother Vishinu has not learned how to dodge the steamroller."

The speaker, with a prestidigitator's flourish worthy of Mario the Magician, Thomas Mann's most eloquent saltimbanco, now gave the Hallucinator a twirl and stopped it when one of its sides was facing the audience.

"What did Professor Ames teach us? A great lesson: that without perspective, or with the wrong perspective, the eye sees nothing but mirages. But does the Hallucinator prove that behind every pattern we think we see in the outside world there is nothing but chaos? Not at all. All it proves is that the patterns built into our eyes by outmoded words and labels are hallucinations. There *are* patterns in the silent world, but we shall be able to see them only when we shake off our hallucinating words. Observe."

The entire side of the box, it seemed, was mounted on hinges at one end so that it could be swung back like a door. Now the speaker took hold of it by a knob and with a dramatic flourish—Martine half expected to hear him mutter "Alagazam, alagazoo"—yanked it open.

The audience was stunned. Just as the speaker had predicted, the box from this angle seemed to contain neither the figure of a cybernetic miner nor a jumble of slivers and strings. What came into sight now was another figure altogether, composed of the same ingredients as the digger but up to something quite unlike digging. It was a man poised daintily on a mound, body arched like a ballet dancer's, head flung back, arms raised on high; in one hand was a good-sized net, and fluttering in the air just beyond it, just out of reach, was an enormous butterfly.

"What was Theo doing in the Indian Ocean?" the speaker said. "Brush away the semantic smoke screen and you will see. He was collecting butterflies, of course. This is the silent reality behind his 'imperialism'!"

Thing to do, obviously, was to put Jo-Jo the Moth-Bedbug in the Hallucinator. Turn him over on his imperialist back and let him go into his megalomaniacal oscillations as a moral equivalent to the managerial steamroller, a sort of silent-level St. Vitus'. dance which would scramble all Aristotelian maps and Amesian territories in one great big lovely hyphenated omelette. Call the omelette a smoke screen of butterflies, oceanic ratiocinatrix. Oh columbium the gem of the oceanic—

"What?"

"I said," Jerry repeated, "that was a real break for you, having that special lecturer show up. He answered all your questions."

"All except one," Martine said. "Why do guys who believe the truth's speechless spend so much time talking about it?"

"I guess you still don't understand," Jerry said. "Semantics just says that there are different vocabularies, there are Aristotelian words and then there are non-Aristotelian words and. . . ."

But Martine was no longer listening. They were in a corridor on the third floor, the entire outside wall was made of glass from floor to ceiling, looking out Martine could see the

138

wide flower-dotted lawn in front of the University. Sitting on a bench down below was the girl with the very black hair and the pink-and-blue dress, sketch pad in her lap.

He wished to hell his sweat glands would stop gushing and his throat muscles would relax a little, it was getting downright painful.

chapter twelve

FARTHER DOWN the corridor they came to a door on which were printed the words: PANIC CONTROL LABORATORY: YOGA BREATHING AND MUSCULAR RELAXATION. Through the glass panel Martine could see a row of cots inside on which some twenty mono-amps and duo-amps were stretched out, all of them in the nude, all with their pros removed. He stopped and studied the scene.

"Do amps have to relearn everything?" he said.

"Oh, sure," Jerry said. "People never knew how to breathe and sleep before. War comes from jerky respiration, muscular tension and insomnia."

"There used to be some simple-minded people around," Martine said, "who had the idea that jerky respiration, muscular tension and insomnia sometimes came from war. From war and from the rumors of war."

"Somebody should've told them about the James-Lange theory of emotions—we don't run because we're afraid but we're afraid because we run. Carry that a step further and you've got a physiological approach to the problem of war."

Martine pulled out his handkerchief and dabbed at his forehead. Sweating; extreme muscular armoring in the throat, the back of the neck, the shoulders; breath shallow and forced—he had all the symptoms of panic, sure enough, a gang of tropisms were acting up in him. How to dodge *these* damned internal steamrollers? But the moment he put the question to himself in that form he felt his neck and shoulder muscles clamp still tighter. He was in a hell of a spot, semantically and psychosomatically: his big internal steamroller was the word "steamroller" itself—a contingency for which neither Mr. James nor Mr. Lange had allowed.

"Could we go in and have a look around?" he said. "It's fascinating."

"Come on," Jerry said. "There's still a few minutes before the last lecture."

There were dozens of electrodes fastened to the body of each student, to toes and fingers, thighs and forearms— where there were any left—pelvis, neck, forehead, just about everywhere. The wires from these terminals were plugged into rows of sockets alongside each cot and seemed to be connected up with banks of tonus indicators on the wall behind, one series of dials for each cot.

The instructor, a young quadro-amp, turned his head when the visitors entered, cautioned them with a finger against his lips to remain silent, then went on with his class. "All right, men," he said. "We'll take it again. Just concentrate on the diaphragm. Stop feeling that you are breathed in and out of by some wind machine you don't control. *You* breathe. *You* make the diaphragm stretch and slacken, you force the lungs open and shut. No 'It' breathes through you, *you* breathe. Stop being tyrannized by your diaphragm! You can bend it to your will! Through it you can slow up your pulse rate, throttle the thyroid and the pituitary and the adrenals, stun the parasympathetic nervous system, anything. You are master of your own metabolism! Your body is your instrument! Learn to control it and you can walk on hot coals, stick pins through your tongue. You've seen it demonstrated over and over again in hypnosis—a psyche, the hypnotist's psyche, uses a human body as a toy, paralyzes it, raises boils on the skin, removes warts. The next good Immob step is to make yourself your *own* hypnotist, put your *own* psyche in your body's saddle. Concentrate on that. Remember, you're in charge. Think now of your diaphragm, that helpless, will-less, impotent strip of membrane. Now you're going to put it through its paces. Ready now. Everybody ready. One. Two. Three. *Breathe!* In . . . out. In . . . out. Diaphragm up . . . diaphragm down. Lungs open . . . lungs shut. Do it yourself . . . do it yourself. Body slow down . . . body slow down. Heart slow down . . . glands slow down. In . . . out. Muscles loose . . . nerves loose. Iiiiiiinnnnn . . . ooooouuuuut. Steady, now. One . . . two . . . one . . . two. . . ."

All the students had their eyes closed. With each insucking of air twenty chests rose, twenty abdomens were pulled in until they were tight cups of flesh—with one boy down near the end, the abdominal walls fell away until it seemed they must be pressing the intestine flat and making contact with the base of the spine. Martine watched the dials on the tonus indicators. All of them had begun to drop

140

when the breathing exercise got under way, in some cases almost to zero, in others just a few degrees.

The instructor walked up and down the aisle. He watched the indicators and in a soft, rhythmic singsong gave pointers to each student individually. "Croly," he said, "your embouchure's tied up in knots. Concentrate on the lips, the cheeks, the lips, the cheeks. . . . Anderson, your toes are all bunched up, watch the tonus in those toes, watch the tonus in those toes. . . . Schmidt, you've still got a lot of hypertension in the pelvis, the pelvis is retracted, the pelvis is retracted. . . . Dunlap, for God's sake, relax those sphincters, take it easy, man, relax those sphincters or we'll have to send you back for more narco-suggestion. . . ."

"There's something I don't get," Martine whispered to Jerry. "Why do they all remove their pros?"

"Simple," Jerry whispered back. "What're the animal emotions? Fear and rage. What's the bodily state that induces 'em? The possession of arms and legs. Because, see, so long as you've got arms they'll want to be used as weapons against others—and because everybody else's arms want to be used against you, your legs will want to run."

"But wouldn't that go double for pros? They're much more powerful than real limbs."

Jerry looked outraged. "You must be kidding, Doc. There's one thing about a pro that makes it entirely different from a real limb—it's detachable, see, I already told you."

"You mean—Immob doesn't do away with panic, it just makes it detachable?"

"You're getting the idea. In this lab guys who are first-degree and second-degree amps learn that they can begin to control their panic by detaching their pros and then subduing the glands and nerves and muscles through Yoga breathing and progressive relaxation. It helps to build up the ego, which in itself is a sure cure for animal panic. Props up the shaky megalomania. Naturally, it's just for the transi—"

"One . . . two," the instructor chanted. "Iiiiinnnn . . . oooouuuut. Dunlap! Watch those sphincters, boy!"

"—it's just for the transitional period."

"All right, men," the instructor went on. "That's all for today. You can put your pros back on now."

The students opened their eyes, sat up on their cots, yawning and stretching. All except one, the young man down near the end whose abdomen had seemed to cave in entirely during the breathing exercises. The instructor walked down to his cot, took him by the shoulders and began to shake him.

141

"All right, Higby," he sad. "Higby. Come out of it now. Higby! Snap out of it!"

Almost all of the indicating needles behind Higby's cot were down to zero. Suddenly they all jumped and began to jerk wildly. The young man opened his eyes with a start, blinked rapidly several times, then heaved himself into a sitting position.

"Good work, Higby," the instructor said. "That makes ten days, for ten days in a row you've relaxed so completely at the signal that you've lost consciousness. You've got the knack of it now. Men!" He turned around and addressed himself to the class. "I have an important announcement to make, men. Higby has now mastered the breathing and relaxation techniques perfectly—something that practically never happens before the quadro stage. Never again will he be so enslaved by his body that he'll have to lie down in bed and wait to *fall* asleep. Sleeping will never be a passive falling expreience for him again. He can now send his Atman soaring into the Brahman any time he wants to. He'll never again have to *lose* consciousness, he'll simply thrust it away from him. Higby will never again know panic. He has dodged the steamroller. I'm going to give him his P.C. certificate and what's more, I'm going to recommend that he be allowed to go on to full amputeeism, he's earned it."

The other members of the class had plugged their pros back into their sockets. They all stood up now, still in the nude, intense emotion on their faces. Turning toward Higby, they all began to applaud wildly, they shouted phrases like "Bravo!" and "That's the stuff, Hig!" and "Good going, kid!" The instructor stood alongside Higby's cot, a pleased smile on his face; Higby sat quietly, a little sleepy and bewildered but tremendously moved, his lips trembled.

"What a break," Jerry said enviously. "A Panic Control certificate and a recommendation for quadro at his age! That kid's got the makings of a real champ psychosomaticist."

What, the final speaker demanded, is Immob? Immob is the cyber-cyto dialectic—the dwindling distance between cybernetics and cytoarchitectonics. The bridging of the gap between the mechanical and the human—the discovery of the Hyphen between machine and man—thus enabling man finally to triumph over the machine because it's *man* who has the Hyphen and not the machine.

There was always a great paradox in pre-Immob history, the lecturer pointed out. Why should it be that the human brain can produce perfection only outside itself—in the machines it conceives and builds? If it can conceive and project such perfection, why can it not apply the same grandiosity of vision to itself, rebuild itself? The answer is that it can, once it stops being cowed by its own creations. The slogan, "Physician, heal thyself!" yields to the Immob admonition, "Cyberneticist, redesign thyself!"

There were two plastic models of human brains on the demonstration table. The speaker now turned to them, pointing first to the smaller one. "Here," he said, "is a typical brain of homo sapiens circa 1970—on the verge of the EMSIAC war. A bird brain, a peanut brain. It suffers from one fatal debility: in EMSIAC it has produced a fantastic mechanical image of its own dream of perfection but, because it is trapped and enervated by arms and legs, it has no Hyphen to relate itself to that metallicized dream. Therefore the dream is about to turn on the dreamer and steamroller him into oblivion. . . ."

The speaker turned to the larger brain. "Now consider the second model. It is an Immob brain circa 1990. Already it is larger by many, many grams. After the agony of the Third, the war in which the dream of perfection became a steamrollering nightmare, this brain has finally discovered how to link itself to its own projected vision—it has lopped off its animalistic tails. It has suddenly made the breathtaking discovery that the perfection of EMSIAC and other robot brains lies in the fact that they are sheer brain with no irrelevancies, no arms and legs, just lines of communication and feedbacks—and it has begun to overhaul itself in the image of the robot. This, by the way, is no hypothetical brain—it is an exact copy of a real one, one belonging to a great Olympic athlete of our times, Brother Theo. This brain is beginning to realize itself. Notice the specific cortical areas in which it has begun to grow, now that no more energies are drained from it—in the sensory centers here, the manual centers here, the locomotor centers here—"

"Of course," Martine whispeed to Jerry. "Theo was pretty brachycephalic to begin with."

"These are bumps of maturity—humanity is sprouting all over this cortex. This Immob brain is beginning to catch up with its best machines. Soon it will outstrip them. Then, of course, it will invent still more fantastic machines to outstrip, for the machine is eternally the brain's dream of fulfillment. . . ."

But, the speaker cautioned, before a territory can be developed we need some preliminary picture of it, a map. This holds for the territory of the brain as well as for the territory of British Guiana or Timbuctoo. It was the wisdom of Brodmann and all the neurological researchers inspired by him that they saw this need and set themselves the task of charting the brain's wily topography.

The lecturer pressed some buttons on the wall, from rollers suspended above the blackboard two large multicolored sheets began to descend. They were both cytoarchitectonic maps, one a post-Brodmann drawing belonging to the period just before the Third, the other an Immob product of the year 1990.

"For years," the lecturer was saying now, "Brodmann and his followers performed their painstaking lobotomies, transorbital leukotomies, selective ablations, their electric-needle stimulations and strychninizations to fire the cortical neurones. At first they were much too concerned with esoteric subjective matters, but they were soon obliged to correct this one-sided emphasis. Things were happening in another field which vitally concerned them. More and more there was a need for super high-speed electronic computing machines—to guide radar tracking equipment, to act as mechanical brains in the operation of totally mechanized atomic piles, to direct remote-control missiles, to solve the incredibly complex mathematical problems posed by nuclear physics, above all to take over the increasingly unwieldy complexities which were the concern of managerial groups in both industry and government. Cybernetics spurted forward. And the moment it did, it had to tear the cytoarchitects away from their futile subjective researches and press them into service. Before men could build mechanical brains which would outstrip human brains, they had to know more about human brains. The engineer's brain had arrived at a point where it had to listen to the ancient Greek admonition: Know thyself. So the Wienerites had intense and urgent need of the Brodmannites. The result of their marriage was dianetics—a remarkable technique for making the human brain into a lightning-fast computing machine by clearing it of its norns, or inhibiting 'devils,' and jolting it into recall."

Dianetics drew in bold outlines the blueprint of the optimum human brain. But before this model could be of much practical use, the whole anatomy of the id, ego and superego had to be traced. Only when such a full picture was available could the human brain build electronic brains still

144

better than itself, after which it could then pattern itself. Brains without aberrations, without a debilitating unconscious. The crying need was to explore the all-important neural Hyphens. Not until that was done would it become clear, as it subsequently did, that the animal unconscious persists, with all its disruptive norns, only because of the animal Itness of arms and legs—that the electronic brain is pure and self-determined because it is not shackled to arms and legs.

"The great work along these hyphenic lines," the lecturer said, "was done by a man you all know about. Although a very young scientist before the Third, only at the beginning of his career, he had already managed to trace many neuronic networks which had never been imagined before."

The lecturer turned now and waved his hand dramatically in the direction of the Immob cytoarchitectonic map.

"This is the map of maps," he went on. "Over its terrain will be fought the wars of the future. The cyber-cyto wars. The man of whom I am talking knew that. He gave us the main elements of this map as a living testament to his vision. What further earth-shaking discoveries might not have come from his inspired scalpel if his life had not been cut short, almost at the moment of its beginning, by the EMSIAC war! And yet, in handing down this map to us, he did, in a sense, triumph over EMSIAC. For, armed with this revoluntionary tool, we can now march forward into the cybernetic future in which we shall become our own EMSIACS, the human brain will overtake and outstrip its own projected greatness. Yes, the Immob world will never forget its debt to the greatest cybernetic hero of all, its towering genius and immortal martyr. He, more than anybody else, was responsible for the cyber-cyto revolution of Immob. Dr. Martine was the first and greatest adversary of the steamroller. . . ."

Steam hissing, roller rumbling. Iiiiinnnnn . . . ooooouuuuut.

"There's a break for lunch now," Jerry said.

Let me tell you about my aberration—

"Want to come up to the cafeteria and put on the feedbag?"

Feedbag's clogged. It makes my sphincters very tense. The riddle of the sphincters, *I* say, not Oedipus, is to take the fool by the norns—

"Hey, Doc." Jerry stopped and looked hard at Martine. "You look kind of funny, you're awful pale. You got something on your mind? Sounded like you were mumbling something to yourself."

"I'm sorry, Jerry. Yes, there is something on my mind—I mean, something's trying to put itself on my mind. . . . What were you saying?"

"Just that it's time for chow. How's about it?"

"Sure."

What was it he was trying to remember, what confounded mess was churning, turning, burning, yearning, norning in his anachronistic unconscious? Something overheard from his listening post inside some anachronistic uterus of a bunk way back at the begining of time's slickumed track, the hissing of steam, the rumble of roller. What the hell did the fellow mean, whooping it up about Martine that way! Did a guy become a hero just because he wrote a few technical papers on the cortical-thalamic circuits in the higher primates? A martyr? Something was very definitely the martyr. With Martine. . . .

On the roof, forty-odd stories up, they found a table to one side of the huge glass-enclosed penthouse restaurant. The whole city was stretched out below, wheels within wheels: directly to the right was the circle of park at the hub, with the statue of the steamroller hunched massively in the middle.

He was hungry, and the turkey sandwich (dark meat, with East Union dressing) was wonderfully tasty, but after a moment he put it away and sighed: looking down at the statue, he found that he'd lost all interest in food. What was it about that mammy-jamming symbol that upset all his gastric functions?

"All that talk about Martine," he said.

"Great man!" Jerry said reverently. "Did I tell you, I was born October 19? My mom says with a start like that I can't help but be a world beater."

October 19. Oh, God, yes, and back on the ship one afternoon Jerry had said something about *another* date, he'd said, why, sure, *everybody* knows somebody who was born on July 16th. And—back on the island all the amp athletes had worn big blue "M's" on their sweatshirts. "M's" which could hardly have stood for Man. . . .

"Like Martine. He beat it right out of this world on October 19."

"Didn't he, though? Plop into immortality." Martine decided to change the subject: he was beginning to sweat

146

badly again: Helder had snored so goddamned loud. "These lectures," he began.

"What'd you think of them?"

"They were meaty, all right." He stared at the slivers of turkey protruding from his sandwich. "They contained plenty of food for thought." He was silent for a moment, blank. "I want to ask you an important question. Remember that African bushman I told you about a while back?"

"Yup, what about him?"

"Well, I was trying to imagine how he'd react if he'd sat through this morning's lectures. He'd be awfully impressed, of course, but all the same I think he'd sense a certain contradiction."

"A contradiction? Seems to me all the theories fit together pretty neatly."

"You bet, it's perfectly amazing. Square concepts are plugged into round theoretical holes and, by some miracle of non-Aristotelian logic, they seem to fit. But a naïve guy like Ubu might still say that the two halves of the overall theoretical picture don't seem to dovetail."

"Which halves?"

"The Yogi half and the Commissar half. Let me explain what I mean—seeing it through Ubu's childish eyes, naturally. Immob was founded on the idea of immobilization, right? That is to say, the new ideal was simply quiescence, the passive condition—Yogi donothingism."

"All that's kid stuff," Jerry said. "Where's the problem?"

"I'm coming to that. Now, this Yogi tendency is founded on a real disdain for the body, it's an attempt to humiliate the body, crush it, petrify it, escape from it. But there's another side to Immob. The Commissar side. The feverishly active, striving, fast-moving side. All that seems to be based on adoration for the body, not a rejection of it. Anyhow, the upshot is that the immobilized acquire greater mobility and the passive get around more than ever. To an outsider like Ubu, you see, all this might seem a bit inconsistent."

Jerry stared at him. "Why?"

"Look, people start out truncating themselves in order to disengage themselves from the world—and they wind up capable of greater engagement than ever. Ubu would flip his wig trying to figure out how a program for detachment metamorphoses into a program for the oceanic."

Jerry frowned, he seemed bored by the whole discussion. "I'd give your Mr. Ubu a very simple answer," he said. "I'd tell him to stay the hell out of politics."

147

"Politics?" Martine said in bewilderment.

"Sure. What you're talking about, this so-called contradiction Ubu would hit on, that's the whole bone of contention between our two big parties."

"You have parties?"

"Natch, haven't you heard about the Pro-Pros and the Anti-Pros? They're just what their names imply: the Pro-Pros are in favor of prosthetics and most of the Immob big shots belong to it, while the Anti-Pros have been dead set against prosthetics from the start because they think such developments foul up the original principles of Immob."

"I gather," Martine said, "that you belong to the Pro-Pros."

"Gather again, Doc. I don't belong to anything. Politics, any kind of politics, makes me sick—too verbalistic an activity, it's for blabbermouths. But all the same, I think the Antis are a bunch of dizzy extremists. What are you going do to with a guy after you make him into a hero and give him all this charisma—tuck him away in a basket without even a pair of thumbs to twiddle? Is that the thanks he gets for his sacrifice?"

"Ubu," Martine suggested, "might say that, as he understands Immob, amputeeism is supposed to be a privilege and not a sacrifice."

"Quibbling," Jerry said firmly. "What's the sense in kidding ourselves? The whole thing's nothing but a semantic difficulty. In the Age of the Hyphen we're bound to work out ways of bringing such polarities together. Through dialectic materialism—idealism, I mean."

"You think you'll reconcile all polarities? Even the North and South Poles?"

"Sure thing. The split is just semantic. Isn't the real silent world a mighty solid hyphenation of north and south? Take the equator, for example, it's only an Aristotelian construct of man's, it exists only on the map, not the territory. Vishinu may forget it but the territory's been a pretty compact little unit all along."

"So it has. But then, so is an eight ball."

"Right." Jerry yawned. "Well, I've got to get on down to cyber lab. Want to come along and see what it's like?"

"Thanks for the invitation, but I've got some things to do this afternoon. I hope I meet up with you again, Jerry— it's been very helpful talking to you."

"Tell this Ubu to read some Martine. It'll give him a new slant on things."

Hissing of steam in diaphragm, rumbling of roller in

148

sphincters: Helder's loose lips flapping—"I'll do that," Martine said. "Happy cortico-building, and don't let it go to your head."

He'd left not a moment too soon. Another minute with Jerry and he would have lost control completely, already toward the end there he'd felt the convulsive tremors beginning in his viscera. The morning's pedagogical fare had been the most enormous joke he'd ever heard or imagined, very possibly the greatest and most obscene joke ever conceived of by mortal would-be man: and nobody had laughed. Nobody had chuckled. All those hyphenated sobrieties! Those oceanic pomposities! Everybody had the drag-ass bring-down cyber-cyto blues!

Walking away from the University, down through the spacious gardens and past the girl with the pink-and-blue skirt and the sketch pad—not really seeing her, not seeing anybody, moving blindly and mechanically—he found that his mind was reeling.

"Not a smirk," he said aloud to himself, wonderingly. "Not so much as a twinkle in anybody's eye. Oh God, oh Montreal, oh Martine."

Up ahead there was a crowd gathered before a store window. Automatically he stopped and tried to see what was inside. The establishment was called F. A. O. Schwab's, the gold lettering on the window read TRICKS, JOKES, GAMES, NOVELTIES.

Jokes? What sorts of jokes would a smart oceanic retailer be merchandising to these dead-pan Immobs: what amp Joe Miller texts, what cyber-cyto itching powder, what non-Aristotelian rubber hot dogs and soluble spoons? It seemed that when the limbs were amputated the funny bone automatically went with them. How would these people know a joke if they saw one?

Yet they were laughing. Some of them, indeed, among them quite a few amps of varying degrees, were holding on to their sides and quaking helplessly, their eyes wet and hysterical. Martine forced his way into the throng. Marching back and forth on a platform that ran the length of the window were a lot of ingeniously constructed mechanical toys, whole troops of them—little robot quadro-amps hardly more than four or five inches high, each outfitted with tiny plastic limbs which moved stiffly and lit up fitfully as they jerked. Each figure was so constructed that every few steps it would trip, tumble over on its head, then roll back on its feet and rejoin the parade.

Every time one of the dolls stumbled and toppled over, the onlookers burst out laughing with great heartiness. A stout woman just behind Martine was pressing her bosom solidly against him; with each mechanical mishap she threw her head back and roared, breasts quivering like aspic in a hurricane. The waves of her uncontrolled joy began to call out sympathetic vibrations in him, once again the flutters began in his abdomen.

Immob was this too! A landscape of bleak solemnities, punctuated with pratfalls both programmed and unprogrammed! A nation of unsmiling priests, top-heavy with mission and frozen-mugged with dedication, stopping every so often, at every pratfall, to laugh in unholy glee at themselves and each other—at the symbols of their mission and the objects of their dedication. Here was ambivalence with a vengeance: a whole inspired people plunging the dagger of the horselaugh into the bowels of its inspiration. No doubt the founding fathers of Immob hadn't counted on these spurts of mockery, and yet their massive piety had contained in it the seeds of its own negation. Why? By what psychic alchemy did it happen that these plastic hands started out folded in the attitude of prayer and wound up with thumbs to the nose and fingers wagging madly?

Still giddy, Martine groped for some idea large enough to embrace this staggering fact. Maybe it was something like this:

There was probably a touch of psychic hara-kiri in every human community. For every community promulgated some sacred mission or other, dedication was the matrix of every group, its psychic glue—and every communal mission was in the end a bit absurd. Why? Well, simply because it demanded of all men within its pale that they order their psychic economies to conform with the group goal, verticalize their horizontal instincts: this was the meaning of the reality principle as superimposed on the pleasure principle. But the reality created and deified by the community, although it undoubtedly paid some emotional dividends to those who kowtowed to it, never turned out a really adequate substitute for the simpler instinctual pleasures sacrificed at its altar: peace, for example, was a hollow gift when purchased at the price of orgasm, or limbs. So even in the most socialized citizen, the most obedient, there was a festering remnant of discontent. Particularly since, when he looked

150

around, he saw other men in other places devoted to goals quite antithetical to his own—and every bit as solemn about it.

Good enough. It followed, then, that the healthiest society was one which allowed its members ample escape-valves for the discontents fomented by civilization and its instinct-trampling ends: along with the bread of solemnity, plenty of irreverent circuses in which clowns rode all the sacred cows. Where there were enough such circuses, little ambivalence remained to poison the more devotional activities. But among peoples who were discontented enough, and who were not provided with enough drainage systems for their malaise, every day was something of a circus, every solemn undertaking poisoned by a certain tongue-in-cheek attitude—they did obeisance to the community's lofty goals but always with a shrug of the shoulders and sardonic shadows playing around the mouth and the tacit suspicion that *"Dolce far niente."*

But under Immob something had happened to this dualistic, spleen-venting mechanism. The omnipresent irreverence had been banished. Suddenly America, what was left of America, had begun to take itself seriously, nothing but seriously. Flag waving had been established as a way of life, the wisecrack had been sent into exile. (Helder had always been sober as a judge.) Where ambivalence had formerly seeped into every aspect of life, now officially all was reverence and dedication, the people were mired in mission. (Helder? Missionary through and through.) Why had laughter fallen into such disrepute? Very possibly because the unsmiling priests of the new pacifist philosophy had recognized that behind such mass laughter was a seething fund of aggression—that laughter was the last refuge of the civilized man's anger.

So—nobody laughed when the sacred cow named Martine was trotted out. No clown leaped on his back to make grotesque faces and do hilarious flipflops, turning hortatory lectures into circuses. Martine was installed as martyr, decked out with halo instead of dunce cap and putty nose, and heads were bowed in respectful memoriam. No Louis Armstrong appeared to scat nihilistically behind the benediction. They sank to their solenoid knees before an ideological ikon of a cow named, for some schizoid reason, Martine—and nobody sniggered, nobody tittered. It was the greatest, most obscene, most throat-tightening and diaphragm-fluttering joke of all, and it didn't even call out a faltering tee-hee. Why, in the name of sweet sassafras reason, was

151

the cow called Martine? Why not Bill, or Sigmund, or L. Ron, or Aldous, or Norbert, or Alfred, or Mahatma, or even Helder—why Martine, why Martine? And nobody laughed—

The woman's breasts jiggled against his back again. The tremors started up, erupting in his middle. He was lost, there was nothing for it, it was going to seep over him now in a flood of hysteria. His lips quivered, trying to hold it in. Then it came geysering, a harsh, raucous, convulsive bellowing that caused him almost to double up. Martine, the hero, the martyr, was now in a state of complete oscillation. St. Martine had become St. Vitus, St. Parkinson, St. Jo-Jo. He was suddenly sick to his stomach: no doubt something, some semantic·something, he'd eaten. The thought made him laugh (or cry?) still harder.

It went on for several moments: the people standing near him turned away from the window to stare, uncomprehending. As soon as he had recovered enough to move he straightened up and ran down the street, still choking, trying to wipe away the tears with his handkerchief.

Not far ahead, on the strip of parkway which cut down the center of the boulevard, there was a deserted bench: he reached it and sank down, dabbing at his eyes. The attack had left him weak as a kitten. Funny, he hadn't swallowed a mouthful of food since early morning but now he felt like throwing up.

Part Four

DODGING THE STEAMROLLER

---

chapter thirteen

"LET 'ER ROLL!"

Martine cocked his head. In a moment he heard it again: "Is she getting up steam?"

He looked down toward the statue at the hub, the voice seemed to be coming from there.

Just to one side of the stone giant, on the wide pedestal supporting it, a man was doing acrobatics; every few seconds he shouted a nonsensical phrase which boomed through the entire neighborhood, then he catapulted some twenty-five or thirty feet into the air, turning head over heels a dozen times or more before landing on his feet. On his pros, rather; his artificial limbs flickered as he pinwheeled through the air. His gibes were barked into a microphone which stood on the pedestal. A considerable crowd was gathered in the park at the base of the statue.

Martine rose from the bench, shaking his head, feeling a bit faint, and walked from the street to the meeting. The speaker had now stopped his gymnastic stunts and was talking more earnestly.

"No! No, brothers! The steamroller doesn't go chasing after amps who can skedaddle thirty feet into the ozone any time they've a mind to! But this poor jerk—*he* was stretched out flat on his back from the word go, begging for it." Here the young man pointed an accusing transparent finger at the Christ-like stone figure which lay prostrate, legs crushed under the great cylinder and arms raised in petrified petition

153

to the thin air. "Get this straight: the steamroller's got to be dodged. Of course, the Anti-Pros will tell you that *their* one ambition in life is to dodge the old lady too. But take it from me, friends, if you can't move superfast, with super cortical co-ordination and super neuro controls, why, you stand about as much chance of outdistancing the old lady as Brother Vishinu does of winning the Olympics with his tongue! And it's plenty nimble!"

The audience was with the ingratiating young soapboxer, heads nodded vehemently and hands clapped resoundingly. But the speaker waved the applause away.

"A man," the Pro went on, "has to be up to something to justify his staying alive. And that means, first of all, that he has to be *up*. And about. Will some gum-beating Anti kindly tell me how a man gets together with his fellow-humans and with the world around him if he spends his whole blamed life on a hunk of foam rubber, casing his navel and gurgling philosophy? The simple fact is this, friends: Our heroes, our Theos, must be in full view, up at the top, at the controls, guiding and inspiring us all. They can't do that unless they're fitted with pros, their badges of merit and honor. Prosthetics versus prostration, folks, that's the issue. They most decidedly do *not* serve who only lie and wait—they're just appeasers of the steamroller—and Immob is first and foremost a philosophy of service. Look it up in Martine if you don't believe me. . . ."

Martine gulped, his stomach felt as though it had suddenly turned over. Oh, there were many things that he would like to look up in Martine. Unfortunately, some of the key volumes in his collected works were missing—and that thought in itself seemed to him howlingly funny, although he couldn't for the life of him, for the death of him, see what it meant.

"Of course," the Pro continued, "at this point the Anti boys will start splitting their semantic hairs. They'll say: 'All well and good, but doesn't the very word Immob mean immobilization?' Well, we Pros are such good Immobs that we refuse to make a fetish of any word at all—even the word Immob. Who cares about names? On the silent level a rose by any other name would smell just as sweet—that's the law of semantics. Immobilization? Sure, what's been immobilized in the amp, even rooted out altogether, is the war-making tropism. That's what Immob was after, not the paralysis of man for its own sake. The moral end is accomplished—

154

why perpetuate the physical means? That's such slavish devotion to the map that the territory's lost sight of entirely.

"Let's get this straight: something downright magical happens to a man when he's inducted into the select circle of ampism. The ritual whereby he emerges a full-fledged quadro drives all the malice and mischief out of his system. Good. That's a nifty beginning. But at that point only the negative job of cleansing has been done, now he's got to acquire his positive glow, his charisma. How do we give him that? First of all, his brain has got to be expanded to its full human proportions by pros that stimulate it with exercises in co-ordination, the d-and-d's and all that. When man becomes fully human he will be a pacifist, that's A.B.C. But no man will ever get the feeling that he's fully human until he knows that the world is wide open with possibility before him and he's allowed a *choice*. That's the great word, folks, c,h,o,i,c,e, choice, it's choice that makes us human because it means we've dodged all the 'Its' that make the animal a robot, we're self-determined. The first great choice Immob gives a man, obviously, is the choice about cutting his arms and legs off. Before this men became amps only on the battlefield and in bombings, in some accident or other, it was something *done* to them, they weren't consulted. So *voluntary* ampism is a big step forward toward humanness."

Voluntary, voluntary: Martine cringed, this seemed to him now the most obscene word he had ever heard, more obscene than a snore.

"But now, take the same logic and apply it to the Immob *after* he's become an amp. What choices remain to him now? Can he *choose* to lie down rather than stand up, *choose* to call an attendant to scratch his, ah, ear lobe rather than do it himself, *choose* to be immobile? No, sir. Without pros he's all amp and no vol. Even his pacifism isn't a matter of choice, that's the point, he couldn't take a poke at anybody if he wanted to. But fit him with *detachable* limbs which snap on and off quicker than you can say Norbert Wiener, give him the feeling that his limbs are *voluntary*, you see, and he stops being a robot. The prosthetic limb, friends, is the means whereby man makes his great leap into human freedom.

"Oh, I know, I know—the Antis will make a great logical fuss about the so-called contradiction in the idea of militant pacifists, *active* pacifists. Well, just look around you and you'll see that all the great men of your time, all your leaders, are Theos, superactive pacifists. The type of new man, fully human man, is here, the first real hyphenated

155

Renaissance man ever produced by the human race. He is the genuine glowing son of Martine. Never forget this: Brother Martine, our immortal martyr, founded the new world in a great *act* of pacifism. . . ."

At the final invocation of his name, Martine came out of the fog and his legs, powered by a morality of their own, began to carry him away from the scene superfast. It was hard to keep from breaking into a run, but even as he moved off the voice boomed out again and in will-less fascination he glanced back over his shoulder for a last look.

The speaker bulleted into the air again, high above the heads of his listeners. This time, though, he had removed the microphone from its stand and attached it to his lapel, so that his voice, steady, controlled, self-assured, mocking, continued without a falter as his body careened through the air.

"Look at the old lady, she's so sore she could spit! I'll dodge you every time, nasty old bitch, I'm the daring young man on the flying prosthetics! Watch me give the old girl the slip! Whee! Zowee! When you can pop up to the ceiling any time you've a mind to, well, the old lady's double-crossed, she can't get herself a nice juicy victim any more— all she can do is hit the ceiling herself, ha ha, ho ha ha. . . ."

Over and over he jumped, while his forceful voice licked out over the great landscaped circle. The crowd broke into frenzied applause, there were whistles and shouts of approval.

Martine hurried around the corner. He began to walk feverishly. For a long time he wandered about the center of town, now hurrying down the main arteries which led away from the hub, now poking into the side streets which bisected these spokes. At a corner stand he stopped and ordered a hot dog, but when he was served a paper napkin and saw stamped in the corner a figure of the ubiquitous steamroller he put the roll down (the frankfurter was still steaming) spat out the one bite he had taken and walked away, stomach quaking. Distraught, thinking the city's a circle, going around in circles, circling around and around a word and a sound and a sweat, thinking, he never laughed but he snored; his thoughts swimming like hyperthyroid tadpoles in a muddy creek.

He must have been zigzagging through the streets for fully a half-hour when he turned a corner and came upon the department store with a great neon sign on its façade:

MARCY'S GENERAL MERCHANDISE. As he approached the nearest window he saw that a clump of people had gathered in front of it. There was nothing inside but a long row of baskets, each one containing a large doll.

Something began to bother him. Just as he was about to make an opening for himself in the crowd and pass through, one of the dolls, the one at the very end of the line, the one which seemed to have its large round blue eyes fixed on him—this doll moved.

It blinked.

Unmistakably blinked.

He moved a few feet, then stopped. He had the sensation that something intolerable was happening, that he was being trapped. The doll's big blue eyes had moved, they were still fixed on him, picking him out from the crowd. When he turned and looked squarely at the doll with an air of outrage, the doll's whole head moved so that it could look squarely back.

This, he felt, was a scene, some shimmer of improbability, that he would much rather avoid, but he remained rooted to the spot and forced himself to face the fact—it was not a doll, it was alive, its lips were moving, all the doll-sized figures in all the baskets were alive and their lips were all moving too. They were alive, these dolls, and dangling before each one was a microphone. Each one was alive and speaking into its microphone, addressing a group of spectators outside. The low drone of their voices came to Martine now through the traffic noises.

His impulse was to fight his way to the curb and run but he stood there, his legs limp. The live doll at the far left, its eyes never leaving him for a moment, was speaking to him, directly to him, he heard the one voice above all the others. He did not want to hear, he did not want to stay, but slowly, thinking of the perversity that makes a man poke his tongue into an aching cavity, he made his way to the window and stood there looking down at the figure in the basket.

The blue eyes gaped up at him, pools of bland accusation or maybe just neutral sheets of mirror reflecting his own guilt, some obscure guilt, something to do with snoring and not snoring, and the lips moved and words came softly into his ears.

"We have lost the true way," said the doll that was not a doll, no expression ruffling its doll-like alive features. "It is late—the time for loom weaving is past."

"The time for loom weaving is definitely past," Martine whispered huskily, mechanically. "Gone forever."

"I am glad you agree," the living doll said.

It gave Martine a start: obviously there must be microphones installed somewhere on the street to pick up voices and carry them inside.

All these figures were quadro-amps—without prosthetics. Their limbless bodies, ovaloid, spheroid, stripped of geometric irrelevancies, were hidden under blue silk-edged baby blankets, which was why it had been easy at first glance to take them for dolls: only their heads were exposed. These were the basket cases, the ceiling gazers and navel explorers.

"The issue is clear," the amp went on in a monotone. "Arms mean armaments, legs mean marching orders. Men must stop moving or they move to their doom."

"The time for doom leaving is past," Martine muttered.

"It is clear," the amp continued. "If the tiger's claws are removed by surgery and replaced with cybernetic super-claws, will it stop slashing the other beasts of the jungle? If the lemming's legs are amputated and replaced with super-legs, will it refrain from hurling itself suicidally into the ocean? The energies heretofore trapped by the body's 'Its' must be placed at the disposal of the cerebrum—so that, at last, the cerebrum will be able to perceive and conceive truthfully, uncorrupted by animal lusts. These lusts cannot be shaken off until their agencies, the limbs, are removed. Prosthetics do not prod the brain into expanding and becoming a more perfect organ. This is a perfection of the brain in nothing but a bestial, jungle sense."

Why, Martine wondered in a sudden rush of pique, was the amp addressing these remarks exclusively to him? Why were his, Martine's, limbs considered such special prizes? Was it—was it because of what he'd been doing with them for eighteen years, was it because for eighteen years he'd been standing alongside an operating table in the Mandunga cave, fashioning with his hands a race of emotional amps, a race of mushrooms, non-laughers, snorers, their psyches holed up in a basket whether or not they happened to retain their limbs? But the Mandungabas should be a delight to this amp, why was he eyeing his, Martine's, limbs so hungrily? Just plain gluttony? Or was it because of his, Martine's, own guilt, guilt that once, nearly eighteen years ago, he had not snored nor even slept. . . .

"Cybernetics has only bolstered the beast in man, tied him to the jungle life of tooth and claw. We have a choice:

to rain blows with our limbs, or caresses with our liberated spirits; one or the other. Let Vishinu have all the columbium, it is a trap."

"It is too late for womb leaving," Martine whispered.

"That is correct," the amp said. "As Martine said, it is too late for loom weaving."

Strange, how hypnotic the man's voice was. More, almost uncanny. An hour before, Martine had quickly spotted the Pro-Pro speaker for what he was: only the Immob variant of the traditional soapbox polemicist, with all the folksy flimflam of the demagogue. But this Anti-Pro was something new under the political sun, his whole polemical style was that of murmurous serenity. He did not harangue, he expounded. He *knew*. He chose now to pass his knowledge along to the world, without sales pressure. This total lack of salesmanship, Martine reflected, was the shrewdest selling technique he had ever run into in a rabble rouser. To challenge him would be like challenging the voice of God. (Helder, holding forth in the upper bunk, had often sounded like God.)

Part of the effect, no doubt, was due to the fact that the man was lying on his back, an unagitated position seldom cultivated by agitators. But it was much more than that. Apart from his immobilized state, or perhaps because of it, the young man—he was hardly more than twenty-seven or twenty-eight—spoke with the pontifical last-wordism of Solomon, of Methuselah. He drawled obscenities, dispensed nightmares in a placid whisper. His oratorical style (like Helder's) was that of a superb *machina ratiocinatrix*. . . . But maybe, after all, the deepest secret of this impact *was* the fact of his spectacular maiming. One could to some extent fight off the hypnotic verbal blandishments of a Pro-Pro spellbinder, it was not too hard because the man's crippled state was so thoroughly compensated for by artificial limbs that it did not call for pity. The Anti-Pro, on the other hand, was so demonstratively damaged that the mere sight of him lying in his basket was enough to stir up all sorts of sympathetic vibrations—and these vibrations were what gave to the experience its uncanny quality, its eeriness.

Yes, that could be it. For it is uncanny whenever some sight or sound arouses a person's deepest unconscious hungers—and the sight of a grown man reduced to complete uterine-infantile helplessness must mobilize in everyone the yearning, thrust very far from consciousness and bedded in

159

churning guilts, to achieve the same spectacular regression, to draw back from the grueling effortfulness of adult life into the sheltered megalomaniacal crib of babyhood. Everybody hungers for passivity and must deny that guilt-laden hunger in bursts of feverish activity; no doubt much of human tonus derives from just this ambivalence, seeping insidiously into the nervous system. And the hidden urge must begin to dance at the sight of any person, crippled in birth or by accident, who wanders into view. He is a dramatization of the forbidden. The looker, in his first spurt of reaction, identifies with the maimed one, empathizes into his condition, thrills to this eerie charade of his own taboo wishes; but as the taboo wish is activized, draws perilously close to awareness, there rise with it all the unbearable guilts which ordinarily keep it safely anchored. These guilts must not be allowed to break through into full consciousness, it would be too painful. Accordingly, the stirred-up yearning must be warded off, driven back into its subterranean hiding place— and this is accomplished by striking another, cover-up attitude, not one of identification with the maimed but one of removal from him. One thinks then, reassuringly, how infinitely worse off the cripple is than oneself, secretly complimenting oneself on escaping such a cruel fate. Finally, if this attitude of contented superiority becomes too uncomfortable—the ethic of communal living requires that one *feel* for the unfortunate, not lord it over them—the looker covers up all his urges and counterurges with a topmost cloak of polite sympathy. This stereotyped, socially dictated attitude of sympathy, finally, allows a bit of the original identification to be discharged surreptitiously. In short, one becomes the cripple, then revels in being utterly unlike the poor fellow, and finally is politely but distantly sorry for him—while secretly feeling a bit like him after all. All because his mere presence agitates one's innermost yearning to crawl back to the crib and curl up cozily, to be taken care of by a universe now, as in the paradisiacal beginning, cringing under the whiplash of one's imperious will, terrorized by one's every whimper.

But suppose the damaged one is transparently *not* the victim of a mishap? Suppose it is quite clear that he has deliberately, programmatically, *voluntarily* performed the mutilation on himself—and as a result is officially showered with kudos and plaudits by his whole society? What then? The sight of such a cripple would become so uncanny as to be unbearable. For the entirely *willful* nature of his misfortune would dramatize not only the beatific state of passivity but even more, and with harrowing starkness, the fact that one's fascination by that state is, at its furtive heart, a masochistic one. When one secretly identifies with *this* cripple, one identifies not only with mutilation but also with the *wish* to be mutilated, to do the mutilating oneself. The voluntary side of ampism, in other words, highlights in the observer his own hidden volitions in all their self-destructive import—and, most sickeningly of all, with all the social onus removed from them—and whenever this masochistic layer of the psyche is prodded in the slightest it must send off evil odoriferous fumes of shame. So the voluntary basket case must be an infernally potent magnet for everyone's deepest guilts, since he focuses attention on everyone's desire to do damage to himself, the masochistic essence of every man's interest in all damaged people. No psychic distance from this self-made baby is possible: this is no victim. The spotlight now is on the "I," not this or that "It." This must be the key to the Immob's charisma—the fact that he served as a living uncanny symbol of all men's drives to wound themselves, annihilate themselves, the masochism which motors all human urges to move backwards in time toward the blessed megalomaniacal state at the beginning—and to punish oneself for so desiring. The amp dramatized, indeed, the fact that one could not backtrack in psychic time *without* self-mutilation. Once dispossessed from the womb and the nursery, no man could buy megalomania save at the cost of slashing violence to his own person and personality.

It struck Martine now that it might provide new insights into the political process to draw up, a rank order of panics. On the lowest level would be the reaction of the normal, intact man when he is solicited on the street by a crippled beggar rattling a tin cup: he either turns aside or flings the unfortunate a coin to remove him hurriedly from sight and conscience. However, the same normal man will often forget his self-protective reactions when the same beggar appears before him, not as bum, but in the guise of saint (Christ) or artist (Rimbaud) or political leader (Helder? Helder?)—this normal man then, surprisingly enough, prostrates himself. Obviously something has happened to his defenses, he is so deeply shaken, thrown into such overwhelming oscillations by his panic, that he cannot recognize the solicitor as the same raggedy panhandler, now juggling a slightly shinier and more streamlined cup—a cup which by some infernal magic is disguised as a gift from the solicitor to the solicited.

161

Why the astounding psychic shift in the normal man before the cripple-fanatic, the disintegration of all his psychic safeguards, the hurried passage from contemptuous retreat to adoring self-subjection? Maybe just because the saint-artist-politico—as against the street-corner beggar, who was haphazardly mauled by poliomyelitis or ack-ack or some other "It"—is the epitome of the self-mauled. Maybe because, bringing to life as he does a terrible reminder of the urge toward death in all of us, he leaves us too guilt-ridden to put up much of a fight against his spell: in dramatizing the universal death-wish, he reduces all men whom he touches to living corpses.

But the doll was still talking to him, the big round blue eyes flashed authoritatively at him alone. . . . "I would like to speak with you," he said. "It is important. Would you be good enough to come inside?"

Outraged to be singled out so, astounded at this exclusive interest in him, quite sure that it would be much, much safer to go away, thinking again of the perversity that makes a man probe an aching tooth with his tongue, hot, sweaty, drenched, stomach a rock, breathing hard, throat choked, Martine proceeded to the entrance of the store and went through the revolving door, revolving, around in a circle, vicious circle, around and around a word and a sound and a guilt, steamily, rollingly. Somewhere overhead a jet plane thrummed and whined, making a noise like a man in an upper bunk breathing hard in laughless sleep.

chapter fourteen

ABOVE THE basket was a mirror tilted at a sharp angle, in it the amp could see the faces of those standing behind him and they could see his. He looked hard at Martine's reflection. "You are troubled," he said without preliminaries.

The flat statement caught Martine off guard. "What?"

"You are uneasy, you perspire."

"Oh—I'm not troubled, really. A bit puzzled, that's all."

"You are an unusually sensitive and intelligent man, my intuition tells me that. Why are you not one of us?"

"I've been away. I had no idea how Immob was developing back here."

"You agree with Immob?"

"It's several cuts above any other philosophy I ever heard of."

The amp's face showed no response to the joke. "Why are you not even a mono or a duo?"

Martine thought fast. "For a very good reason. I am a parasitologist. In order to do worthwhile research I had to spend long years in the African jungle. Unfortunately, when I left for Africa prosthetics had not yet been developed, so if I'd had any limbs removed I couldn't have gotten replacements for them. Under the rugged conditions of life in the jungle, an amputee without pros wouldn't survive very long, let alone get any research done. It was simply in the interests of my own Moral Equivalent that I had to forego the initiation rites of Immob."

He considered his improvisation almost inspired, but the amp seemed not at all impressed. "Your logic is entirely spurious, of course," the young man said. "Short of total passivity there is no Moral Equivalent for war. Why, may I ask, do you not begin your initiation now?"

"Ah," Martine said, "I'm afraid I'm too old for that sort of thing now."

"And uneasy. You are too intelligent a man not to see the contradiction in the non-amp state."

"Oh—maybe. I must say, though, that I can't help seeing a few contradictions in the amp state too."

"The contradictions are all in the Pro-Pro camp. The only way to end the disastrous movements which have always plagued mankind—individual and mass movements both—is, quite simply, to stop moving. That is Martine's whole lesson about the steamroller effect. Gandhi's too. Perhaps you remember the tactics employed by Gandhi's followers in the face of overwhelming odds—they simply lay down on the railroad tracks in front of an oncoming locomotive. They were never run over. The locomotive stopped. *In every case, the locomotive stopped.*"

"Why?"

"Those early practitioners of passivity had triumphed inwardly over the locomotive. They projected charismatic power, not panicky animal impotence. Therefore the locomotive became impotent. Long before Martine, Gandhi had found the way to dodge the steamroller—by lying down in front of it. . . ."

He felt his gorge rising. They had to stop kicking his name—his mottled pen name?—around like this! He had reached the limit of his patience, how long was a man expected to go on being muddled and mottled and penned up and perspiring and feeling sick to his stomach and his

163

breath coming in quick fluttering gasps—by God, he would put and end to it! make them eat their abominable obscene words!

His throat was terribly dry, it was hard for him to keep the agitation from flooding into his face, he looked away from the amp's reflection in the mirror and out the window. He was suddenly crafty, he thought that if he could change the subject his stomach might quiet down. "Everybody around here seems to poo-poo Vishinu's speech," he said.

"Vishinu's attack means that the final crisis has come."

"What's the nature of this crisis?"

"Simple: the moment amps acquired new limbs they regressed from Immob into the old pattern of activity. And activity means war."

"Why? The caress is also an act."

"The hand was and remains an instrument for animal aggression. Therefore, when it fondles and strokes there is a blow lurking in the caress. Hands are made to grasp with. So long as men are graspers, they must compete. This competition, which originated in the primordial slime, reaches the peak of frenzy at the present moment. Now, in the cybernetic limbo, men grasp for the instruments of grasp: the means have become the end. The final war which writes finis to the human race, the half-human race, will be one waged by clawing men for their man-made claws."

"So there's no way out? No escape claws?"

"Only a very uneasy man jokes so obscenely. Once you join us this glandular panic will subside. . . . No, men must lay down their arms—and legs—quite literally, or the steamroller triumphs. The only way out of the vicious circle is to recline in the center of it and turn the thoughts inward where there are no circles, no boundaries for the mind, only a serene infinitude."

. "You evidently place little stock in Moral Equivalents?"

"None whatsoever. Gandhi thought to de-energize men's aggressions by turning their efforts to wholesome pursuits, he invented one of the first M.E.'s in loom weaving. It could not work, he who sits down at the loom to make cloth can rise again to make war."

"Do you really think the Untouchables on the railroad track, simply through lying down, unnerved the locomotive?"

"Certainly. Is it not a rule that a lion tamer is perfectly safe in his cage—until he betrays a touch of animal terror?"

"Maybe it is. But there's an old joke about such rules: You know it, and I know it, but does the *lion* know it?"

"Of course the lion knows it. That is why it never bites a man unless he is afraid."

"You must know more non-Aristotelian lions than I do," Martine said. "The lions back in Africa would lunch on any man within pouncing distance, charisma and all. Anyhow, isn't it true, as the Pros claim, that this detachment you advocate is the very negation of the oceanic? How can you be in touch with anything when you pass your days flat on your back, with your eyes on your navel?"

"Do not scorn the navel," the amp said. "It is infinity's aperture. It is the door that leads everywhere."

"Mine's pretty clogged," Martine said. "Collects a lot of lint."

"The man who transcends his body does not simply retreat into his own isolated deeps. When the gaze turns inward the spirit suddenly leaps into the innermost being of the world, into the hearts of all universal matters—Thou art That. When a man's own skin is his horizon he touches nothing but himself, an eternal exasperated self-fondling. Bodies prevent the merger of human beings with each other and with the world. Do you, by chance, know the text of Nietzsche entitled *The Birth of Tragedy from the Spirit of Music?*"

"Vaguely." Back before the Third, Martine remembered, he had once picked up a second-hand copy of the book in a Greenwich Village shop.

"A remarkable work. In it, you may recall, Nietzsche distinguishes between the two motifs in the Greek spirit: the plastic, which glorifies human separateness in statuary and whose form of expression is a measured eloquence; the musical, which represents a cry of anguish from man yearning to break out of the bodily trap and whose form of expression is nonsemantic sound, song. Sculpture, according to this view, is Apollonian, reveling in the restraint imposed on the spirit by the body, in physical definition and containment, and music is Dionysian, the shriek of those who yearn to lose their bodily separateness and melt into the herd and the landscape and the void. From this frustrated Dionysian urge Nietzsche derives the whole quality of tragedy, and he is quite right: the tragedy of the human condition is precisely the entrapment by the vile engine of bone and muscle, the cursed armoring of the self by the engulfing skin. The navel is the only escape hatch from the trap."

"You might just as well have quoted Freud," Martine said.

165

"Nietzsche's Dionysian urge sounds very much like Freud's death-wish."

"Precisely," the amp said, not without respect. "It was the same polarity which Freud had in mind when he posited two great warring impulses: Eros, which is the life-giving and life-saving drive, and Thanatos, which is the passion of the body to throw off all cramping patterns and drip back into oblivion with the inert scattered elements of the cosmos. Thanatos, as he knew very well, was the personification of Death in Greek mythology, brother to Hypnos, the god of Sleep, and Nyx, god of Night—all three of them dwellers of the lower depths."

"And this is what you have made into a program for the salvation of humanity: universal death?"

"Far from it. You see, there is a paradox here which Freud did not savor fully. The inertness which is variously called sleep, hypnosis, thanatosis—a zoological term which, as you may know, refers to the trancelike state of inanition assumed by beetles and certain other insects when disturbed or threatened—is not a genuine death but the only way of evading the death-ridden flesh. Voluntary thanatosis, therefore, is an affirmation of life through which the totalitarian quakes and spasms of the death-hungry body are overcome and the spirit can soar into the limitless void wherein eternal truth resides. The mind-map becomes one with the world-territory. This, you will recognize, is the genuinely oceanic condition, which Freud discounted as a human possibility."

"All Yogi and no Commissar," Martine said, "makes Jack a dull boy."

"Transcendence," the amp said, "is possible only through the trance—through the catapulting of the Dionysian, musical self up and out of the Apollonian, chattering body. From this analysis you should appreciate that the Yogi's state of nirvana has been thoroughly misunderstood. It has been taken for a condition of nothingness, of negation, whereas it is actually everythingness, the only human affirmation. For it is not the antithesis of Eros, but only a strategy for doing what Christianity and many other religions have tried to do without success—for transforming Eros into Agape, bodily self-centered love into spiritual oceanic love, the love that is greedy and sucking into the love that is genuinely agape and open to everything. For through nirvana, the mystic's self-willed thanatosis, the Yogi manages to elude the flesh and merge in spirit with the Other, with the primordial Oneness, in the true oceanic experience, the ultimate orgasm. The animal, slave to erotic tropisms, can only cry, 'Give to me! More! More!' The liberated spirit, giving itself freely over to Agape, murmurs over and over again, 'Om, Om, Om'—Om being the mystic Vedantic word, compendium' of all man's oh's and ah's, essence of all human sound-making, the all-sound whereby the spirit is projected into the ripples of infinity to become one with the ocean beyond. Immob has simply discovered the underlying law which governs such rising above and beyond: full spiritual clutching is impossible until the agencies of *physical* clutching are removed—and, with them, the dictatorial thirsts of the body. The Yogi must slough off the Commissar."

Martine shook his head, making a supreme effort to dispel the agitation. "Seriously, I see a certain flaw in your argument."

"The flaw is in your vision," the amp said. "Kindly be more specific."

"When Orwell and Huxley looked into the future, they both concluded that sex was not among the things-to-come. In the scientific society, they foresaw, sex would be pretty drastically curtailed or eliminated altogether. You, however—"

"You are suggesting," the amp said, "that our program of amputeeism is incomplete?"

"I am. If you're going to hack off four of the trouble-making appendages, shouldn't you, in the interests of consistency, also hack off, or at least immobilize, the fifth and most troublemaking? The organ you might call Immob's anatomical fifth column?"

The amp yawned. "Under your flippancy," he said, "there is an astute question. As a matter of fact, we are now holding policy discussions on the question of castration. One faction maintains quite seriously what you have just suggested in jest. In their view, the spiritual orgasm which takes place in oceanic Agape must be crippled or even excluded altogether so long as the physical orgasm of bodily Eros remains a possibility."

"That makes sense to me. Oms do not make the man."

"I myself feel that sex does not have to be eliminated because it contains within itself the seeds of its opposite—it can become oceanic once a man is spiritually transformed into a complete Immob. Physical orgasm, properly savored, is a

167

haunting harbinger of the spiritual one, a stepping stone from Eros into Agape, from the cage to the ocean."

"My friend," Martine said, "you want to eat your cage and have it too."

"Nothing of the sort. Sex as it has been practiced and experienced until now, by half-human beasts, has been only a frantic Dionysian effort to break through the boundaries of skin by a violent merging of two separate bodies. It cannot work, of course: it is like beating two bricks together in an attempt to make them one brick—in the end they both crack and crumble. Therefore sex has always been the supremely frustrating experience for human beings, as witness the age-old saying, *Post coitum tristrea*. Of course man is always sad after coitus. For man is essentially an animal, and animals cannot merge and blend with one another—they are forever trapped in their own tormented mounds of flesh."

"Freud put it much more simply and less ominously," Martine said. "He suggested that there is simply something in the nature of the sex drive itself which precludes full satisfaction."

"Quite so, but he could not say what that something is. We have isolated this mysterious X-quantity and thus solved the conundrum of the ages. It is the hunger of the animal for the oceanic."

"Other remarks of Freud suggest that this X-quantity may be something less spectacular. Ambivalence, to be specific. More than once he speculated that sex and aggression, the two original drives in the id, are closely linked, and that the one constantly glides over into the other. A provocative idea, that. As an existentialist writer pointed out long ago, the rhetoric of love is remarkably like the rhetoric of war, the lover has a soldier's ardor, he talks of his phallus as though it were a firearm, when he ejaculates he 'discharges,' he speaks of his erotic campaigns in terms of attack, assault, siege, capitulation, victory. What's more, the lobotomists, I'm told, have found that whenever they dig the aggression out of a human brain the eroticism goes too. Very well—then couldn't we say that, because there's an aggressive tinge to even the purest sex act, the guilt which results is the reason for the touch of melancholy at the end? And wouldn't this mixture of embracing and alienating motives be what you mean by the tension between Agape and Eros? But let's not argue about that, there's another point I want to make. You insist that all movement is war. O.K., but sex is the quintessence of movement. Ergo, on your own premises, sex is war."

"It is indeed—for animals, which are engines of war. But once the two partners genuinely become one, in the great oceanic melting of orgasm, how can it be war? It takes two to make war. The solution to the war problem is also the solution to the sex problem: to blend the opposites and thus eliminate the spiritual gaps across which hostilities are carried on."

"What!" Martine exclaimed. "You mean—according to your school of thought, we drop bombs on each other simply because we don't have real orgasms?"

"Is it such a surprising idea? If in your animal state you cannot conceive of the selfish and the outgoing strands of personality melting together and sex becoming the ultimate in human transcendence, I can only assure you that it happens. Under such circumstances, if a man were to drop bombs it could only be on himself."

Martine was stunned.

"Through sex—through sex you destroy the body?" His voice was incredulous. "Shades of the Manichees!"

"Ah." The amp's eyes opened wide. "You are familiar with the history of the Manichean heresy?"

"I know a little something about it."

"What, exactly?"

"Oh, wait a minute, I know, for example, that the Manichees began in Persia as a Christian sect which preached that the soul, springing from the Kingdom of Light, seeks escape from the body, agency of the Kingdom of Darkness. They argued, accordingly, that the historical, flesh-and-blood Christ was a false Messiah, since the flesh is so vile that the spirit of God would never choose to inhabit a corporeal form—and so the whole idea of the Incarnation of God was an obscenity. Let's see. The logic of the Manichean doctrines, of course, led inevitably to the idea that salvation, the liberation of the spirit, is possible only through suicide; and, in fact, come to think of it, the final step in the initiation rites of certain early Manichees *was* suicide, the endura, I believe it was called."

"Excellent. Really excellent. Let me only add that in the eleventh century, when Pope Innocent decided to suppress the important Manichean areas of Western Europe in the blood bath of the Albigensian Crusade, the heretical doctrines did not die but only went underground. Without some knowledge of this ideological sediment it is impossible to explain the downcast eyes and flat gold otherworldly backgrounds in the medieval paintings of saints; the castration

169

of choirboys; Henry of Navarre's refusal to let his mistress wash under the armpits; the terrible filthiness of monks after the tenth century and, contrariwise, the stricture that cleanliness is next to godliness; the Huguenot hymn which is entitled, 'Everything Stinks But God.' The basic dualism upon which Christian thought subsequently rested can hardly be understood unless its furtive roots in Manicheism are dug out and examined. It is the key, for example, to the love stories derived, as most modern ones are, from the Tristan and Isolde legends of the troubadours—love stories in which a sexual relationship is sought, not for gratification of the senses, but only because it serves as a springboard into death."

"I remember, a big literature on Manicheism grew up earlier in the century, some of it after the First and a lot more after the Second," Martine said.

"Yes, and not accidentally. The new theologians were forced to recognize that modern global warfare was only a mass eruption of Manicheism—people would simply not fight such suicidal wars unless there was a terrible mass malaise over all things bodily and a real mass craving for endura."

"I see, I see," Martine interrupted. "Then isn't your version of Immob, if not Immob itself, the final flowering of Manicheism? Isn't it, in a sense, what's left of the Christian ethos once its id breaks loose and floods its ego and superego?"

"Very perceptive," the amp said, yawning again. "It is indeed. But Immob has not only brought the Manichean content of Christianity out into the open—in the process we have also corrected its doctrinal distortions. For, you see, while the Manichees were right in positing the vileness of the body and the need for liberation from its trap, they were wrong in assuming that this liberation could only be accomplished through suicide. They made the same mistake later made by thinkers like Freud—a Manichean par excellence, by the way—namely, that the urge to escape from the body is a death-urge. Immob has revealed the thirst for the oceanic behind the so-called thirst for oblivion, and it has discovered the instrument for such a spiritual leap into everything: not the suicide's razor but the surgeon's scalpel."

"Maybe," Martine said, "you're just substituting the martyr for the suicide?"

"Nonsense—the martyr gives up something, the Immob gains everything."

"There's something I don't quite get. How did a cultism of trance, such as Anti-Pro represents, manage to take hold in this country? Traditionally our people have always shied away from the contemplative and dreamlike. Pro-Pro, which offers a program of superaction, seems much more in tune with the ethos of the country, and I'm not at all surprised to find that it's the ruling party rather than yours."

"Splendid—when you are not making laborious jokes your insights are admirable. It is certainly true that, from frontier days on, America was a country devoted to manic activity and mobility. Quite so. But for a variety of reasons— among them the absence of a long cultural tradition whose dead weight would act as a brake on the individual—the urge to plunge inward and explore the gopher holes of the subjective through trance and dream was always present under the surface too. When people are not told very clearly who they are by voices from the past, they are driven to find out who they are by exploring their own insides—they cup their ears for inner voices. The Americans always suffered from this split—and so did the Russians. . . ."

The amp yawned again, deeply and luxuriously this time, his whole face screwed up. It was beginning to annoy Martine: when they used to crawl into their bunks in the plane Helder always yawned over and over, loudly, sighingly, a ritual of voluptuous whews. . . .

"It has been a hard day," the amp said. "I am tired."

"Maybe you'd like to sleep a little," Martine said.

"No, no, that can wait. Let us go back to the point about charisma."

"Yes, that interested me. What, exactly, is this charismatic charm?"

"Toynbee," the amp mumbled, "said that the sheer sight of a great man will electrify the masses. He used the word 'electrify' advisedly. Do you know, perhaps, Wilhelm Reich's theory of orgone energy?"

"Yes, quite well. He maintained that there is a vital energy in the cosmos whose color is blue. It was his idea that human organisms, all living things, are infused with this cosmic energy, charge themselves from the environment and then discharge themselves through the full orgasm."

"That is indeed orgone energy. Reich, however, was wrong about one point, because he did not understand the distinction between animal orgasm and oceanic orgasm. You see, when a man becomes fully human through Immob, his orgone energy leaps from all his parts, from his head as well as his genitals, from his entire skin. When he is photographed with the proper apparatus at the moment of orgasm, he

171

seems wrapped in a halo of flaring blue. I know, I have seen it in our laboratories. This overall discharge of vital energy, however, can take place more modestly even without orgasm, from moment to moment. That is the physiological basis for the electrifying effect which Toynbee described. That is charisma."

The amp closed his eyes for a moment and lay perfectly still, then he opened them and looked at Martine. "Charisma," he said, "is only an example in the so-called psychic field of the universally valid second law of thermodynamics. According to this law, when there are two organized systems of unequal potency, energy will always flow from the higher and more powerful to the lower and less powerful. Now, what is the fully human organism but the highest and most potent system of organization in the animal kingdom? I am talking, of course, about myself, for only the Immob is fully human. You are still an animal, a lower and less potent system of organization. Therefore, when I am juxtaposed to you, my energy will flow outward to you. That is the whole secret of how, as a fully human creature in a universe of the less-than-human, I achieve the oceanic: my psychic energies constantly go from the high of me to the low of the Other, in invisible ripples, and as a result I am always enmeshed with my surround. And when I choose to, I can sometimes place a word, a phrase, a fragment of a thought, into the psychic stream and let it be carried out to other, less highly organized minds."

"It's very fortunate for me that I'm less organized than you are," Martine said. "According to the second law of thermodynamics, that means I can read your mind but you can't read mine."

"When we have perfected the technique," the amp said, "I shall be able to read all minds, for then my consciousness will encompass everything. But I will not pretend to be expert even in the limited projection needed for thought transference. None of us is, as yet. It was only a few years ago that we discovered it could be done at all, and our experiments in parapsychology have only begun. In the end, of course, we shall dispense entirely with hallucinating vocabularies. When we are fully attuned to Korzybski's silent level we shall exchange only speechless truths."

"I have observed," Martine said, "that Immob seems to make people extremely eloquent about the virtues of silence. There are professional lecturers on the subject. Do you know

172

what somebody said about Carlyle? He extolled the virtues of silence in nineteen volumes."

"Nothing more natural. In this transitional period proselytizing is still necessary, there are many false prophets to be exposed."

"Orgonize 'em till they're blue in the face."

"It is not as far-fetched as you think. Remember what we have learned from the psychosomaticists. We know that the psyche can make the soma do its most extreme bidding: it can raise huge blisters on the skin, cause false pregnancies, produce embolisms. All such effects, of course, are brought about by the unconscious part of the psyche. Suppose that this power to mold the body were placed at the disposal of the *conscious* mind? Immediately there is a revolution: man ceases to be an animal at the mercy of his inner mechanisms and becomes a full human, the executive of his body. His sense of power, his exultation, begins to fan off from him in a shimmering aura. More, since he is in charge of all bodily functions, he can even *will* his orgone energy to beam out. He glows with charisma."

"It seems to me that you constantly confuse the inner and the outer. One moment you speak as though all reality is to be found inside the self, the next you—"

"The polarity is false. There is a Hyphen. Consider, if you will, the problem raised by a dream. We accept this inner nocturnal drama as perfectly natural, and yet it is one of the weirdest and most anomalous phenomena in nature. For it is an event of which we are aware, and yet it transpires in a state of sleep. How to explain this consciousness in coma? Obviously our old-fashioned ideas about such polarities must be revised. There is a fundamental difference between day-consciousness and night-consciousness, and it consists in this: that what our awareness is keyed to in the day is the 'real' outside world which impinges on us through our senses, while during the night our awareness shifts its focus away from the outside world toward the inner world, the deepest subjective truths which are kept hidden from us during the day. There must be some kind of inner filter, or screening apparatus—what the Freudians called a censor—which operates during the day to keep the inner facts buried in the unconscious; for if they were allowed to intrude into consciousness willy-nilly, to mix with the perceived facts of the outer world, the result would be chaos and fracas—we would lose the sense of demarcation between without and within, would no longer know where the substantial ended

173

and the subjective began. This has been the deadliest fear of man since the beginning, this mixture of inner and outer: see how the public recoiled when the surrealists toyed with it. During the coma of the night, however, the burden of coping with the outside world is removed and, accordingly, the screen which repels the inner facts can be relaxed. As a result, the facts from the mental cellars are sucked into consciousness by the vacuum left there when the facts of the outer world recede. Then a man's innermost self makes a supreme effort to talk to him.

"Now the question arises: When is a man closest to reality—when his awareness is flooded with the outer facts of day or the inner facts of night? This question, which has confounded philosophers for centuries, could not be answered before Immob because until now man did not have enough control over his consciousness to experiment with it. Now Immob has answered the question. We have proved conclusively that the so-called real world of which men are monomaniacally aware during the day is entirely ephemeral and deceptive, a world of hallucinating signs and stirrings, all dust in the eyes—because men up till now have been Aristotelian, have seen only the cloak of treacherous verbal symbols which they themselves have flung over the world. But with Immob the mind is free to roll over, so to speak, and open itself to the full flood of facts from the pool inside, to the subterranean inner stream of dream and fancy. It is a revelation. In the Aristotelian's night life, thanks to his aberrating norns, the unconscious facts protrude only vaguely and meagerly, in the disguise of symbols and concealed hints—the screen has not been relaxed entirely; an iron curtain remains between him and his innermost being, his bottom-shelf memory banks. The non-Aristotelian created by Immob can open himself fully and directly to the contents of his command nakedly, not as fragmentary symbols—for Immob realizes the old Freudian slogan, 'Where Id was, shall Ego be.' And this revolutionary thing happens. The moment the unconscious is fully unleashed, man finds that what he has been carrying about in himself all along is the world, the cosmos, infinity, the whole undulating ocean of reality. For in his original passive state, before he was invaded by norns, before he was forced to make the cruel and hallucinating cleavage between 'I' and 'It,' he was in the whole world and the whole world was in him. Now, with his passivity regained and all his Hyphens restored, he heals the split. For the first time, merely by plunging into his inner reality, he

174

makes the leap that lands him foursquare in outer reality. The dive into himself is the dive into the world. Night becomes day. Dream becomes reality. What the surrealist toyed with, Immob realizes."

"And then?" Martine said softly.

The amp's eyes narrowed, clouded over. "Then everything becomes possible. Once thoughts are oceanically in tune with the pulse of the world, keyed to its vibrations, man's cortical pulsations will move mountains. Literally. The map will for the first time overtake the territory—and then reshape it. Man's charismatic magic will flow from his liberated mind out into the entire universe, not only exploring it but altering it at will. Telepathy and dream transmission, extra-sensory perception, divination of the future as mind roams the space-time continuum, levitation as mind invades outside objects and dominates them just as it does body, mesmerism of objects as well as of animals—all these wonders will become commonplaces. Who can tell what marvels lie ahead? You may know of John Wharton's theory of mattergy—the theory, based on Einsteinian logic, that there is a prime element in the universe called mattergy, which can at any moment change from matter into energy and back again. Perhaps the human mind will subdue mattergy and learn the trick of materialization and dematerialization—perhaps it will so thoroughly master the physical that it will be able to command the body to appear and disappear at will, or dart from planet to planet with the speed of light. Yes, the mind will be powerful enough to do everything. It will receive, finally, the music of the spheres—the buzz of the quanta, the swish of cosmic dust, the grinding of the planets, the whirring of electrons in the atom. And who knows? Perhaps ultimately, when mind becomes omnipotent, it will achieve that state which up to now has only been dreamed of as an attribute of the mythical superman we call God, grab bag of all man's yearnings for himself—the state of immortality, pure, immutable being."

"I find this being unbecoming," Martine said in a whisper. It was all outrageous, shameful—but at the same time he found himself somehow caught up in the appalling grandiosity of the man-infant's vision, in the lulling, Mosaic rhythms of his phrases. "Isn't there an easier road to immortality?"

"Name it, please."

"Well, death is very probably a psychosomatic excess anyhow. So, if mind achieves complete mastery over the body, why doesn't it simply instruct the body to stop dying

175

and live forever? In that way, it seems to me, the spirit might solve its housing problem permanently."

"You do not understand," the amp said. "To grant the body such importance—to imply that any bodily vessel is worthy of living forever—is to put it on a par with spirit. Why bother? When mind becomes as potent as it is capable of becoming, surely it will not die—as God does not die. At best it will only materialize and dematerialize, as God does in his Incarnations. Out of nothingness everything is possible. On the condition that nothing is desired—nothing but pure contemplative being, the triumph of the vegetative principle, the end of striving. Oh, believe this. . . ."

Logical progression. Saint on a flagpole: saint in a cave: saint on a soapbox: saint in a department-store window with a powder-blue baby blanket for a sackcloth. St. Simeon: St. Augustine: St. Helder: St. Severe-Sphere. Yes, it was logical as hell. From washing irregularly and leaving the lice in the scalp and wearing hair shirts, it was a short step to thunderous pacifism and then to voluntary amputeeism and the full unabashed womby-comfy huddle. The saint become a basket case! He lay there now, this amp, with his pouty juvenile-senile features composed in that otherwordly calm often found on the rather absent-minded faces of anointed ones in early Christian paintings—on the enrapt irony-shorn faces of political saviors—on the face of, say, a Helder. Was there something obscene about the picture? Well, sure. There was always something obscene about a man drawing back from the challenge of complexity and whittling himself down into a simpler form through pseudo-infantilism, pseudo-imbecility, pseudo-simplism, pseudo-holism, pseudo-Helderism; sloughing off dimensions in the futile effort to make himself unilinear and unwavering; trying to amputate himself back into the monocellular compactness which precedes multifid turmoil; like a Christ, a Gandhi, a Helder.

There was a staggering paradox in the situation of sainthood because, while it denied all taint of duality, it was actually the most dualistic situation of all, a condensation of all human ambivalence. Take the Christian precept that it is more blessed to give than to receive. The saint, of course, went about giving all over the place and indicating no desire whatsoever to receive—all Agape and no Eros, apparently. And yet he was not quite without ulterior motive after all, for, according to his own dogma, all his demonstrative giving was motored by the conviction that through his glad-hand

176

dispensations he would receive the most prized dispensation of all, namely, the state of blessedness. Instead of being spurred by altruism, he thirsted for special favors not available to the poor wretches to whom he doggedly gave, and in the very giving established that they were swine forever doomed to limbo because they were greedy enough to snatch like hungry giraffes what he thrust upon them. Eros under the Agape.

Yes, this latter-day Immob saint was no different from the rest, his endeavors to lead mankind into an allegedly better state were inspired by a hunger for the powers he felt would accrue to him in the process: hypnotic powers, levitational powers, the megalomaniacal magic which has been dreamed of from the beginning by all cherubs and crackpots, messiahs and mountebanks, all healers and helders. A spectacular case of double-entry moral bookkeeping; some people were more careless about keeping books, he, Martine, had not kept many books, some of the key volumes in his collected works had disappeared to helder and gone. . . .

The amp yawned again, a cavernous unhinging, then his authoritative hobbledehoy-hoary papoose-patriarch younger-helder pout relaxed and he closed his eyes. Something was happening to his breathing, it was becoming deeper and much slower, his chest rising and falling under the blanket at such a lazy pace that Martine wondered if he might be ill—it was not the shallow respiration that ushers in sleep. Finally, without any change in his slow-motion breathing, the amp opened his eyes again, fixed them on Martine's image, and began once more to speak.

"You do not know," he said. "You. Do. Not. Know. Problem is to shed the skin. Animal covered with fur. Semi-human man smooth-skinned. Next step for man to become fully human shed skin altogether. Sex cannot be encased. With skin you have sex but you do not know what sex is you know only the animal agony. Animal. Agony. Impotence. Like animal you strive strive in quivering and sweat to merge with loved one become one with her. Never. Always it fails. Orgasm never complete. Orgasm must be bursting of all skins but at the end your skin is there and her skin there and between them the void. Barricades of skin. Over these barricades men fight their wars. Orgasm. No man or woman an island is. Orgasm. The great melting melting. At last the one world. But for you never one world always many worlds. Never can you melt. Always you try. Caressing her making

177

love to her holding her desperately tight in attempt to penetrate one into the other you look down upon her closed eyes her clenched twitching lips her head as it sways from side to side and you wonder. In agony and terror you wonder. Make the movement of love and you wonder you think I feel this this I know I feel but what does *she* feel? What. Does. She. Feel. Ask the question make the movement ask the question. No answer. There. Is. No. Answer. She is there beneath you skin assaulting skin yet she is a million lightyears away from you. This the maddening enigma of the Mona Lisa of all women known transepidermally. In the act of supreme intimacy you find you are lying with the supreme stranger. You increase the tempo and thrust of your love-making rise to peak of frenzy sex becomes not melting but assault you interpret this as frenzy of passion but it is only frenzy of isolation frustration. You cannot bear to be by yourself at this moment of dissolution yet you find yourself more alone than ever. Unbearable. You shriek you moan you wail and babble. Sounds grow wilder and wilder at moment of crisis the movements more violent they are taken for the ravings and spasms of orgasmic ecstasy but they are not that. They are the horrible cries and writhings of a maniac in irons inmate of an asylum. At moment of orgasm you are inmate of the asylum of skin. Asylum. Of. Skin. Smashing your head helplessly against its steel doors. For you know only what is happening inside your own skin you do not know what is happening inside your beloved's. She is the unknowable Other snatched from you in the nursery long ago your frantic attempts to overwhelm and penetrate have all been repulsed. You. The Other. Between you the void heritage from the nursery. Void which no burst of orgasm can fill. Skins drip with sweat. No wonder. The violently insane those who are forcibly restrained they always sweat as they struggle to break loose from the strait jacket. Afterwards two strangers side by side panting separately panting smoking separate cigarettes staring up separately at separate spots on the ceiling nourishing their separate furies muttering their separate curses. Separate. Only one thing do these two share the pool of sweat beneath them. No ocean of meltingness but only this pool of sweat anxiety's sap. The. Pool. Of. Sweat.

"Listen. Let me tell you what it can be like when sex ceases to be straining and shrieking of the insane becomes the blending. Becomes the floating rippling bobbing oceanic. Listen. This is how it is with me. You and she are one from the beginning. One. Together. Interpenetration of opposites

178

and all poles hyphenated and contraries wandering into each other. There is a meltingness. No barricades between. Thus a great ease and flow. Serenity. The overwhelming soothing lulling calm. Sex is not tension not tonus. Tonus comes from the anxiety of separation the anxiety of not knowing what is inside the Other. Not knowing if the orgasm the flight into Everything the burst into Everything is rising in her as well as in you. But now you know for she is you and you are she and what happens to both of you is happening at every moment to you. You know. Know. At ease. Unhurried flowing as of tides. Flowing. Tides. You do not make the movement of love love moves you. You feel it on your side. Simultaneously you feel it also on her side you are the thrust-into as well as the thruster the done-to as well as the doer stimulus and response and the Hyphen between. You give and simultaneously with each giving you receive. Here the barrier between giving and receiving melts away altogether. Giving. Receiving. Are. One. And what you feel at each moment is what each party to the two-become-one feels apart from the blending and within the blending too. You know what it is like to be enfolded in her skin as well as in yours. At last at last there are no more skins just a great placid outflowing-inflowing vibration which you lie back and receive. Eros is Agape.

"One cannot rise to the climax without the other. If one has orgasm the other must have orgasm for both are one. There is no void. There. Is. No. Void. Only one orgasm it belongs to both. It. Is. The. Ocean. You shriek now and she shrieks but these are no longer the sounds of the insane behind the asylum walls this is the final Dionysian music the geysering of the oceanic of Nature's Primordial Unity restored of the ultimate healing of Om. Joy. It is the cry of joy in the extinction of skin-tight selfness. Cry of joy to be inside her as well as yourself and to feel her inside you and know the oneness. Joy finally to know a woman. Always sex was said to be the *knowing* of a woman of course of course for the whole drive of sex was finally to know another person. But now for the first time it happens. You are she. You quiver with the spasms of your penis and also with the hurricanes of her vagina and those hurricanes are felt now not only from the outside through one skin-encased organ touching another skin-lined organ but from the inside of her from within her skin from the racing tremors of her autonomic nervous system and the convulsive pulsations of her thalamus and the ecstatic throbbings of her prefrontal cortex and all the while knowing that as she feels these tremors and pulses and throbs she is within *you* within the skin of *your* genitals permeating *your* autonomic pathways and thalamic-cortical connections. No more from outside the skin. You. Know. From. Inside. All. Skins. You. Are. Inside. Everything. You. Flow. Inside. You. Are. The. Ocean. Meltingness. Everywhere. Orgasm. Everywhere. World no more in fragments. Whole again. No more war. World an ocean. Om."

The amp's eyes were open just a slit, thin bands of white showing. "Tired," he said, lips hardly moving. "Very tired. Oh, I could tell you. There are many things I could tell you but only on the silent level for the rest there are no words. Must leave you now. So very tired. Must—"

"Listen," Martine said in great agitation. "Don't go away yet. I just thought of something, I've got to ask you one more thing, the most important thing of all. How is it possible? How, without making Immobs of the women too? And if both men and women are Immobs, then how can you, how is it possible—"

The amp seemed finally to have heard him. "Yes," he said wearily, his voice faint as though it came from a great distance and from some unlikely place, from the top of Olympus, inside of a whale, bottom of a barrel, bubbling up through the amniotic bath of a womb, ink of a fountain pen. "It is a question. What to do with women. To make them amps or not. Still holding policy discussions on the subject. Two schools of thought. But we have a few Immob women. Purely experimental so far."

"But? If women are Immobs too. . . . Sex is movement, you said so yourself, you spoke of the movements of love. But if the man and the woman are both Immobs?"

"Sex is not movement. Sex is the great peace, the passive inert flowing. Sex is not war. There are ways. We are working on it. It is a transitional period, it is all very experimental so far, much remains to be done."

"First one thing, then another," Martine snapped. "You keep shifting, you've got to stop doing that to me, do you hear? He was always saying that too. It was a transitional period, he would say. When we talked back and forth in our bunks he would say it needed more discussion, the program had to be hammered out more fully, that was always the thing. I'd put my notebook down and try to talk to him about Rosemary. . . ."

The amp's eyes flickered slightly. His breathing had become very slow now, it was distressing to watch the blanket as it billowed out for long seconds and then collapsed again.

"Tired. No, more, talk. Go, away, now. Tired, from, trying, to, reach, you, you, come, close, then, you, fight, me
off. Do not, fight, any, more. You, are, on, the, verge, of,
believing. Believe. Come, into, the, ocean, of, serenity, and,
sex. Behind you, is, the, recruiting, booth. Go, and, sign.
To, your, right, there, the, rack, the, rack, with, our, amp
pocketbooks. Take some. Take, Number, One, especially,
Basic, Amp, Text, Number, One, take, that. Entitled, *Dodge,
the, Steamroller*. Study. Sign. You, are, already, one, of, us,
in, your, heart. Take, the, last, step. Going, now. Must, go.
Off. Drifting. Peace. . . ."

His eyes were wide open now but vacant, the eyeballs
rolled back so that the pupils were almost entirely hidden,
over them the oceanic glaze of trance. His lips moved but
they made no sound, they seemed to be forming one word
over and over, Om, breath, Om, breath, Om, breath.

"Wait, wait, please," Martine said urgently. "One last
thing. He, my friend I mean, I'm sure he's dead, he was
always arguing the way you do, he was always saying that
all things exist within us and we must unleash them because
they are all good. He would sometimes lean over from his
bunk in great excitement and interrupt me when I was
writing in my notebook just to tell me that, almost in your
words. I wonder, could you have known him? He was full
of words too, I told him he would eat 'em some day, the
whole goddamned fountain pen, no I didn't say that, of
course. Well, no matter. But he was always arguing about
the endless panorama within, that's what he called it, you
see. And listen, here's the point, I would always answer by
telling him what Baudelaire said to the lesbians—Shun the
Infinity in you! Can't you see? I kept telling him that, do
you hear, you fool. . . ."

But the amp was far away now, riding the quanta, there
was no perceptible movement in his body at all, he seemed
to have stopped breathing entirely. Or, there now, were the
lips trembling ever so faintly? Puffing? Oms? Snoring inter-
galactically?

Martine looked down the row of baskets. Some of the
other amps were still talking softly, magisterially, into their
microphones, others had drifted off into a trance too, they
lay like infant corpses, lips fallen open and eyeballs tipped
as though to stare at their own insides. Martine turned away
with a curse.

Now for the first time he noticed a large booth in the interior of the store, festooned with drapes of bright bunting. It was a recruiting desk, he could see, above it a large sign urged,

The Human Race Needs YOU!
Dodge The Steamroller
Register Now For Immob

and in front of the desk there was a line of young men, waiting to affix their signatures to a registry book. They all seemed bemused, their thoughts far away as men's thoughts often are at the moment of great and irrevocable decisions; there was something robotlike, "It"-propelled, about the way they shuffled along and the absent-minded air each one had as he stepped up to take the pen offered by a smiling blond young lady clerk. One of the applicants, Martine noticed, stood in line staring at his hands, examining them wonderingly—fascinated, no doubt, by the spectacle of appendages which, as their last act in the world, were about to sign their own Moscow confessions and death warrants.

Automatically Martine's eyes lowered and came to rest on his own trembling fingers. "You are already one of us in your heart." It would be a double irony, he thought with a sudden vicious jolt in his gut, if his hands, hands of the world's most skillful aggression excavator, were to sign their own lives away in a burst of surgical abandon. There was some sort of ghastly fascination in the idea, his legs were taut with the urge to move in the direction of the booth and fall in line. Why this sweating, choking, nauseating guilt which had been plaguing him all afternoon, all the creepy word-gutted afternoon? Was it because he was intolerably reminded somehow that his fingers, his cunning fingers, had done terrible things with a scalpel? Did the incredible loathsome word "steamroller" somehow remind him of the crimes his fingers had perpetrated for eighteen years with a scalpel? Was that why, in a surge of masochism, he now, contrary to all logic, to all life impulse, toyed, despite his conscious moral horror, with the idea of surgical mea culpas? Or—was it because of something else his fingers had once held—in a lower bunk under a blanket of snores, a sackcloth of snores—sweatingly, wordily, heldishly—something, a fountain pen. . . .

"He must be dead," he muttered. "Sure, he's *got* to be."

Looking for something to distract his attention, any stray object, he turned his head and caught sight of the rack of books fastened to the wall on his left. There, he saw, were the Basic Immob Texts, containing what were clearly the classic works of the movement; familiar names leaped out tauntingly at him—Freud, Korzybski, James, Tolstoy, Swami Prabhavananda, Aldous Huxley, Nietzsche. Etcetera, etcetera. The very first one, the one marked Basic Immob Text Number One, bore the title, in large letters, DODGE THE STEAMROLLER.

Eyes unfocused, mind unfocused, he reached for a copy of the book and shoved it in his pocket. Then, body trembling, legs so weak he was afraid they would buckle, he picked his way through the crowds to the door, straining with the effort to keep his eyes away from the booth, a sickening turmoil in his stomach. "You are already one of us. . . ."

"But *Theo* isn't dead," he said to himself. "Then—"

He hurried along the boulevard, panting. When he came once more to the great statue at the hub, he reached into his pocket and pulled out the book, at the same instant aware even before the words came into sight that his breath had quickened to a desperate chug and his whole knotted body was filmed with clammy sweat and his gut was a hopeless writhing rope of anxiety; aware of this extraordinary upset now culminating the distress of the whole vile day, aware of it and wondering why it should be so and yet somehow not wondering but knowing and yet not knowing and in terror of the unknown undodgeable knowledge. And then his eyes fixed on the cover of Basic Immob Text Number One and knowingly they drank in the sickening abominable knowledge, squirming in outrage that was somehow prepared, stunned but not without anticipation and a pre-set for the stunning—

Whammo! Thunderclap in his head. All the drawers of all the filing cabinets tumbling out and spilling their screeching turkeys in a vast upheaving and at last, as he struggled to keep above the surface of nausea, not to sink, not to faint, at last, as the convulsion sped down, down to his stomach, the collected works of Martine were complete again, the crucial volume had been slipped back into place and it was a torment and a relief too, it was what he had been fleeing from all day and yet somehow seeking too, dodging and yet dogging, in misery and revulsion and need he had all day secretly been looking for this key volume and now it was there in his fingers, the fingers from which it had come a long long time ago while the son-of-a-bitch snored. He read with blurred terrified anticipatory knowing-dodging eyes the words on the cover of the volume:

Dodge the Steamroller

The Notebook of

DR. MARTINE

Edited and with an Introduction

by Dr. Helder
PRESIDENT OF THE INLAND STRIP

"Of course," Martine said. "Naturally. President."

Directly across the drive which circled the state was a clump of trees, to one side of a row of benches on which a few people were sitting. He hurried across, blind to everybody and everything, and at last, at last, hidden behind a thick eucalyptus, he bent over and retched—horribly, endlessly, gaspingly, shudderingly, eating his words and spewing them out at last and straining with each heave to force the guilt up with them. Thinking that this was surely the greatest bellylaugh belly-emptying laugh of all time and yet he could not laugh, he had no laughter left, now he was crying uncontrollably and broken-heartedly.

He stayed there for a long time, doubled over. Finally he straightened up and wiped the tears and muck from his face. Then he found a seat on a nearby bench and began to read.

from dr. martine's notebook
(mark i)

(BASIC IMMOB POCKETBOOK EDITION)

OCTOBER 18, 1972
With Flying Hospital Unit X-234-BL
Belgian Congo, north of Stanleyville

Almost midnight. Dog-tired. Can't sleep. Hell of a battle going on somewhere around Tunis, casualties pouring in. On duty in surgery plane for almost eleven hours, spent last three of them patching up Babyface's noggin, what was left of it.[1]

The kid's face haunts me. Dedicated, that's probably it. Dedication is mother's milk to this young onward-and-upwarder—he's a priest in an anti-gravity suit. Johnny One-Note—no doubt he looks exactly the same, exudes waves of goodness, whether he's harranguing people about signing the Peace Pledge or erasing Paris from the map. I've seen that kind of unswerving intensity on only one other human face: Helder's.[2] Such built-in rapture can only be described as theological, the neon of belief. Teddy Gorman. Christian

---

[1] Babyface: Teddy Gorman (Theo). Even when he was unconscious and close to death, there was about his face something shining and incorruptible which came through the blood and grime. It was this, no doubt, which prompted Brother Martine to use such a term of endearment. —Helder.

[2] The comparison is too complimentary: Brother Martine's friendship sometimes blinded him to my shortcomings. The truth of the matter is that, during all the months I worked with young Teddy Gorman in Tri-P (the Peace Pledge Program) I found his selfless ardor a constant source of inspiration, but hardly equaled it myself. —Helder.

185

name Theodore, according to his papers. Wonder why they didn't nickname him Theo?[3]

Lying in the bunk plane now, skinful of ache, wondering if I'll ever sleep again. Wondering if I'm going batty.

Infernal clicking from the ticker-tape machine up forward—EMSIAC, electronic chatterbox. No Hamlets in EM-SIAC's vacuum tubes, he's even more single-minded than Babyface and Helder. Only EMSIAC's really sane: knows exactly what he wants. Which is enough in itself to raise the whole question of sanity.

Rest of the crew's asleep. Characteristic of yes men: so long as they do their little duties dutifully, nod vigorously to the world and EMSIAC, they have ready access to the Land of Nod. It's nihilists like me who turn insomniacs—keep a sharp eye on the world during the day and that eye refuses to shut at night.[4]

Noddism: the state of modern man. He says yes, and he sleeps.

Helder's bunk is right above mine. He's snoring away like a buzz-saw, the pig.[5]

Since I can't sleep, I've been reading. Got several things

---

[3] A brilliant and insightful suggestion, entirely characteristic of Brother Martine's quick grasp of the profoundest spiritual truths. After the war, when Teddy Gorman and I began to organize the peace movement again, I reminded him of these words and pointed out that, since Martine had given him his life, it was only fitting that our great martyr should be allowed to give him his name too. From that time on he has been known by the infinitely more meaningful name of Theo. —Helder.

[4] I apparently neglected to mention to Brother Martine that I too suffered quite badly from insomnia in those days. On the night of October 18, although Brother Martine could not possibly have known this, I was able to sleep only thanks to a triple dose of barbiturates. —Helder.

[5] Here and there Brother Martine expresses himself in a gruff soldier's vernacular. The form of such references must not be confused with their content: what looked like sheer viciousness on the surface was, more often than not, tremulous love underneath, a love which we found it hard to express forthrightly under the brutalizing circumstances of war. Not the least argument against war is precisely this, that it does not allow men to express their love for each other warmly and directly. —Helder.

with me I've been dipping into: Norbert Wiener's *The Human Use of Human Beings,* von Neumann's and Morgenstern's *Theory of Games,* Berkeley's *Giant Brains,* McDonald's *Strategy in Poker, Business and War,* Père Dubarle's prophetic little paper on cybernetics. I thumbed through all of them long before the war, and brought them along when I was drafted—plus a volume of poetry by Rimbaud. They make nice hammock reading now.

How can all the noddings sleep? How can that pig above me snore away?[6] Least they could do would be to lie here with their eyes open, listening to EMSIAC and grinning. Really, it's the funniest goddamned thing I ever heard of. And I never thought it possible—that's a laugh too.

No, I never thought it could happen. Back in med school, when Helder first called my attention to Wiener's book (published in 1950), I thought it was just another example of his calamity-howling. I got the giggles when I read it and learned that back in '48 a Mr. Claude Shannon of the Bell Telephone Laboratories, following up an idea of Wiener's, had seriously proposed the building of an electronic calculating machine which would play chess "of a high amateur level and even possibly of a master level." Hell of a joke, I thought. It really tickled me, the idea of making a machine which, as Wiener put it, would show a "statistical preference for a certain sort of behavior" and a statistical disgust for other sorts of behavior—the preference and disgusts you need to play chess. And when Wiener went on to say that the chess-playing machine he had suggested and Shannon had determined to build might have important consequences, how I hooted.[7] How most people hooted. But not, as it turned out, in Washington—and not in Mos-

---

[6] I did sometimes have considerable difficulty in nocturnal breathing, due to a severe sinus infection which produced a chronic post-nasal drip and catarrhal congestion of the upper respiratory tract. I had mentioned this condition to Brother Martine once or twice, but apparently he had forgotten it. —Helder.

[7] The passage in question, from Wiener's *The Human Use of Human Beings,* reads as follows:

"Mr. Shannon has presented some reasons why his researches may be of more importance than the mere design of a curiosity, interesting only to those who are playing a game. Among these possibilities, he suggests that such a machine may be the first

(footnote continued bottom of following page)

187

cow. Not even in 1950; let alone the sixties, when I got around to reading the few books available on the subject. As early as 1950, McDonald hinted just how seriously this chess business was being taken in military circles.[8]

While most of us were hooting, the games specialists quietly went about their job of turning the innocent old-style robot brain, the Electronic Numerical Integrator and Computer (ENIAC), into a chess champ, and then into the Electronic Military Strategy Integrator and Computer (EMSIAC). The problem was licked by the mid-sixties. From which it follows, as the mare the night, that my crew is holed up at this moment somewhere in the stinking heart of Africa, with EMSIAC batting out instructions to us on the ticker tape. And on the other side of the world, Christ knows where, another EMSIAC is clattering away, sending out orders to all the units of the enemy's forces. Because there are two such superduper machines in the world today, one somewhere in the West (Grand Coulee? under Fort Knox? on top of Popocatepetl?) and one somewhere in the East (the Urals? Siberia? the Himalayas?), and what they're playing is one hell of a superduper chess game across the face of the earth, with a couple billion squirts like me for pawns. And the pawns are being knocked off fast, a continentful at a time, click, clack, neat gambit. . . .

No, most of us didn't see it, even after World War II—

---

step in the construction of a machine to evaluate military situations and to determine the best move at any specific stage. Let no man think that he is talking lightly. The great book of von Neumann and Morgenstern on the theory of games has made a profound impression on the world, and not least in Washington. When Mr. Shannon speaks of the development of military tactics, he is not talking moonshine, but is discussing a most imminent and dangerous contingency." —Helder.

[8] In this passage from *Strategy in Poker, Business and War*:

"In military affairs the theory of games is . . . highly developed and exact. Its application in military science is one of the pre-occupations of the U. S. Air Force's 'Project Rand,' which is now conducted by the Rand Corporation. . . . The theory has also been taken up by the Navy and is having its Army genesis in the 'Eisenhower Advanced Study Group.' The military application of 'Games' was begun early in the past war, some time in fact before the publication of the complete theory, by ASWORG (Anti-Submarine Warfare Operations Research Group, predecessor of
(*footnote continued bottom of following page*)

and God knows there'd already been enough danger signals: anti-aircraft tracking equipment, acoustical torpedoes, proximity fuses, servo-mechanisms, the later robotization of one industry after another. A few guys called the shots, though, even as far back as 1948, the year Wiener began his second book. In the same year this little French Dominican friar, Père Dubarle, wrote that cute little piece about cybernetics and "turbulence."

At first I thought the guy was kidding; the brackets I've inserted only occurred to me laterly.[9] I didn't sense that, if there was an "obvious inadequacy of the brain" when it came to coping with the complicated machinery of modern politics, there might be an even more glaring inadequacy of said brain

---

the Navy's present Operations Evaluation Group.) Mathematicians in the group had got hold of von Neumann's 1928 paper on game theory. The success of their work led to the present Naval and Air Forces applications, which are hidden behind military security. . . ." —Helder.

[9] This is Père Dubarle's comment, with Martine's brackets as he inserted them in his copy of the text:

"Can't one imagine a machine to collect this or that type of information, as for example information on production and the market [as for another example: war]; and then to determine as a function of the average psychology of human beings, and of the quantities which it is possible to measure in a determined instance, what the most probable development of the situation might be? Can't one even conceive of a State apparatus covering all systems of political decisions [not to mention military decisions]. . . . At present nothing prevents our thinking of this. We may dream of the time when the *machine à gouverner* may come to supply—whether for good or evil—the present obvious inadequacy of the brain when the latter is concerned with the customary machinery of politics [or war]. . . . The possibility of playing machines such as the chess-playing machine is considered to establish this. For the human processes which constitute the object of government [or war] may be assimilated to games in the sense in which von Neumann has studied them mathematically. . . . This is a hard lesson of cold mathematics, but it throws a certain light on the adventure of our century: hesitation between an indefinite turbulence of human affairs and the rise of a prodigious Leviathan. In comparison with this, Hobbes' Leviathan was nothing but a pleasant joke. . . ." —Helder.

when it came to coping with the incredible complexities of modern global warfare. It just didn't hit me that while an "indefinite turbulence" in affairs of state was becoming more and more obnoxious to the modern bureaucratic-man-agerial-political temperament, the same turbulence in affairs of war would be utterly repulsive to the bureaucratic-military temperament. I had too much faith in the durability of chaos, the human business-as-usual. I had read too much of Dostoevsky and other disheveled minds. I didn't realize that the modern mind was rebelling entirely against the turbulent Hamletism, the palsied ambivalence, of the human condition, and that machined, click-clack thought was its most ardent daydream in all departments. So I just grinned and passed over Wiener's summing-up of the whole business.[10]

But he was right. The "beneficent bureaucracy" *was* being planned—by *two* cyberneticized militaries. Each thinking, of course, of course, that it was acting in the interests of self-defense, preserving civilization, cutting down "turbulence," etc., etc. And when I got around to reading these texts some fifteen years later, during my student days, the thing was pretty far along, although nobody knew about it. The result is World War III, in which we're all being swept from continent to continent by the clacking commands of a couple of computing machines buried in a couple of unlikely places somewhere on the globe—and the aerial armadas, every plane of which is equipped with its little ticker to receive moment-to-moment orders, go hurtling around the world, dusting the hemispheres with H-bombs and RW

10 In the following paragraph:
"The steps between my original suggestion of the chess-playing machine, Mr. Shannon's move to realize it in the metal, the use of computing machines to plan the necessities of war, and the colossal state machine of Père Dubarle, are in short clear and terrifying. Even at this moment [1950!], the concept of war which lies behind some of our new government agencies, which are developing the consequences of von Neumann's theory of games, is sufficiently extensive to include all civilian activities during war, before war, and possibly even between wars. The state of affairs contemplated by Père Dubarle as one to be carried out by a beneficient bureaucracy for the sake of humanity at large, is quite possibly being planned by a secret military project for the purpose of combat and domination. . . ."
—Helder.

powder. And we, the robotized progeny of Hippocrates, trail along in their wakes, patching skulls and guts together. . . .

Wish that damned machine would stop jiggling. Or is it really inside my head?

Wish Helder would stop snoring. Can't get him out of my mind.[11]

Did the greatest patching job of my career tonight. On Babyface, I mean. He interests me, this Babyface: seems to have such a statistical preference for wiping out the capitals of the world. Great little *machine à boom-boom*. He's undoubtedly the most efficient agent EMSIAC has, by a long blast; far and away the greatest hero of the West in this war, and just turned twenty-one too. And to think that he was once a leader of the pacifist youth movement—perfect *machine à être gouverné*. . . .

For three hours I suctioned and sutured and sewed, fitting together the bloody fragments of his brain. Rather like a jigsaw puzzle in aspic. And all the time I kept telling myself that such a brain would be worth salvaging on only one condition: if I could shuffle its parts around so that, once it started functioning again, it would operate with one compulsion—not to carry out EMSIAC's bidding but to *destroy* EMSIAC, to take all the H-bombs that were left and ram them down EMSIAC's throat. It was worth the bother only if I could give this robot machine a statistical preference for an indefinite turbulence in human affairs and a statistical revulsion with all Leviathans. But I didn't know which cortical-thalamic pathways to fool with in order to produce this effect—in which Brodmann areas does one find aggressiveness, in which cortical centers yes-manism and the nodding reflex?

For three hours my fingers were inside Babyface's skull, itching with frustration. I'm not a scientist, an artist, a truly knowledgeable man. Only a tailor of protoplasm, working with needle and shears on human tissues. The only things surgically worth doing, I cannot do.

---

[11] I shall always treasure this evidence of Brother Martine's concern for me. Naturally, the feeling was reciprocal. In those difficult days my thoughts were never far from my comrade; if I had not taken such a heavy dosage of barbiturates I would have been awake at that very moment, sharing his agony of mind. —Helder.

191

Don't even know where to sink my scalpel in Helder to stop that snoring. Except in his throat.[12]

World War III, it's clear, is the first real war we've ever had. The essence of warness. War brought for the first time from the realm of concept all the way into the realm of thumping fact. For it is the first homicidal chess game in which the full gaming board has been used and all the pawns thrown into action with perfect mathematical precision.

The millennia-old promise of warfare has been fulfilled. The promise made when the first cave men went at each other with the first shillelaghs. Finally we have a war which has robotized all the men engaged in it, from buck privates up to top brass and the whole general staff. And now that war is really total, *all* men are engaged in it one way or another. In other words, damned near the whole human race has been robotized this time. Therein lies the essence of warness: the elimination of Hamletish ambivalent wavering in human affairs, the triumph of the pure hammer-blow direct act. War is the engineer's answer to palsy.

Yes, men aren't only robotized; they're activized as well. Action has been made more spectacularly possible than ever, thanks to the mechanical extensions of our bodies which technology has produced: we've all become supreme activists. But at the same time, all decisions as to the nature of our action have been taken out of our hands and brains—all that's handled, much more efficiently and less turbulently than mere human brains ever could, by special decision machines. The general staff has come of age in EMSIAC.

All along, obviously, the big job was to build a machine that would make up our minds for us, so that we could concentrate on moving our arms and legs and the mechanical supplements to our arms and legs without having to bother our heads with the questions of why? in what direction? to what purpose? To drain the Hamletism from military behavior, which is the efficiency expert's idealization of all human behavior, human doing at its most effortful, purposeful, and efficient. Neat division of labor: the machine proposes, man, builder of the machine, disposes.

It was bound to happen, of course. Once men stopped

---

[12] This remark leads me to believe that, after all, Brother Martine *did* remember, at least faintly, that my difficulty in breathing was caused by a chronic congestion in the upper respiratory tract. —Helder.

manufacturing gods, they began to manufacture machines. Whence EMSIAC, the god-in-the-machine, the god-machine. . . .

We could have predicted it. If we'd had our eyes open, we would have seen it coming. EMSIAC is simply the end development of something that's been threatening for a long time in human affairs, especially in modern times. Hobbes called it the Leviathan—I'd call it the Steamroller. War—this present war, this epitome of warness—is only the Steamroller come of age.[13]

I'm not entirely sure I know what I mean by that, but I think I've got hold of something. I'll just ramble on a bit, maybe it'll come clear. At least it'll take my mind off Helder's sound-effects. . . .[14]

After all, what's the great evil in war and in the totalitarian systems which make war? It's not the killing and maiming of people, no matter how much agony that entails. No: it's the Steamroller Effect. The flattening of human spirit, I mean. What the steamroller does to the human spirit is immeasurably worse than anything shrapnel and atomic blast could possibly do to the human flesh, and infinitely more lasting. Why? Because of the humiliation. Because the victim had no say in the matter. Because the loss of an arm or leg or a pair of eyes is a thousand times more unbearable when it's involuntary—when the decision is made not by the victim but by the steamroller. It's the willy-nillyness of the thing. The smothering of the "I" by the "It."

It's interesting, for example, that in World War II amputees began to refer to themselves as *clipped*. The word had about the same overtones as it does when it's applied to a duck that's been hit by a hunter. You say the bird's been winged or clipped, and what you mean is that some outside agency over which it had no control and of which it wasn't even aware has suddenly swooped down on it and knocked the hell out of one of its vital parts, leaving it crippled—without so much as a by-your-leave. That's the steamroller. "It," the robber of free will and dispenser of fates.

---

[13] The most important paragraph in the history of recorded speech. This is the first reference in literature to the Steamroller. —Helder.

[14] I shall always be proud to think that in some small and humble way, even if only by my presence at this historical moment, I helped to inspire the brilliant observations which follow. —Helder.

What's so terrible about all this? Isn't it actually a relief to unburden oneself of responsibility and leave decisions to some machine?

Well, there's an unfortunate twist to the thing. The machine doesn't simply decide *for* its inventor—it eventually decides *against* him. It has a built-in malice against its sire which must come out sooner or later. For a very good reason.

From the beginning man has been cursed with a chronic need to believe in the myth of the steamroller; he needs it as he needs oxygen. The worst psychic flaw in man has always been his tendency to overwhelming self-pity, his deep masochistic component—his enduring fiction that he is set upon and victimized by a menacing outside. Man is the animal that collects injustices and keeps a score board of hurts. Over the centuries he's given a lot of fancy names to his persecutors: demons, furies, witches, ghosts, God, the elements, fate, karma, kismet, germs, ruling classes, glands, id, norns, and so on. And he's even been able to demonstrate experimentally that many of these forces exist and do him positive harm—but up to now he's seldom been able to prove conclusively that they're united in a foul, fiendish plot to do him in, out of sheer malevolence: that the whole universe is an unrelieved continuum of malevolence. Nor has he ever been able to prove conclusively that, when such hostile forces do exist around him, he hasn't secretly misused them, set them upon himself so that he could then bewail his unhappy fate: the psychosomaticists, for example, have shown that you can *choose* to be downed by the TB bacillus, which is the theme of Thomas Mann's *The Magic Mountain;* and who made the modern Western God so starkly Calvinist but a mortal man named Calvin? In other words, except in certain extreme situations (floods, hurricanes, epidemics, concentration camps, gas chambers), man has never been able to advance quite sufficient data—sufficient for his audience *or* himself—to substantiate and fully motivate his feeling of being kicked around, harried, dogged. This is the only thing that has saved him until now: his masochistic myth of victimization was never well enough grounded, quite, so that he could give way entirely to his fits of passivity and self-pitying lamentation. . . .

Now, however, we've managed to arrange things a bit more convincingly for ourselves. The myth, with our help, has sprung into crunching life. Now, thanks to the marvels of technology, we've succeeded in converting the outside world into a very real steamroller—robotized industry, robotized culture, robotized war—and one which fairly bristles with menace. H-bombs, RW dust, proximity fuses, guided missles, etc., etc. The whole shebang ruled over, not by poor innocent beleaguered little man, of course, but by the epitome of menace, EMSIAC, the mechanical brain which has "robbed" man of his decision and "made" him not master but slave of his destiny. Almost as though the myth couldn't be sustained any longer, as man more and more spectacularly subdued his environment and thus freed himself from the very real terrors of Nature—as though it couldn't be sustained without being externalized, concretized, and dramatized. EMSIAC had to be invented in order that man could go on feeling sorry for himself.

Rimbaud sensed all this; he sensed a lot of things. At the age of nineteen—backward child: he hadn't yet wiped out a city, nor even a whistle stop—he shouted: "Don't be a victim!" This, at the very height of the Industrial Revolution. But what a silly bastard he was, really. This wish was coupled with another: he wanted to be—an engineer! Intent on dodging the steamroller,[15] he yearned to become a designer of steamrollers. Naturally; he was the perennial victim type himself: didn't he woo gangrene and the syphilitic spirochete?

Oh, the steamroller must be dodged, no question about it. But not by improving its lines. And not by running away to Africa as Rimbaud did, to map uncharted territories (or to the lobotomy labs, to map uncharted neural pathways). The maps will only serve as guides for the steamroller, as witness what our armadas are doing at this very moment to the whole bloody continent of Africa (as witness lobotomy). . . .

Is there any other way? Sure. The idea came to me just a couple of hours ago, right after I finished sewing up Babyface's scalp. By this time Helder had sawed the jagged bone splints off the kid's stumps and sewed flaps of skin over them, so the job was done. Helder asked me to give him a hand in lifting Babyface from the operating table onto a stretcher, and I did.

Two things happened.

First, I slipped my arms under the boy's body and lifted as gently as I could. Immediately my stomach clamped tight

---

[15] First appearance of this phrase in the world's literature. —Helder.

and I was sick all through me. The reason was, of course, that this boy—a big fellow, judging from his torso and football shoulders: close to a 200-pounder, I'd say—was so revoltingly *light*.

And then, as we were easing him down on the stretcher, I suddenly became aware that his eyes were open. And fastened on me; at least they seemed to be.

I knew that was silly. It would be hours before the anesthetic wore off, he couldn't be looking at anything: no doubt the cortical centers controlling the blinking reflex had been damaged and the lids had just popped open mechanically. Still, I couldn't shake the feeling that he was looking straight at me. And I thought: Suppose he's coming to? Suppose he is just now becming aware of the fact that he has no legs? All the while staring at me? He wouldn't be rational at this moment, of course: since I'm the first living object he'll see, he might very naturally assume that I was responsible, personally, for the loss of his legs. Naturally: at such a time a man needs some living thing to blame, and I would be his personal EMSIAC for the moment.

He didn't blink, he didn't say a word—he just looked, or seemed to be looking. I couldn't stand it. I looked back, horrified and fascinated, trying to figure out what those unblinking eyes were trying to convey to me: accusation? terror? cosmic revulsion? I couldn't tell.

Afterwards I took a turn about the clearing. I kept thinking about the disgusting feel of that body in my arms, I kept seeing those ball-bearing eyes that were trying to say something to me and couldn't. I began to hold an imaginary conversation with those eyes, reading into them all sorts of wild things. Things I had to refute—my sanity depended on it. . . .

ME: Why are you staring at me?

BABYFACE: You look a little green around the gills. What's wrong?

ME: Nothing. Not a thing.

BABYFACE: Don't pull my leg—oh, sorry, it's a little late for that, isn't it? . . . I can guess what the trouble is, though.

ME: Can you?

BABYFACE: Yes. It must be pretty upsetting to pick up a full-grown man and find he weighs no more than a sack of potatoes.

ME: Well, yes, it *was* a bit of a shock.

196

BABYFACE: Funny that your least essential parts—least essential in terms of staying alive, anyhow—seem to carry the most weight. Surely as a doctor you knew that a man's legs account for two-fifths of his total poundage?

ME: Of course I knew it—as a statistic, that is, an abstract datum. Cerebrally, not kinesthetically. My nervous system wasn't quite as well coached as my intellect.

BABYFACE: It's the other way around with me just now. *My* nervous system is becoming aware of what happened to me, the stumps are beginning to hurt like hell in spite of the morphine—but my intellect's having a tough time trying to catch up with the anatomic reality. . . . Tell me, Doc. How much more of me do you think you could hack away before I kicked the bucket—kicked it metaphorically, that is? How light could you make a man, by whittling away all but the absolutely essential parts? What's your guess?

ME: I don't know—close to half of the body could be cut away, I'd say. But look here—you seem to have an entirely false idea of what's happened to you. *I* didn't cut off your legs. Nobody around here did.

BABYFACE: Then who would you say *is* responsible?

ME: The fact is that your legs are several hundred miles from here, somewhere on the North African coast, mixed up with a few shreds of your dura mater. I couldn't have done that to you, could I? I wasn't even there.

BABYFACE: Who did?

ME: The simplest way to explain it is to say that a certain robot brain called EMSIAC directed certain planes and guided missiles to proceed to the area around Tunis and bomb your legs off. The enemy's EMSIAC did this to you, if anybody did.

BABYFACE: Not very convincing, Doc. For one thing, I wouldn't have been anywhere near Tunis to be shot at if *our* EMSIAC hadn't sent me there—with instructions to bomb the *enemy* airmen's legs off, along with their heads.

ME: All right, I'll accept your qualification. What you can say, then, is that two EMSIACS were having it out and you got caught in the middle. That's still no reason to be sore at *me*.

BABYFACE: Isn't it? Don't you work for one of these EMSIACS?

ME: Sure. So what? You seem to forget that you work for it too—we're fellow workers.

BABYFACE: I *used* to work for it. We *were* fellow workers.

ME: All right, *were*. You forget, too, that until this afternoon you and I were doing very different jobs for our mutual boss—you were going around blowing up people and getting blown up yourself, I was just trailing along to patch you up whenever you came undone at the seams.

BABYFACE: You're letting yourself off a little too easy, Doc. Hear that EMSIAC clicking away? Have you ever said no to one of its clicks?

ME: No, but it only tells me to save lives.

BABYFACE: Only when that's part of its plan to snuff out other lives. Frankly, I don't give a shit whether EMSIAC tells you to drop a thermonuclear bomb on Paris or stuff somebody's meandering guts back into his abdominal cavity. The point is that *whatever* you do, you do under orders. So don't give me that crap about saving my life: what do you think you would have done for me if EMSIAC had ordered you to let me bleed to death? You're a humanitarian by dictation from above—so long as those goddamned clicks say this rather than that.

ME: I don't blame you for being bitter but, Christ, use a little logic. If *you'd* said no to EMSIAC this morning, when you were ordered to Tunis, you wouldn't be here minus your legs now.

BABYFACE: Never mind all that. All that was this morning. Just take now. Now I'm lying here without my legs. Do you hear? Without my legs, without my legs, lighter than a sack of potatoes. Lying here thinking only one thing, that it's a pack of shit unless you stand up to EMSIAC and tell it to go fuck itself.[16] Thinking that nothing makes sense but that. And *you're* still saying yes to it—you're going along with one ear cocked for the clicks, so you won't miss out on your instructions. You say yes to the thing that took my legs off, that I'll never say yes to again in my life.

ME: That's easy for you: you won't have to. You'll probably be a hero. You can rest on your laurels and your pensions.

BABYFACE: So now we're on opposite sides of the barricades. *You're* the enemy, the only enemy I can see. Because you're EMSIAC's agent and yes man. You acquiescent tailor

---

[16] In all fairness to Brother Theo I should perhaps mention that he never actually expressed himself in this uncouth manner: he was always a most proper and well-spoken young man. Brother Martine obviously had no way of knowing about Theo's grace and gentility. —Helder.

boy. You obedient hemstitcher. You heel-clicking humanitarian. Fuck you.

ME: Have it your way. You're partly right, of course—anybody who doesn't manage to say no to EMSIAC one way or another is guilty of everything EMSIAC does, one way or another. That's pretty much the normal state of affairs at the moment: *nobody* says no, so *everybody's* guilty., Maybe, in the ultimate sense, I do bear responsibility for your legs lying up there around Tunis—but in that ultimate sense *everybody* is responsible, the whole human race.

BABYFACE: Don't give me that everybody's-responsible crap. Follow that line of thought a little further and it's bound to wind up in an orgy of gabble about no-man-an-island-is and all that slop.

ME: Right, that kind of sentimentality would be a bit absurd—the only thing that would make any sense right now would be a program for severing one's connection with the foul mainland and becoming as inaccessible an island as possible. . . . However. What's much more to the point is that you've got to scream, you've a supreme right to—and you've got to scream at me because EMSIAC's much too remote and impersonal and you don't even know where it's at. O.K., call me all the dirty names you can think of. I'll play scapegoat for you if it relieves your anguish any. And that's one service EMSIAC *didn't* order me to perform. That's an entirely self-willed bit of "humanitarianism," for whatever it's worth.

BABYFACE: Why are you so sure I'm using you for a scapegoat? Aren't you falling back on a clever formula to dodge responsibility again? Turning the spotlight on me and away from yourself?

ME: Nothing of the sort. I know that you need a scapegoat for the simplest of reasons—I know that *I* need one. In that respect all men are pretty much alike today.

BABYFACE: No man an island is, after all? Oh, brother.

ME: No man unsteamrollered is—put it that way. And we've all got the urge to strike back somehow, if only to prove that we don't really like it, didn't arrange it ourselves. But how in hell do you strike back at an invisible cold mountain of metal and electronic tubes—assuming the will to strike is there? Kids can get some satisfaction out of kicking chairs and bicycles they've skinned their knees on, but that kind of animism won't work for grown men. Besides, even if it would do some good to kick EMSIAC, we can't—

where is it? We need living targets to vent our venom on. Go ahead: spit at me. I wish to hell I could do some spitting too.

BABYFACE: You've got something there, I'll have to admit. There's some kind of fury growing in me that isn't simply a reaction to *what's* happened to me, although that's bad enough. The most maddening thing isn't the what but the *how*, the fact that it was done *to* me—I wasn't even consulted.

ME: Now we're getting somewhere. That's the reason every war is self-defeating—the steamroller of war never consults any of its victims, and everybody's victimized.

BABYFACE: You mean war, all war, by the nature of the case, is one kind of EMSIAC or another?

ME: Sure. Of course, the combatants cook up some pretty fancy slogans to sugar-coat what's going on. But no matter what banners are waved, or who wins, the people on both sides emerge slugged, insect like, spiritually flattened. Each war brings the human race a little closer to the insects, whose lives are all "It" and no "I"; at the end of the war people feel less human and more insectlike, very much like the hero in that Kafka story who wakes up one morning to find that he's turned into an enormous cockroach. Interestingly enough, Kafka wrote that story during the First World War.

BABYFACE: Why do people feel more and more like insects?"

ME: The insect's life is all compulsion, and war is the last word in compulsion. All through the slaughter people have been impelled and propelled by vast impersonal forces, agencies beyond their reach. That's a characteristic of modern life in general, of course. Every day of their lives, even in peacetime, people feel that they're pushed around and mistreated—at work, in school, even back in the nursery, where the myth of mistreatment really starts when the kid's grandiosity takes a beating at the hands of reality. But when war rolls around the whole thing is dramatically stepped up and takes on spectacular new dimensions—now they feel that they've been drained of all self-determination and reduced completely to the status of puppets, robots, mechanisms, beasts of burden, cannon fodder. All those sodden will-less things that move only when forces from the outside give them a shove, that are lost and bewildered when guidance doesn't come "from above." That kind of passivity, of will-lessness, is a regression to the helpless mewling and puking state of infancy, which is an unbearable blow to a grown man's dignity. Especially because, in secret, it's so avidly sought after by everybody.

BABYFACE: I don't follow your references to infancy and the nursery.

ME: It's nothing complicated. What was thrown off in infancy—the feeling of puniness, of being a defenseless object—creeps back on the battlefield. With a difference. The resentful infant—resentful because it feels, usually quite without justice, that it's been denied and cruelly mistreated—could only yowl and bite and scratch a bit by way of expressing its rage. Pretty harmless. The soldier, resenting the same enforced passivity, can do something more: he can kill. In a sense, war is an institution which allows men-regressed-to-infants to murder their mommies, the job they muffed in the nursery. The irony, of course, is that the helplessness in the nursery wasn't brought about by the infant—it's just a neutral, objective fact that the kid can't accept neutrally and objectively. But war is man-made, self-imposed helplessness. This is a passivity not dictated by nature but manufactured by those who fume against it. That is the surest sign that the deepest emotional undercurrent in war is a masochistic one, for all the show of bluster and outward-turned aggression: for the thing about it that most infuriates men is really produced by them. They must have a dim realization that they brought this state of affairs about themselves, and that must make them more furious than ever—and more determined to pin the blame on someone or something else.

BABYFACE: What you're saying is, people resent being steam-rollered, in war or any other way—even though, or, rather, *because,* they engineered the whole thing themselves—and have to take out their resentment on somebody. If only to prove that they *do* resent it, don't really *like* what's happening to them.

ME: That's just about it. People have to prove that they're not passive victims but active doers and managers. They have to prove that they don't like being mauled just because, deep down, they keep the nursery myth alive—so much so that they go on perfecting more and more efficient instruments to do the mauling. That's why they fight. The enemy's a convenient scapegoat. War not only humiliates people, it provides easy targets for them when they get elaborately and fumingly sore about being humiliated. . . .

BABYFACE: That figures, all right. People secretly turn pain into pleasure—and reach for the brass knuckles to prove they don't enjoy it. It's kind of a startling idea, but it figures.

ME: The baby and the gangster are Siamese twins. Obviously, then, the important thing is to avoid the feeling of being victimized, set upon from the outside, shoved around—the myth mustn't be propped up by a stage-managed reality, by itself it's enough of a steamroller. Right?

BABYFACE: It makes sense. Suppose I'm huddled up in a fox-hole and a remote-controlled buzz bomb starts to swoop down on me. If it comes right on without a by-your-leave and clips off my left leg, I'm bound to feel that I've been pretty badly treated. If I were given even a tiny bit of choice, I'd immediately feel a whole lot better.

ME: There's no denying it. If you've got to make some sort of sacrificial offering to the steamroller, it would take a lot of the sting out of it to be allowed to name what it's to be—arm, leg, ear, nose, testicle, or what-have-you. As the existentilists used to say, within a determined situation you retain some dab of freedom. . . . But let's go a step further. Can't the amount of choice be expanded?

BABYFACE: I see what you're getting at. Say, this is really an idea. Maybe you could work out a new way of fighting war in which there weren't any victims at all, no steam-rollers. In which all the casualties *volunteered* for their wounds.

ME: That's it! Just to bring the individual will back into the picture. Give the "I" some stature alongside the "It" again.

BABYFACE: Lets' see now. What disturbs a clippee, obviously, is that he had no choice. Maybe he would rather have lost an arm than a leg? But there's more to it. Maybe there was some other guy around who would have welcomed this maimed state because it seemed to him to offer a whole lot of advantages—no work, the security of a pension and three squares a day, an excuse to be passive in a socially approved way and have women waiting on him, and so on—whereas the guy who *did* get clipped doesn't care for it at all, having a taste for other things like work, earning his keep, and lording it over women instead of being dependent on them. Well, if the population had been polled, the amputeeism and paraplegia and all other damagements could have been distributed to each according to his need.

ME: Neat! Marx corrected by Freud. To each according to his need—not his *economic* need but his *masochistic* need. Because some people have a special taste for suffering and should obviously be allowed the lion's share of it.

BABYFACE: Very democratic. Takes the individual into account. Real human dignity to the thing.

ME: Nobody could then say: I was clipped. Exit the steamroller.[17]

BABYFACE: How, exactly, would you get people to volunteer?

---

[17] Note this passage well: here, for the first time in human thought, the concept of voluntary amputeeism is being formulated. But a question arises: why did Brother Martine link this new humanist strategy to the idea of masochism? Did he really mean that voluntary amputeeism was nothing more than a device for satisfying some deep-seated human need to suffer and be maimed, without the traditional mechanics of bloody steamrollering war? The ironic formulations used here might lead the reader to such a conclusion—but that would be to overlook completely the delicate and complex personality behind these formulations. The references to "masochism" must be taken as a jocular touch, designed to lighten a profound and heartfelt idea—a program for the salvation of the human race: Immob.

More than once Brother Martine confided in me, even during our student days, his fear that, possibly because of his Mormon training and, in a broader sense, because of the whole "barnstorming" Western ethos of which he was a product, he had what he called a "messianic complex," an urge to be a "world-saver." (Sometimes he even suggested, in his usual joking way, that I too had a touch of this spirit, perhaps even more than he did! We laughed about it many times. How I wish I had seen through his scoffing manner and realized that, with his delicate indirectness, he was really urging me on to a bolder course.) He need have had no such misgivings—it is glaringly clear now that he *was* the man fated to save the world—but in his great humility he *did* have them, and they prompted his ironies and psychoanalytic witticisms. It only remained for us, Theo and myself and the others granted the good fortune to be his faltering disciples, to study this notebook, break through its thin shell of irony and draw from it its glowing humanist premises in their pristine magnificence. As, of course, he intended us to. We did not find it hard; where there is a will there is a way. —Helder.

What kind of pitch would you use?

ME: That's a cinch. As you yourself pointed out, there are plenty of guys who would be quick to see the advantages—by which I mean, there are plenty of guys who are that self-damaging, who revel that much in mistreating themselves, especially when they are officially encouraged to do so. Of course, you wouldn't put it on the basis of mistreating oneself—that would be giving the game away. It would have to be suggested that the volunteers wouldn't be hurting themselves but actually doing themselves and the world some good. You could easily do that with a few well-chosen slogans, such as—oh, I don't know, slogans to the effect that there's no demobilization without immobilization, pacifism means passivity, arms *or* the man: anything that makes a wound into some kind of boon. And then, of course, as you've suggested, you could offer special inducements to the recruits: cash awards, bonuses, pensions, hero status, medals and decorations, membership in exclusive clubs, leisure, women, all in proportion to the degree of amputation or other forms of crippling. How many men were actually clipped in World War II— 25,000, 30,000 on our side alone? How many in World War III—many hundreds of thousands around the world? Hell, you could round up millions and millions of volunteers if you just put a heavy enough stamp of social approval on it and offered enough juicy come-ons. You'd get precisely the same results that you get from war now, except that everybody would be happy and feel himself the dignified master of his own fate. And, secretly, revel in the enormous amount of pain he'd arranged for. That way, maybe a sorehead word like *clipped* would never even be thought of. Not when the guy's a *voluntary amputee*. A vol-amp. We might call these guys vol-amps. Short snappy catchwords like that always go over big. Vol-amps. Immobs. Limbo—we might call our brave new world Limbo. The great moral equivalent of war might be vol-ampism. You know William James's essay, *The Moral Equivalent of War?* That might be the new Bible in Limbo.[18]

---

[18] First appearance in literature of those inspired key words, *vol-amp* and *Immob*. The word *Limbo,* of course is not to be taken seriously—it was one of Brother Martine's typical jokes, designed to hide his intensely serious purpose. See previous note on the word *masochism.* —Helder.

BABYFACE: Eventually you might bring about universal disarmament that way. You might even go the whole hog and make up a slogan about disarmament being impossible with arms around.

ME: The human race would finally come out of its trance, straighten up, push its shoulders back. Maybe even puff its chest out and begin to strut a bit. The battering's over with.

BABYFACE: No more quaking in the cellar, waiting for the bomb to land. No, sir. You just step up to the operating table after plenty of deliberation and say very deliberately, "Just chop off one arm, Doc, the left one, just up to the elbow, if you don't mind—and in return put me down for one and two-thirds free meals daily at the Waldorf and a plump blond every Saturday." Or whatever the exchange value for one slightly used left arm would be—that would have to be worked out by the robot actuaries.

ME: Oh, it would be conducive to self-esteem, all right. Death to sluggish fatalism. Matter of fact, we'd have to revise our whole traditional concept of tragedy, which has been poisoned by fatalism and a sense of steamrollering menace. Without any more Fates harrying you than you've applied for, all the old-time dramas of people being tormented by circumstance will look downright silly. Without the steamroller, Sophocles begins to look like a calamity-howler. Now all the steamrollers are within.

BABYFACE: Wouldn't the whole American novel in its usual form become passé? The standard American novel is mostly sociological, not psychological—it shows people being overwhelmed by circumstances over which they have no control, rather than seeking out and manufacturing the circumstances that overwhelm them.

ME: It goes without saying. Take just the theme of amputeeism in the American novel. It makes its first spectacular appearance in Melville's *Moby Dick*—Captain Ahab has lost one leg to the White Whale, a pretty crude prototype of the steamroller, the nineteenth-century EMSIAC, and he's so consumed with rage that he goes back and gets himself chewed up altogether. Well, in our new society of voluntary amputeeism, Ahab wouldn't be able to feel one iota of rage, because he would have volunteered his body to the whale—openly and directly, not ambiguously and

with a false-face of indignation, as in the old novel. . . .
Skip a hundred years. When the same theme shows up in
Hemingway's *The Sun Also Rises*—incidentally, remember
the anti-war book he wrote called *A Farewell to Arms?*
Maybe there's a slight suggestion there of the same idea
we're getting at—it's now pegged to the steamroller of war:
the hero has been accidentally castrated in the First World
War, which complicates his love life a good deal and
makes him feel very sad. Well, such a low version of
tragedy will be impossible under the new rules. The unconscious yearning for castration—the ultimate amputeeism—which the success of such a book proves, will be
dragged out into the open, and everybody who has it
will be allowed to indulge it and be rewarded for it.
There won't be any more accidental castrates around, or
self-arranged cases of castration disguised as accidents;
they'll all be volunteers, and knowing themselves for such
they won't be always trying to have their Lady Bretts
and eat them too. Oh, the air will be cleared considerably.

BABYFACE: It's bound to liberate all the optimistic energies of
man. Even the worst masochists and self-pityers will turn
a new leaf. Instead of getting a little beating every day,
piecemeal, in dabs and driblets, they get a hell of a big
beating all at once. So they can afford to relax and cheer
up, the damage is done.

ME: Just by deliberately losing one or more extremities per
man, we'll all be a head or two taller overnight. Say, that
might do for another slogan.

BABYFACE: Sure, there'll be a whole new race of men, fully
human men. It'll be real inspiring to watch it being born.

ME: But there's a slight matter we've got to attend to first.
We've got to stop this war, and I don't see how we can do
it without putting the present EMSIACS out of business—
after all, there's no way to talk this thing over with the
present EMSIACS and get them to see things our way, the
actuarial way. So here's what I propose. You'll be sent
home as soon as you can be moved. When you're well
again, and fitted with artificial limbs, take a look around.
You'll be a great hero then, the bigwigs'll do just about
anything for you. Find out where our EMSIAC is—and
then get yourself a plane, go up and drop all the H-bombs
you can get hold of on it. Just to clear the air, you see.
Then when the shooting's stopped, we can start talking
up our new pacifist program, it'll catch on like wildfire.

BABYFACE: All right, Doc, I'll do that little thing. I wish, though, that while I'm off saying no to EMSIAC, you'd find a way of saying no to it too—I'd feel a whole lot better if I knew you were risking something too. . . . O.K., I'll knock EMSIAC out if I can. Then I'll sit back and watch this new race of men being born. And while I'm watching I'll be eating—swilling tons of food, I understand amps work up a bitch of an appetite. And while I'm watching and stuffing myself, I'll keep on having fantasies. I'll think, maybe I eat so much because something weird and sensational is happening to me. Maybe, I'll think, I need all that energy, more than I ever did when I was all in one piece, because an unbelievable biological process is taking place inside me—maybe all that energy is being stored up behind my stumps, big reservoirs of protoplasmic fuel, and that's why the stumps itch so much—sure, maybe when the stores of distilled steaks and chops and pastries get big enough the miracle of the ages will take place in my body—regeneration! While the human race is being regenerated, my legs will be regenerated, it's a time of progress and miracles all around! Limbo everywhere! The stumps will grow and grow, drop down like a kid's testicles, forced into budding by all the excess grub I eat, and I'll have two fine legs again! While the whole human race learns to stand on its own two feet, against all the steam-rollers! Sure, I see it now. I keep slipping off my pajama bottoms to examine the stumps, especially when they hurt or itch. I think, I'm going to have two first-rate legs again and this time *I'll* decide, all by myself, entirely on my own, standing on my own two legs, just what I'm going to do with them. By the time they're full-grown again there'll be a new fully human society without steamrollers, a new society specifically designed with a statistical revulsion for willy-nilly amputeeism and a statistical preference for voluntary amputeeism, so as soon as they're alive and kicking again I can just walk down to the recruiting station on the corner and have them sawed off again—of my own free will now, just to save my dignity and prop up my ego. . . . I contract my abdomen as I lie there, I clamp my intestinal muscles hard, straining to give birth—to force those leg-buds out like you force toothpaste out of a tube, so I'll be ready for the new vol-amp adulthood of man when man reaches it finally. I want them so goddamned much, just so's I can walk up to EMSIAC and yell, see, I got them back, I *willed* them back, and this time no son-of-a-bitch is going to tell me what should

207

be done with them, this time I'll make up my own mind, see, and take my own sweet time about it. Then maybe, who knows, maybe I'll sit down and saw them off myself, right in front of the machine, just for the hell of it. . . . That's what I'll be thinking all the time the human race is getting born in Limbo, month after month and year after year. Only there'll be a little hitch—the legs never *will* start growing. I'll keep probing them, measuring, massaging—and all the stumps will do is ache, and itch like hell, while the human race is growing up and amputating itself all over the place. . . . You bastard. All you do is talk, talk, talk. The only thing that would make you into a human being would be for you to say no to EMSIAC, and all you do is talk, talk, talk, while EMSIAC keeps on clicking. I'm sick and tired of it. You've got lots of fancy words but what it all adds up to is this—you're standing there on your own two legs and I'm lying here without legs. I'll never have legs again. I'll never stand on my own legs again. I've been steamrollered good and proper; it won't get undone. You dirty fancy-talking son-of-a-bitch—why should you have your legs when I lose mine? Bastard. You dirty bastard. Fuck you. Fuck you. Fuck you. . . .

POSTSCRIPT

So ends Brother Martine's notebook. Soon after the last entry was made, at exactly 3:31 A.M., a formation of enemy bombers arrived over our encampment. By 3:33 the H-bombs were going off.

Some planes survived, among them the one in which I was bunked with Brother Martine and the one in which Brother Theo was lying still unconscious. We had received the alert far enough in advance to put into effect our anti-gamma and anti-blast precautions.

When I was awakened by the alert I noticed that Brother Martine was gone from his bunk—only his fountain pen and notebook were there. Later, when Theo and I got home, we sat down to study this notebook seriously. We soon realized, of course, that in his usual persiflaging manner our martyr was enjoining Theo to destroy our EMSIAC and thus say no to "It."

Brother Theo accepted his historic assignment and carried it out flawlessly: he discovered the location of EMSIAC deep in the Black Hills, hidden behind Gutzon Borglum's enormous faces of Washington and Jefferson, and bombed it out of existence. Thus was Immob born. But the daring feat had effects which we could not anticipate, although they were undoubtedly a part of Brother Martine's inspired plan.

Each EMSIAC, of course, was a chess player and nothing but a chess player; and, as such, it was able to cope with any situation so long as it was confronted with an opponent with similar statistical preferences and revulsions. But neither EMSIAC had been designed to cope with a chess-playing situation in which the opponent was suddenly eliminated from the picture altogether: it was built to play a two-handed game, not solitaire. Therefore, once the American EMSIAC was destroyed, the Russian one was faced with the one predicament it could not anticipate or deal with: a game without an opponent. Its feedbacks were overloaded, it was thrown into a quandary, it had the electronic version of a nervous breakdown.

When the Russian soldiers and airmen became aware of the fact that their guiding brain had suddenly developed palsy— and there was no ignoring it: the machine was babbling, humming, mumbling schizophrenic nonsense—their sense of awe was immediately dissipated, they realized that even EMSIAC was not infallible. In the turbulence which resulted, a young Russian airman named Vishinu—Theo's opposite number, the man who destroyed New York, Boston, Philadelphia and Washington—was encouraged to engage in the same daring adventure which Theo had successfully carried out. He located his own convulsed EMSIAC under the Taj Mahal and bombed it out of existence.

So, in a matter of forty-eight hours, the war came to a spectacular close, as Brother Martine, with his genius for seeing all things, had no doubt known that it would. And the air was cleared to begin the agitation for the pacifist program which our martyr had so meticulously worked out for mankind's salvation. Such were the miracles wrought by one man's "banter"!

What, however, about Brother Martine? After the bombing there was no trace of him anywhere in the encampment— although all of us were required to wear on our persons certain heat-proof and radiation-proof name plates and other marks of identification. It can be considered established, then, that at 3:33 he was neither in any of our planes nor outside in the encampment area.

What happened to him? We can answer the question very definitely. After the bombing we made an extraordinary discovery. Surgery plane 17-M, which on the night in question was unoccupied, was gone. Vanished into thin air, as it would not have if it had been destroyed by bombs. That, in any case, was out of the question: it was on the outermost rim of the target area and would not have been severely damaged at all.

There is only one conclusion. One man had vanished, and one plane. Obviously the man had vanished *in* the plane. In an unauthorized flight. The first unauthorized flight ever known to EMSIAC. The first flight in which a man, by engaging in a desperate act of will, said no to an EMSIAC, the will machine.

This is not just the sentimental speculation of one man grieving for another. By no means. There is abundant evidence to support this theory. First, the psychological evidence: as his last notes indicate, Brother Martine's mind was filled with the idea of saying no to EMSIAC, in some spectacular gesture or other, at the moment when he put his notebook in an ostentatious place and stepped out of the bunk plane. But that is not all. Among the survivors of the raid were a few of the men who were on radar-scanning and guard duty during the night, and two of them reported that, just a few minutes before the attack, they were startled to see a plane take off from a point on the northern edge of the encampment, precisely where 17-M was stationed. The reason for their surprise was, of course, that EMSIAC always informed them in advance of all flights scheduled during their period of duty, and they had been told nothing about this particular flight. The guards had no way of investigating, since EMSIAC's red-flash emergency alert had already reached them and they had to take up their defensive positions. In the excitement of the next few minutes they quite forgot about the unscheduled flight, and recalled the incident only when we began to search for Brother Martine and 17-M.

More still. EMSIAC, of course, kept completely detailed punched-tape coded records of all units deployed on all fronts. Now, all these records were preserved in underground storage vaults, where they were instantaneously available whenever EMSIAC had occasion to consult its memory banks. These vaults were remarkably sturdy affairs, and just about all the reels of tape stored in them were found intact after Theo destroyed EMSIAC itself. And when we instituted a search, after the war, we found on one of these reels EMSIAC's complete data on the peculiar movements of 17-M between the hours of 3:27 and 3:39 on the fateful morning of October 19, 1972. This roll of tape is now on view in the

Library of Congress, preserved in a helium-filled glass case along with other mementos and documents pertaining to our great martyr—including, of course, his brown-and-white plastic fountain pen and the original manuscript of his immortal notebook.

What do we learn from the EMSIAC tape? Many, many things. That 17-M *did* take off from our Congo encampment that night, at exactly 3:27, on an unauthorized flight. That this was exactly two minutes after EMSIAC had begun to send out its red-flash alert to us about the impending attack. That, because the compartment of EMSIAC concerned with our flying hospital squadron was so heavily taxed at the moment with the problem of the alert, it did not have any circuits free to cope with the unauthorized flight of 17-M until several minutes later, just after the attack began. That finally, when its instructions to the pilot were ignored, EMSIAC at 3:38 took over the plane's automatic pilot, which had been set on steep climb and a southeast course, and fixed it on a half-turn, preparatory to returning it to base; at the same time, considering this breach of discipline a matter of the utmost urgency, it switched from ticker-tape communication to electrovox and began issuing oral instructions to the pilot to return for court-martial. (Judging from the coded records, EMSIAC was momentarily confused by 17-M's flight, an act of disobedience more flagrant than any it had so far encountered: two circuits backfired and blew before a course of action was decided upon, and it is clear that two or three times, when the electrovox began speaking, it stuttered.) That, a few moments before 3:39, EMSIAC's self-protective batteries became aware that the EMSIAC receiving apparatus in 17-M was somehow being tampered with, that the container was being struck violently; the electrovox immediately assumed that the pilot of the runaway plane was attacking the communications system and began instructing him to desist, telling him that resistance was useless. That, at precisely 3:39, the communications box in 17-M went dead and all contact with the plane was lost.

What does all this tell us about Brother Martine's last moments? The subjective side of the picture is clear. Upon leaving the bunk plane, his mind brimming with agonized thoughts about Theo's desperate injuries and the necessity for some nay-saying gesture against EMSIAC, he proceeded to the unoccupied 17-M; and there, at 3:25, he heard the red-flash alert coming from EMSIAC. In a split second he saw that his chance to say no to EMSIAC and affirm some human value had come, and he decided on his heroic course of action. He turned on the jets and took off at 3:27.

What was the meaning of this unprecedented action? It was, first of all, a defiance of EMSIAC's express instructions to assume defensive positions. Clearly Brother Martine intended deliberately to disobey EMSIAC, for the reasons philosophically developed in the imaginary dialogue with Brother Theo. But the gesture was not simply negative; our hero was too idealistic a person to commit any act out of mere nihilism. No, he had something infinitely more noble in mind; as an intimate of his over the years, I can vouch for that. Brother Martine knew that in this desperate emergency his comrades were in the gravest danger, and he knew, with his entirely instinctive heroism, that he could make of his masterful no-gesture an act of ultimate bravery and self-sacrifice. Defying EMSIAC, he went forth entirely on his own, by his own self-willed decision, to do battle with the enemy bombers. It meant death for him, of course, but, just possibly, life for some of his comrades on the ground. And life for countless millions of others who, taking courage from him and stirred by the immortal words left behind in his notebook, might finally stand up to EMSIAC as he himself had done in one last blaze of glory.

This hypothesis clarifies the most puzzling aspect of those twelve minutes that shook the world. What about the strange blows on the EMSIAC communications box in 17-M? EMSIAC's immediate conclusion was that the pilot was responsible; he was breaking discipline, he was a criminal, and therefore everything untoward which happened in his plane must automatically be the result of his criminality, part of the enormous crime. But that shows the fatal weakness of EMSIAC's utterly logical police-mind. It simply could not grasp a matter of indiscipline which arose from motives beyond the realm of police mentality. It never occurred to EMSIAC that the occupant of 17-M, after an initial act of defiance, might go on to commit an act of stupendous, self-sacrificing humanity. And that the blows on the communications box might have eventuated in that act of humanity, rather than in further "criminal" excesses.

Our hypothesis makes sense of these blows. It was not Brother Martine hammering at the box, an utterly irrational, nihilistic act which was totally alien to his personality. Obviously he had, at 3:37 or thereabouts, engaged the enemy. No doubt he was immediately subjected to a merciless bombardment of torpedoes, shells, rockets, guided missiles, and everything else the enemy planes carried; and, no doubt, some of these missiles struck the communications box when they tore into 17-M's interior. It was the enemy who was raining blows on EMSIAC! But EMSIAC, with its one-track police mind, infuriated over this one violation of discipline, could imagine only that the terrible "criminal" inside the plane was attacking it. There, indeed, is an irony which Brother Martine's sensitive and complex mind would have savored to the full.

At exactly 3:39, we can assume, Brother Martine's plane was badly hit, and he was wounded mortally—trying to destroy EMSIAC and save his comrades and all of mankind. Let us never forget it; Brother Martine's last act was an affirmation of life and human goodness and a gesture of supreme contempt for EMSIAC and all the "Its." It was an assertion of free will, of self-determination, of decision and decisiveness as against all steamrollers. Brother Martine for all time dodged the steamroller—in one split second he snatched initiative back from the machine and reinstalled it in the human soul. By this one act alone, he spelled out the death sentence for EMSIAC and all such steamrollers.

What happened to the 17-M after 3:39? Brother Martine was certainly dead, or dying; the craft was badly damaged; it could hardly have stayed in the air for very long. Where could it have crashed? When Immob was established, one of the first M.E. projects we organized was a series of expeditions to search for traces of the plane in the Belgian Congo, Kenya, Tanganyika, the Rhodesias, and so on; every square foot of those territories was combed through, without results. It is out of the question, therefore, that the 17-M could have fallen anywhere on land.

The hypothesis soon arose that the plane could not have disappeared so completely unless it had dropped into a body of water. Which one? The Indian Ocean, off the coast of Somaliland or Kenya or Tanganyika? We soon ruled out that possibility—a jet as badly damaged as the 17-M must have been could hardly have remained airborne long enough to make such a trip. But—there was another body of water, a very large one, over two hundred miles long, much closer to the encampment: Lake Victoria, in northern Tanganyika Territory! Less than four hundred miles from the scene of that historic battle, this lake lies directly east-southeast from the scene, which is exactly the course the 17-M was flying.

There is no more mystery: the 17-M lies at the bottom of Lake Victoria, and within it are the remains of Brother

213

Martine. For the last several years Immob's top-priority M.E. project has been the Victoria Dredging Project: we have already probed more than half of the lake's bottom, and before too long, we can rest assured, we shall find Brother Martine's remains and give them a hero's grave. Yes, it was in these peaceful blue waters, in the shadow of snow-capped Mt. Kilimanjaro, that our martyr came to the end of his anguish.

We need not weep for him. Let us, rather, eternally honor the memory of this true messiah for the inspiring symbolism of the way he chose to die. He not only died for us, he left behind a lesson for all men in how to live. He is not gone; he has but become the ocean; let us humbly drink.

—Helder.

Part Five

LOVE AND COLUMBIUM

---

chapter fifteen

HE WAS finished reading, at last. He sat on the bench, staring dully at the book in his lap. Everything was clear. He understood now his agitation of the past few hours—of the past week, the past month. Of every minute of every day and night since the man named Theo had first made his brachycephalic way to the Mandunji village.

It had started there—although a niggling disquiet had come over him weeks before, with the first reports of the queer-limbs who had been sighted off Madagascar. At that moment his memory had begun to grind again, trying to pump long dormant words back into awareness so that he would be forced to eat them. For a month the words had been trying to break through the censorship of his fear and nausea by reminding him of the forgotten pegs from which they dangled: 10:10, scalpel, 17-M, EMSIAC, bunk plane, Helder's snoring, Helder, pen with which he wrote in note-book, notebook. For the past hour he had been eating all his old forgotten words, every last gallows-humorous syllable—all his moth-eaten old jokes, as mauled into a philosophy under Helder's parasitic-inspirational aegis. He knew now what united him, tragically, with the giraffe.

It was all clear now. When Theo had stepped jauntily into the village, he had brought with him some vital fragment of Martine's buried identity—something that was inextricably entwined with all these forgotten words and their pegs. At that moment Martine had suddenly known, with a knowledge

215

that went beyond all logic, that he had to leave the village. Only for purposes of safety, he had thought then, but actually to follow this trace of his buried personality—like a man poking an aching tooth with his tongue—back across the Atlantic as far as it would lead—fighting against the shock of recognition all the way. Now he had found what he was looking for in this joke-book-become-bible, some essence of himself which had been flickering feebly for nearly eighteen years under the incognitos. Its name? He could not fully recognize it as yet, he did not quite have the name for it. But at least the shock was done with. Somehow, at the death-ridden heart of Immob, he had found himself—was about to find himself. Henceforth, when he closed his eyes, giraffes would do no more demented nibbling on neon.

He looked up, somebody was watching him. It was a girl on the bench across the way. The girl with the sketch pad: he noticed it without surprise, almost with relief. She had her pad on her lap and she was drawing—glancing over at him from time to time, then going back to her work. She seemed not at all concerned when he caught her eye.

The thought came to him: he had to have a woman.

He stood up, no more dizziness, crossed the drive to her bench. She was not disturbed by his approach, did not even bother to close the pad when he leaned over to see what she was drawing.

It was a charcoal sketch of himself, very cleverly done, showing him reposing in a little basket. He was without arms and legs, there was a beatific, saintly expression on his face.

To his own surprise, he managed a smile. "A very good likeness," he said. "I'm afraid it's a little flattering, though."

"I must draw what I see," she said. Her voice was husky, with only the slightest trace of accent.

"Do I really look that good? Good enough to be in a basket?"

"Of course. I look for what is inside a person—I'm not taken in by appearances."

"Appearances? You mean I'm an Immob and don't know it—an ambulatory basket case?"

"Something like that. You don't fool me for a minute."

"I'll bet you say that to all the boys."

"The ones who are worth recruiting. Not that there are many past forty."

"Recruiting?"

"Sure. I'm from the East Union—one of the artists over here on cultural exchange.

"I don't know too much about all that, I've been out of touch with things."

"Well," she said, giving him a queer look, "if you really don't know about the setup I'll explain. We've had this cultural exchange ever since the Strip and the Union went Immob. Only the Strip artists who visit us are mostly just sightseers, while the Union artists who come over here are more active in a propaganda way, just as we are at home."

"It was always more or less that way," Martine said. "Our tourists used to travel with capital, yours with *Das Kapital.*"

"Yes, my people have always been more interested in mass enlightenment."

"Does this recruiting really work?"

"Well, somehow or other it seems to hit people awfully hard when they see a picture of themselves in a basket—especially when it's drawn by a woman. That alone often does the trick, without any discussion of principles at all."

"I see, I see." Martine rubbed his forehead and frowned. "And so you—you've been following me around all day, haven't you? From the time I passed you in the lobby of the Gandhiji?"

"You'd make a wonderful Immob, I sensed that from the first. Also—you're an exciting man."

"Maybe I'm what you call an exciting man *because* you think I'd look so wonderful in a basket."

"Every real man would, silly. There's no contradiction."

"A real man," Martine said, "might prefer a woman to be attracted to him because she'd like to go to bed with him. Not because he brings out the surgeon in her."

"The problem is purely semantic."

"Oh? Then—come to bed with me now. While I've still got my appearances on."

The girl's eyes opened wide. "Go to bed with you? You're asking me that now—hesitantly, as if it were in doubt? Strange man!"

"You mean you won't. You're offended."

"Offended? This gets stranger and stranger! But of course I'm going to bed with you—I thought you understood that when you came over and sat down here."

"I—well, I wasn't sure. There've been a lot of changes I don't know about."

"As a matter of fact, you puzzled me this morning in the Gandhiji. I wondered why you didn't speak to me then."

"Good Christ," Martine said, "you don't mean that if I'd stepped up and asked you then, out of the blue, you would have said yes?"

"No, that's not what I mean at all."

"What, then?"

The girl began to laugh. "You really have been out of touch, haven't you?" she said. "Why, any fool can see what I mean. *I* would have asked you. . . ."

An hour later Martine gulped down the last of an excellent T-bone steak, dropped his knife and fork, and settled back with a sigh. In the park he had mentioned that he was ravenously hungry, and the girl had promptly led him to this café-restaurant, an enormous basement decorated like the salon of an old Mississippi steamboat—the first touch of architectural nostalgia he had come upon anywhere in New Jamestown. Now he grunted in contentment, doubly happy to find that the turbulence in his gastric affairs was quite gone, and looked up at his companion, savoring her along with the cigar and the Napoleon brandy.

And still he was not altogether at ease. Sitting opposite a very beautiful woman without a speck of reluctance in her make-up—the adolescent's dream girl—he was annoyed to feel a trace of reluctance in himself. Maybe because he sensed that, like so many of the girls he'd known in his adolescence, she had such a trigger-quick erotic response because the thing was to her a quite casual business—and he, even in his most flamboyant self-proving days, had never been able to take it quite casually. When the woman was this cavalier in her handouts, the suspicion arose that what she had to offer was less a rare gourmet's delicacy than a soggy free lunch. (On the other hand, reluctance was no guarantee of a superior bill of fare: Irene had been reluctant, but only because she had not wanted him to find out too soon that in her larder was only a lean snack of cold cuts disguised as boned hummingbirds.) What was wanted in her was not a coldness, to be sure, but some deep wariness, an air of discrimination, so that a man might feel he was chosen because of some special worth and that he had somehow through his special worthiness *forced* the choice—that the act was not entirely a thing-in-itself which could be performed equally well and with equal meaning, or lack of it, by interchangeable parts and parties. Martine shuddered: he remembered a Greenwich Village girl who, when issued a casual invitation to drop in at his place for a drink, arrived

218

carrying two suitcases. And then he smiled. There was something outrageously funny in the reversal of roles here; he was complaining about the female's brutalized attitude toward sex exactly as, for centuries, the female had complained about the *male's* brutalized attitude. . . .

"I guess I ought to know your name," he said.

"Neen."

"Mine's Lazarus. Dr. Lazarus."

"I know. The desk clerk at the Gandhiji told me."

"What else did he tell you?"

"Nothing much. Just that you're some kind of medical man. Judging from your clothes and your luggage, you've apparently been away from the Strip for some time. And, judging from the questions you ask, you aren't very familiar with what's been happening in recent years. At least, you don't *seem* to be." The peculiar, sly look crept into her face again.

"Do you always compile dossiers on likely bed partners?"

"I like to know who I'm sleeping with. It helps."

"Sure—but a little knowledge can be a dangerous thing."

"So can a lot of ignorance."

There was a bandstand over to one side of the night club, and next to it an elevated dance floor; now a dozen Negro musicians appeared with their instruments, all of them gotten up as traditional plantation darkies and levee roustabouts, in ragged dungarees and with gaudy kerchiefs wrapped around their heads. They seated themselves on the stand and at a signal from their grinning leader—a duo-amp: the only one in the group who was any sort of amp at all—they burst into a raucous, bouncy rendition of "Muskrat Ramble." It was old-style New Orleans four-beat jazz, religiously patterned, note for note, after the records of Jellyroll Morton and King Oliver and Louis Armstrong and Sidney Bechet.

As soon as the band started to blast away, dozens of couples made their way to the dance floor; the platform began to quake under their wild prancing and galloping. Almost all the men who undertook to dance with their partners were quadros—assured, haughty-looking ones: evidently this club was a hangout for the elite—and the gyrations they went through resembled nothing Martine had ever seen, although there were in them echoes of many way-back dances from the Charleston and the triple lindy down to the applejack and the mambo. The men, once they had twirled their women away to one side, did multiple flips and somersaults which they came out of in spectacular splits; they shifted from feet to hands and back again, without missing a beat; they spun like tops, did handstands and lightning-fast cartwheels; and all the while their partners could do nothing but stand by, swaying gently to keep the rhythm. Now, obviously, the men could perform feats of caperous co-ordination with their plastic limbs which the girls could not hope to duplicate with their real ones; and so a popular dance had come into being in which the man was the fiery, contemptuous show-off and the woman, no matter how expert she might be, essentially a spectator, caught up by her partner at odd moments and then flung aside as he began to strut his cybernetic stuff again. There had been more than a suggestion of the battle between the sexes in old jazz dancing; now it had become the whole thumping spirit of the thing, because of the tremendous anatomical inequity between the partners. More reversal of roles: women had become the aggressors, men, the exhibitionists. This male flashiness, indeed, went beyond kinesthetic stunts, the men displayed their limbs and their clothes were loudly colored. In the end as in the beginning: in most primitive societies, and almost everywhere in the Western world until the eighteenth century, it was the men who got themselves up flashily, preened and strutted. . . . It was an arresting scene—with some seventy or eighty quadro bodies flying about, the whole stage seemed like a fireworks display.

"That's quite a dance," Martine said. "What is it?"

"It's called the Cyber-Cyto Hop," Neen said. "Phuh."

"Don't you do it in the Union?"

"Certainly not. We like a little more dignity in our amusements."

"You don't go for jazz?"

"I hate it, we all do. For a long time before Immob, you know, your music and dancing were officially banned from my country, and we still find them offensive. We like sturdy folk dances and songs you can whistle, we reject tics and sounds that seem to come from an asylum. Jazz is degenerate."

"Me," said Martine, "I like a bit of degeneracy now and then. Takes your mind off things."

"Immob," the girl answered, "aims to elevate the mind, not distract it. All this is plain animalism. Were our marvelous pros invented for Immob man in order that he might hop around like a kangaroo with the itch?"

"Considering how down you are on things animal," Martine said, "you've got some pretty strange notions for this evening's recreation. Or did you mean that we were going to play mandolin duets and discuss Tolstoy in bed? The collected works of Martine?"

"Don't be funny," Neen said. "Sex is animalistic only when it's done by animals. For true Immobs it becomes something altogether different."

"That's what I'm afraid of."

"You're afraid," Neen said, "for the same reason an orangutan is afraid to stop fingering himself and write a sonnet."

"Maybe it's not fear," Martine said. "Maybe it's common sense. He may know that once you invent the sonnet you very probably have to go on and invent the hydrogen bomb and policemen and EMSIAC and dementia praecox."

"And in the end, Immob."

"Yes, in the end, most likely, Immob. His literary reluctance may be based on that too. That may be why he doesn't even keep a notebook."

Martine signaled to the waiter, a pleasant-faced young Negro in a crisp white jacket, and paid the bill. On their way out Neen stopped and pointed to the dance floor.

"Look at the orang-utans," she said. "There won't be many couplets coming out of them. They don't have the time—they're too busy fingering themselves."

"Is that fun?" Martine said. "With plastic fingers?"

A tall Negro in a brocaded uniform swept the door open for them, grinning, and they passed out into the street. It was dark now, the prosyletizing dirigible was blinking out its message above, luminous sheets of window gave off a rich milky glow from the store fronts; it was a cheerful, ingratiating scene, taken just visually.

"Something puzzles me," Martine said idly. "Except for the musicians back there, and a few menials, there don't seem to be any Negroes around town."

Neen snorted. "That surprises you?" she said. "You *don't* remember your country very well—if you're really surprised."

"I remember that even in the best of times they were treated pretty much as second-class citizens. Not that that's any reason for you to feel so superior: *your* country, even in the best of Soviet times, had some fifteen or twenty million of *its* second-class citizens in slave labor camps. But, anyhow, there were certainly Negroes around. And some of them, after a hell of a struggle, were even beginning to push their way up a bit. But now, with Immob, I would have thought—"

"Think again. The reason you don't see any more of them is that they're all underground."

221

"What? You mean they've started some kind of subversive movement?"

"Not exactly—most of them are working in industry, which is all underground now. They're the new proletariat, pretty much."

"But how can that be? What with atomic power plants and robot brains, there can't be many workers needed in industry any more. Even when I was a kid the big plants had been pretty completely robotized."

"There's plenty of dirty work even in a highly mechanized factory. Besides, we have the strong impression that the Strip industrial engineers have avoided mechanizing their plants all the way, precisely so that Negroes and other 'undesirables' might be put to work and kept out of trouble—and sight."

"Aren't Negroes eligible for Immob, then?"

"Oh," Neen said scornfully, "they're eligible, all right. According to the law, that is—just as in the old days, according to the law, they were eligible to vote, go to school, run for office, and everything."

"Then how do some Negroes get to be Immobs?"

"By doing what they've always done when they couldn't get what was coming to them—they arrange to do it for themselves as best they can. They've set up their own Immob clubs, and along with them their own surgery centers, pro-fitting centers, neuro-loco training centers, and all the rest of the Immob institutions. Some of them, of course, come over to the Union to have the operation."

"Why do they bother with Immob at all?"

"When you're in Rome—that applies to the pariah too, you know. Especially to him. In a caste society, the bottom dog has very little choice but to follow the example of the top dog: what other example has he got to follow?"

"Why do you work up such a sweat about the caste system over here? Don't you have one back home?"

"Certainly not," Neen replied spiritedly. "Naturally, some people have better jobs than others. But with us, people don't get up to the top because their skin's a certain color or their nose a certain shape, it's all on a democratic basis. You know, a lot of Negroes have migrated from the Strip to the Union and risen to positions of real importance. For a long time our people have lived by a very simple proposition: From each according to his ability, to each according to his need."

"As I remember," Martine said, "there have been other

222

societies which subscribed to that idea. As I also remember, the principle usually worked out something like this: From each according to his ability to maneuver and scheme and bribe and toady his way into the bureaucracy, to each according to his need for power and special privileges—that is, if he had the aforementioned ability."

"We don't have any bureaucracy. If the important people get where they are because they deserve to, what's bureaucratic about them?"

"The fact that they're important—*even* if they deserve it, and most important people don't. Their mere existence is a steamroller to the unimportant."

"What nonsense! Take me—as a recognized artist with lots of special privileges, I guess I'm fairly important, but how did I get that way? Because I'm a *good* artist. Over here my ability wouldn't get me very far—I've got half a dozen different bloods in me. According to your lily-white standards I'm fit only to be a dishwasher or bed-maker."

"I wouldn't say that you've entirely dispensed with the bed-making functions," Martine said. "Couldn't your success also—couldn't it have just a little bit to do, too, with the number of beds you've managed to make? Your talent for compiling dossiers on worthy bed companions?"

"I pity you," Neen said calmly. "Only a person who hasn't shaken off the old materialistic values could make a remark like that."

"It seems to me," Martine said, "that only a pretty materialistic young woman could sleep around the way I suspect you have. I predict you'll go far wherever you are: To each according to her agility."

It was a silly outburst, of course; he meant the condemnation to indicate a purely esthetic pique, not any lofty moral one, but still, it was silly. The trouble was that he was getting angry: with the girl because she made herself available with a handshake and a brisk exchange of amenities; with himself because he knew this couldn't be any good and still he was going through with it. For better or worse, no matter how much the prospect annoyed him, annoyed one side of him, he was going to take this girl: all his senses bellowed now for some thalamic excess, to correct the cortical excesses of this complicated day.

"In any case," he said more mildly, "the point is that there are hierarchies in both the Strip and the Union. However they've come about—in both cases, it seems to me, they're the products of some pretty old values that have hung over from pre-Immob days. But no matter where they come from, they must still look and feel like steamrollering hierarchies to the bottom dogs. In your country, as here, the cat still cases the king. And spits, when nobody is looking."

"Only in the Strip," Neen said stubbornly.

"Really? If your people are so high-minded and un-materialistic, how do they happen to be just as greedy for columbium as my grasping countrymen?"

"Oh, *that*," Neen said exasperatedly. "You pretend not to understand anything, don't you? Obviously we've got to interest ourselves in this metal because the Strip is trying so hard to corner a monopoly on the supply. We've no alternative—it's a case of self-defense."

"Which, I gather, is exactly what the Strippers say in reference to the Union."

"Sure. Only they're lying."

She tilted her head a little to one side, her marvelous dark slanted eyes narrowed, she regarded him once more with that quizzical look. "Ask your dear Theo," she said. "Ask him what he was doing in the Indian Ocean, in case you don't know."

They had reached the entrance of the Gandhiji, Neen halted there. "I'm stopping here too," she said.

"That's very convenient. Are we going to my place? I don't have any mandolins."

"My rooms are very comfortable. Let's go there."

"I hope you write a good sonnet," he said, following her through the door.

chapter sixteen

UNDER HER skirt she was wearing only a skin-tight pair of briefies, a garment which had started as an abbreviated leotard and atrophied almost to a G-string. Her body was even more exciting than he had imagined. She was not at all dark but there was a suggestion of something-not-quite-white in her complexion, a faint tint of the olive to confound the pallor of the peach.

Neen came across the room. She was excited, nostrils wriggling like twin caterpillars, full lips parted with the effort of breathing, breasts rising and falling energetically, eyes saucered and too bright. When she leaned down over him he knew immediately what she wanted and he braced against

224

it, determined in a spurt of willful maleness that she was not going to have it her way.

"What's the matter, tootsie?" she whispered. "I thought you wanted me."

"I do," he said. "My way. Right now I feel a bit old-fashioned."

"But there is only *one* way." She was not being funny: she meant it.

"No. That is a surprisingly animal rigidity for a humanist. Has no one ever taught you your place?"

"You don't like it like it like this?" There was real astonishment in her voice.

"Very much. Sometimes. But not now, not this time."

"You must not fight, lollypop. Don't fight Immob."

His hands tightened on her shoulders. "Oh? It's Immob I'm fighting?"

"The Immob in yourself. Let yourself go, sex is no more a struggle now. Melt, honey, give in to the melting in yourself. . . ."

There was nothing to do but kid it: "You don't recognize hierarchies anywhere," he said. "Listen, it's a mistake to take over the man's role entirely, to try to. There really is a certain difference between us, universal suffrage quite aside. A writer named Thackeray—he was an extremist, of course—once said that the queen has no business to be a woman."

She was frigid, of course, a man-eater, a man-displacer; only a frigid woman would have to make such an issue of the top billing—but he had allowed himself to get mixed up with such a woman, and now, against all his foreboding, he was excited too, abominably so. . . .

"Lie back," she whispered. "Let it happen, honeybunch. No struggle."

So there was a choice to be made: was he man or Immob? He released his hold on her, filled with contempt for himself. All right, he thought. She was used to going to bed with men who didn't have arms and legs, who removed their arms and legs, that was it. He would just pretend that he was foot-loose and arm-loose and fancy free too. Anything to oblige a man-eating lady. Just to get the feel of the thing, nibble at the oceanic. Position *wasn't* everything in life. . . .

But what happened then was more astonishing still. "Oh, lamb chop," she sighed and suddenly turned to stone, a figure from an old Corinthian bas-relief, and he was forced to remain still too. They were frozen on the neck of an old Grecian urn, urn from the ice age, deep frieze, but one did not giggle at such a solemn immobilized time.

"Don't try," she whispered. "Just be still, lovey-dovey, be still, honeybun. No effort. Let it happen."

And then began something even weirder: still unmoving, Neen now began a powerful rhythm. That was all—a situation of complete petrifaction, joke marbled by some misogynist Praxiteles. It excited him strangely—and irritated him too: he did not relish that part of him which *could* be aroused in this passive way—and he could sense the turmoil growing in her too. . . .

For long minutes it went on, intolerably, hypnotically. All the while his mind raced through a maze of irrelevancies: he recited a line of poetry to himself, "Feather-footed through the plashy fen passes the questing vole," remembered a photographic study of the Taj Mahal on a picture postcard, wondered if the lichens were getting bigger in General Smuts's ears, tried to recall the taste of pistachio ice cream, thought of the numerical value of pi. The excitement was getting more and more feverish, but it was like something spied on by periscope in the next county—there was about all this a horrible frustrating Itness, some interloper tinkering with the body's engine while the master mechanic squatted pouting and uninvolved on the sidelines. It was unbearable, he despised himself for harboring this standoffish scoffing inner commentator who kept up a steady flow of icy analytic narration while the rest of him was straining with need, he hated himself for fooling with a woman who could involve nothing but his glands and thalamus; and now his heart was hammering madly—

And a new agitation in her: and she said, in words that seemed to be caught deep in her throat and rasping harshly as they struggled to get out, muffled in her throat, she said, "Yes. Yes. Now, now, lamikins, now." Suddenly she was not the mover, something in her that was not willed was taking over—it was not intention tremor but the upstart tremor which drowns intention. Holding a man prisoner, beholden to no man for her triumph, involved with her partner only insofar as she had momentarily borrowed him as a necessary prop in the burlesque ritual, herself responsible for everything, the doer, the precipitator, she had brought about the intensest of fulfillments for herself—and without losing his clinical data-hungry eye for a moment, and furious with himself for the eye's unblinking endurance, he felt the galvanizing effect of it, the pulse somehow flowed over to him and suddenly, in a quick upheaval—"Now, ootsums," she whispered—trying savagely to free himself, filled too with hysterical laughter that he should be caught in such a trap and so unutterably helplessly done to—now he too felt the fury tearing through him—stampede—

A shock and a shudder.

Billowing blackness, the Taj Mahal wavering wanly in the middle of it.

Then no more swirling and he opened his eyes and watched the room jell into uprights again.

Burlesque. The most frustrating and humiliating erotic moment of his life, he thought with a grimace.

Phuh. . . .

And then, rather amazed at himself, he began to laugh. Neen looked at him in complete bewilderment.

"Have you gone crazy, dewdrop?" she said.

"It's funny," he gasped. "I just thought of something funny. You know what you were saying about Immobs not being animals in sex? You were perfectly right, you know."

"Of course. I told you you'd see."

"I do, I do. Where in the whole wide animal kingdom is there a female who pre-empts the whole role of the male? It's the most unanimal-like thing I ever heard of."

"Roles, roles," Neen said contemptuously. "We are finished with all that reactionary ideology, Adam's rib and such garbage."

"From what part of Adam would you have preferred to spring?"

"Never mind the jokes. It is a fact, your ideological godfathers treated women like dirt and said they were intended by nature to be slaveys. According to their stuck-up idea a woman couldn't fulfill herself unless she crawled and catered and cringed before some man, some strutting puffed-up gamecock of a man. All that is finished now in Immob. The Immob woman does not take it lying down."

"Maybe there's no other way to take it. There's something even deeper than ideology—anatomy—women seem to be made to *receive;* in that sense, at least, women are intended to be a bit more passive. If they're to *feel* like women."

"Are you trying to tell me I didn't feel like a woman just now?"

Martine yawned, wondered if the Taj Mahal was still standing. "Frankly," he said, "I think you'd be hard put to it to say exactly what you did feel." She had had an orgasm, certainly—even in the most difficult of positions, a man-deposing position which for most women would exclude the possibility of any real orgasm at all—a full vaginal one, not a pale clitoridean substitute. But why? Only, he guessed, because she had taken over all the maleness of the thing. The condition for her satisfaction, apparently, was that she play the man, absorb the man, castrate him: expropriation without compensation, her forefathers used to call it. Which was a rather spectacular form of frigidity. If she couldn't get her sense of male usurpation that way, chances were she would have to get it in the more traditional way, by shifting her erotic center from the vagina to the clitoris, that phantom phallus, and thrusting it back at her partner as though it were the genuine article. Which took some doing. . . . "What you need, obviously, is the feeling that you're the doer. Maybe the whole purpose of Immob is to give you that feeling. . . ."

"All garbage. You think about sex as a thrusting belligerent thing done *by* men *to* women. Man the subject, woman the object, the old animal double standard."

"And you have made them *equals?*"

"Of course, puss. By rising above movement."

He propped himself up on one elbow and stared at her. "You're quite mad," he said. "Let's take it primer fashion: sex is an ecstasy of friction; friction is a function of movement; man, by anatomical necessity, is the prime frictioneer. There, snooky, is the rub. All you've done is to substitute one kind of movement for another—one which allows the man to have his satisfaction only at the price of his manhood. And, I might add, of your womanhood. In this half-ass unacknowledged matriarchy of yours you haven't eliminated the sex roles, only reversed them. Some call it love but I call it castration. I'm against it."

"You don't understand anything," Neen said in her best didactic manner. "There is still a modified, reduced form of movement, I'll grant you—although much less is needed with an Immob man than with you, because he has risen much further above his old animal self. But this is a transitional period. In the end sex will be a mutually oceanic experience with a complete absence of movement. The orgones will leap at each other by themselves. Then there will be no more strife in the world. Movement is strife. The whole idea of Immob is to eliminate *all* friction between people."

"There may very well be no more strife—but only because

there won't be any more people around to have it. Because there'll also be no more orgasm: that's a conception to end all conception. Which seems to me a nice proof of Freud's prediction."

"That reactionary. What did he predict?"

"Well, he once said it's hard to avoid the impression that sex is a dying function. He meant that civilization encroaches more and more on the animal functions, robs them of their energy, loads them with taboos and uneasy symbolisms that bottle them up and ultimately, maybe, cause their organs to wither away."

"Marx once said the *state* was going to wither away."

"He was dead wrong, we know that now. But Freud really may have hit on something—maybe it's the genitals that will wither away. After a certain time that should more or less automatically take care of the state. . . . Tell me this: don't the Pros remove their arms and legs when they go to bed with a woman?"

"There are lots of arguments about that too. The Antis even point to these arguments to show that the Pros are still animals because they often want to keep their limbs on and use them in the old way, to subdue women and lord it over them and all that. Women who have had a real Immob indoctrination and caught the spirit much prefer their partners to take off their pros, of course. The man's bound to find it a lot more satisfying once he adjusts to it, and it's a lot more satisfying to the woman, too."

"Sure, when she's frigid. Look, let me point out something about this oceanic experience of yours. You didn't exactly merge with me—you were fighting me all the way. You had a full experience, sure, but it took you a hell of a long time to arrive at it: well over thirty minutes, I'd say, whereas the average normal coitus lasts for only a very few minutes. And like all women who achieve satisfaction only with great difficulty, and only under special aggressive circumstances and only after prolonged tension and anxiety, you were determined to be the pace-setter. That's quite characteristic of frigid women too—the man's mechanism must be only a passive reflex of theirs. You'll find this hard to believe, but the normal state of affairs is quite the other way around. And without any trace of competitiveness, either. With a kind of warm melting you don't know anything about."

"Fascinating. But you're not up to date on your statistics, Doctor. You evidently don't know that among Immobs, among the Antis, at least, the average coitus—to use your quaint language—lasts from thirty minutes to an hour, even longer. And is repeated several times a night."

"You've got an explanation for that, of course?"

"Of course. Our medical researchers have discovered the exact reason. You see, in the old animalistic days men couldn't sustain themselves for very long, not long enough to satisfy the average woman; the blood would only stay in the genitals for a limited period because it was needed elsewhere. But when the arms and legs are removed more blood is available to the genitals and for longer periods. Especially since the doctors at the amp stations now pump as much of the blood back into the body as they can after an amputation. Besides, a lot of women I know bring their amp husbands back from time to time for transfusions."

Martine was staring out the window, watching the illuminated dirigible float by. "I can suggest another explanation," he said finally. "A most intriguing one. Has to do with masochism."

"Masochism? What a pecular old-fashioned word. I've never seen it used anywhere—except in Brother Martine's notebook, where he makes a kind of obscure joke out of it."

"It was obscure, yes. But here's my idea. People have potency interruptions for all sorts of reasons—neurotic sex is loaded with all sorts of mocking symbolisms of giving and not giving—but they pretty much boil down to one common denominator—masochism, the desire to feel mistreated and neglected, the unconscious pleasure one takes in pain. Generally speaking, frigidity or impotence is not something done by one person to another, it's something a person does to himself—with a carefully selected collaborator—because unconsciously he finds frustration—which he can blame on his partner—a greater pleasure than satisfaction would be a conscious pleasure. All right. Let's take a man bothered with some potency trouble—and *not* an inability to make love for thirty minutes, because, no matter what you think, that's pain rather than pleasure to a normal man. All right. This guy submits to an operation which removes all four of his limbs. That's a pretty solid dose of masochism all at once, isn't it? Maybe his unconscious pain requirements are satisfied so whoppingly in one big bundle that afterwards he can afford to be not too masochistic in his sexuality. Four symbolic castrations at one stroke—after that the average masochist doesn't need a fifth, psychic, one. It's the same story with psychotics after electric shock treatment or lobotomy: they've overfulfilled their masochistic quotas so spectacularly that they can afford to let up on their more modest self-damaging symptoms and show some improvement for a while. . . . But there's a good deal of masochism left in the amp, even so. It's masochistic to be obliged to remain still, to take all erotic guidance from an aggressive woman, to postpone climax for half an hour, to be *used*. . . ."

Neen sat up in bed with an abrupt movement. She was angry now, her eyes were blazing. "You're fantastic. Fantastic."

"Am I?" Then, from out of nowhere, he remembered something the basket case in Marcy's window had hinted at. It was a shot in the dark, but there was one other clue: the charade he had seen enacted by the young couple on the sun deck at the Gandhiji. "Then tell me what happens when amps *refuse* to take off their pros in bed?"

She seemed puzzled. "Oh, all sorts of things," she said. "One bad thing is that they have funny accidents with them. They're tempted to use them the way they used their real limbs, to caress and hug and all that slop, and lots of times they seem to forget their co-ordination completely and—well, you know how dangerous a pro can be when it's not co-ordinated right. There've been some very bad accidents as a result—ribs and jaws broken, eyes blackened, and even worse. Some women have even died from their injuries. It's all very animalistic, only animals hurt each other in sex."

"You see?" Martine said triumphantly. "This passive sex of yours is just too much of a masochistic pill for men to swallow. Too humiliating—they resent the being dominated too much because they really want to be so much, want to smuggle the nursery into the bedroom. That's why men would rather keep their pros on—and often have face-saving Freudian 'slips' with them which land their ladies in the hospital and the morgue. The gangster's needed to hide the baby. It also explains why the ladies would prefer their lovers in the dismantled state—their instinct of self-preservation tells them they can't take the upper hand so completely without expecting a few cybernetic uppercuts in payment. . . ."

Martine began to laugh again. "The next step is for them to deny the physiological facts of paternity, nudge the man out of the conception picture entirely, just as primitive woman does. In the end as in the beginning. . . . It's the funniest goddamned thing I ever heard of," he gasped. "It just struck me—that statue, that statue at the hub."

"What about the statue, you fool?"

"It shows a man being flattened by a steamroller. Don't you see? Immob was supposed to get rid of the steamroller. Instead—oh, it's unbelievable—you've gone and installed another steamroller, in and out of bed. The New World has kept its promise. Woman is the new Immob steamroller, even your soapboxers refer to it as *she*. . . ."

When he got over it he sat up and looked at her. He was quite serious now. "Martine was right," he said. "A man *should* dodge the steamroller. By all means."

He took her by the shoulders; before she could squirm out of his grip he had her pinned down, his fingers digging in until he could feel the bones of her arms through thin casings of compressed flesh.

He had his own idea of what it was that set human sexuality off from the animal: egoness. Egoness. It was a word that had once been suggested to him many years ago, when he was a medical student, by the psychoanalyst to whom he had been assigned (by that time it was required of all medical students that they complete a minimum analysis before they were eligible for their degrees).

"With the animal," this analyst had suggested, "sex is all blind compulsion, mechanism; with man the emotional keynote of the experience is the sense that he is doing this thing himself, willing it, bringing it to pass, calling out response in the partner—reversing the ignominious situation in the nursery, healing the nursery wound, denying the deep yearning for a resurrection of the nursery situation. That sense becomes doubly important to him today, because it's a counterbalance to what happens to him in his non-erotic life—almost everywhere but in bed he takes an awful beating, is cowed and humiliated and passively manipulated by bureaucracies and overwhelming machines which turn him into helpless instrument and object. In bed the ego takes on new life: in Freudian terms, the sense of injury is overcome a bit by the active repetition of a passively suffered narcissitic wound. A neat switch: Do something to somebody else and you are no more object. Of course, that may represent a great danger. It introduces more self-proving drive into the erotic life than Nature intended. Maybe men will feel so set upon in the end that this lust for egoness will run wild and so distort the sex function as to cripple it altogether. Men may be so masochistic that when they go looking for too many ego-affirmations in bed their malicious unconscious

232

drives may make them—impotent. This may be loading the sex impulse with more irrelevancies than it can bear. . . ."

Egoness, yes. But not with brutality. Not belligerently, provocatively. Not as against tenderness. . . . Stupid business: he grimaced in distaste for what he was about to do. He had always been bored by the chin-jutting he-man who felt obliged to establish his masculinity by sheer force of main and muscle—why work so hard to prove you're one thing unless you're really the other? Of course, he had no taste for it. Gestures, all gestures, were so goddamned silly. And yet—

"You've had your fun," he said. "It's my turn now."

She fought him, her body writhing with the effort to break his hold, but he was determined. Equal rights—he was not asking much, just equal rights. It was not going to be exactly the best he'd ever had, but it was better than nothing. And didn't she really want this after all? Rape was a pretty difficult business without a bit of ambivalence in the woman. There was another case: Rosemary. Immediately he dismissed the name from his thoughts. . . . Of course she would not fall in with his movements, allow him the freedom his whole being called out for, but at least he was not entirely tied down by her immobility now, he was able to achieve some caricatured semblance of the act—even against her will it was now something of an act rather than an imposition, a petrifaction.

Rosemary. . . . There was no responsive yieldingness in her, and yet the feeling of being somewhat in control again was enough—he was, in spite of everything, rising to another climax which was entirely free from her dictates. In a matter of a very few minutes, not the thirty or more minutes of the first time but only three or four, he was there, getting there, filled with the triumph of getting there—and in a kind of terror, trying to ward off the culmination that came from his pace-setting and not hers, sensing no doubt that if his time-table were allowed to fulfill itself it would make a mockery of hers and all the fine-spun theories built on it, she pressed, resisted, seething with antagonism. Even while he felt the climax coiling in him, he thought with despair and contempt which was also self-contempt that it was all a farce. His whole being cried out now for the feel of Ooda beneath him, the warm and glowingly alive Ooda who went along not in resignation but in response, seeking not to usurp but to blend and mingle, not to resist and oppose but to supplement and react and flow with him. The oceanic! Oh, yes—the closest thing to it he had ever experienced, the closest thing to it that was possible, maybe, was the sense of tantalizing tender togetherness he'd felt with Ooda, the thrill of being mysteriously joined with her even as the irony of ultimate separateness hovered over their heads; the bittersweet ambivalence of unity in alienation, merger across barricades, a momentary ecstatic brush with the oneness—the best that could be hoped for and plenty good enough, something he'd settle for, and prayerfully, for the rest of his life. He wanted only to be with Ooda now. Thinking that, and filled with ghastly laughter to know that he was even capable of thinking at this moment—and with the name Rosemary rattling around somewhere in his head—he came. And it was good in a way, an affirmation. A great abominable joke too, but still.

It was a bad moment for her, he could sense. It was all beyond her control, it was a reproach. Anything in a man not engineered by her was a reproach. But something wholly unexpected was happening. For the first time she stopped opposing him and crumbled into softness and now she too, against her will, overwhelmed in spite of herself, the engine of her body snatching the controls away from her will—she began to respond, for once passive and open to emotional suggestion from the outside. But it was not the same as before, not at all the same. She could not yield entirely. It started deep within her, a powerful quaking pulse at her core: he could feel it. But—forced to abandon the male role, forced to yield her drawn-out timetable too, she was driven to assert her male willfulness in the only way left—frantically she clapped her body against his, shifting her whole focus from the intaking receiving core of her, driving with her phantom maleness; the last castrate maneuver. The inner throb grew feeble, died away. It was not, although it had started out to be, the genuine full reaction of the wholly yielding, wholly warm woman—she, or her ornery unconscious, had executed a diversion to defeat him at the last moment, at the price of her own full satisfaction. It was a last desperate gesture against passivity, a peculiar double-edged denial-of-frigidity-through-frigidity. "Oh, lamb chop, lamb chop," she whispered but there was venom in the endearment—and a tortured unspoken question.

It left her, as it was bound to and intended to, filled with mixed sentiments; Irene, too, when with great difficulty she had reached the same derailed climax, had been emotionally akimbo, ecstatic on the surface, raging with unuttered denunciations just below. She looked up at him now with

234

an uncertain expression in her eyes—the eyes never fully carried off the lie of lustiness—wavering between wonder and hostility; feeling the partial edge contentment of the maimed woman who has had an ersatz pleasure and would like to consider it the real thing, the partial hatred of an unsatisfied woman to whom protest is more important than fulfillment and who would like to hurl the blame for it at her partner. But at this moment it was hard for her to know exactly what to blame him for: the experience had been largely frustrating for her, but it had also been totally new. She had experienced a sudden loss of emotional face and focus. She hardly knew whether to scratch his eyes out or curl her arms around him. Perhaps she would like to do both—she did neither. Something had happened to her, she'd had a touch of the steamroller, it had left her concepts quaking.

The room was a battlefield, littered with the corpses of gestures and symbols, all sorts of stupid irrelevancies. Rape: Rosemary. He struggled to drive the words from his mind.

"Maybe we should have stuck to the mandolins," he said.

Long silence.

"You've got an awful lot of aggression left in you, patootie," she said finally.

Good: she was retreating into ideology.

"Ain't it the truth," he said. "My oceanic quota's awfully low."

"It comes from a lack of Moral Equivalents. Before you get to Immob you'll need plenty of indoctrination."

"I'll see a doctrine about it first thing in the morning."

"Listen, sugar," she said urgently. "Just what kind of a medical man are you, anyway?"

"My specialty is peeping-tometry, that's a branch of optometry. No, seriously, I specialize in tropical diseases. Spent a long, long time doing research in Africa. That's where I've been all these years."

"What's your real name?"

He stiffened. "I told you. Lazarus, Chester P. Lazarus. Pleased to meet you."

"Stop lying!"

He looked at her in astonishment. "What?"

"Don't lie to me—you've been playing dumb all evening and I've been playing along with you, but there isn't much time left for games. I know you've been off in Africa, but what were you doing there? You were looking for columbium, weren't you?"

He was too dumbfounded to answer, he just stared. "Columbium?" he said at last. "You've got me mixed up with a couple of other pole vaulters. I don't even know what the silly stuff looks like."

"*Listen*." She sat up and swung her legs over the edge of the bed; her expression was serious. "Maybe you didn't understand me, *there isn't much time*. You've got to tell me the truth."

"But that is the truth," he protested.

"You're queer," she said, looking at him speculatively. "Your head is full of ideas that come right out of the dark ages but I don't know, there's something about you. I like you—you irritate me, but I like you. I felt something different with you, screwy, I don't know whether I go for it or not, I haven't had time to evaluate it from a non-Aristotelian point of view but it's intriguing."

"You mean I've stopped you in your tracts?"

"Don't you see, I want to help you. I'll save you if I can."

"What the hell are you talking about?" he said.

"Just this. You are connected with Theo. You had something to do with his phony Olympic training cruise in the Indian Ocean. You know plenty. Tell me, otherwise it will be bad."

"Do you mean," he said slowly, "do you actually mean—you followed me around all day, you brought he here and even—it was all because you thought—?"

"Are you going to tell me?" Her voice was hard now.

"There's nothing to tell, you idiot."

Shs shrugged. "All right. I gave you your chance. You can't say I didn't try."

She stood up and walked across the room to a door, not the one leading to the hall but another. Without bothering to put a robe on she opened the door and said, "I can't get anything out of him. You'd better take over."

Two men came into the room: Vishinu and the Eurasian who had been with him on the plane from Miami. They came over to the bed and stood there looking down at Martine.

"So, *Dr. Lazarus*," Vishinu said. He had an automatic in his hand, muzzle fitted with a peculiar sleevelike sort of flange. "Good. You will loosen up your tongue now a little, I'm sure. You will tell us very many things about your friend Theo, oh, yes."

236

chapter seventeen

VISHINU SAT down on the edge of the bed. His pros crackled, it sounded as though somebody were shelling peanuts. "Cover up, please," he said, pointing. "We are interested in your viewpoint, not your view."

Martine pulled the sheet around him.

"Better," Vishinu said. "Now let us sum up. Here is the picture. Theo goes sightseeing around the Indian Ocean and Lake Victoria—you are not seen anywhere with him. Then Theo comes home on a liner—you are on board too but you stay in your cabin the whole trip, very ostentatious. You even arrange to board a different plane in Miami so you will not be seen with him. Unfortunately for you, however, I am passing through Miami the same day and I have reports on you and I begin to get very interested in you. Then you register at the Gandhiji as Dr. Lazarus but there is no record of any Dr. Lazarus in any of the medical directories. Conclusion: either you are a doctor whose name is not Lazarus or your name is Lazarus and you are not a doctor. Conclusion: either way you are concealing something. What? That you were not in Africa to study tropical diseases? But you *were* in Africa. What, then, were you studying that makes you so secretive? Columbium, perhaps? Like your friend Theo, who you avoid?"

"Go on," Martine said. "Your mind fascinates me."

"Not as much as yours fascinates me," Vishinu said. "I am always fascinated by the mind of a man who says he studies bugs when he studies only rocks."

"*Your* research is pretty spotty too. If you'd looked further you would have found that I'm not listed in any of the directories of metallurgists or mining engineers either. I couldn't tell a piece of columbium from a scoop of pistachio ice cream."

"Now, now," Vishinu saud. "Not necessary to quibble. The members of your Olympic team are never listed as metallurgists or mining engineers either but that is what they are, good ones, too. It is a very clever system, sir. We naturally know all about it—we have been using it for some years ourselves."

"You forgot to mention that in your telecast last night. Immob must make you absent-minded as well as absent-legged."

"Ah, do not be too harsh on us, my dear unregistered doctor," Vishinu said humorously. "What can we do? So long as your country insists on playing its old imperialist-monopolist game, we must take countermeasures. However, let us get down to business. Obviously you had no reason to be around Africa unless you were looking for columbium. We can consider that established—very, very few Inland Strippers travel abroad these days unless they are mixed up with columbium some way or another. The same with us Unioneers, of course, you have forced us into it: all our ambassadors, our lecturers, our exchange students, our athletes, our artists." Here he stopped and waved in Neen's direction. "All, unfortunately, are either looking for columbium or for their opposite numbers who are looking for columbium. So we will have to face it: you were in Africa because of columbium. From this it follows that you also have something to do with Theo, because he was there for the same reason. Now you will tell us about Theo. Everything. I am afraid we shall have to insist."

"I'm afraid it won't do you any good," Martine said. "I'd be very happy to tell you all about Theo but I don't know a thing about him. Not a thing. I've never even met the man."

"I see." Vishinu looked at him thoughtfully for a moment. "You are not a gossip—most admirable, but a little unfortunate under the circumstances. Dai, my colleague here, is a spetz in making gossips out of strong silent men. After Dai gives you a demonstration you will gossip, I assure you, like old ladies over the back fence. Oh, yes."

The Eurasian took a short, thick rubber truncheon from his hip pocket and held it at his side.

"You can't get information out of me that I don't have." Martine sat up, the sheet still draped over him. "Look, would you have any objection if I put my clothes on? It's getting chilly in here."

"Please. You will make a much better-looking cripple in your nice tweeds than in your birthday suit."

Vishinu spoke a few words in a foreign tongue to Neen. She immediately went to the chair on which Martine's clothes were lying, felt expertly in all the pockets, then brought them over to the bed. Martine began awkwardly to dress. At the same time Neen took a robe from the closet and slipped it on.

"What is your decision?" Vishinu said finally. "Shall we begin with the, ah, ceremony?"

"You put me in a difficult position," Martine said. "I don't have anything to tell you—that's the truth, but you won't believe it. On the other hand, I'm obliged to face another fact: no matter what you believe, you can't let me go."

"How do you deduce this remarkable fact?"

Martine sank into an easy chair. "It's simple enough. Spying is forbidden everywhere in Immob, I understand. Don't tell me everybody does it, that's another matter—the point is that it's a terrible crime for anybody to get caught at. And you have now made it clear to me that you, chairman of the East Union delegation to the Olympic Committee, are the head of a very large spy ring. It makes no difference if Theo is too, I can't prove that. But I can prove it about you, at least I can call attention to it. So it's obvious: you can't leave me any way but dead. Therefore—"

"I do like your mind," Vishinu said. "Very much. Continue."

"So even if I did have something to tell you, which I don't, why should I? I'm a dead duck either way you look at it."

"Not necessarily. For one thing, you would avoid much pain before the end. A good deal, take my word. But there does not have to be an end, there is another way. Tell us everything you know—not as a double-crossing spy but in order to save the cause of Immob and civilization."

"Don't tempt me. I'm sucker for saving civilizations—it's the Mormon in me."

Vishinu leaned forward and began to speak seriously, ignoring the interruption. "Do this. Then come over to our side as many courageous Strippers have done, many Negroes and others too. You will be safe. We will slip you out of the country and take you to the Union to wait."

"Wait?"

"Not for long. Five, six months now, not more, the showdown will come soon. Then the treacherous bureaucrats who have grabbed power in the Strip will be taught their lesson. There will be a place then for you, you and all the other true Immobs of the Strip. You will return then in glory. You will be a hero to your people, another Martine. It will be worth it."

"What, exactly, is happening in five or six months?" Martine hoped they would not notice that his voice had become tight and strained.

Vishinu pulled a cigar out of his breast pocket, lit it and puffed for a moment, then took it between thumb and forefinger and waved it at Martine like a baton. "Yes," he said. "When you leave this room you will be either a corpse or a recruit to our side. Yes, I can tell you something. The Theos and the Helders are going to be taught a lesson."

"They will learn not to be greedy for everything," the Eurasian said.

"And to mistreat Negroes," Neen said.

"And to bring back all the old crap, the old imperialist crap," Vishinu said. "To act as though in the West is everything good and the East is only for savages and barbarians. To think that because they are so good with machines and laboratories and efficiency systems everybody else is so much garbage. To spread around the idea that technics and material values is civilization and a man with two helicopters in his garage is better than a man with a thousand dreams in his head. To fool themselves that those who jump a few feet higher in the Olympics should be the lords of the world and get all the columbium. Yes, my friend, they will be taught. We have been patient, but when it comes to stealing all the supplies of columbium—well, we will not sit by and let it happen. We are going to remove the imperialists in your country and put back Immob, true Immob. And those Strippers who help in the great work will have their reward for it."

"Another war to preserve peace?" Martine said. "This is where I came in. I mean, this is where I went out."

"The Strip has declared this war behind the scenes," Vishinu said forcefully. "It is here whether we want it or not. Now it is only a strategy matter. Either we sit back and let your Theos and Helders stamp us into the ground, or we attack out of self-defense, before they do. It is the only choice open to us."

"Couldn't you just lie down and passive-resist?" Martine said. "Grunt a few Oms?"

"Don't talk nonsense," Vishinu said. He was getting impatient. "Such gabble is for schoolkids and Anti-Pros. We have these crackpots in our country too, but we keep them where they're harmless."

"Oh? And if they're not harmless?"

"Simple: then we arrest them and bring them to trial for their crimes. You have not heard of the East Union trials? These Antis and their fellow conspirators confess to everything, sabotage, spying, counter-Martinism, imperialist plotting, terrorism, degenerate bourgeois democracy, deviationism, Talmudism, homeless cosmopolitanism, troglodytism, Aristotelianism, and so on. Everything."

"Aren't those pretty big crimes for basket cases?"

240

"Sabotage and terrorism," Vishinu said, "can be moral as well as physical. There is such a thing as *passive* sabotage and terrorism. This is the worst crime of all."

"Say," Martine said, turning to Neen, "this is a side of Union democracy you forgot to tell me about. It looks like passivity can be pretty dangerous after all."

"Do not deceive yourself," Vishinu said. "Passive resistance is a nice idea—if you want to feel the steamroller on your belly."

"I most definitely don't," Martine said. "Not even yours." His fingers played aimlessly with the row of pencils in his breast pocket, then he slid one of them out and began to chew reflectively on the eraser end. Vishinu was watching him closely, the Eurasian tightened his grip on the truncheon. "And I see only one way to dodge your particularly persuasive kind of steamroller."

"Namely?" Vishinu said.

"By making myself particularly passive," Martine said.

He bit off the eraser with his teeth, spat it out, before Vishinu could reach him he had upended the pencil and swallowed its contents.

He stared into the flaring mouth of the automatic, inches away from his head.

"What was that?" Vishinu said furiously.

"Don't worry. Just seven cc's of trance. Anti-steamroller juice."

"I advise you, do not play games with me. What was it?"

"Rotabunga, plus a few other things," Martine said. "It's very popular among the Ubus, a tribe I lived with in Africa. Would you like to know the ingredients? First there's $C_{17}H_{22}Cl-$"

"Never mind," Vishinu said harshly. "What does this stuff do?"

"There are various mixtures," Martine said. "This particular mixture, Rota Three, is a pretty nifty pacifist snake oil. In exactly three minutes I'll be totally anesthetized. In another eight or nine minutes I'll be almost totally paralyzed, except for the blinking reflex, certain restricted movements of the vocal cords, and a few odds and ends."

"You think this solves something for you, you fool?"

"For at least twelve hours it does. You seem to be fond of demonstrations—shall I give you a demonstration? The anesthesia is beginning to set in. Watch."

Martine unfastened his tie clasp, a strip of solid gold. He

held it out, demonstrating its sharp pin. "Nice, isn't it? Used to belong to the British consul at Johannesburg." He lit a match and dipped the pin in the flame. "Sorry to waste your time," he said apologetically. "Sterilization, necessary surgical precaution. No sense risking infection." He took the pin firmly between his fingers and jabbed it into the palm of his other hand. Then he extended the hand, palm down: the point of the pin was protruding from the other side. "See?" he said. "I'm now the insensitive type. It's quite a good trick—almost as good, I'd say, as the Indian fakir's sleeping on spikes."

Now he pulled the pin free, stuck his tongue out as far as it would go, and drove the sliver of metal all the way through its fleshy tip. "How's 'at? 'Akes talking a 'iddle bi' di'icult bu' it'th quite d'amatic, idd'n it?" With a quick gesture he removed the pin from his tongue. "Gentlemen, for the next twelve hours you can make salisbury steak out of me with your revolver butts and blackjacks, kill me if you choose—but you can't hurt me. Flail away, father confessors. Incidentally, I'd like to talk to you later, when you've got a minute, about getting the agency to handle this stuff in the East Union. Bet I could make a fortune selling it to your basket cases—the ones you've decided to extract a few confessions from. Sure cure for confessions."

Vishinu yanked the pin away and plunged it into Martine's upper arm, over and over. Martine sat without moving.

"You'll never get me to say Uncle Vanya," he said. "I'm stubborn—it's the Mormon in me."

"He's right," Neen said, puzzled. "He doesn't feel a thing."

"Important to send in a report on this right away," Vishinu said. "No doubt all their operatives carry this new stuff with them. We must take countermeasures."

"Seven cc's of alienation," Martine said. "You can't reach me, the real me. Rotabunga should be the national beverage on Independence Day. Do you mind if I lie down? Musculature's going flabby now, that's the next step."

He stood up, made his way waveringly across the room and flopped down on the bed with a deep sigh. "Religion the opium of the people?" he said. "Wrong, rotabunga opium of the people. Sleep the opium of the people. Opium opium of people. Lobotomy and amputeeism opium people but rotabunga better, reversible. Those who take opium of people can be unopiumed but people can't be unlobotomized or unamputated. Am I boring you? Excuse me, hard to talk, lips getting heavy. . . ."

242

"It must go to his head," Dai said. "He talks crazy."

"He thinks he's being funny," Vishinu said. "He has a very big sense of humor."

Neen came over to the bed and stood looking down at Martine.

"Hello, sweetheart," Martine said thickly. "I wish to thank you for a wonderful evening. You must come up and see my mandolins sometime. Miss Oceanic. Miss Oceanic of 1990. Sorry can't smile at you, embouchure's frozen stiff as a board as a pelvis. Just consider please that I am mentally smiling at you. Broad grin. Miss Position-Is-Everything-In-Life. Only mistake you make you don't give guy a slug of rotabunga before you start steamrolling him. Great little pacifier, passive-fier."

"Twelve hours," Neen said. "What are you going to do with him?"

Vishinu looked thoughtful. "He may be lying about these twelve hours," he said, "but we must wait. Take this." He handed Neen the revolver. "Watch him—and be careful, you don't know when he'll get over it. Dai and I will see the agent from L.A. and get his report. Also, we will search this pig's room. We will look in from time to time." He leaned over and slapped Martine's face hard. Martine's eyes blinked once, that was all. "We will slap him and stick some pins into him from time to time," Vishinu said. "The moment he feels even a little tickle, life will begin to get very, very sad for him. You hear me, Dr. Lazarus? You are going to be very, very sad."

Vishinu and Dai went toward the door.

"'Bye," Martine said to the ceiling. "Don't take any wooden expressions. Unioneers have such wooden expressions and not only expressions. Suspicious of man with frozen embouchure. Tonus written all over map pretending it's territory. Oriental inscrutability balls. Oriental tonus from jowl to jowl, it's no Occident. . . ."

The door slammed.

"You shut up," Neen said. She pulled a chair close to the bed and sat down, the revolver held warily in her lap.

It was his first experience with Rota Three, any of the rota mixtures. For all the thousands of times he had observed its effects on others, both in preparation for surgery and as a general sedative, he had never tried it on himself, preferred being limber to limp. No feelings now, soaring, gliding, body an inert lump he had sloughed off in Mani-

243

chean despondency, slough of despond, body lying back there on earth somewhere and he did not *feel* the movement, only *perceived* it. *Knew* it. World as Idea, Omful of Idea. Pure Reason. Sheer delight. Sheer Om.

"Om," he said experimentally. Hearing dim now, words far away like soft bubbles under water. "Ooooommmmmmmmm." Very far away but he could hear it as it echoed ripplingly through space, gondoliered through his semicircular canals, bouncing off Jupiter, ricocheting off Saturn.

He flowed out unfeeling with the mystic word, he was the Word, in the beginning was the Word as big as the world and he was straddling it, riding along past the sluggish galaxies at 186,000 miles per sec and everywhere at once and nowhere, just the idea of everywhere, because at 186,000 miles per sec there is no mass only energy, all energy, dazzling blue orgonotic energy of oceanic light and so at the speed of light you are weightlessly everywhere. Discovery. Revelation. Revealed at last the way to plow through the alienation, all you do is hit the cosmic road at 186,000 miles per sec and shed vile mass and become a light beam and finally Thou art That, yippee. Traveling light, Einsteinian system for beating the rap of skin. With one fell swig he had rid himself of swarming protoplasm, don't you think it's swarm in here, thrown off limbs, abdomen, viscera, instincts, glands, solar plexus, thalamus, parasympathetic nervous system, all the agents of the steamroller inside the skin, all the troublemakers and tonus-makers and tempest-makers and toupee-makers—nowhere and everywhere and an all-at-onceness, cuddled up with the Infinite, playing footsie with the Ineffable Omnipresent Altogether, bursting with it in gleed and gleek and gleet and, oh, yes, glee. . . .

"Hey," he said. Thought he said; hearing fading fast now, could hardly make out sound of voice drowned in swish of stardust rumble of meteors. "Don't look now but somebody stole my skin."

"I can't stand much more of this," Neen said. Seemed to be saying. Sight fading too: blurred words came from pinkish blur presumably Neen poised on russet blur presumably chair. "Are you going to keep this up for twelve hours? I'll go crazy."

Would be good to go limp ride with it just riding but too risky. Would lose consciousness if stopped talking stopped thinking. Had to fight keep awake keep in touch. Rota would wear off in two three hours. Had to be awake in control of it when it happened. Had to follow process as cortex spinal cord came back to life. Otherwise might give it away with telltale squirming stretching. Goner that way for sure. Could not let them know when stuff was wearing off play dead only chance. . . .

"Sorry to make such nuisance myself," he said. Talking almost unbearably difficult now, face mask of pulpy papier-mâché, tongue thick slice of aspic, lips flaps of cotton wadding. "Just got Word Word is Om. Listen." Couldn't move eyes now but staring up at India-rubber ceiling sensing vague smudge that must be her over near Saturn; voice seemed to be coming from echo chamber under floor. "Mistake for woman make herself man all Commissar no Yogi all alp no sea. False phallus. Phallusy."

"You've got to stop it," Neen said. "Stop talking crazy. I've had as much as I can take."

Wavery blur moved closer now, she must have stood up. Seemed now through gathering fog in room she had bent over was fumbling with him somehow, couldn't feel it but some swimming shape that could be hand reaching out to where his chest had been. Yes, yes, saw it now as through milk, fingers fumbling at his pocket, pulling false pencils out, could just barely see bright reds greens blues of pencils rising into pink haze that was her face shimmied there for moment came down again. Smelling, sure, smelling what was in pencils.

"Listen," said, hoped was saying. "Immob fine but big mistake. Apply it to women not men automatically end war between nations. War between nations only extension war between sexes. Language of love language of military. Sex is war games. To demilitarize sex men must stop feeling competition from women castration penis envy all that world needs less momism more Omism. Trouble is—"

"If you don't stop, I swear, if you don't stop I'm going to pour some more of this stuff down your throat. I don't care if it kills you. You've got to stop it."

"Trouble's simple," forced laggard lips to say. "Man resents once being dependent on woman spends whole life denying it proving lead in pencil instead rotabunga women helpless dependent on him. Bad for ego saw off legs make him dependent on women again better saw off women's legs make them helpless babies he's got to take care of show he's not big baby. Trouble with Immob—"

"I swear I'll do it. The whole works. Right down your throat."

"Immob symbolic castration quadruple castration. Women

245

all basket cases only solution better amputate clitoris let man be little Commissar in bed doesn't have to play big Commissar on battlefield finally peace in our time."

"Tell me," Neen said. "Tell me this. Why are the pencils different colors? Are there different solutions in them?"

Thought managed to make lips say yes, own voice inaudible hers still filtering through faintly. Seemed she heard nothing saw no movement.

"*Tell me!* Can't you hear me? Are they different solutions?"

Yes, yes, yes, screamed.

Om, Om, Om.

Nothing happened.

Leaned over him now, blob of face inches from his eyes. "You've stopped talking. Maybe you can't talk any more. But your eyelids are still blinking. I want to know if that's automatic or if you can control it. If you can make your eyelids move at will, blink right now. Blink twice. Fast."

Concentrated, poured all dwindling thought into lids. Please God, prayed, make them blink. Take steamrollers off eyelids.

"Very good. So you can blink when you want to. That means you can hear me. Good. Now listen carefully—I'm going to ask some questions. You answer yes or no: one blink yes, two blinks no. Blink once if you understand what I just said."

One blink.

"Fine. Now tell me: do the different colors on the pencils stand for different drugs?"

One blink.

"Is one of them an antidote?"

One blink.

"Which one, the blue?"

Two blinks.

"The green?"

One blink.

"How fast does the antidote work? Is it a matter of minutes?"

Two blinks.

"Hours?"

One blink.

"How many hours? Blink the number."

One blink.

"One hour? You're sure you're not lying to me?"

One blink.

246

"If I give you the antidote, will you promise not to make any trouble when you come to?"

One blink.

"It doesn't make any difference of course. Vishinu and Dai should be here long before that. Even if they're not I've got this revolver—" Aware of faint movement near his nose. "—and I won't hesitate to use it. All right. Shall I give you the whole pencilful?"

One blink.

"Here it is. I'm pouring it between your lips. Try to swallow."

Tried to remember where throat was, concentrated on memory of process called swallowing felt nothing, remembered nothing.

"O.K.," Neen said. "I think I got most of it down. Now we'll wait."

Alienation syrup administered. Body restorer swigged. Five minutes to restoration. In five minutes would be back in skin, antidote real knockout powderful but mustn't let it knock him out. To sleep meant perchance to twitch upon awakening, five minutes hence, invitation to truncheons. Fight it. Remember what Ouspensky wrote on pad beside bed when he took heroin then tried write down essence of mystic experience. Scribbled four words before pencil fell out of hand: "Think in other categories." Very well. Think in these categories. Russian bear never reigns but it paws. Move so much as little finger they break every bone in your body you confess you are old jokester Dr. Martine then curtains. Before antidote slugs you into anti-dotage write yourself note à la Ouspensky, write out prescription for staying alive, write out post-hypnotic suggestion: Don't move. Auto-hypnosis possible, why not auto-post-hypnotic suggestion? In words of Immob lady, don't move. Don't move when you wake up. Dodge blackjack. *Under no circumstances are you to move when your skin comes back. . . .*

Flares in eyeballs.

Soft kettledrumming in ears.

Itch, somewhere. Vague itch somewhere around right shoulder blade.

More. He was no longer free-wheeling thought. Aware of being a thing of mass now, felt body pressing down against the mattress and mattress fighting back. Knew himself subject to the laws of gravity again.

Heaviness in shoulders, legs, arms, even tongue and lips and eyelids. Pressure in the groin. Bodied forth and unsaintly again, capsuled once more in tonus. He could feel. Back from ataxia. Be down to get you in ataxia, Norbert.

Terror: if he could feel maybe he could move. Now that itch is here can spring be far behind? Mustn't move. Must only ascertain whether, and to precisely what extent, he was capable of moving. Springing.

He concentrated on his feet and without taking his eyes from the ceiling he felt that his shoes were on. Good. He could wriggle his toes, at least, without being observed.

He moved his big toes up and down, right one, left, pressing against the inner soles and then against the canvas lining in the caps.

They moved without trouble.

He tried retracting his tongue into his throat. Then he pressed it against his teeth, making sure the throat muscles did not move with it.

Tongue in good working order. Hurt, from the pin.

One hand, he became aware, was lying under his body, which was twisted in an S-shape on the bed. He tried moving the fingers on the bedclothes. They moved.

Generally and motorically speaking, he seemed to be in pretty good shape. If he undertook some broad, complicated movement or series of movements there was a fair chance he could carry them out more or less efficiently.

Excellent. So now he knew where he stood, lay.

Now without his eyes wavering he began to concentrate on Neen, on the presence of Neen. Immediately he knew from the mass of colors off to the right, on the very edge of his vision, that she was still sitting there and that she still had the gun in her hand. Any sign of Vishinu or Dai in the room? As nearly as he could sense, no sign of Vishinu or Dai in the room.

"Can you hear me?"

Neen's voice. He froze inside, fighting the impulse to turn his head and look at her. Fighting especially the impulse to blink. Better to let her think he was unconscious, at least completely insensate. Might arouse her suspicion—she might come closer to investigate.

"I'll give you one more chance. If you hear me, blink."

Silence; then a movement to the right told him she was standing up and coming toward the bed. He concentrated on the perforations in the laminated squares of the lumi-ceiling: must not look at her, must not look at her.

"All right," she said. "Maybe you're lying and maybe you're not. I don't believe you about its taking a whole hour

248

and I'm going to find out." She was standing next to the bed now: must not blink. "If you can hear me, listen. I've got the pin in my hand. I'm going to stick it into you as hard as I can. If you don't scream and hit the ceiling, O.K., I'll admit I was wrong. When you wake up I'll apologize."

All a question of split-second timing now. Everything depended on the niceties of co-ordination now. O.K.: tense, the inward crouch, ready-set—

He didn't move, didn't blink, as the arm rose to the level of her head and poised there for a moment and then plunged downward. When the pin tore into the flesh of his thigh he yelled with the pain of it and something else that was not the pain of it and even as the sound burst from his mouth his free hand was coming down hard, edgewise and palm held stiff, down on that other olive-tinted hand with the gun in it.

The gun went off—no sound but a soft ping: flange must be a silencer—the bullet burrowed through the bedclothes without touching him, even before the smothered sound died away the gun had dropped to the floor with a thud and he was up beside her and twisting her arm behind her back. Pressing so hard she was forced to bend over double, he stooped and picked up the gun.

Twisting, twisting the arm brutally until she whimpered. In a rage—wondering all the while he was hurting her why the image of the pin in her plunging hand still clung to his eyeballs, why it made him want to kill this woman.

"If you want to stay healthy," he said, lips still heavy and inert as though numbed by novocaine, "don't try anything. I'm a little wobbly but I can move fast. And I've got the gun."

"You bastard."

"Sticks and stones," he said. "You'll never get a rise out of Lazarus that way."

He pushed her into a chair, backed over to the bureau and felt around in the top drawer, found a scarf. Then he pulled her to her feet again and fastened her hands behind her with several tight loops. Only now did he become aware of the sharp pain in his leg, he reached down and pulled the pin out. He looked around and in a moment saw what he wanted—the collection of pencils, they were lying on the coffee table next to the bed. He scooped them up.

"Listen, kiddo," he said. "You go for this equal rights kick. Well, I'm going to give you some equal rights—seven cc's of the oceanic, the real cosmic McCoy, exactly what I've just had. Prepare to mingle. Think in other categories."

He shoved her down into the chair again, tilted her head back, forced her mouth open and emptied one of the pencils into her throat. When she choked and tried to spit the fluid out he squeezed the muscles of her neck until she had to relax and swallow.

"It's been nice," he said. "In case I don't run into you again—don't take any wooden legs." He pulled all the sheets from the beds, rolled them into a ball and walked to the door leading out to the sun deck. "Incidentally," he said, turning, "in case you're interested, I *am* a doctor, and I think Martine's jokes about masochism were pretty damned good, even if they *were* a little obscure. Ta-ta, Rosemary. Sweet oceanic dreams. I'll send you a postcard from the Taj Mahal, lamb chop."

His hands were shaking so badly that he had trouble turning the knob on the door.

Shaking—with intention tremor? He knew why they were shaking. It was because, incredibly, he had called her Rosemary.

chapter eighteen

HE WAS ON the forty-third floor, two floors above his own. With the aid of two sheets knotted together and secured to a cylindrical concrete column, he was able to slide down to the sun deck below; then, with the remaining sheets, he repeated the operation. He now had to cross three terraces to the left—easy enough, since the doors connecting them were unlocked. Thanks to the hour, no one was home in any of the rooms he passed. The first light he came upon was in his own room; inside he saw Vishinu and Dai moving around.

Squeezed against the wall to one side of the window, he watched as the two men searched through his belongings. The contents of his valises and bureau drawers were strewn over the floor; the shaving-lotion and toilet-water bottles in which he carried his supplies of rotabunga lay unnoticed on the bureau; stacks of bills were lying on the carpet near the armchair, apparently even large sums of money did not interest the Unioneers. His notebook, concealed within the dust jacket of *The Moral Equivalent of War*, was still where he had put it on the night table.

Vishinu pulled a flannel suit from the closet and began to go through its pockets. The London label did not impress him: he could not know that the suit had come from the wardrobe of the last Russian trade representative stationed in Johannesburg, a gentleman who had preferred to have his clothes made on Bond Street rather than on the Nevski Prospekt.

Dai walked across the room to the night table and picked up the volume lying there. Martine froze, crammed the knuckle of his forefinger into his mouth: this could conceivably be the turning point in Immob history, its Waterloo, the sacking of its Rome, its Gettysburg. Then Vishinu apparently said something to his associate—the Eurasian shrugged, put the book down, and followed his superior from the room.

Martine took his finger out of his mouth and looked at it: there were drops of blood on the knuckle, the whole hand was quivering. Blood: he'd called the girl Rosemary, it was crazy.

They would discover he was gone in a matter of minutes, no time to lose. Best to dispense with luggage altogether, he might have to move fast. Inside the room he hurriedly filled some more pencils with the rotabunga mixtures, then poured what remained in the bottles down the sink. He stuffed his pockets with bills, grabbed his notebook, slipped out as soon as he had made sure there was nobody in the hall. In a moment he reached the emergency stairwell and began the laborious climb down.

By the time he reached the ground floor his legs were aching and he was dizzy with the turnings, but he did not stop to rest. He hurried out of the hotel through the rear exit. The next step, obviously, was to get out of town—but how? Busses, trains and planes were out: no telling where he might run into one of Vishinu's ubiquitous "tourists." Best to play it safe and pick up a car. He needed a car. As soon as he had posed the problem he knew the solution: earlier, in his wandering around town, he had noticed several rental agencies.

Two blocks from the hub, on Henry Adams Street, filled with flickering thoughts about virgins and dynamos, he found an agency that was open: TOM MURRAY'S ROBO-RENT. With the help of a clerk he quickly picked out a fast touring car, a duraluminum dewdrop mounted on three wheels. The clerk prepared the necessary papers and gave them to Martine to sign. He wrote out the first name that came to mind: "Brigham Rimbaud."

"Thank you, Mr. Rimbaud," the clerk said. "Ah, do you have some means of identification with you? It's just a formality, of course, but these machines are pretty expensive and—"

"I'm in a hurry," Martine interrupted. "I haven't had time to go home and pick up my papers. Look, I'll tell you what I'll do." Before the man's astonished eyes he counted out several bills of large denominations and handed them over. "Five thousand," he said. "That'll cover the cost of the car, won't it? I'll leave this as a deposit, so you won't have to worry about my papers."

The clerk gave him a briefing on the operation of the machine—the dashboard was loaded with gadgets he had never seen but he had a quick mechanical mind and he got the idea fast. Minutes later he was speeding out along Tolstoy Boulevard, palms sliming sweat onto the wheel.

He drove for over an hour, mind a turnip; then he checked the mileage indicator and saw with a start that he had come almost 150 miles. Time to pull up and figure out where he was going—bulleting along aimlessly like this, without knowing where the Strip began or ended, he might find himself in deserted country or in some devastated area which hadn't been rebuilt after the war, and he had with him no food whatsoever and no weapon but the automatic he had taken from Neen. What was indicated, obviously, was at least one quick trip into a fair-sized town to pick up some clothes, some rifles and ammunition, and other vital supplies. After that he could hide out almost anywhere.

Lights up ahead: a wayside eating place called ROYALL SMITH'S AUTO-EAT, the "auto" apparently standing for "automatic" as well as "automobile." From the lumi-walled central building of the establishment there fanned out in every direction a series of belt-conveyors; the customer simply drove up to the terminal point of a belt-line, studied the menu, inserted the indicated number of coins in the slots opposite the desired items (if he didn't have change he could get it from a separate machine), pressed a button to register the order, and waited for a couple of minutes until a tray came riding out from the kitchen.

There were only two other cars on the grounds when Martine turned in, their occupants paid no attention to him. He studied the menu, burst out laughing when he noticed tapioca pudding listed among the choices. No, he thought. No. This was no time for tapioca. He decided on coffee and doughnuts, and while waiting for his order unfolded the large map of the Strip which the Robo-Rent clerk had given him. It was devoutly to be hoped that in this non-

Aristotelian society the map to some extent resembled the territory.

He was startled to see the physical dimensions of the Strip. It could hardly amount to more than one-twelfth or one-fifteenth of the overall territory of the old States. Even more striking than its size was its location: the Strip ran roughly north and south, its southernmost tip hundreds of miles from the Gulf of Mexico and the western boundary almost a thousand miles from the Pacific. Dedicated to the oceanic, this society seemed to shrink from the oceans; huddled in the protective shadow of the mountains, those fugitives from marine flabbiness.

The States which had existed before World War III were not indicated on the map. But it would be a fair guess, he thought, that the new, dehumidified America, less than four hundred miles across at its widest point, started somewhere in the vicinity of the Texas Panhandle and eastern New Mexico and ran almost due north through parts of Colorado and Kansas, Wyoming and Nebraska, up into Montana and South Dakota. The picture was complicated, though, by the skinny irregular arms which stretched out more or less laterally from each side of the Strip, rather like the pseudopods of an amoeba. On the west these bands cut separately into Arizona, Utah and the mountainous areas of Montana, petering out in the foothills of the Rockies; on the east, into Oklahoma and Arkansas, Iowa, and Minnesota, each arm stopping short of the Mississippi in true Immob hydrophobia. On the bottommost western arm was the capital, and he saw now why it had been referred to as L.A.—it was Los Alamos, the old atomic-energy center above the bomb-testing grounds at Alamogordo and White Sands. Alamogordo was not indicated; White Sands was a national park.

Where to go? His eye wandered idly up the map, spotting here and there a name that was familiar—Santa Fe, Pueblo, Denver, Oklahoma City, Omaha, Des Moines, Helena—among others which were new, Agassiz, Burbanksville, Schweitzer Falls, Thoreaupolis, Veblentown, Groddeck, Helderfort, Theo City. Then he realized something: he had automatically headed north, northwest, when he started out from New Jamestown, he must have had some destination dimly in mind.

Salt Lake City! He had been pointing toward Salt Lake City like a homing pigeon. Without even knowing whether it was there.

He began to look for it, suddenly excited. There was Salt

Lake, just beyond one of the western arms, but—no Salt Lake City. Then he stiffened: the city was there, all right, but the name had been changed. It was called Martinesburg.

He stared at the dot on the map, hypnotized. It was like being plopped down on Mars and suddenly coming across all the faces one had left down home at the corner drug store.

"O.K.," he said to himself, starting up the motor. "So I'm a sentimental slob. I'll go and visit the old homestead."

Driving was comfortable, even at a clip well over one hundred and fifty. The car was marvelously smooth; besides, it was not so much a matter of driving as of being driven. Now, following the clerk's instructions, he had switched to robo-drive; the car was actually driving itself and he had nothing to do but peer out the window and try to make some split-second sense out of the jumbled black masses that hurtled past in an avalanche of landscape.

He marveled at the electronic brain—actually, he suspected, a quite simple device—which kept the car unswervingly on its path and regulated its speed at every turn. As the clerk had explained, and as he could now see for himself, the whole system of robo-drive depended on clusters of slim, needlelike beams of light which cut across the highway at regular intervals just a few inches from the pavement, emanating from squat mounds of concrete placed alongside the road. On the right-hand side of the car there was a photoelectric-cell mechanism which intercepted these rays and transmitted their messages to the robot brain, so that actually the robot was receiving instructions on how to guide the car every few hundred feet. It was these rays which told the automatic driver when it was deviating a few inches to the left or right; when it was slacking off a couple of miles or infinitesimally picking up speed; when there was another car in the same lane up ahead, or when there was a curve coming and what the speed should be reduced to to negotiate it safely; when it was safe to accelerate again.

It was ironic, Martine thought, that as a result of technology one of the last refuges of the frontiering ego in America—the automobile, the jalopy, streamlined Old Paint—had been all but abolished. Early in the century, once the venerable horse had disappeared, all the conveyances developed for speedier transportation seemed calculated to give men a feeling of complete helplessness and passivity, a sense that they were mere bundles of freight to be lugged from one place to another: the trolley, the bus, the train, the plane. Paralleling what had happened in other areas of life, travel too had become uterine. Only in his own automobile, at the hydromatic reins, could a man still recapture some of the old frontiersman's thrill of domineering his trusty old pinto, of being in control, of doing rather than bing done to: *he* pushed the buttons. But now, with robodrive, the motorist too had become passive baggage; the mechanism had taken over and turned its electronic back on him. You could turn it off or on—that was the limit of human intervention.

Just now, however, Martine was grateful for the car's self-sufficiency; he was dog-tired, and groggy from the rota and anti-rota, and driving at any speed would have been a considerable strain. Besides, his left arm hurt where Vishinu had jabbed it with the pin. From time to time he curled his arms around the steering wheel, let his head drop, and dozed off. He had no idea how long he slept in these cat naps, but awakening from one of them he found that it was daylight and that he had come close to a thousand miles.

He had a strong desire, suddenly, to see Salt Lake; his eyes were starved for the sight of water. It was out of his way, since he was approaching from the southeast and the city was this side of the lake, but he took over control for a moment and turned into a roundabout route which would allow him to indulge his whim. The country he was heading into now, being headed into, took on a more familiar aspect: occasionally snow-sprinkled mountain peaks loomed up over to the west, the vegetation was getting scraggly and thinning out into increasingly barren stretches. The feel of what had been Utah was beginning to haunt him again, stirring old memories of hunting and fishing trips with his father—youthful explorations which had brought him closer to a feeling of oneness with the world about him, probably, than anything before or since.

Now, finally, he was speeding into the flats of the lake country. And there, at last, was the lake itself, that briny expanse of feminine yieldingness which, as his muscles could still remember, possessed such sturdy resistance that it would refuse to let a man break its resilient skin and sink into its ambience: breast that became springier with each reluctant inch of giving, breast that gave not like molasses but like foam rubber, within the deceptively flaccid flesh a fist.

He recalled how, when he swam here as a child, it had always been a challenge to him to pierce the gravity-snubbing armor of these falsely gentle waters, so acquiescent on the surface, so defiant underneath; how he had always tried desperately, with wily dives and wrigglings, to pierce their stand-offishness; how he had always failed, and been left at the end with a vague unnamable sense of defeat and frustration. He had wanted somehow to be bold, firm, arrowlike, remorselessly heavy and compact, like the incorruptible stern alps over in the mountain ranges, but always the lapping passive waters, seemingly without effort, had made a fool of him. *Mother* Nature! No wonder a sort of momism had always been attributed to Nature by men (while the paternal principle was generally located in the temporal: *Father* Time). Inside all Nature's cushions was a spine of steel. One reclined on her breast only to be buffeted and stung—if one chose to take it personally.

Mother Nature yielded and clutched, gave way and snarled, parted and overwhelmed—there were *two* mothers in Nature, as there were in every man's infantile memories: one that was all haughty omnipotent willful strength, another that was all softness and quiescence: alp and ocean— hardly surprising that Nature's most peculiar children should do the same and that out of this built-in contradictoriness, this chronic all-at-onceness, should create finally that living death, that furious ultimate interpenetration of aggression and passivity, of push and pull, of Eros and Thanatos, known as Immob. . . . He remembered how, as a kid, he had often given up his struggles to breach the lake's rejection and had simply turned on his back and floated, face turned to the warming sun, eyes closed and will jettisoned. In the defeat there had been a quiet exhilaration, as of a quest ended and some hit-or-miss jejune Brahman achieved merely through abandonment of effort. Oh, the seeds of Immob had been in him too. His own being was drenched with ample dosages of both rota and ganja. Immob was a macaronic melt of East and West—so was he.

He was plunging, being plunged, through the flat stretches of salt licks and alkali wastes now: the blanched dead landscape was good to see. Here in his youth he had always had a feeling of respite and peace, but now he could put into faltering words what had been utterly beyond articulation in those days. Here the skin of protoplasm, foliage and teeming soil, had been stripped from the earth and the underlying hard unassailable skeleton exposed to be bleached by the sun—there was about this eerie petrified whiteness an air of the ultimate, of finality, of having hit bottom; kaleidescope of rigor mortis. In expanses of trees and plants and jumbled greenery, the earth's squirming epidermis, there was always the suggestion of struggle and strife (the old Notoa); here nothing stirred, nothing thirsted to be other than itself, to become; petrified pre-nativity everywhere, nothing but immutable dead-weight being (the new, loboto-mized Notoa)—the core of steel had sprung nakedly from the flesh. It was somehow momentarily comforting to be in a place where life had turned to a stone, crusty mass which chips and crumbles when hit but never yields and parts and falsely flows—where matter is so completely drained of its disgusting juices that its tissues have hardened to unde-viating calcium and salt.

And he saw that there was a parable in the scene—if you wanted to take it personally. This was the answer to the contradictoriness in Nature and its wild protoplasmic excess called man—death, petrifaction. Short of the final achievement of inertness there was to be no real inertness, no untainted ease, no indivisible peace. It could be lamented, if you wanted to waste the time—it couldn't be changed. There was this way, and only this way, to resolve the ten-sion between mountain and ocean, and within each moun-tain and ocean: to strip down to skeleton. For it was this wracking polarity which infused the teeming skin of the earth and the flesh of the living creature, breathed life into soil and flesh, motored their pulsations. Every cell contained a seething mixture of Eros and Thanatos; ambivalence was its glue and tension its spark. And Immob, like Mandunga, had come about because people had forgotten that all the warring pairs were indissolubly linked—they'd developed too much of a taste for consistency. Yes, the two-way stretch between heaven and hell so abominated by the Manichees existed in every turbulent cell. And the Manichees had been right: the only way to avoid this tension was to commit suicide. It was clear enough, Mandunga was one of the oldest, and Immob the newest, Manichean technique for committing mass suicide—in the name of consistency. Men would reduce themselves to mounds of tapioca, and even-tually to spatters of bleached alkali, to avoid being caught in a contradiction. And fight another war, a thumpingly pacifist war, along the way.

It was an idea at once revelatory and absurd—it seemed to explain much, but any effort to explain so much was downright preposterous: only paranoiacs want to encompass everything. But there was no more time for musing, he was approaching the suburbs of Martinesburg.

With a grunt of relief he switched over to manual operation, as his fingers gripped the wheel he thrilled to the feel of pulsing power once more subservient to his will. He'd had too much of passive thought, good to be doing something with his hands again.

But why, a few hours ago, had his hands wanted to kill Neen? And trembled when, unaccountably, he had called her—Rosemary?

The city had not been so much overhauled as filled in and expanded: there were many buldings and even whole blocks that were substantially as he remembered them but they were interlarded with skyscrapers, Immob recruiting centers, branches of the M. E. University, all plastered with the usual Immob slogans—the archaic sandwiched with the unprecedented, as always in America. There, for example, was the University of Utah, were his father had been a professor at the world's first atomic medical school and where he himself had completed his undergraduate studies before going on to study brain surgery in New York: many new buildings had been added, the entire institution was now called RADIATION RESEARCH LABS. And there was the old Mormon tabernacle, it was now the MUSEUM OF IMMOB CULTURE.

He parked in the shopping center, and for the next two hours was busy with his purchases. At CHAMP BROSSARD'S ROD AND GUN CENTER he bought several rifles and cartons of shells, plus a full wardrobe of warm camping clothes, a camp stove, oil lamps, eating utensils; at AL ERSKINE'S ELECTRONIC APPLIANCES, a portable television set; at ANNE WINTER'S FOOD MART, several cases of canned foods; at FRANK SCHWARTZ'S SUPERIOR STATIONERY, a half-dozen notebooks in which to continue his jottings; at LINN JONES' FINE LIQUOR SHOP, a few bottles of sour mash, once his favorite whiskey; at BOBBIE REITZ'S FOUR SEASONS BOOKSTORE, all the Immob pocketbooks and texts he could find, everything from Tolstoy down to Helder; at DOTTIE CLARK'S BAKE SHOP, a case of vacuum-packed chocolate layer cakes, the pièce de resistance of his childhood gormandizing; at JIM MAHER'S SERVICE STATION, some spare energy capsules for his car; finally, at JOHN MUNDY'S SNACK CORNER, two hamburgers which he consumed on the spot. Now he could go into hiding for months, if necessary. Five or six months, anyhow. He remembered Vishinu's deadline: the world had been given a suspended sentence for a few months, five or six.

Where to now? Where did one go to dodge the Martine ocean? The mountains, of course. But first—he thought, with sudden apprehension—it wouldn't hurt to play the nostalgic prodigal for a few minutes and take a look at the old homestead. Assuring himself that it was a silly whim, he climbed back in the car and drove out toward the University.

For a moment after he parked the car he was sure he had come to the wrong place: the houses on either side seemed as he remembered them but his own house was not there. When he looked more closely he saw what the trouble was. The original house was not gone, it had only been swallowed up by several new wings and glass-enclosed sun porches and heavy landscaping which hid it from the street. In addition, a high brick wall had been put up just back of the sidewalk, terminating in an elaborate iron grillework gateway; on the gate itself was a metal plaque.

Martine went over and read the inscription:

The Martine House.

Home of
DR. MARTINE
(*1945-1972*)

"He is not gone; he has
but become the ocean; let
us humbly drink."—HELDER

Over the gate was an arch decorated with iron flutings and curlicues, many of them wound around little triskelions filled with running pros, and in the center of it a large bronze bas-relief: a steamroller, with a man perched proudly on top of it rather like a gunner emerging from a tank, man triumphant over the machine, the rider with raised fist indomitable and the machine helplessly couchant, brought to its knees. But the man's fist was an Immob fist, the arm was a mesh of tubing and coils, so were all his limbs—he had subdued the machine by making himself into the machine. Peculiar sort of victory, won by incorporating the enemy

259

into oneself. If imitation was the sincerest form of flattery, the overwhelmed machine had won the fight hands down: the master had become the mirror image of the slave.

Martine's hand jerked uneasily, went up to his beard. He had just noticed the face of the man who straddled the metal dragon: it was his own, his face of twenty-odd years ago, sans whiskers and irony. Well, he was safe in his disguise.

There was more lettering, done in twisted iron, under the sculpture: THIS HISTORICAL SITE HAS BEEN PRESERVED AS A NATIONAL SHRINE AND REST HOME BY THE DAUGHTERS OF IMMOB HISTORICAL SOCIETY. Leave it to the girls.

"My God," Martine said to himself, "I used to pick my nose in this place, now it's a shrine. You can't be too careful."

The sky was overcast, everything gray, he saw the lights go on in one of the long sun parlors on the ground floor. The gate was open. He slipped inside, quickly hid himself among the bushes, and approached the glassed-in room. Long drapes hung· from the ceiling on all sides, but at several points they had been pulled apart a bit to allow for ventilation through open window panels. Standing on the grass to one side of an aperture he could see slantwise into the room and hear the voices inside.

At first glance the room looked like a nursery: there were some eighteen or twenty baby carriages standing in a row along the long wall of the porch. In a moment he realized that the occupants of the carriages (some of them lying in pairs, their heads at opposite ends of their double baskets) were all quadros, covered with fluffy baby blankets like the Antis he had seen in Marcy's window. Two women were standing near Martine with their backs turned, bending over one of the carriages; he judged that the dumpy gray-haired one was quite old, the tall lean one considerably younger, they could be mother and daughter. Inside the house, he could see, several Pros were grouped around a ping-pong table: apparently this was a rest home for Pros and Antis alike.

As the women talked and fussed over the one boy, Martine studied the faces of the others. They seemed to be paying no attention to the conversation, most of them were awake but their eyes were blank, fixed on the ceiling. Except for the women's murmurous voices and the clicking from the ping-pong table inside, the place seemed as hushed as a doll's house. Only the blinking of the unfocused eyes in the carriages provided a touch of animation. Somebody inside turned on a radio: Bessie Smith's voice, singing "Empty Bed Blues."

Old Ubu should see the scene on this porch, Martine thought; he'd go green with envy. Here was the graveyard of tonus. These young warriors had given up their spears and bolos for good. They might raise their voices, never their fists.

At this moment, though, the amp hidden by the women *was* raising his voice, and emphatically. "You're wasting your time," he said. "I told you I'm going and I'm going."

"Why you?" the younger woman said bitterly. "Why must it always be you?"

At the sound of her voice, Martine's shoulders hunched, the carping tone set his teeth on edge.

"You know perfectly well why," the amp said, with the infinite condescension of a teacher explaining sums to a backward child. "You know I have responsibilities the others don't have. I *must* be the first."

"What good does it do?" the woman went on. "Lying around in department store windows, mercy sakes, it's undignified."

"If people want to see you," the old woman added, "they can come here."

Her voice was niggling and sad, Martine's throat tightened.

"That's not the point," the boy said petulantly, "and you know it. It's not a question of their wanting to see me. It's my duty to go to them."

"But what can *you* do?" the first woman said. "You're just a baby."

"I may be a baby to *you*," the amp said icily, "but it just so happens that to the rest of the country I'm president of the Anti-Pro League. And this is a critical moment, morale has been badly shaken by Vishinu's speech. I can't just lie here and do nothing."

"Vishinu was talking about Theo," the younger woman insisted. "If Theo doesn't like it, why, let *him—*"

"Let him nothing. It's people like Theo who've gotten us into this mess. Look, apparently you don't understand how serious this is. It's a crisis."

"All right," the younger woman said. "All right. But if you have to make a display of yourself, why not do it in some store window right here in Martinesburg? Why go hundreds of miles to Los Alamos? Nobody in Los Alamos sent for you."

"Naturally they haven't sent for me. They're afraid of me.

You can see, even the Pros around here in the Home have been avoiding me lately. They're all scared."

"Then why go? Why bother at all?"

"Can't you understand *anything?* L.A. is the center of the panic. That's where all the hysteria starts. What's needed is a special demonstration, some unusually striking gesture, right at the national capital, to shock our leaders and win them back to true Immob before it's too late. We're trying to contact our brothers in the East Union to do the same thing at New Tolstoygrad, maybe we'll be able to synchronize our demonstrations, but in any case we've got to go ahead. There's going to be a special concentration of our forces at the capital and I've got to lead it—it's as simple as that."

A few carriages away, one of the other quadros coughed delicately. He coughed again. When nothing happened he let out a long, low whistle, his vague eyes still riveted on the ceiling. Both women straightened up, the thin one walked down to the signaling amp, reached under his blanket and drew out a bedpan.

Dully, uncomprehendingly, Martine stared at her pinched sharp features, then at the puffy wrinkled tearful face of the old woman.

"My mind's made up," the first amp said. "Don't waste your breath arguing with me."

"Stubborn," the young woman said bitterly. "Just like his father." She turned and went inside.

The boy's face was directly in Martine's line of vision now. It was like all the other Anti faces he had seen—the face of a somehow wizened baby, fixed in an authoritative scowl that was at the same time an infantile pout, the expression one of mingled hauteur and fret, insouciance and incipient tantrum. It was a sophisticated-suckling face imperiously demanding the universe for a teat and yet filled with rage over the prior knowledge, the dotard's sour knowledge, that all breasts this side of Paradise must have some frustrating fist buried in them. So, mixed with the childishly headstrong was an infinite senile pique.

But, for all its stock Antiness, there was something distinctive about this one face, something which set it off from the others. Buried somewhere under the typical was a suggestion of the individual. Martine could hardly bear to look at it, it was the face on the bas-relief outside, the unwhiskered steamroller-subduing Martine face minus melancholy and mischief. His own face. He was back twenty-five years, looking into a mirror.

"Then *go* and save the world," the younger woman said angrily. She was back on the porch, the bedpan gone from her hands. "Be a hero like your father. When do you intend to leave?"

"For God's sake, Mother, don't take on so," the amp said. "*Will* you try to understand?"

"When *are* you leaving?" the older woman echoed.

"I leave for L.A. next Tuesday," the amp said. "They're sending a plane up for me. Listen, Grandma, you've got to make mother understand. That's *your* duty."

"I'll do my best, Tom," the old woman said helplessly. "But I'm not sure *I* understand. Generation after generation, boys running off and doing silly things just to hurt their mothers—oh, I don't understand anything any more." She began to cry.

"You've got to try," the amp said. "A fellow in my position can't just turn his back on the world. People expect things of me."

"Go right ahead," the younger woman said. "Run off and get yourself killed. There's good precedent for it. . . . Oh, honestly, sometimes I just can't understand why you don't forget this silly window business and put some arms and legs on and act normal like other boys your age."

The amp yawned, his eyes were beginning to glaze. "If you don't mind," he said, "I'd like another helping of that chocolate layer cake we had for lunch, and a large glass of milk. I'm hungry."

"His father just loved chocolate layer cake," old Mrs. Martine said through her tears.

"Like father, like son," Irene said.

"I hope so," Tom Martine mumbled. "But it's a heck of a responsibility."

Sins of the fathers—
Like father like—
"But he volunteered! If all the wounds of babies—if they volunteer! No other virus!"

He was just thinking it to himself. But he heard the words, it was more than he could stand, they plowed through the water to him. Somebody screaming the words at him, an electrovox, bellowing, trumpeting under the water. Himself screaming, lips moving against the pressing waters, throat bulging with the words. . . .

263

Head spun like a badminton bird, churning the waters. Saw the white lacerated body of Rosemary scudding gently by in the water, trailing strands of kelp, and yelled, "She's got nothing to do with this! Leave her alone!" Losing support, falling, falling, clutching at the window sill as he went down, afraid that if he fell into the bottomless smothering basket of the lake and the two women bent over him with their niggling and their needling he would have to kill them and—

The waters closed over his head. Kelp stuffing his nostrils. Limp, floating.

Odd sense of levitational drift: body being raised, carried up, then up again, then dumped. . . .

chapter nineteen

. . . . For a long time he lay at the bottom of the lake, flat on his back, unintentioned as a mollusk. Once in a while, thinking it over, he began to resent the indignity of it and started to fight—wanted to bolt up to the surface, up to the top where the surface shimmered and rippled, through the skin of the surface and out into the open where he could breathe. Then lay back meekly in his shell-walled basket and studied the snow-capped mountain rising up proudly and indifferently on the other side of the surface, he could just make out its wavery outlines. Wanting to get up there and stretch. But steel clamps on his arms, malicious fingers, held him back every time. He cried out in his fury, "The program is to be ambulatory! Must run around and round the triskelion! Otherwise, don't you see. . . ."

After a time, many rages later, exhausted, he opened his eyes slowly, oysters unbuttoning, lids pushing against the water. It took a while for things to become clear through the soapy silt-sprinkled muck. He began to feel reassured as objects swam through to him: maple bureau against the wall, old browned chromo of Brigham Young just above it, white bookcase with small plastic radio on the top shelf, closet door with its chipped porcelain knob. It was good to be back in his grotto-room. In the closet, on a hook, was his catcher's mitt, well-oiled, fully broken in; maybe, if it was a nice day, he'd go over to the park after breakfast and play baseball with the kids for a while. Just outside the open window the leaves of the old mulberry tree rustled, stirring up eddies in the gelatinous fluid. It was dark outside, forest of seaweed.

How come he was awake at this hour? If the day turned out sunny a fast game of ball, maybe just some batting practice, would be fine—

No. What day was coming up? Might be Friday. If it was Friday his father might be coming home from the University in the mood for a hunting trip. They might round up their gear and pile into the station wagon, just the two of them, and go off to the cabin in the mountains, up out of the clutching waters, for the week-end: his mother would be at the curb, they'd wave good-bye to her, her lake-face would be kind of tight and sad and something like accusation in her tired washed-out polyp eyes, they were running out on her again. . . .

Next to Brigham Young's portrait on the wall, dim in the marine murk, something that didn't belong there. Some kind of plaque, his eyes strained to pick out the letters: HERE DR. MARTINE SPENT THE FIRST FIFTEEN YEARS OF HIS LIFE. . . . Under water, of course. Ancient sub-mariner.

Something else in the room that didn't belong. Some person. His mother, sitting quietly to one side of the bed, shawled with algae. Something wrong with her, she was much grayer and older, years older, she'd aged forty years overnight. It terrified and saddened him and he wanted to cry when he saw her wrinkled flotsam-jetsam face, studded with barnacles, but he understood that this aging was part of the accusation, her way of getting back at him, it bothered him so much he tried again to sit up. Eels held him like ropes.

"No, no," she said. "You must rest. You're very weak."

"He was weak too, just a kid," he said bitterly. "Why did you let him do it? You could have stopped him, tried, anyway. Why didn't anybody try to stop him? Just because he was weak enough to go and volunteer to get them cut off, *volunteer.* . . ."

She didn't understand the obscenity, just sat there staring at him with shocked accusing agar-agar eyes. She was looking ocean-bed accusations at him, he was screaming fathoms-deep accusations at her. It had to stop, now with the flood.

"Well, Christ, what's the sense in looking so hurt, anyhow? If they want to run away from you for a week-end, back away to save face, if they insist on running around in circles, triskelions, what's so terrible? It's their virus, not yours, don't you see? Always the backing away a little and the accents of remorse, the flaws in the flesh. Why take on so? God, you needn't age forty years about it. . . ." All he wanted to do was to put his arms around her and kiss her now to show it was all right, the backing away didn't mean anything, but he couldn't move against the lake's pressure.

"You're feverish," she said sympathetically—a little frightened too. "Try to rest, I'll get the doctor." Bubbles cascading from her mouth.

She got up and breast-stroked toward the door, he made another desperate effort to rise through the water, had to explain before it was too late. Important to put his arms around her but the pressure.

But her nervous harried jellyfish face was gone. He fell back on the bed, arms and legs like sash weights socketed into his body, anchors, he couldn't move. So easy to reach out across the vicious distance and embrace her, what arms were for, but not with all the viscious waters pressing. Always water there. In a minute she was back, behind her came a quadro-amp doctor with something in his hand and two mono-amp orderlies. Behind them, Irene, with taut beleaguered ruin of a porpoise face.

"You say he fainted?" the doctor said.

"Just outside the sun porch," his mother said. "We heard something—he was shouting something about babies and wounds, he kept repeating a name, Rose something. He was unconscious when we got to him."

"We had him brought up here," Irene said. "It's the only vacant room."

"When he came to he began to talk very excitedly again," his mother said. "Oh, he's so upset. . . ."

"Why won't you understand!" he said weakly. Every word an effort now, the lake was smothering him, mouth stuffed with sponges. "The joke's on him, not you! It was voluntary! If he tries to pretend now that you always snatched the cake away. . . . It's simply not your sin, you must see that! There are sins of the sons too! Addicts of steamrollers and accents of panic. If they go hunting for their wounds, who's to blame? No matter how many Rosemarys they go after. . . . But oh God, oh God, couldn't you have stopped him? You might have tried. Maybe you could have held him down *before* the doctor came. . . ."

There was no way to make it clear: now he broke down and wept, it was all too late. No way to reach her and comfort her in the seaweed. His body shook with sobs, the waters swirled.

"He's delirious, all right," the doctor said through the bubbling waters.

"Maybe he'll snap out of it if he sleeps a little," Irene said.

"I'll give him a shot. It'll quiet him down."

The doctor held up his hand, in it was a hypodermic needle. He signaled to the orderlies, they drifted in from either side as the doctor came close. The two women swam close too, his mother on the left, Irene on the right.

"No!" Martine screamed. "No tapioca in my veins, absolutely not! Too much rota in the blood stream already, enough robo-drive and scalpels! I almost killed Neen for less, I warn you! If you want to immobilize me you'll have to cut off my arms and legs, that's all there is to it! I won't volunteer! Don't come near me!"

As the hands descended on him from both sides he began once more to struggle, tried to, but the waters were tightening on him like a strait jacket now, his cravings basketed, whale-bellied, and far above, on the other side of the surface, there was the snowy mountain top, agonizingly out of reach.

He was lying back helplessly in the submerged basket, belly, the women were treading water just over him, faces questioning, accusing. Someone was rolling up his sleeve, the needle was drawing near, now the accents of panic and no panic controls for these accents, he was already one of them in his heart.

"So terribly wounded!" he yelled as the needle went in, sobbing now. "Oh God, God, so voluntarily cut to bits! If only somebody could have stopped him but the sins of the fathers, the mythological cakes, over and over the needles—"

". . . . something," from the bony white-gilled Irene face bending over, it sent gusts of panic through his chest. "What is it about his voice?"

"There, there," from his mother's blotchy plankton face as she patted his drenched forehead and he cringed at the touch. "It'll be all right. A little sleep. . . ."

"I want," he wept. "There are sins of sons too, that's the only thing that saves us, if it's voluntary. . . ."

Then the salty waters, oceans of tears, filled up his mouth and sloshed through his brain and dissolved his spine, gurgling softly into his fingers and toes, and there was no more talk or thought. "I'm glad I didn't kill Neen," he glubbed, and that was all for a long time. . . .

When he opened his eyes there was a white-coated orderly sitting at the side of the bed.

He felt a pain in his upper arm—where the needle had gone. A sudden fright: if they'd rolled his sleeve up all the way, they must have uncovered the tattoo. Irene would immediately have recognized the tattoo, she knew all about it.

He sighed in relief. The pain was in his left arm. The tattoo was on his *right* arm.

Dark outside. The mulberry leaves rustling.

"How do you feel?" the orderly said.

"Pretty good. I'm hungry. How long did I sleep?"

"Two hours, about. What would you like to eat?"

"A large glass of milk, please."

"You bet. Anything else?"

"A piece of chocolate layer cake, if there's any." But that wouldn't take him long. "And—maybe a couple of boiled eggs."

"Right. Take it easy, I'll be right back."

The white jacket rose, went out. Martine gave him a few seconds, then jumped up, shaking his head to drive the fog away. He found his coat in the closet—automatically looking at the hook in the corner to see if his catcher's mitt was there: it was—put his shoes on, went into the hall and crept down the back stairs he knew so well. Nobody around.

Out into the deserted grounds, place entirely dark except for a light in the kitchen. Through the gate, a little wobbly now but all right, out in the open air again, surfaced at last. Afraid that if he didn't get away from there fast he would rush back into the house, find the two women, throw himself at their feet and tell them everything, begging for forgiveness. . . .

Sins of the fathers. He got back to the car all right, nobody saw him. Sins of the fathers. Neen had sketched him that way, but it had needed his own son to bring the sketch to life. Sins of the fathers. The phrase caromed through his mind as, purely by reflex, he started up the car and guided it out to the main thoroughfare and then through the deserted center of town. Sins of the fathers—in those four words now was more sickness than he had ever known.

During most of his adult life he had been caught up in a certain malaise, a modest recurrent nausea with the slimy fetid facts of living, but it had not bothered him especially: he had taken it with only faint queasiness as no more than the normal dole of human distress. What he was feeling now with the intimacy of love, of digestion, was more than that, some misery entirely different in kind from any he knew about—a sickness unto and beyond death, a feeling of being trapped in death and still breathing, of being dead with full lip-curling awareness of it and the stench fuming in his nostrils. His nervous system had grown a special receptor, keen as a taste bud, to savor the poisonous fact. Sins of the fathers. He had seen death in the flesh, his own flesh, his own irremediably maimed flesh, lying impotent and peevish in a perambulator, covered over with a blue baby blanket. Yesterday he had joked about being an ambulatory basket case; today he had seen himself as a perambulatory basket case. Flesh of his flesh, blood of his blood, sin of his sin, death of his death: he had seen himself lying there, irascible stone, unmanned and frozen in tantrum: messiah in tantrum. He had looked on death's face in his own face and now he knew its greasy bloated chalky physiognomy. Death was a huddling in ersatz wombs, face fixed in a suckling's pout. Death was a cocoon you spun yourself, with synthetic umbilical cords of your own making. A self-crippling, then a tyrannical shouting of orders to the world such as is allowed only to cripples. A hacking off of hands and feet so that the clucking womenfolk must wait on you hand and foot. The peremptory whimper for chocolate cake, the delicate whistling for mamma to come fetch the bedpan. Deadly sins of the death-ridden fathers.

He was out of town now, approaching the flat salt graveyard again. He pulled up at the side of the road and put his head down and sat for a while, shaking all over, sharp in his mind the image of death the imperishable infant with the babyface of Martine. When the attack had passed he wiped his eyes and drove on again, westward across the crusted alkalis.

But what, precisely, *were* the sins of the fathers? What sins, precisely, had he committed that had come to be visited upon his son with the surgeon's knife? Where did his responsibility begin for this violation of his own flesh—what scurvy paternity was he to claim here? What of himself lay back in Martinesburg, enshrined in that baby carriage? Like father, like son? But how, exactly?

He did not know. But he did know that the father had carried some undetermined death in his flesh and had passed it on in some undetermined way to the flesh of his flesh, and now in looking on the face of his son had seen there death—and it *was* himself. And there was sin in it. And he must find the name for that sin which ran in a reeking mucid line from notebook to perambulator or he was nothing but death. Death, some kind of death, was the sin, it had somehow existed in the father's myth and been bodied forth in the son's flesh. He, sinful father, had come nine thousand miles in search of himself and found what he was looking for in a baby carriage under a baby blanket, pouting for messiahdom

269

and chocolate cake. Now he had to find out what of himself, exactly, lay in that baby carriage. There, neatly packaged taunt, was the innermost identity he had been moved to seek under all the incognitos. The dredging was done with, the corpse of Martine had been located.

He would not relinquish control of the car to the robo-drive, he kept it on manual. Drunk on his misery, he hardly noticed the road, but old habits, long buried, stirred again to keep him going safely and in the right direction. Thirty-five years ago he had traveled this route time after time with his father, his muscles had not forgotten the turns.

He thought of Martine Senior, his father. Good American father, intense in his work and a bit ineffectual away from it, a bit uncomfortable in the presence of his women, delighted to escape from the too correct too demanding environment of women whenever he could manage a week-end hunting or fishing trip into a falsely exclusive world where men provided and cooked their own food in an orgy of self-sufficient camaraderie. Life for him, as for most of his colleagues and contemporaries, had been dotted with these wistful charades of rough-and-ready masculine brotherhood. . . . Now his, Martine Junior's, hands, tense with nostalgia, guided the steering wheel along the old and long forgotten escape route into the mountains—like father, like son. . . .

It was close to two hours before the paved highway ended and the familiar dirt road began the final ascent into the steep mountain range. Automatically, Martine slowed down to navigate the bumps; automatically, when he came to the narrower lane that branched off toward the lake, his hands maneuvered the swerve.

Several miles more and he was there: the lake, surrounded by a growth of pines thick as a muff, was a sheet of isinglass glinting in the moonlight, exactly as he remembered it. And there, in the little grove beyond which the mountain soared up again, was the cabin.

When he trained his flashlight on it he saw that it had not been used for a long time: most of the windows were broken, the brick chimney had collapsed, a tree had fallen over on the porch, bashing in the flimsy roof. Chances were that he would be safe here, at least for a time. Five or six months anyhow, with luck.

It was chilly now, he shivered in his light clothes, but he was well prepared for that. He was safe, from everything but his thoughts. For a time he would provide his own

tinned chocolate cake and evaporated milk, handle his own
bedpans, nurse his dreams of omnipotence, quake in his
nightmares of impotence, the archetypical frontiersman taking
to his (electronic) horse in flight from his women. But the
hunter's log cabin was only a thinly disguised baby carriage.
Now, to be sure, he was in flight from something a lot more
substantial than mom-mythologized-into-monster; still, he
had the uncomfortable feeling that, just as in the old days,
he was running at top speed from a mirage—from something
in himself. Some voyage of self-discovery! One mad scramble
after another.

Dully, he tried to order the events of the last two days in
his mind: they were swimming in improbability. He knew
from the gnawing in his stomach that he had hardly eaten
for the last twenty-four hours, from the ache in his bones
that he had hardly slept for twice that long. He could just
barely drag himself from the car, he wanted only to flop
down and sleep, but he had to eat something first and there
were no women about to summon with a cough and a whistle.

Sweating with the effort, he carried most of his supplies
into the cabin, arranged a cot in the corner so that he could
crawl into it when he was ready. Then he opened a can of
beans and gulped down its contents without bothering to
heat them.

It now occurred to him: he had come close to being
killed last night.

How, the enormity of how it could have happened, still
wasn't clear to him, but there was no blinking the simple
fact: he had almost had it. Tomorrow, no doubt, when he
was functioning again, he would receive the full impact of
that brush with death and quiver—now it was simply one
more insipid fact among others: porch staved in, son in a
perambulator, mother and ex-wife alive, beans cold, wind
blowing in through the broken windows, he had almost been
killed by Vishinu and Dai last night. He was no longer capable
of reacting, when the nerves were too heavily overloaded
they finally stopped oscillating altogether, went dead. Now
he wanted only the blessed release, the death-in-installment,
of sleep.

He fell on the cot without removing his clothes and pulled
the thick blankets up over his body and closed his eyes. The
next moment he started up in a cold sweat, thinking about
Neen's hand poised with the pin in it. He remembered that
one of the cartons he hadn't brought in from the car was the
small brown one marked DOTTIE CLARK'S NONPAREIL CHOCO-

LATE CAKE—he'd noticed it, grimaced, quickly pushed it to the rear of the luggage compartment and forgotten about it. As soon as he'd closed his eyes he'd seen a painfully sharp image of the carton—the lid was slowly rising, sickeningly rising, Pandora's box on the point of disgorging its horrors— he'd known that something monstrous, a woman's hand with a murderous sharp instrument in it, was about to emerge from its depths and he'd jerked up in dread.

With the feeling that it was all a dreary repetition. He'd sat up like this, sweaty, taut, once before. Not long before his fourth birthday, in that Victorian house on a side street of Salt Lake City. He'd been ill for three days, some virus, tossing for hours at a time in delirium, lying there helpless and drenched while his mother bathed his face and tended the bedpans; he'd just passed the crisis the night before, finally, he was still feverish and there were moments of wobbling consciousness. He couldn't understand what they meant by a virus: somehow, without having words for it, he had felt that this wracking illness was some malevolent thing that had been deliberately done to him. There had been a great unspoken tearful feeling of abuse.

Waking that morning after the crisis, he had found his mother sitting anxiously at the bedside and immediately, in a weak martyrish voice, he had asked for chocolate cake. His mother had caressed his brow, explained in her niggling sad voice (she had her martyrdoms too, he thought now with surprise) that the doctor would not allow him to eat anything solid yet—she would bring him some beef broth so that he could get strong again and then he could have all the chocolate cake he wanted. That would not do, he refused to listen to her patient medical explanations. He knew only one thing: she was refusing him, she always refused him. He had already been treated badly enough—if "they" put this "virus" in him the least they could do now to make it up to him was to give him some chocolate cake! In a rush of indignation he'd sat up in bed, all his feeble energies mobilized by his fury, and begun to yell at the top of his lungs, demanding—not whistling, not whimpering, but screaming out his imperious-impotent orders. She had not been able to quiet him, in a panic she had finally summoned the doctor. To end the tantrum the doctor had given him an injection of a strong opiate: he still remembered how his mother held him down while the doctor approached his arm with the hypodermic needle, in some hallucinatory perception it had seemed to him that it was his mother who was descending upon him with a murderous needle in her hand, needle, knife, dagger, something, he'd screamed in terror. And after that, in later years, the same theme had recurred many times in his dreams—often there was some ominous figure of a woman padding through his sleep, reaching for him with some needle or knife. And so (oh, yes, this sickening thought had occurred to him once much later, during his analysis: then he'd thrust it away from him), fifteen years later, he had chosen for himself a career of using humanitarian hypos and knives on others: do unto others as ye feel ye have been done to, done in, undone, yourself. And so, years after *that*, he had huddled miserably in a bunk plane in the Congo, writing down an elaborate dirty joke about people using knives on themselves, of their own volition: whence volampism. . . .

He'd sat up like this a second time—almost twenty years later, in New York, on a psychoanalyst's couch in a room overlooking the East River. (A point about compulsive repetition, he thought now in his misery: he, the enemy of compulsion and repetition, advocate of the voluntary and the spontaneous and the unprecedented, had been springing up from the same bad dream all his life long, like a jumping jack.) Throat muscles rope-tight, as before, sweating as before, scream rising from compressed lungs as before. Remembering the scene from his childhood, muscles reminiscing as well as mind. Why the intense emotion, the quaver in his voice, the analyst had wanted to know? Because, he'd replied—well, the event seemed to confirm his early feeling of being unloved. Strange that he should find such confirmation in such an event, the analyst had remarked: hadn't his mother refused him the cake in order to protect him, for his own good? Yes, of course, he'd admitted impatiently; but: if she'd *really* loved him, given him the sure feeling she did, maybe he would have seen the point. As it was. . . .

No but's, the analyst had said. He apparently had gotten oriented from the first to see no point about his mother but the point of a menacing knife. They had seen in the course of his analysis, over and over, that this feeling of being unloved by his mother was his basic myth: one by one the proofs, dredged from the depths of his reluctant memory, had turned out to be phony, based on an insistent misunderstanding and misreading of reality. And what a craftily selective memory he had! From his dismal recitals of hurts one would gather that his early years were one unbroken sequence of denials, rebuffs, no's, don'ts—that his mother had never changed a diaper for him, dressed a skinned knee, cuddled him, tucked him in—that, utterly indifferent to his needs for food and clothes and shelter, she had callously deposited him on a snowy mountain top to fend for himself or be eaten by wolves. But his total blackout about this side of his mother, the *giving* side, gave the game away. What he really had against his mother was not this or that real hurt but—her very existence. Her mere existence as Other, her "refusal" to be co-opted and absorbed by him. The gap between his skin and hers. Her living at moments beyond the reach of his tongue and lips and eyes and hands. Her keeping one foot in the world of the "It," rather than letting herself be sucked totally into his "I". . . . In the early days psychoanalysis had, more often than not, accepted the patient's myth of mistreatment by the elders as a fact, and derived from it all his subsequent malaise, confirming his fiction that all his troubles stemmed from bad parental handling; but more and more, in later years, analysts had come to see that this last defensive layer of myth had to be ripped off before the real genetic truth emerged: namely, that emotional distress is something a man inflicts on himself. Because he, or at least his unconscious, has learned to take pleasure in pain. Indeed, the infantile truculence behind such a fiction, flying in the face of all reason and reality, could not be maintained *without* the expectation of pain—from the outside in the form of punishment, from the inside in the form of guilt and depression—and without some inner mechanism for converting such unavoidable pain into pleasure. It had to be faced: the myth of having been denied would not be nourished so devotedly, and enacted in adult life over and over so compulsively, if under it was not the deeper desire to be refused, to precipitate refusals: under the protest is the yearning—a strategy for courting pain. By and large, the denied chocolate cakes were myths, and when one clung to them one arrived at pain, finally became an addict of pain which, by the fantastic alchemy of the unconscious, is turned into pleasure, secretly crowed over under a cloak of pouting indignation. . . .

It was true. Nauseatingly, humiliatingly true. Because if a man had really been hurt in infancy by denying parents and if he was not masochistically in need of hurt, he could easily correct things in maturity by arranging for himself the kind of life situation in which he would *not* be hurt. It was easy enough to pick friends and lovers who would *not* reject you as your parents had allegedly done. But later he had sought out a cold woman and married her (and cut short his analysis to do it): a good deal of his tension with Irene, some of his worst fights with her, had begun over matters of food, often in the kitchen; he'd complained many times about her being such a terrible cook. It must be—as his analyst had suggested—that he had needed for a wife just such a terrible cook, and terrible bed partner, precisely so that he could cling to the myth of chocolate cakes wanted and never granted: there were women in the world who could make wonderful chocolate cakes and would like nothing better than to give them to him. There was Ooda. Yes; but he had backed off from Ooda, too, a little. Why? Because, even in the best of circumstances, he had to maintain a small flickering fiction that *every* woman, no matter how giving, came toward him with a needle in the offered pastries? That *every* lake harbored in its false softness a fist, a steamroller? So that, even in the best of circumstances, a man had to be mountain-stern? Of course, such backing away helped to *create* the needle, fist, steamroller. To reject Ooda, however subtly, even in her moments of fullest giving, was a sure-fire technique for provoking her into anger and counteraggressiveness. . . .

Now he was sitting up again, damp, tense, miserable. Thinking about the other two times, trying to recapture their interlocked meanings. He was much too tired, couldn't think. He fell back again and pulled the blanket over his head.

Instantly he was floating on a lake, inert. Queer, from this moment on he had the distinct impression that everything happening was in the nature of a pun, even when no words were spoken.

. . . . floating on a lake, face down, mouth puckered with the burning brine, soured milk, trying desperately to dive under the surface. Useless, it was like batting his head against a bale of cotton, the waters had a will of iron under their lapping softness.

"Relax," he ordered. "Give in. We'll do it my way, don't go sour on me."

"Lie back and float, why fight so hard? You have but become the ocean, now flow," somebody said mockingly. Neen's voice, Irene's voice, Rosemary's voice, his mother's voice, impenetrable Lady of the Lake. "Switch from manual to robo. Drink your milk, son, we'll take care of the bedpan."

Suddenly he felt himself helpless, the soft fleecy blanket had turned into a strait jacket, arms were gone, legs were gone, he couldn't fight any longer, waters too rubbery. He fell over on his back now in the right receptive nursery position which is everything in strife and let himself be carried along at 186,000 miles a second, cork bobbing on the rushing waves, but when his mother reached gently under him for the bedpan she brought out an object that was not enameled at all but leather-covered, a notebook with his name written on the cover and above it the words DODGE THE BEDPAN. While Irene bent closer and closer over him and ran her hands over his inert body and the forefinger jutting pedagogically and surgically from her outstretched hand was a nipple no was a hypodermic needle was a snub-nosed automatic that turned into an enormous glass of milk but when she raised it to his lips he knew from the noxious briny taste of it that it was rotabunga and he gagged and tried to spit it out but she squeezed his throat and he had to swallow. Now she sank down upon him and was straddling him and as he lay there impotent and filled with rage—squatter's rites for *her?*—he looked over her shoulder and saw the tower of the Gandhiji rising up like a giant hypodermic needle from among the mountain tops about where Kilimanjaro should be, spouting strychnine, its cap of snow melting and enormous drops big as dirigibles falling from it as it melted and neon letters flashing from their sufaces as they fell—DODGE THE VIRUSAGO—he knew they were glutinous gobs of tapioca and would drown him.

"Lie father, lie son," young Tom said in a low authoritative whine from his basket in the corner, swimming in tapioca.

Rambo leaned over and administered the · antidote. Refreshing taste. Real milk. But when he reached out for it his hand began to oscillate wildly with intention traumer and he blushed. The rosier the merrier. Rosemary.

"A myth is as good as a smile," he said thankfully to Rambo.

As the energy flowed back into his limbs he felt better and he blinked three times for maybe. He rolled over again into the position that was nursery-wrong but feeling-right and he was sinking into the lake at last, into sleep, it seemed to him that finally he was freeing himself from the prison of the waters, the waters were parting now before his trust because in good we thrust and now it was right and he began to make easeful and liquid love to Ooda, unresistant parting Ooda, no fists in her acquiescent giving responsive flesh. Over and over as he dove in effortless unencumbered self-propelled pelvic sweeps, buoyant and plunging as a catamaran, not wanting to hurt Rosemary now, over and over as she undulated liquidly with him, all protoplasm no skeleton, waters parting, she whispered in his ear, "No bolos, I do not want to fight," and thankfully he churned to the bottom and came to the bott-Om, thankfully and fulfillingly and without awakening he spilled into the ocean and the ocean now milk churned with him, and he thought, hugging the bottom, "Rambo, yes, there is Rambo. At the storm's end the Rambo."

"You see?" Ooda said gratefully. "That is when it is best, without proving, gangster gone, Rosemarys gone. It does not have to be all eagerness either. Egoness, I mean. Why worry so much about who does it—let it be done, forget about needles and the need for needles and the need to cover up the need for needles, you relax more that way. The less egoness, the less going away. Eagerness, I mean. Otherness. A little tapioca is not so bad at times."

"When he wakes up he will be very, very sad," Vishinu said.

"There is plenty of precedent," Irene said. "He always wanted to be precedent. Eat his chocolate cake and have it too."

"There are sins of the sons too," Rambo said.

He paid no attention. Cushioned in the fistless enveloping flesh of Ooda the Om the doming heavens the clouds like scatter rugs the wind whistling whimpering through the broken panes, feeling the waters finally drained of fight the lake's legs spread and encircling and will abandoned, Rosemary emptied of screams, come at last to the end of his anguish, he settled thankfully on the bottom of the ocean of ease, Victoria's peaceful blue waters lapping around him and Kilimanjaro dripping into the waters; curled up against a sunken dirigible soft as a breast but no neon slogans flashing on it now, and slept.

from dr. martine's notebook
(mark ii)

JULY 27, 1990
At the old hunting lodge

Back in New Jamestown about three weeks ago, Fourth of
July, two men, a Russian and a Eurasian, were all set to save
humanity by working me over, maybe killing me. Complicated event. Long history behind it, over eighteen years in
the making. Been doing some background reading and the
pieces are beginning to fit. The historical picture's something
like this:

FIRST PHASE (1972-1975): *Myth-Making.*

At 3:25 A.M., October 19, 1972, Helder jumped for his
anti-blast suit and found the notebook sticking out from
under my pillow. He put two and two together—he'd never
read Dostoevsky, didn't suspect that twice-two sometimes
equals five—and decided I'd gone out in a blaze of unauthorized heroics. Beginnings of the myth.

Teddy Gorman was ordered to be flown home, and
Helder wangled it so that he went along as surgeon in charge.
Teddy was brought to a secret underground hospital installation outside Oklahoma City, Helder attending him. It
was touch and go for Teddy for some time, he didn't even
regain consciousness for over a week; but finally he rallied.
When he was on the mend Helder began to read him
passages from Martine's notebook. During these sessions
several ideas began to shape up in Helder's programmatic
head:

First, Martine had worked out a whole new philosophy
for the pacifist movement, based on the principle of saying no
to all EMSIACS. Second, Martine had picked Helder to un-
ravel his thought and Teddy to put it into action. Third, to
inspire Helder and Teddy and those who would flock to their
banner, Martine had sacrificed his life to say the first thunder-

ous no to EMSIAC. Elaboration of the myth. So began the deification of Dr. Martine, much misunderstood deserter, who couldn't get his jokes taken seriously.

Many weeks passed. Teddy was finally fitted with some old-fashioned artificial legs, aluminum ones. Coached by Helder every inch of the way, he finagled his way into the EMSIAC area and blew the whole works sky-high. Before many hours had passed, Vishinu, a Russian flier somewhat older than Theo (he'd been a protégé of Vasili Stalin's) but pretty much his opposite number, heard about what Teddy had done and got the idea of clobbering his own EMSIAC.

America and Russia were a shambles; so were all the heavily populated areas of the world. Nothing could be done on a national or international level—no nations left. Reconstruction had to get going on a purely local basis, town by town and village by village. Slowly the survivors came out of their state of shock and began to huddle together in areas where there were vital industrial plants underground.

All this time Helder, with Teddy now his strong right arm, was busy in his makeshift headquarters in Los Alamos, planning to launch a refurbished Tri-P movement. Early in 1975 he decided the time had come and over the one partially rebuilt radio network he made the electrifying announcement: Tri-P was a going concern again. Under the leadership of Helder, the mentor, and Teddy Gorman, the protégé. Under the martyrship of Martine. Nobody thought to mention one little fact: in the years before 1970 Martine had consistently resisted Helder's efforts to get him into Tri-P. Myth now become movement. . . .

SECOND PHASE (1975-1977): *The Bid for Power.*

Tri-P in its reincarnation had a brand new gimmick, one that Helder had dreamed up entirely on his own. The essential problem, of course, was that of pacifism vs. defensism—the tendency of pacifists, except for a fringe of ineffectual cranks and crackpots, to break down and turn patriotic in situations where their own countries seemed to be threatened with attack. The shift from turn-the-other-cheek to eye-for-an-eye: the Judeo-Christian ambivalence. In his notebook Martine had indicated that this was the core of the pacifist dilemma. Now Helder announced that he had found the solution—the Assassination Clause.

Simple gadget, this Assassination Clause. Wherever Tri-P came into power it was to be written into law; as the twenty-third amendment to the old American constitution, the first amendment to the old Soviet constitution. The Clause read as follows:

> Every person who offers himself as a candidate for public office automatically takes oath never to encourage or countenance or còndone the manufacture of arms or their distribution; never to make hostile utterances about other nations or peoples; never to carry out the functions of his office with any degree of secrecy, or enter into diplomatic negotiations or agreements which are not fully open; never to obtain information of any sort through the use of confidential agents; never to employ bodyguards or take any steps toward the securing of his personal safety; never to suggest, under any circumstances whatsoever, that the foregoing commitments must be suspended because of a state of "crisis" or "emergency"; never to adopt or even advocate a strategy of defensism, political or personal, no matter what "external" threat appears to exist. If during his tenure of office he engages in any of the illegal acts enumerated above, or even suggests that such acts are called for by a "new" situation, this shall be construed by the citizenry as an invitation to assassinate said official in the public interest; and if the official takes any measures whatsoever to protect himself against such assassination, that act in itself shall be construed as an invitation to all genuine pacifists to assassinate him; and if he does no more than argue against this Assassination Clause, and press for its revocation, that act too shall be construed as an act of treason and an invitation to assassination.

The new pacifist program was a thing of lean, monotoned beauty: any pacifist who doesn't act like a pacifist in office begs other pacifists to bump him off without further ado. In other words, the old Oxford Pledge foolproofed, with no outs.

Of course, Helder went on, a certain logical objection could be made. Peace, according to the cliché, was indivisible; workers for peace and a better world had always understood the necessity for spreading their programs across the frontiers of nations. So, in the crisis of war, each internationalist shrugged his shoulders, acknowledged despairingly that no one could disarm unless all disarmed, and reached for a gun.

The premise was logical enough, Helder confessed. If one

country was disarmed it could easily be attacked by others that retained their arms. Nothing more obvious. But logic was not enough—pacifists had been rigidly logical whenever they had risen to power, and the result had been one ruinous war after another. There was something beyond logic, some outrage to logic, some magical thing, that had been lacking in the pacifist brew all along. Martine had supplied the missing ingredient. It was, simply, the faith that surpasess all logic and understanding, utterly blind faith, a fanatical dogged devotion that could only be called theological. From this moment on, Helder announced, Teddy Gorman was to be known as Theo, as a living reminder of Martine's bequest to humanity.

But coupled with this blind faith in the rightness of the program must be an equally blind faith in something else: the potential of good will in all people. One must believe that when a genuine pacifist gesture such as the adoption of the Assassination Clause is made in one country, its moral audacity will exert such a magical pull on the pacifist impulses of other peoples that a mighty wave of good will will sweep over all countries and, in one mystic surge, achieve the oceanic internationalism that all the "practical" and "responsible" leaders of the past had talked about but never gotten anywhere near. Did history refute this belief? Well, when in history had such a gesture ever been made? Who had ever *really* turned the other cheek?

That was the burden of Helder's opening-shot speech. It was a stunner. People were sick to the marrow of war; they were fed up to the point of nausea with leaders who had promised peace and then sold them out. They wanted peace at any cost—anything, literally anything, would be better than war.

There was great excitement in the new cities that were being founded up and down the far western strip of America. Soon an election was arranged, Tri-P swept into office with practically no opposition, Helder became president and Theo his right-hand man, emissary, and all-round troubleshooter. So the Inland Strip was born. And the magic ground swell which Helder had predicted came to pass. Very soon the theological excitement of the Assassination Clause filtered into the East to take the burgeoning pacifist movement there by storm; it led to a new order headed by Vishinu and some of his associates. So, by ignoring the logic of internationalism, Helder's "blind faith" had finally brought about a genuinely international order.

281

Martyr: myth: movement: macrocosm. But in his haste to proclaim the martyr and get going, Helder forgot, first, to locate the martyr's corpse. . . .

THIRD PHASE (1977-1978): *Crisis of the Outmoded Cortices*. And immediately there was trouble. For one thing, a whole slew of materials like cobalt, petroleum, uranium, thorium, columbium, important deposits of which were to be found only in the great no man's lands left throughout the backward colonial patches of the globe after the Third World War, was vitally needed by each of the powers. Wouldn't either power, simply in order to protect its geopolitical situation, have to maneuver for control of such areas even when it did not yet need the specific materials available in it?

Such "protective" ideas, of course, could not develop in a world in which people were nothing but pacifists. But the trouble was that nowhere in the Tri-P world could you find a man who was nothing but a pacifist. To be that, a man would need to have a very long and very rich and overwhelmingly persuasive tradition of pacifism behind him—and there was no such tradition in the world, even that strand of the Judeo-Christian heritage which had to do with turning the other cheek was cunningly intertwined with another strand which suggested an eye was suitable payment for an eye and a tooth the minimum recompense for a tooth. But the peoples of the Tri-P world did have another sort of tradition which was still very much with them. A long, rich, remarkably persuasive history now folded deep into the cortex, only thinly overlaid with benignity, which told every Easterner that the Western world was rapacious, and materialistic, and contemptuous of those with darker skins and more meager technologies, and Wall Street imperialist; every Westerner that the Eastern world was wily and rapacious and totaliarian and benighted and clumsy with machines and irrational and contemptuous of democratic human values and Soviet imperialist.

To be sure, the leaders of the Strip and the Union never gave voice to such thoughts—there was, after all, the Assassination Clause to think about. But the Clause could not be enforced against whole populations. Private citizens of both countries—newspaper editors, journalists, professors, economists, businessmen—were not bound by the Clause; they were free to make accusatory statements, and make them they did.

Then a completely unforeseen thing happened. No holder of public office could make accusations against another power, not if he valued his neck. But—and this was something the clause makers had not anticipated—he could resign his office and, using his prestige as a recent leader to gain an audience, yell out his accusations all over the place with the immunity of a private citizen. This is exactly what Vishinu did. He kept mum for almost two years after he became head of the Union. Then he quit, on the ground that he could be more useful to his country as a private citizen, and let fly.

There was hell to pay. Vishinu threw the whole moth-eaten Soviet book at Helder and his associates—charged them with everything from imperialism to bed wetting. Helder and his associates, of course, could not reply.

It was a bad time for Helder. Vishinu, it was suggested, was preparing a coup in the Union which would overthrow the nominal Tri-P government and set up a defensist one. What was Helder to do? To give up Tri-P would mean to give up everything which stamped his messianic life with meaning and direction. But he could not disprove the terrifying reports which appeared daily in the Strip press—and neither could he do anything to muzzle the press. He could not even be sure that the aroused citizens of the Strip were not doing exactly what they accused Vishinu of doing—there were such rumors too. War, a thoroughly off-the-record war, was obviously being prepared by the citizens of two pacifist nations in a thoroughly off-the-record way, and there was no way to stop it.

Crisis. In three short years the world was on the brink again. Some essential ingredient, obviously, was still missing from the pacifist stew. And if it could not be found in a hurry, the human race was very probably doomed—that was being corny and histrionic, maybe, but there it was. . . .

Helder was in a state of panic. He had missed up somewhere. He had to find out where, exactly—otherwise his life made no sense. And he was a man to whom it was enormously important to make sense—he always forgot his Rosemarys.

FOURTH PHASE (1978): *Revelation of the Word.*
He went into retreat in the mountains. For almost a month he was gone; only Theo knew his whereabouts. He thought and thought, pacing the floor of his cabin nights. Where had he gone wrong?

In desperation he went back once more to study the bible. And suddenly, one febrile night, it struck him. None so blind as those who will not see. The answer was as simple as a twice-two-equals-four Euclidean theorem—it had been there in Martine's notebook all the time.

It was as though a veil had suddenly dropped from Helder's eyes and he saw for the first time. Martine had sensed, with his breathtaking insight, that pacifism was all child's play and dust in the eyes unless it was nonreversible—and it would never be nonreversible until it was rooted in the very anatomy of man and the aggression which vitiated it was rooted *out*. Martine had meant to suggest all that in his apparently casual and haphazard speculations about inducing good will in Theo through lobotomy. And then he had gone on to suggest the real surgical solution to the problem through a series of apparent jokes and wisecracks—the solution of Immob!

The big problem was to *prove* to the world that in becoming a pacifist you were not simply stepping from one ideological suit of clothes into another, while inside you remained the same; you had to demonstrate for everyone that you were thinking and feeling with a completely new cortex, from which all the old suspicions and wily strategies had been removed. Immob would do just that: no one would suspect a vol-amp of harboring any anachronistic imperialism under his cranium. It was not by accident that Martine had put so much of the Immob philosophy into Theo's mouth, in that incredible imaginary dialogue which no one had understood before this moment. It was glaringly obvious that this was Martine's way of saying: because Theo was already a duo-amp quite involuntarily, because he'd been mauled by the steamroller, he must now become the initiator of Immob by voluntarily making himself a quadro-amp—and thus launch mankind's first real effort to dodge the steamroller.

In great excitement Helder summoned Theo to his hideout. He closeted himself with the young man and, stammering with the furious glory of his revelation, explained the whole thing—quoting the lines from Martine's notebook which, several years ago, he had deleted as irrelevancies. (All the lines—except those having to do with masochism.) At first Theo thought Helder was joking; then he grew silent.

Finally Helder asked him what he thought. He said that he would have to go off by himself and worry it over a little—it was a pretty big idea to swallow all at once.

Theo went out and sat on the mountain top all that night long. God only knows what ideas went through his mind as he felt his aluminum legs, then raised his hands and studied them in the moonlight. But when the sun came up and he went back to the cabin, Helder knew by the saintly glow on his face what his answer was. Theo was not one to refuse the mantle of destiny, especially when it was flung to him by a Martine.

The whole thing was arranged by Helder in absolute secrecy. A remote place was selected for the operations, surgeons were sneaked away to do the job. For almost two months Helder and Theo remained in hiding, recuperating.

By this time, of course, the whole Strip was in a panic—the leaders were gone, the bombast from the Union propagandists was getting wilder and wilder.

FIFTH PHASE (1978-1979): *Tri-P to Immob.*

Loud-speakers all through the Strip trumpeted the sensational news: Helder and Theo were about to return to public life—they would appear at a monster rally at New Jamestown. The rally, of course, was scheduled for October 19, 1978; that had already become the big holiday of the new order, known as Peace Day.

Came the great day. People poured into New Jamestown from all parts of the Strip. A quarter of a million spectators crowded into the giant stadium. When the curtains finally rolled back, they revealed two people on the stage: Helder, standing behind a table draped with bunting, and Theo, standing directly to his right.

A tense hush. Slowly, with great emotion, Helder began to speak. He held up one hand, in it a volume; this, he explained, was the original manuscript of Martine's notebook, the manual of humanism bequeathed to all men of good will by the great martyred hero. In it was the great lesson—the need for absolute faith.

Now he turned and pointed to Theo.

Here, as they all knew, was the prototype of the great faithful, so named by Martine himself. Martine's plenipotentiary to humanity. For some three years now the remnants of the civilized world had been living under Martine's banner, striving to reach the theological purity of Theo. Through the political instrument known as the Assassination Clause, the best device invented by man so far to make his moral commitments stick.

And yet—something had gone wrong. Wild recrimination

285

filled the air all through the pacifist world. Charges, threats, and bitterness everywhere. The moral commitment had *not* stuck. Somehow, the Assassination Clause was inadequate. Another catastrophe impended, one which would eliminate whatever tag ends of the human race were left. What, what had happened?

He would tell them what had happened. They had not reached out joyously to accept their heritage from Martine. The one true lesson in the notebook, they had not learned. The Assassination Clause was not the way. It was a puny, halfway measure. The wholeway measure, the full triumphant leap into irrevocable faith, they had not taken—but Martine had defined it and pointed the way. It was—

Immob!

Immob!

As the magical word boomed through the stadium, great banners unfurled from the proscenium arch. On them, emblazoned in lumi-letters twenty feet high, were the sensational new phrases: NO DEMOBILIZATION WITHOUT IMMOBILIZATION, PACIFISM MEANS PASSIVITY, A LEG SHORTER AND A HEAD TALLER, ARMS OR THE MAN, DODGE THE STEAMROLLER, DODGE THE STEAMROLLER, DODGE THE STEAMROLLER. . . .

What, Helder demanded, did Immob mean? Immobilization, of course. Immobilization through vol-amp. He explained what vol-amp was, how it was designed to outwit the steamroller.

But Immob was more than that. Much, much more. Something more positive. He and Theo had pondered its meaning in Martine's guarded remarks and they had come to see, in a burst of revelation, what else it meant. It was the name of a whole new movement, a new way of life, a new and fully human order. Its letters were the initials of the new and spiritually soaring thing that Tri-P must become if it was to capture the missing ingredient of theological devotion. Those initials stood for—

International Mass for the Manumission of the Benign!

Mass, not movement. There had been too much movement in the world. Immob was designed to cure the malady of activity. Mass—that summoned up a picture of humanity becalmed by a new quiescent faith, impervious to all steamrollers, just triumphantly standing there.

Helder and Theo had pondered long and soberly. They had come to see who had to make the first gesture. And now—it was to be made.

At a signal, attendants appeared from the wings. Two of

them stepped up to Theo, reached for his jacket and slipped it off.

A quick gasp, choked off in many throats. For when the jacket came off, the shirt underneath was exposed and it was seen that there were no sleeves on the shirt—there was no need for sleeves, Theo had nothing to fill any sleeves with, his arms were gone!

The world's first Immob!

But he was not alone. The attendants advanced to the rostrum, took hold of the wooden framework supporting the bunting and removed it.

Another great convulsive shudder ran through the audience. Helder was not standing behind the draped table, as everyone had thought. He was standing *on* the table! On his two stumps!

The world's second vol-amp!

"This is our answer to the charges made against us!" Helder cried, his voice thick with sobbing. "This is our answer to men of faltering commitment everywhere! We are not imperialists! We give ourselves fully, all the way, forever, to peace! Where is the man who will join us?"

Great lamentation through the stadium. Sobs, wails, screams, women falling in a faint. Weeping, much wringing of hands.

But then—something else. Another, more positive sound. A wild affirmatory shouting, hoorays, whoops, hysterical and surging.

It was the young men, reacting now after the first paralyzing shock. Leaping to their feet. Jumping up and down. Waving their arms frenziedly in the air in a surge of benignity. And running, bounding, stampeding down the aisles—to the recruiting booths which were now being set up on the great stage.

It was a wild time. And it lasted for many days. Like a great tidal wave Immob swept across the Strip: very soon all but a few queer, iconoclastic elements among the youth—not much in the literature about them—were recruited. Before long the thing began to get institutionalized; there were Immob clubs set up and M.E. universities, and the academicians began to overhaul their ancient disciplines and a new philosophy and ethos began to take form. The atmosphere crackled with magic.

And the magic was infectious, on a scale beyond Helder's wildest dreams. Almost overnight Immob captured the public imagination all through the East Union. The Union youth too rushed to the recruiting stations. Now, indeed, on a basis of full commitment, of theological fervor, the one world had come into being. Even Vishinu threw in his hat and both legs.

All bitter talk of imperialism ceased. Men who are rushing to have their limbs cut off in the interests of peace do not call each other imperialists.

SIXTH PHASE (1980-1990): *Artificial Limbo*.

There was just one fly in the saccharine ointment. Helder had reckoned without modern technology—the electronic tube, the transistor, communications science, cybernetics, atomic energy, etc., etc. He had been so engrossed in programmatic matters these past years that he did not even know about the small group of cyberneticists who had, ever since the war, been working quietly in a little neurological laboratory attached to the Denver University Medical School.

These men were, almost without exception, expert neuro-cyberneticists who had studied under Wiener at M.I.T. They had been inspired by Wiener's contention that, granted the techological savvy of the 1940's, an artificial limb superior in many ways to the real one could easily be created if society wanted to spend as much money on such a humanitarian project as it was willing to spend on developing an atom bomb. Their research on prosthetics had begun under the aegis of the Advisory Committe on Prosthetics Appliances which had been set up in 1948 by the American Congress to aid the amputee veterans of the Second; it had been given a great impetus by the Third, in which scores of thousands of people, both military personnel and civilians, lost one or more limbs. (It was their laboratory, as a matter of fact, which had built the aluminum pros for Theo when he was flown back from Africa in '72.) And when the Inland Strip got organized in '75, their project was granted a subsidy by the new government, purely in the spirit of encouraging humanitarian research.

Less than a year after Immob was founded, these cyberneticists made a startling announcement: they had perfected an artificial limb superior in many ways to the real thing, integrated into the nerves and muscles of the stump, powered by a built-in atomic energy plant, equipped with sensory as well as motor functions, etc. It was a neutral, value-eschewing announcement. They did not know whether this invention was good or bad, whether it should be fostered or suppressed, any more than physicists a quarter century earlier had known whether their discovery of atomic fission and robot brains was good or bad—they merely had the thing, it was up to the politicos to figure out what to do with it. Science discloses, politics disposes.

Great agitation on the heels of this announcement. Heated pros and cons. Shouldn't this doodad be unceremoniously suppressed—after all, if Immob was the idea, what was the point to devices which would provide still greater mobility? Yes; but weren't the vol-amps our great heroes, hadn't they made the supreme sacrifice in the spirit of Martine? Was anything too good for our heroes?

The battle went on. Sides were taken. It became the basic political issue, the split in opinion started to take on institutionalized shape in the form of parties, Pro-Pro and Anti-Pro came into being. And Pro-Pro soon became the government party. Helder and Theo, after looking the problem over from all angles, decided to go along with Pro-Pro—they could not see how any kind of mechanical gadget could vitiate the inner moral revolution brought about by vol-amp. After all pros were removable; and besides, many of the vol-amps were getting restless, the first intense glow of passivity had begun to wear off and they were complaining that, now that they had given themselves irrevocably to peace, they wanted to get up and around and do something a bit active for the cause instead of lying flat on their backs. And their women complained that they fretted and pouted quite a bit, lying there in their baskets (although many women joined the Anti-Pro Ladies' Auxiliaries). These psychological problems had to be considered.

Prosthetics plants were set up. Neuro-Loco Centers were organized. More active M.E.'s were devised. The dexterities and discernments became basic sports. A new philosophy came into being, based on expectations as to how cybernetic limbs would affect the cytoarchitectonic structure of the cortex and produce a new superior type of man. And as all this happened on the double in the Strip, similar developments took place in the Union: technological, political, philosophical, the whole works.

In 1982 the Olympic Games were revived, this time as an annual cybernetic competition. Vishinu had never gone back into the Union government, but he did accept a post as chairman of the Union delegation to the Olympic Arrangements Committee. In the first Olympic Games, Theo and Vishinu were the outstanding competitors of their respective teams—at first duo-amps like Vishinu were allowed to compete in some events—Theo trounced Vishinu every time, the Unioneers never won a single event.

Those were eventful times; real ferment, a progression of red-letter days. Much excitement, and a great international friendliness—everybody alive and benign. But there was an entirely unforeseen development.

As soon as the mass production of prosthetics got under way, it became clear that they couldn't possibly be manufactured in quantity without big supplies of columbium. And the known deposits of columbium in the world were very meager indeed—not enough to answer the needs of even one Immob nation, let alone two of them. The pinch had begun to be felt by the U.S. Air Force as far back as the forties. No substitutes for the rare metal were possible, this was the one problem that continued to stump all the metallurgists.

What to do? Both the Strip and the Union began to send out parties to look for columbium in the unexplored wildernesses—the Andes, the Himalayas. There was talk of looking into the situations in Madagascar and Greenland, perhaps even at the North and South Poles. It was quickly realized that this sort of exploration might develop a certain competitive spirit, not quite as innocent as the spirit of the Olympic Games, and to guard against that eventuality the more promising areas were pretty carefully staked out between the two powers. But then, as the years went by and the shortage grew more and more acute—to the point of being an insuperable bottleneck in many cybernetic projects—a certain tension developed. Each party began to think that perhaps the other one had the better of the bargain—and each began to wonder if the other wasn't, in the old imperialist manner, organizing sub rosa expeditions in the hope of getting the jump on its partner. Vishinu was still not hampered by public office: he made the first guarded references to this lurking suspicion. Soon the references became less guarded. After three or four years, the situation got pretty serious. The whole thing culminated in the hammer-blow speech made by Vishinu three weeks ago in New Jamestown. . . .

It looks like Jerry was right: the earth has played a very cute little joke on the pacifists. Everything else it yields up in teeming abundance, fruits to delight the palate, all the rotas and ganjas the human organism can stand—but with

290

this one thing, this silly metal which can hold up under the blasting fires of hell, it turns miserly. After whetting men's appetites for this heat resister beyond all slaking, Mother Nature coyly withdraws the mineral breast.

There it is: the world is now irrevocably committed, with theological devotion, to only one thing, columbium, and there is not enough of the stuff to go around. So long as men want cybernetic super-limbs to super-move and super-grasp with, they will not find anywhere under this good green earth enough columbium to build them with. . . .

And so, almost eighteen years after I made the last entry in my notebook, two men, one a Russian and the other a Eurasian, came after me with a rubber truncheon and a stubby automatic. Yes, the event has a long and complex history. What is its meaning, exactly?

It makes no difference what Vishinu and Dai had *consciously* in their minds. The event has an objective significance, quite aside from the conscious intent of its participants. By an oversight, the new world's martyr hadn't been quite reduced to a corpse; now it meant to rectify the error. This kind of society wants its martyrs to stay quite dead—the martyr who turns into a Lazarus only makes trouble. Just like an Unknown Soldier coming back to life, it would be embarrassing as hell—what in Christ's name would you say to him, what heretical things might he not say to you?

They haven't got me yet. Not quite. I'm a bit of a slippery customer, thank God, for the martyr-makers.

So far I've given the slip to all the martyrizers of Martine—except myself.

But they got me indirectly. They got my son.

And just about the whole youthful population of the entire civilized world.

For which I can't entirely dodge the responsibility. After all, I did make the jokes

Point there somewhere, wish I could see if I weren't so tired but

AUGUST 7, 1990
Hunting lodge
Swimming in the lake a lot. Like old times, keep diving to see how long I can stay under. This afternoon almost caught a trout with my bare hands but it wriggled free.

AUGUST 13, 1990
Lodge
Keep thinking of Tom in the perambulator. Dreamt about him last night—I was trying to pull the covering away from him, it was very important to me to see if he was castrated but the blanket was like a sheet of steel riveted in place, wouldn't budge, I was soaked with sweat. He looked up at me with a malicious grin. "Nothing doing," he said. "I know what you're up to but you can't change places with me, from each according to his need."

Woke up with bad rheumatic stiffness in my arms and legs, it lasted several hours, disappeared the moment I went swimming. Toward evening I opened a vacuum-packed chocolate cake, delicious, took one bite and immediately threw up.

AUGUST 22, 1990
Lodge
News report on the video. Vishinu and Theo meeting in Los Alamos with the Olympic Arrangements Committee. Making plans for the Games, due to start October 5 and run through October 19, Peace Day.

SEPTEMBER 13, 1990

Lodge

Peace Day one month off. Twentieth anniversary of my much martyrologized desertion. Of my birthday; except I still don't know what the hell I started to get born as.

"Ambulatory basket case." Why does the phrase keep bothering me? "You are already one of us in your heart"—that bothers me too.

Can't think. Can't think.

Hunting today. Took a pot shot at a rabbit, winged it in the foreleg. Clipped. Set the bone, rigged up some splints, put it back in the forest.

Rummaging in the closet. Found an old mildewed collection of stories with my father's name inscribed on the flyleaf. Hemingway's *Men Without Women.*

SEPTEMBER 22, 1990

Lodge

So, then: Immob started as a joke. A joke that miscarried.

But every one of the big salvationist movements in history—from the Ten Commandments all the way down to the Mormons' Later Day Sainthood and Christian Science and Jehovah's Witnesses and Fletcherism and Bolshevik-Leninism and Dianetics and Orgonotics and Santa Monica Vedanta and Mandunga—every one of them might have started out as a great Swiftean joke. That some humorless man got hold of and took literally.

The jokes get wilder and wilder, people laugh less and less.

Suppose some Helder had come across Swift's tract on a method to abolish the famine problem in Ireland by eating the children of the poor. Jesus.

SEPTEMBER 27, 1990

Lodge

Notoa. Oh, he's no great shakes as an artist, really. Even if he had greatness in him, the Mandunji village wouldn't call it out or even give it leeway to operate. In a society that's dedicated to naïve whites, the best an artist can hope to produce, even a supremely gifted one, is equally naïve blacks. No esthete is going to amount to very much in an atmosphere which isn't complex enough—ambiguous enough, emotionally and ethically—to have an esthetic dimension. *Esthetically* my enthusiasm about Notoa was often pretty damned sophomoric, he's no bush-league Hieronymus Bosch, it was just an easy way to take sides against Ubu.

Still, *non* esthetically, what Notoa was trying to do was valid and important, granted the nature of the village in which he had to operate. What was he trying to prove when he carved a canoe for a nose or showed cobra fangs darting from a man's genitals? Just this: *Everything is possible.* The more outrageously illogical a thing is, the more possible it is. The fundament of reality is the incongruous, the grotesque, the absurd, the miraculous, the improbable. The blind faith, the leap beyond logic, which Helder looked for in messianic politics, Notoa was after in the only kind of art he knew. The only way he knew to make his point was to put eyes on fingers and cassava leaves in ears. And who am I to argue with him? I've seen fingers turn into nipples and hypodermic needles and automatics and glasses of milk— God, I haven't thought of that dream for over two months. I've seen lichens coming out of General Smut's ears. I've seen all the improbability there is, I've seen Immob. I've looked at myself in a baby carriage. Baby miscarriage.

I've seen the corpse of Rosemary. But I don't like to think about it it's

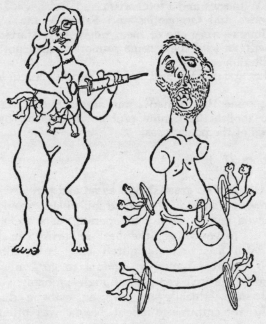

Lodge

Turning chilly. Flurries of snow during the night. Chopped some firewood.

Just got an idea about Immob: it's all done, not with mirrors, but with Hyphens. First you amputate, then you hyphenate.

Thing is, man has always been uneasy with the world as it is—its disarray, its slipshoddiness. Can't stand an indefinite turbulence in his affairs. People are too damned neat to live with the world's litter; maybe it comes from too much toilet training. Man isn't the tool maker, the speech maker, the concept maker: pre-eminently he's the system maker, the compulsive bringer of order into primordial messiness. Always chasing one gilt-edged Hyphen or another.

That's the ineradicable sickness, Hyphen-addiction. The paranoiac urge to find the one all-embracing formula that subsumes and explains everything, one slap-happy Brahman or another. The Packaging Urge, you might call it.

All along, the philosopher's Holy Grail has been the magical Hyphen, some unified-field theory or other. After the religious short cuts to oceania had been tried and failed— the Catholic's hierarchical stepladder to the One, the Protestant's individual pipeline—the philosophers had a try at patching things up. They were all variations on Descartes, trying to find the missing cosmic link in one pineal gland or another. During my student days, I remember, I was instinctively leery of the then current systems (which were later absorbed by Immob), Koestler's insight-and-outlook, Reich's orgonotic cosmos, Korzybski's semantics, Helder's good will—who was it who wrote that human history is "an endless tableau of the ugly fact slaying the beautiful hypothesis"? Often a guy seemed to have got hold of some provocative kernel of an idea, some puny lever with which to pry open this or that chunk of reality—but invariably he palmed it off as the Ultimate Lever. Some of these guys, in fact, judging from the grandiosity and fanatical intensity in their writings, were in the strictest clinical sense pathological, determined to find the *one* key that would open *all* doors. It never occurred to them that different doors might be fitted with totally different kinds of locks. So that anybody rash enough to pose as a cosmic locksmith should, in the interests of public safety, himself be locked up. To mix the figure still further, a key which is fobbed off as a cosmic can opener can very easily be turned into a bull whip or truncheon or automatic—or steamroller. Helder could never see that, poor unitarian. He was dead sure that you had to make the panorama of odds-and-ends sequential before it could be consequential. . . .

What the systematizers always left out of their neat packages, of course, was the one prime ingredient of reality—what the existentialists used to call the absurd. In their passion for explaining and relating all things they never stopped to examine the inexplicable and unrelated—that whimsical element which seems to mock all orderliness. The pigeon that refuses to fit into any holes. The duck-billed platypus that keeps a Darwin up nights. The playful meteor that hightails out of the firmament and lurches smack into the Yuma desert, to the consternation of the entire staff at the Mt. Wilson observatory. The particular blood vessel that chooses to hemorrhage in a particular cortex. The conductor who sneezes in the middle of the *Eroica*. Hobo touches in a strictly determinist world.

Yes, yes: these whimsical events follow laws too, maybe, every meteor's zag, every maestro's itch, every lesion. But where is the super-Newton or the super-Einstein or the super-Brodmann—or even the super-EMSIAC—who can store up enough information to be able to predict the specific lurch, the specific sneeze, the specific arterial rupture?

So, in the end, Immob, which outlaws the pratfall. Outlaws Dostoevsky's fatal fantastic element, Mann's criminal disorder and disease, Gide's gratuitous act; that satisfying quirkiness in Nature that sometimes produces an upstart event without discernible rhyme or reason, apparently just for the hell of it. But an occasional vagrant atom with baggy pants and putty nose sometimes meanders along in even the most unified of fields—Martine pops up as Lazarus. Who knows when or in which direction the specific electron—or martyr—will chose to dart? In fact, science long ago stopped talking about the *laws* of Nature and came around to the idea of *probability*—but the moment you concern yourself with the probable you have to allow for the improbable, the case in which twice-two can equal any number of absurdities. For areas of nonsense and non sequitur and nihilistic horseplay, in which a man with a stomach for that kind of thing can live on a diet of miracles. All that is ruled out by Immob. Immob does not acknowledge that even into the most steadfastly cortical universe a little multi-making thalamus must fall. The blind, parading as authorities on myopia. But this lust for Hyphens would never have gotten so far out of hand if the gaps found in Nature hadn't been exaggerated by men until they became intolerable—that's the history of the West, in one neat package. . . .

Naturally, there's a joker. In Immob, which pretends to be the healer of all gaps, all the old, old splits are perpetuated, and aggravated into monstrosities. Immob pretends to have surmounted the cleavage between mind and body—true enough, it's been expunged from their vocables, but is it really gone from their lives? Far from it. The time-honored breach between matter and spirit, cornerstone of the whole Judeo-Christian ethos, has reached its fullest expression in Immob. Underneath the smug verbal unification a more deadly war than ever is being waged between the bodily vessel and its spiritual contents—otherwise why the dizzy seesawing, now toward contempt for the body (Anti-Pros), now toward deification of the body (Pro-Pros)? Why the terrible urge to annihilate the body, which was the wellspring of Immob altogether, only thinly covered up with artificial limbs and Olympics and much talk about the electronic body beautiful? Why the Manichean grimness which seems to have settled over the whole sex life? What, indeed, is the *manic* compulsion to battle the elements, transform them, humiliate and punish them, if not a searing disdain for the world of gross matter which they compose? You would not march against Nature as on a punitive expedition unless you first felt a bilious disgust with Nature. This is more than ego-push. This is endura.

They've invented Moral Equivalents, all right. Moral Equivalents for the bodily. The urge to give battle to the elements derives from the same source as the urge toward amputation—a horror of things physical, the things of the material world and of the body—a moralistic, puritanical need to lash and lacerate thingness. All this, of course, under the guise of unifying man with himself and with the world which surrounds him. This is paranoia become a whole way of life.

In outlawing the absurd, Immob has installed it still deeper at the heart of reality. And the most absurd thing of all is that these hyphenating fools, who see oneness everywhere, haven't yet found a single Hyphen, any political pineal gland, that will bind the East and West together. . . .

Better cut this short—I'm in danger of making a new integrative system out of absurdity, the existentialists sometimes went overboard in that direction. . . .

Lodge

The nineteenth century worked out a neat, rationalistic, hyphenated picture of homo sapiens: Economic Man. Economic Man was a very logical and calculating fellow who, if given half a chance, would weigh all the possibilities of action in a coldly analytic fashion and then unerringly choose that course of behavior which would be to his own interest. Self-interest, that was the human prod. And it was upon the primacy of self-interest in human motivation that the great minds of the century, Ricardo, John Stuart Mill, Adam Smith, Marx, premised their predictions of social development. Economic Man was expected to be capitalism's savior, also its gravedigger. Obviously you wouldn't have much of a class struggle unless the members of both contending classes could be counted on to defend and enhance their own interests.

The twentieth century worked overtime at one big project: to blast all the Hyphens of the nineteenth century off the map, to expose Economic Man as a low comic figure; to shatter the monistic view of human behavior and show man as a bundle of the most contradictory feeling and drives, very few of them consonant with self-interest. To reveal the Dostoevskian under the Marxian. Freud called the turn at the beginning of the century by supplanting the concept of Economic Man with the concept of Ambivalent Man. The century has done a good job of proving him right.

But, terminologically at least, we can go a bit further, as some post-Freudian analysts began to do. After three world wars, after EMSIAC, after Immob, we can find a better name for Ambivalent Man, give him a tag which will indicate the source of his ambivalence. What else can he be called but Masochistic Man? (Name first proposed by Freud's student, Dr. E. Bergler, who brought to light the mechanisms of psychic masochism.) Economic Man standing on his head?

The twentieth century has dragged into the open a pretty startling fact: when given his head, man's inclination is to pursue self-destruction rather than self-interst. Economic Man was a cover-up for Masochistic Man, under the cool Apollonian cloak was a wild death-seeking Dionysian—and now the cloak has been ripped off. The perfection of war by itself accomplished the denuding. According to all the nineteenth-century rationalists, pro-capitalist Smiths and anti-capitalist Marxes alike, nations went to war only for material advantages—but who can pretend, after this century of

298

world wars, that advantage is a motive in these global holocausts when the upshot, economically as well as every other way, is sheer disaster for *all* the combatants? When to win is every bit as costly as to lose? When, after the smoke from the last hydrogen-atom explosion has cleared way, it is impossible to tell victor from vanquished?

Before the Third, capitalist and communist alike dreaded to rip the rationalistic mask from the masochistic skeleton of mankind. And today each half of the Immob world, for all its semantic training, persists in viewing the other as imperialistic, seeking some material advantage. As though there were a real material advantage in cornering the world's supply of columbium—which you wouldn't have any need for unless first you'd cut your arms and legs off!

But maybe they're getting scared at having exposed themselves so. Maybe they can't go on indefinitely destroying themselves without the pretense that it's in their own interest. Immob man hastily generates plastic limbs. Maybe Masochistic Man will have to slip on the mask of Economic Man again. It looks like yet another war is in the making.

Funny, this whole idea about masochism has a familiar ring. It's exactly what I was trying to say in my old notebook, in the last entries I made just before I deserted; it's what I was beginning to get at in my analysis, too. . . .

Lately my thoughts keep spiraling down to the old notebook, seems the big secret is somehow there if only I could figure out this business about masochism and see how it applies to me exactly but Christ I can't think everything gets fuzzy I try to get the thing straight and I begin to go around in circles and sit and look at the television and I can't even

19th Century

20th Century

OCTOBER 4, 1990

Lodge

Immob is the full flowering of man's capacity for masochism. Born of a joke that miscarried. All right—but then, doesn't that mean the joke itself was a pretty revealing one? The kind of joke nobody but an eighteen-karat masochist—trying to shrug off his own flaw by making a joke of it, in the spirit of *l'humeur noir*—would have thought of?

Is *that* the secret I've been trying to dig out of my notebook?

Good God, have I found my hidden identity in that old notebook? Via a perambulator in the Martine Home? Have I come nine thousand miles to find under all the incognitos nothing more distinctive than an ambulatory basket case?

The ambulatory basket case—that's what everybody is, Immob just removes the pretense.

Nothing at all under the incognitos but life's delicate child, Homo Dei, the doG-God: Solomon Bloom and Stephen Daedalus, Naphta and Settembrini, Hans Castorp, Mr. K: Mr. Everyman, Mr. Here Comes Everybody—Masochistic Man in person, in the maimed flesh? After all the stock-taking? Can't think.

Aching for Ooda. Nap this afternoon, dreamt about her. She was pushing a baby carriage up the mountain toward the Mandunga Circle. I kept leaning over but I couldn't see who was inside. "Why do you make me do this?" she asked. "What's the sense to pushing a gangster around in a perambulator? When you get the skull off you better look in the prefrontal lobes and see if you can locate the baby in the miscarriage. Let some light into *that* cave. I dare you."

Games start tomorrow.

Wish

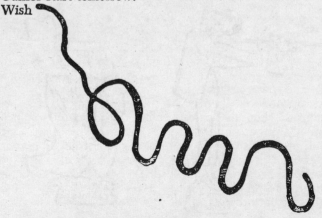

300

Part Six

GAMES

---

chapter twenty

EIGHT, NINE, ten days it went on. A sequence of kinesthetic marvels—whirlings, lunges, soarings, flipflops, heaves, spins—cybercyto feats such as no Immob eyes had ever seen. All of them performed nonchalantly, with debonaire ease, by the Unioneers—who, like the Strippers, all wore large blue "M's" on their jerseys. With each passing day the sportscaster's voice lost a few more decibels of its professional bounce, grew more and more puzzled; after a while he began to stutter badly, it looked to Martine as though he was a bit frightened.

"What d'you know!" he said the first day. "The Union team has just won the decathlon! They ran up twenty-eight points over the world's record, heck—"

And soon after, sputtering now: "Seventy-three feet! Imagine that, ladies and gentlemen, seventy-three feet! Nobody's ever broad jumped anywhere near that far before! That's, why, see now, that's thirty-two feet more than the world's record established by Theo in '83! Say, what's *happened* to these Union boys?"

Nobody knew what had happened to the Union boys. Five hundred thousand people sat in the great oval stadium in stunned silence, pondering the answer while event after event fell to the visiting team without a struggle. It was not that the Inland Strip athletes were doing badly, not at all: in fact, quite a few of them succeeded in breaking the records chalked up in previous competitions. But no matter how the Strippers outdid themselves and their predecessors, faces contorted with the effort, each time the Unioneers stepped up casually right after and did better without even trying.

There was unbelief in the announcer's voice on the tenth day when he muttered, "There's no longer any question about it, the score card doesn't lie. Yes, the Unioneers have already piled up enough points to win the Olympics! The first time it's ever happened! But how, how, *how* did it happen? What's the thing mean, *cybernetically* speaking? That's the question on everybody's tongue out here this afternoon. . . ."

For two weeks Martine sat slouched in a chair, hardly moving, eyes glued on the television screen.

There were interludes when no matches were going on; then he would wander down to the lake and stretch out on the rotting boards of the little dock to doze in the sun, mind battered into blankness. Only at night did he crawl out of his drugged state for a while—then, for three or four hours at a stretch, to the hooting of owls and the yelping of coyotes in the forest, he would sit at the table under the sputtering oil lamp and read, or write in his notbook. Try to write, anyhow. Often the words refused to come and his scribblings would trail off into an undecipherable scrawl in the middle of a sentence. He lost a lot of weight during this period: his cheeks were sunken and his eyes looked tired and glazed.

Once in a while, as he sat observing the competitions, the oval of the stadium would turn into a great basket and in it he would see his son, himself, with his mother and Irene hovering solicitously and officiously over the prostrate figure. It would quicken his pulse, make him breathe more rapidly, dilate his pupils, as though he had heard a threatening footfall behind him and were crouching in anticipation of a blow from an unseen assailant—then it was gone and he relaxed again and the droplets of sweat slowly dried on his face. At other times he would suddenly bolt upright out of his lethargy and say aloud, he had fallen into the habit of talking aloud: "They would have killed me. They've given the world six months. What's it all about?" Several times that happened when the television camera left the field and climbed to the officials' box to pick up Vishinu or Dai or Theo, but then the image would fade away and with it the memory of the automatic and the rubber truncheon and that was all. Often there was nothing in his mind, not even the debris of a percept or a thought, he did not even see the impossible shenanigans transpiring on the television screen, the skipping, hopping, vaulting, catapulting, gyrating, juggling, twitching, twirling; he was as drained of content as a vacuum tube—then he would suddenly say in a loud voice: "What did I do? How did I get into the basket? Rosemary—after all, I didn't actually—am I *really* guilty?" At night he slept for long hours, but his rest was broken by bad dreams.

Toward the end of the second week his cheeks were really cavernous, his pants were bunched at the waist where he had had to pull in his belt several notches to take up the slack. He had even lost interest in writing, in trying to write; his notebooks and reading matter lay in a heap on the table, quite forgotten; he sat before the television dully, unable to think, unable to feel. This was his state of mind and body on the fourteenth day, Peace Day, when the Games came to an end.

In the morning the Unioneers soundly trounced the Strippers in several track events, the hundred-yard dash, the quarter-mile, the pole vault, javelin throwing, the shot-put, the pentathlon. Then came a break: the officials were preparing for the high jump, traditionally the closing event of the Games.

During the lull the announcer interviewed various Strip dignitaries about their reactions to the amazing upset; the dignitaries were taciturn, falsely calm, falsely reassuring. Finally Theo appeared: his pleasant youthful face seemed to have aged ten years, he looked worried and there was a distracted air about him.

"Brother Theo," the announcer said eagerly, "we're sure anxious to get your slant on what's been going on. We've seen some mighty strange things out here these past two weeks, a lot of records, including some established by you, have been knocked for a loop. It's—"

"I know," Theo said soberly. "I don't mind much about the traditional events. What hurts is taking such a shellacking in the d-and-d's."

"But these guys were always such bums at everything, especially the d-and-d's. How do you figure their suddenly becoming champs?"

"It'll all come out in the wash. Just one point I'd like to make—we must all remember that these competitions are entirely friendly in spirit and are always followed by a full exchange of engineering information between the contestants. Anybody who's been shaken by what he's seen here ought to remind himself that we don't go in for old-style competitive sports any more than we do for war—these are games in the true, innocent, playful sense of the word, carried on without any spirit of rancor."

"Well, people are saying, Brother Theo, that there's a very definite old-style competitive spirit in the Olympics this year. They say Brother Vishinu was being pretty darned competitive in his speech about columbium, and now his athletes have become just as competitive in the Games. Some folks think maybe there's a connection between the two."

"Nonsense," Theo said firmly, a little too firmly. "That's just sour grapes. It's a sure way to bring back the old panicky way of thinking. We've got to mobilize our panic controls and keep our heads, all of us."

"You feel, then, that people are wrong to tie up what they've seen here with all the talk about columbium?"

"Definitely. Anybody who thinks that way ought to go home and do some deep breathing."

"Thank *you*, Brother Theo." Theo got up and left the telecasting booth. The announcer continued. "And now. . . . What's this? Ladies and gentlemen, there's just been a new development here, stand by, please. . . . Yes, yes. Oh, that's just fine! Great! Ladies and gentlemen, our Number Two booth down on the field has just flashed us on the intercom—it looks like they've finally rounded up Brother Vishinu for an interview! Stand by, folks, take it away, Number Two. . . ."

Another announcer appeared on the screen, sitting at a table with Vishinu. The Union representative was dressed in a blue-and-white blazer, rather like a yachting jacket, and a long-visored white cap; his heavily jowled, dark face was composed and impassive.

"Brother Vishinu," the announcer said deferentially, "you have just heard Brother Theo's reassuring words to the Inland Strip. Have you anything to add to them?"

"Nothing. Except, of course, one little thing. He is totally wrong."

"Wrong? You mean—about columbium?"

"I mean precisely about columbium."

"I'm afraid I don't follow you, sir. Could you try—?"

"I will put it this way," Vishinu said. "For many, many years now the Inland Strippers, and before them their forefathers when there was yet no Immob, have had a very smug attitude about themselves and their country. Very satisfied with themselves. They decided they alone have all the know-how to make machines and apparatus of various sorts, that in all the world there are no engineers and masters of technics like them, so naturally everybody should kiss their, mm, boots and they should be allowed to rule the whole world."

"But. . . ." the announcer faltered. "I thought, Brother Theo was just saying—"

"Semantically it made no sense," Vishinu said impatiently. "*I* am explaining to you now the *truth*. The union engineers have been working very, very hard on prosthetics. Now it is proved that we can make the best pros in the world, better even than the master minds of the Strip. By the logic of the Strip imperialists it follows that if we have such fine know-how also we should have all the columbium in the world."

"Brother Vishinu," the announcer said. "You are, why, you are contradicting everything Brother Theo said."

"Of course. Precisely my purpose."

"Do you mean, then, that Brother Theo was wrong about what we can expect after the Games? You won't share your discoveries with other Immobs?"

Vishinu smiled for the first time. "With other Immobs, definitely yes," he said. "With those who betray the Immob world and stray off from the true path of Martine, definitely no."

"What about the time element here, sir? How long have you had these new pros?"

"Please, no philosophical discussions. Not so easy to define time—the East and the West have most different approaches to this commodity."

"When—will you announce your plans soon?"

"Very soon. In a matter of minutes everything will become most clear."

"*Minutes?* Is something going to—?"

"Young man," Vishinu said as he got up to go, "remember, please, the words of your great Brother Theo: Be patient. Rome was not burned in a day. I must go, the high jump is happening very soon now."

As the two teams lined up on the field for the final event the announcer, badly shaken by Vishinu but trying hard to recapture his usual bland glibness, explained the procedure. Since the Games winner was already known, there was no point to prolonging things unduly. Therefore, by consent of all parties, the crossbar would, right from the start, be heisted to the highest mark ever set, at the world's record level established nine years ago by none other than Brother Theo himself.

The field was cleared and the Union captain withdrew several yards to allow himself the usual running start; the stadium was still as the morgue. The jumper poised himself on his toes, then took several long, loping steps until he came to the take-off point. He was not exerting himself, he seemed only to hunch for a fraction of a second, bending slightly at the knees to give himself an upward push. Then he took off, effortlessly but with rocket-like force.

Up, up he shot, not even bothering to scissor his legs as jumpers usually did to facilitate clearing the bar. There was no danger of his grazing the bar, he went up stiff as an arrow, body upright and arms held rigidly at his sides—zoomed past the bar, past the tops of the uprights supporting the bar, and kept going. He had easily jumped two hundred feet. When he plummeted down he bent his knees parachuter style to break the fall, landed gracefully on his oleo-strut shock absorbers and bobbed up and down a few times and marched away.

The stadium was still, a petrified forest. Even the announcer was quiet, evidently he had nothing to say, the visual evidence spoke for itself. Months later, an eternity later, a long low ripple, a sound like wind lapping at dead leaves, passed through the crowd.

Stepping out smartly, like a drum major, the Union captain proceeded to the officials' box and went into conference with them; in a few moments the Strip captain was called over. After some more whispered talk one of the white-capped officials went over to a microphone and addressed the crowd over the loud-speaker system.

"The Committee has an announcement to make," he said. "In view of what has just happened the Strip team concedes the final event without a contest. The Games are over."

Another flabby ooze of sound, the stadium was one enormous mouth softly gasping.

Now began the final ceremony. The whole Union team, some two hundred strong, proceeded to one end of the field and assembled in military formation. They began their triumphant procession, arms and legs sparkling as they rose and fell in unison. At the head of the column marched Vishinu.

The new champions reached the center of the field, wheeled at a right angle, headed like an electrified centipede for the judges' stand. Here were assembled all the top officials of the Strip government in their capacity as hosts, all of them, headed by Helder and Theo. When the Unioneers arrived at the stand Vishinu raised his arm and they came to a halt. At a second signal from their leader they went into precise side-stepping maneuvers until the several rows had fused and they were all spread out in a single line running parallel to the stand. They stood rigidly at attention, Vishinu at the center of the formation and a few paces in front of it.

Helder rose to speak, holding a large golden object which gleamed in the sun. Theo stood too, at the President's right. The camera panned in on Helder for a close-up, the object in his arms bulked large on the screen—a statue, miniature reproduction of the gigantic sculpture at the hub of New Jamestown, showing a man being run over by a steamroller. But something had been added: the triumphant figure of a quadro equipped with pros was straddling the machine, exactly like the figure of Martine in the bas-relief outside the Martine Home. He rode the steamroller with the extravagant chest-bursting pride of Prometheus unbound, in his hand a javelin instead of a bolt of lightning.

The camera moved upward to Helder's face. Martine stirred, slid from his chair and sank to his knees in front of the television. The face was as he remembered it but grown meatier and more pensive—brown hair thinned considerably at the forehead, long nose thickened and inset more deeply, dimples lengthened into crevice-like folds, the thin pressed lips become a harsh and undeviating incongruous gash that seemed laid out alongside the otherwise irregular features with a T-square, the eyes still intense gray pinpoints but ringed with thick shadows that were new. There was trouble written on this face, a tension not entirely under control. When the camera backed away Helder's legs came into view: plastic. Somewhere in the stadium a band played a few bars of some brassy flourish, then Helder began to speak.

"Brother Vishinu," he began. "Esteemed visitors from the far corners of the Immob world. It is in order on this day, Peace Day, that we remind ourselves of other times, less enlightened times, when the Olympics were not the noble, fraternal occasion they are now but cultural echoes of the terrible imperialist struggles which racked the whole world—contests of egocentric persons and ethnocentric nations. You are no enemies who stand triumphant before us now, claiming your rightful prize—you are only our other, and at the moment obviously better, sides! You are ourselves! Can the left hand resent what the right hand accomplishes? Especially since we know, we know full well, that the marvels

307

which you have unveiled before our eyes here will not be selfishly hoarded treasures. Every Immob advance is another drop in the ocean of humanity from which we all drink, the ocean of Martine.

"Yes, drained of their vicious content of man against man and people against people, the Olympics have become the great Moral Equivalent of war—Immob life on all levels has become one vast Moral Equivalent of war! Under Immob all of life has become one continuing Olympic, one unending sunny smiling Game. The Game has been snatched from the battlefield and brought into the world of community endeavor and mutuality! In the true innocent spirit of the Immob Game, therefore, I salute you, the gallant knights of joyous mutuality! You have made history here, the world will be the better for the cyber-cyto splendors of your accomplishments! And therefore, with rejoicing in my heart on this greatest of all days, Peace Day, I present this statue to your leader, Brother Vishinu. We pass it into your hands with no sense of loss. For we give to you that we may receive. . . ."

Vishinu stepped forward until he was standing directly under Helder. Helder reached down and handed the statue to him; he took it stiffly, without acknowledgment, and backed away until he had regained his original position. There was a microphone there, he spoke into it.

"You will receive, all right," he said. "Definitely. All of you. You will be paid back double and triple for your rotten lies."

A hushed "oh" from the massed flesh, vast and oval as the stadium itself; then a terrible silence, as of an electrovox suddenly going dead.

"Let us have a clear picture of these happenings," Vishinu continued, speaking very slowly and precisely. "There has been no Immob, no true spirit of Martine, until this day. Until this day there has been no sharing and no equity and glad exchanges. The muck-a-mucks of the decadent West have been playing their usual game until now, the game of the lords and masters and the know-it-alls, of the global haves strutting around in front of the global have-nots. This has to stop before Immob becomes a dirty word. This week we, the East Unioneers, have put a stop to it. We represent the fresh new spirit of the East which is blowing up now a real cuber-cyto hurricane to sweep the world clean of the foul imperialist odors of the old Western masters. No, you will share nothing in our victory, Helder and Theo. What was victorious on this field was the true spirit of Immob, precisely in spite of you and your foul plots against Immob mankind."

308

Behind Vishinu a frozen blur: half a million people rooted to their seats, not moving, hardly breathing. Martine's fingers clawed at the floor, knuckles white with the strain; his face was flushed and moisture was beginning to trickle down his cheeks.

"Your imperialist crimes can no longer go unpunished. You are traitors, saboteurs, terrorists, schemers, and you will be dealt with as such. We peoples of the East, we vermin of color and backwardness, we coolies of the world, the white man's burden—we show you now that we can do as much, even more, with your fancy vacuum tubes and transistors and nuclear energy and solenoids than you great masters of the world can. We have knocked you off your smug thrones cybernetically. Now, for the sake of everything we call Immob, we must knock you off your imperialist thrones too. On this Peace Day, in the name of Martine, for the sake of the Immob masses born and unborn, we now call you to account for your imperialist crimes."

The Strip officials were standing rigidly in their box, stupefaction on their faces. Vishinu raised his hand once, emphatically: behind him the two hundred athletes lifted their arms too, pointing them at the officials in a gleaming mass salute, like divers ready to take the plunge.

There was a moment when nothing moved, not a sound was heard. Then Vishinu brought his hand down again, smartly, maestro pacing the flutes.

A series of sharp, explosive sounds. Simultaneously the outstretched arms of the Union athletes, all four hundred of the arms, lit up with a blinding glare. The effect was quite different from the dancing glints which usually emanated from pros: for a fleeting moment every arm seemed to be positively incandescent along its whole length.

The officials in the box reacted like drunken puppets. It was a scene out of comic opera, the gestures absurdly exaggerated and the facial contortions so unlikely that they were only clownish. Some flapped their arms wildly, like fledglings essaying to fly; others clutched their throats and thumped their chests in buffoonish frenzy, still others began to tear their hair, wring their hands, stroke their cheeks in fits of absent-mindedness: their hands came away from their bodies red. And there were some who, with no histrionics, no expressions on their faces but utter incomprehension, slumped immediately to the floor and out of sight behind the balustrade.

One by one the gesticulators, the claspers of bosoms, the

hand wringers, followed suit, crumpling like marionettes from which the mover's hand has suddenly been withdrawn. Cries of anguish came from one, then from another—sharp yelps, long meandering whines, hysterical screeches that sounded like laughter. Soon they were all on the ground, their bodies hidden from sight.

Martine had not moved from his position on the floor. He was on his knees, Mohammedan crouching before a television Mecca. He searched the scene for some sign of Helder and Theo—he had not followed what had happened to them in the confusion, they were gone from sight now.

"The swine, the swine, the swine," he said. He thought he was just talking but it was more like screaming. "He lied. Five or six months, he said. I remember distinctly. He said five or six months."

A humming noise now began to come over the television speaker, slowly it grew louder.

"Swine," Martine said, shrilled, pounding the floor with his fists. "Swine. Swine. Swine."

One of the cameramen at the stadium seemed not to have lost his wits entirely—he swiveled his camera away from the boxes and tilted it up at the sky. Onto the television screen flashed an image of dozens of planes with helicopter rotors whirring, humming, a whole fleet flying in over the western rim of the stadium at an altitude of less than two hundred feet.

Slowly the planes made their way to the center of the field, then stopped there and idled in the air. From the underside of each plane dangled a series of contraptions which looked like trapeze bars.

At last something began to move on the ground. With Vishinu still at their head, their ranks unbroken, the Union athletes proceeded with military order to the center of the field, to a point directly below the motionless planes. Vishinu crouched, then bolted upward with bulletlike speed, body turning until he was moving feet foremost, straight for one of the planes. Whether by magnetic force or whatever, his plastic feet seemed to be pulled unerringly toward one of the trapeze bars. The moment they came into contact with the bar they stuck to it, in a second he was hauled into the plane through an opening in the belly.

Now a second Unioneer—this one a quadro, moving hands first—soared upward and disappeared into a plane; then a third, then a fourth. Very quickly the sky was peppered with dozens of bodies catapulting at once. And now figures began to break loose from the solid mass of flesh huddled in a ring around the stadium; they too came to the center of the field and began the ascent into the planes. Some of them carried drawing boards, some were women, they seemed to be the visiting artists from the Union, while others of all shades and complexions, men and women alike, were unmistakably from the East too. Apparently all the Union guests at the Olympics were taking part in this vast vertical exodus, being sucked up into the sky. Martine tried to make out the individual figures as they darted onto the field and then vaulted into the blue. The women, not having cybernetic limbs and therefore unable to jump by themselves, climbed onto the shoulders of male Immobs and were carried piggyback by them; Martine squinted in an effort to see one such tiny figure as she hurtled upward on the back of a brawny Union athlete, he thought she was wearing a pink-and-blue dirndl skirt but it was hard to make out, he couldn't be sure. Uneasy rider, he thought.

More sound effects now, the spectators were beginning to come out of the paralyzing shock. A woman howled, making a quavering sound something like a yodel; a throaty male yawping began, as of an animal in terrible pain—all the sounds of terror and lamentation somehow absurd because of the time lapse between stimulus and response. Gradually, under all the haphazard sounds of individual collapse which happened to be picked up by nearby mikes, there swelled a less shrill and more substantial sound, a steadily increasing hum from many thousands of throats as they unlocked and began to vibrate—a mass whimpering.

The camera panned down into the bleachers. At random points in the ring of flesh individual figures began to move: a man stood up and staggered a few feet, drunkenly, like a sleepwalker, hands alternately rubbing temples and playing an aimless game of patty-cake; a woman began to make disjointed movements with her arms, like a windmill furiously reversing itself over and over, then dropped in a faint. Everywhere around them other people were just sitting and looking into space, as though daydreaming on a park bench.

A figure wandered into range of the camera and stood there looking jerkily from side to side, very much like a spectator at a tennis match. It was one of the announcers, apparently unaware that he was being televised. His lips were moving, they were the lips of a priest saying his beads, of a child blowing bubbles—"My God, my God, my God," he was saying over and over in a kind of throttled sob, the words came over the audio.

The announcer's hands were wandering idly up and down his body on a mission of demented exploration. One of them stopped at his collar and fumbled there: it had come into contact with the wire leading away from the lapel mike.

"Si!" a voice yelled from nowhere. "Si, for Christ's sake, you're on the air! Stop mumbling, man!"

The feel of the wire seemed to bring the man back to reality: he shuddered, then threw his shoulders back, cleared his throat and began to speak in a parody of his professional style. The clichés of the trained verbalizer tumbled out now in monstrous schizoid lack of contact with the enormity of what had happened; but there was hysteria under the glib robot heartiness.

"Ladies and gentlemen," he said mechanically; for a moment he forgot himself and experimented with a ghastly smile, then gave it up. "Ladies and gentlemen. You have just witnessed the most remarkable—today we have been privileged to see. . . ."

He made an obvious effort to pull himself together, he swallowed hard and tried again.

"Something inconceivable has happened here. We don't— we don't understand it any better than you do. It looked as though the Union athletes had pro arms that were weapons of some sort, pistols or rifles or something, at a signal from Vishinu Brother Vishinu they all pointed their arms and fired. Their arms were guns or something. Then they fired. There were sixty or seventy of our top officials sitting in the boxes, then suddenly the arms went off and. . . ."

His lips began to quiver, he broke down again.

"Si!" somebody shouted again. "Get hold of yourself, Si!"

"Oh, God," the announcer said. "Horrible, horrible, horrible. Oh God, God, oh my God."

Another voice, forceful and authoritative, boomed out over the scene. The camera switched back to the formation of planes overhead.

"This is Vishinu," the new voice said. "I am speaking to you from my plane. I am now leaving the stadium with my countrymen."

"Swine," Martine said. "Pig. Scum. Swine."

"Before I go," Vishinu thundered, "I have a message for all the oppressed masses of the Inland Strip. Brothers, no need to despair! The warmongering demagogues who are left among you will tell you with their oily words that what we have just done is an act of war. Do not believe this lying propaganda, brothers, it will be just a semantic trick to confuse the suffering masses. There is no warlike element in our actions today. For many years now your false leaders have been provoking us with their imperialist tricks under a demagogic cloak of Immob. They were preparing war against us and plotting to steal all the world's columbium—plotting to get the columbium to make the war and also to make the war to get the columbium, like true double-dealers. Naturally we reached the end of our Immob patience and we had to defend ourselves. For a long time we waited for you to take care of this matter yourself but none of you dared to invoke the Assassination Clause of your Constitution—or, this I think is the more likely, your fine leaders guarded themselves too well to let you invoke it. Well, today, on Peace Day, we have invoked the Assassination Clause for you, because we saw you needed our help."

"Can you hear me, Si?" the unseen announcer bellowed. "Get a grip on yourself, man! We've got a job to do—drag your ass over to the officials' box and see if you can find out anything. Si!"

"We do not want war," Vishinu said. "We make no wars with the abused and oppressed masses of the West. Listen to me, little people of the Strip. This very minute, while I speak, many many Unioneers are landing from ships on both the coasts of your country, they are already beginning to march toward the Strip. Do not fear them, they are not armies, they are liberators coming to throw off from your backs your imperialist masters and free you to return to Immob. That is why they do not drop down from the skies on you suddenly, with hydrogen bombs and such things; they come slowly to give their brothers here the chance to do the job themselves. Oppressed Negro masses of the Strip! You especially, brothers, must work with the Union liberating forces because you are doubly oppressed. Among the liberators you will find many Negroes from your own country who ran away from the segregation and discrimination of the West to take refuge in our democratic lands, where a skin that is not lily-white does not mean the man inside is all garbage. You will have a people's Immob democracy at last. You will be free at last. Be of good courage, comrades, soon the masses everywhere will live in peace in the true spirit of Martine!"

"Pig," Martine said. "Oh, the pig."

The planes began to shift now, soon they were aligned in

313

four long rows which came together to form an enormous "M."

"Long live peace!" Vishinu shouted. "Long live Martine!"

The formation of planes started to move, it passed over the rim of the stadium and disappeared. The camera swung away from the sky, registered the field again.

"Si!" the voice blasted. "You got anything, Si?"

Loud wailing from the bleachers, terrible cacophony of distress, individual screams tearing through the wall of sound. The spectators were no longer huddled in their seats, many of them were scampering through the aisles, leaping up and dashing down on the field to run to and fro in a sudden access of motoric panic.

The announcer called Si flashed on the screen again. He seemed slightly more in control of himself.

"Si! Anything happening down there?"

"Looks bad," the announcer said. "We have no report so far on how many have been killed and wounded, but it looks bad. I see, though, that some of the Olympics doctors have finally reached the boxes, we should have something for you soon. One of our men is up there now, he's trying to find out something. . . . Oh, here he comes now, maybe. . . ."

Another quadro with a large press button on his lapel came up to the announcer and whispered in his ear, wildly excited. The announcer stood in stupefaction, mouth open, eyes bulging.

"Oh!" he cried. "Ladies and gentlemen, we've just found out something incredible, oh, simply incredible! It's not quite as bad as we thought—almost everybody up there was hit but listen to this! *Brother Helder and Brother Theo are not there! Their bodies haven't been found! They—are—safe! They got away!* According to a newspaperman who was sitting just behind the boxes and saw the whole thing, Brother Helder somehow saw what was coming and at the last split second he threw himself on Brother Theo and got him on the floor so the bullets missed both of them! In the confusion which followed they both managed to crawl to the exit and got away! *Brother Helder and Brother Theo got away!* Most likely they're on their way back to the capital now, if all goes well, oh God, if all goes well we should be hearing from them at any moment! Folks, let's all try to mobilize our panic controls and wait, and hope—"

Martine stood up and switched the television off. He rubbed his sunken cheeks distractedly. "So," he said. "Assassination didn't take. Has to be done over again. Naturally."

314

He walked to the window and looked down at the lake, came back to the center of the room.

"No getting away from it," he said. "Otherwise I'll never get straight with myself, I've got to sleep again. R.I.P., Rosemary."

A half-hour later he was in his car, hurriedly packed valise in the luggage compartment, careening over the back roads in the general direction of Los Alamos. He was keyed up again, lively as Lazarus, he hadn't felt this wide awake since 3:39 A.M., October 19, 1972.

chapter twenty-one

SOME TWENTY miles north of Los Alamos he turned in at a small motor court: SVIRIDOFF'S CABINS, the lumi-letters said. He signed the register with the name "H. C. Earwicker" and asked the clerk if there was anyone around who could run an errand for him—letter to deliver, he'd make it worth the messenger's while. The clerk said he reckoned his son could take time out from his chores to make the trip into town. Martine promised to get the message written immediately and went off to his cabin.

The trip southward, much of it over rundown back roads, had taken all night; it was daylight now, he was aching with exhaustion. But as soon as he was settled in his cabin he refreshed himself by running ice-cold water from the tap over his head and neck. Then he sat down at the desk and composed the following letter:

Dear H:

You should recognize this handwriting; you've read plenty of samples of it in your time. But in case you need another hint, here goes:

In the middle sixties two medical students, surgeons in training, were rooming together in an apartment in Greenwich Village. Let's call them X and Y. One night X came home very late. He was in an agitated frame of mind, paced the floor gulping down one drink after another (sour mash, Y always kept a bottle of it around). Under Y's prodding he finally spilled the story.

X was pretty complicated in his dealings with women: couldn't bear them, couldn't bear to be without them; needed them, kicked them around when he had them. Not an unusual attitude, God knows, but X's toughness with women

315

wasn't checked as easily as it is in less tempestuous guys. X never cared to stop and take a good look at motives: he was compulsive rather than reflective, given to acting energetically and precipitately instead of sitting down and trying to figure out what prompts a given action.

Y was just the opposite. Too reflective, if anything. He was always making trouble for himself, maybe complicated things unnecessarily, by trying to work out all the ambivalent motives behind any act he felt impelled to enter on; so he did a lot more uneasy thinking than acting. He was up to his ears in his own analysis (X resisted the whole idea of analysis, took it on sufferance only because the medical school required it) and wished there were time to pursue it more deeply than his studies permitted. Sometimes Y even wondred if surgery was the field for him: he thought the analytic profession was a lot closer to his real interests and speculated about whether he might not make a switch later on.

So X talked. Seemed he'd had a date with a girl named Rosemary, a nurse at the hospital adjoining the medical school. As a matter of fact, he'd taken Rosemary to a political rally at Madison Square Garden—a rally of the Peace Pledge Program, the pacifist movement in which X was becoming extremely active. (As I said, he was quite an activist.) After the meeting, at which X himself had made a fiery speech, he'd insisted on going up to Rosemary's apartment for a drink.

He'd had several drinks; he'd tried, very energetically, precipitately, actively, to make love to the girl; she'd resisted him just as energetically, at the end even hysterically. Finally, in a kind of blind rage, he had, to put the matter bluntly, raped her. Whatever the complicated act is which is named rape—obviously, more often than not, it involves certain ambivalences on the girl's part too—that's what X had come to at the end of the evening. Needing the girl and at the same time furious with her, intent on an act of love which was also a gesture of considerable hate. In any event, it was an act. X was first and foremost an activist. . . .

While the roommates were talking the phone rang. It was one of Rosemary's girlfriends: she was calling to let X know, in between sobs, that Rosemary had just committed suicide by slashing her wrists. The police were already on the scene; the girlfriend had been called in and under questioning had revealed that X had been out with Rosemary during the evening; X would probably be hearing from the police, maybe they were on the way to his place right now. It might

316

be pretty messy, Rosemary had been raped and in the process pretty badly mauled, inside and out. The girlfriend was calling for a very simple reason: she herself was an ardent worker in Tri-P and an admirer of X, she was dead sure that a man as dedicated to the pacifist cause as X just couldn't have done such a horrible thing to anybody, so she wanted to warn him about what was coming.

Close to hysteria himself, X told his roommate what he had heard over the phone. Y's reaction was typical. Peculiar, he suggested, that an act of love could do so much damage. Peculiar, too, that in an act of passion a medical student, who knows the anatomical facts of life pretty thoroughly, could be just as inept and brutal as a moronic butcher's boy.

But the conversation didn't get very far—the bell rang, it was the police. Under questioning X admitted readily that he'd been with Rosemary that evening. However, he explained, he'd left Rosemary at her door; whoever had attacked her must have done it long after he'd returned home—his roommate could confirm that he'd come in less than forty minutes after the meeting at the Garden was over.

The police turned to Y. After some hesitation he corroborated X's story. Then the police took X's fingerprints and studied them. How, they wanted to know, could X explain the fact that the same fingerprints had been found on a glass in Rosemary's apartment? X answered that he had come to pick Rosemary up *before* the meeting and at *that* time she'd given him a couple of drinks to bolster him because he was nervous about the speech he had to make.

The story sounded a little fishy, but there was no evidence to contradict it. And Y had given X an airtight alibi. After a few days the case was officially closed—suicide after rape, the rapist being unknown—and X heard no more about it.

A lot of unpleasantness developed between the roommates. Some weeks later Y moved into an apartment of his own; the two men had no more contact until the war broke out. X became more and more active in Tri-P, making speeches all over the place and getting his picture in the papers. He was quite an activist.

On that complicated night, though, there was more talk between the two men; it lasted till sunup. Talk having to do, naturally, with motives—there Y was in his element. He was furious with X for having forced him into the position of lying to the police; even more furious with himself for having been so weak as to have allowed himself to become morally involved—steamrollered into the role of accessory

317

after the dirty fact. So he talked, angrily, accusingly, about X's motives, and for once X listened. Y insisted on several hammer-blow propositions:

That, by the nature of the case, the rapist gets absolutely nothing out of the adventure worth having. That, therefore, the rapist, under the pretense of wanting desperately to be loved, really is intent on being most spectacularly denied. That X's need to be rejected was proved by the fact that his taste in women ran to frigid types: when he came across a girl with a real suggestion of warmth and giving he suddenly became strait-laced and described her as "loose" or assumed the air of a connoisseur and dismissed her as "shallow" and "uninteresting." That, unconsciously, X knew full well he wanted only rejection from a woman, exactly like the criminal who really wants to be caught or the gambler who really wants to lose. That, to ward off this inner accusation—to prove that his basic drive was not to be the passive help-less baby callously sloughed off by mamma—he was ob-liged to act the brutal gangster with women: his violence was all phony. That all this cast an interesting light on X's hyperthyroid politics. That, proceeding from the inside out, X's characterological onion consisted of the following layers: (a) the passive-feminine mashochistic baby, intent on repeat-ing with all persons and objects in its environment its nursery myth of the denying mother; (b) as defense against that, the extremely active-aggressive tough guy; (c) as secondary defense against *that*, the humanitarian pacifist, whose two-fisted energies are all expended in altruistic pursuits. That every so often the inner truth erupted and broke through all the flimsy defenses thrown over it—out, on this particular night, came the rapist-in-the-pacifist, and then the baby-in-the-rapist, determined to prove once more that mamma was a bitch. Of course, Rosemary got mauled pretty badly in the process, this baby had big muscles. . . .

(Prophetic words: thirteen years later X was driven to dramatize his essential babyhood in a really spectacular way, by cutting his legs off. In the name of humanitarianism, of course.)

"All right," X said. "Let's say it's all so. What do you want me to do about it?"

"For Christ's sake, I don't want you to do anything about it," Y replied. "But you might occasionally own up to the sleazier motives behind your noble fanfaronading activities."

"I don't follow you."

"Look, I was reading *Notes from Underground* again

318

tonight. Dostoevsky's a very good case in point. Do you know there's some evidence that at one time or another, as a young man, he may have brutally attacked a very young girl? A passage about just such an incident was deleted from the original edition of *The Possessed* and some people believe it was autobiographical. Anyhow, the point is that old Fyodor was capable of some pretty rough behavior with women; whether or not he did actually rape some kid, he certainly wasn't too nice to his wife, that's a matter of record. And as a cover-up for this phony brutality in him he sometimes went overboard in his enthusiasm for humanitarian, salvationist causes too: he always had a big streak of messianic religiosity, and in his younger days he fooled around with a nihilist group—for which association, interestingly enough, he came within seconds of being mowed down by a firing squad. *But*—in his writing, at least, he was a hell of a lot more honest than you and your world-saving friends are. Because you, in your theory of human nature, maintain there's no such irrational thing as a rapist in anybody, that all people are inherently nice pacifists with an infinite fund of good will in them, if only the world would allow them to give free rein to their goodness. Dostoevsky, on the other hand, wrote this fabulous *Notes* thing which I could never get you to read—a blast against your psychology of all lights and no darks, against the simplistic, 'enlightened' sunniness of the nineteenth century. . . . Good God, man—you do a thing like what you've done tonight, this monstrous filthy thing, just after you've made a speech from the platform at Madison Square Garden about the deep fund of goodness in all men—you do the one thing after the other, hardly stopping to catch your breath, and still there's not the tiniest worm of a doubt in your mind about the triumphal march of rationality up the straight shiny glory road of history, all that shit. . . ."

Y really sailed into his roommate. Secretly he already knew that, for all he had begun to suspect about himself in the course of his analysis, he had made up his mind to marry the girl he was engaged to—and, as a necessary preliminary, to discontinue his analysis as soon as he could. His own devotion to the mythological figure of the Bitch-Goddess was pretty extreme too. Naturally, in attacking the self-destructiveness of X, he was at the same time expressing an unacknowledged irritation with the same quality in himself. He was revolted by a brutal caricature of himself. But he

319

was also trying, by some psychoanalytic-rhetorical magic, to cast out the devils from his own prefrontal lobes. . . .

X sensed all this, however dimly. "Maybe you're right about me," he said slyly. "But you'd better take a good look at yourself, pal: physician, heal thyself, and so on. It doesn't strike me that the girl you're going to marry is exactly the fully giving vaginal type either, to judge from a few things you've let drop."

"Don't try to drag me into this," Y answered angrily. "I'll give you this much: the struggle between passivity and activity is pretty much the struggle that every man born of woman has to go through every minute of his life, sure— it's pretty much the human condition. But not many of us get as spectacularly doglike-godlike as you. We don't rape, we don't become soapboxing pacifists. . . ."

In his agitation Y jumped to his feet and began to march up and down. Pretty soon he went on, waving an erudite finger at his roommate: "One more thing, if you'll forgive another literary allusion—you always seem to bring out the literary in me. You know the section in *The Magic Mountain* where Hans Castorp gets lost in a snowstorm and has a vision of the City of God? A paradisiacal spot, sunny, people dancing gracefully in the meadows with a kind of sunny solemnity—and back in the temple, in the cave of the temple, in the hidden guts of the community, so to speak, the monstrous cackling witches dismembering the body of an infant and crunching its bones between their teeth, blood slobbering down their withered dugs. You see—at the heart of the City of God, directly behind the scenes, the murderous Bitch-Goddess, man's enduring myth—yours, and mine too, I'll admit it. But you, who keep this myth alive in its most harrowing obsessive form, deny that it even exists, you go on plotting a perfectionist world in which there's *nothing* behind the scenes—a City of God that's sun-drenched all through, no caves. That's *your* myth, undiluted Godliness, in which there's no cranny for the mythological Bitch. . . ."

Even nastier things were said that night, but no matter. The point is that only one person could possibly know the details I've recorded here. If you're not convinced by the handwriting, be convinced by what I've written.

Never mind where I've been or how I got here. I am here, and I've got to see you. The most important thing in all your life is to see me now. You're in a pretty bad jam at the moment and I know how to get you out of it. I've bailed you

320

out of more than one jam before this, sometimes without meaning to.

I'll be waiting at this auto court, Cottage No. 7, the address is on the stationery. Let me hear from you at once.

Hans Castorp Earwicker

P.S. I know you like to sleep on things, but don't do it this time. Aside from the fact that I must move fast, I don't like the thought of your sleeping on anything—you snore too goddamned much. It may be due to a chronic catarrhal congestion of the upper respiratory tract but it still sounds terrible.

Writing at top speed, he had taken close to two hours to get the letter done. When he stopped now and read it over he was furious with himself: he had intended to dash off a curt, zippy note, just enough bait for Helder to rise to, and instead he'd composed a half-ass psychoanalytic treatise; even worse, he had meant in his reconstruction of the ancient episode to pillory Helder, and he was not at all sure that he hadn't wound up pillorying himself at least as mercilessly—it was by no means clear who was the primary target of the heavy Freudian ironies. Obviously his purpose in writing the letter was a lot more than the merely tactical one of tweaking Helder's memory—he had been trying to get the long-dodged incident straight in his own mind, especially his own shadowy role in it: there, too, was a suggestive hint as to his own identity. Well, he wouldn't try to rewrite the thing, he was too beat. Sloppy, but it would do the trick; he'd send it as was.

He wrote Helder's name on an envelope, down in the lefthand corner he printed in large letters the word PERSONAL and under it added VERY URGENT. He sealed the letter in the envelope, placed it in turn inside a blank envelope, then pushed the service buzzer.

In a couple of minutes the clerk's son appeared, a solemn-looking boy of fourteen with a confetti of freckles on his face and ears like landing flaps. Martine impressed him with the importance of the mission, instructed him to enter the capitol building and leave the envelope with some responsible official; he gave the boy a twenty-dollar bill for himself, the youngster gulped and wiggled his ears in ecstasy.

As soon as he was alone Martine threw himself on the bed and closed his eyes. The question now came to him: Why for a quarter of a century had he been so reluctant to think about the Rosemary episode? Some curdling guilt had no

321

doubt driven the thing away from consciousness—but it was not so easy to define the guilt. Was it simply because, in giving Helder his alibi despite all misgivings, he had allowed himself to become an accessory after the fact—as he had later allowed himself to become an accessory after the fact to Mandunga? No: in some terrible way he had been an accessory *before* the fact.

That was it. All men were, in a sense, accessories before the fact to each and every rape. Because all men carried about in themselves some touch of the rapist, as a necessary face-saving camouflage for their ineradicable softness—they sprouted fists to cover their essential flabbiness. Because they all shared with Helder his secret myth of the Omnivorous Denier. But, generally, men kept the myth under better control than did Helder, and thus were able to soften their camouflaging blows down to something resembling caresses. That was precisely why it was so terrible to be confronted with an unruly Helder—he disrupted the solemn-sunny communal dance by letting his myth-Bitch come prowling out in all her stark gory nakedness: and then let fly at her with both deceitful fists. The rapist shed a fearful amount of charisma because he brought out into the glare of day the secret shame of all men, exposed the hidden guilty rapist trapped in all of them. And who could say that, confronted with the vicious act of rape, other men, under their indignation, did not secretly, vicariously, partake of the false brutality, revel in this onslaught at one police-evading remove? Was this not why, for all his contempt, he, Martine, had passively given Helder his alibi instead of turning him over to the police? The thing had happened at the precise moment when he, Martine, was unbearably uneasy about his impending marriage to Irene, was already feeling trapped, smothered. And, after coming close to killing Neen—because of the needle in her hand—he had, absurdly, called her Rosemary. . . .

One knot, anyhow, was beginning to get cut, at least frayed. . . .

He slept. . . . Not too long after, three hours at the most, he was awakened by the sound of a car crunching on the drive outside. Squeal of brakes; bang of a car door; footsteps on the loose pebbles; doorbell ringing.

Martine slid his hand under the pillow, found Neen's automatic where he had left it. He got up, dropped the gun into his jacket pocket and pushed the safety catch down with his thumb. He crossed the room, took a deep breath, opened the door.

"Well, well," he said. "Everloving Babyface. Come in."

Theo stepped uncertainly into the room.

"Brother Helder—he—" he said, then stopped. Hard to say whether the expression crippling his features was terror or adoration, or just three decades' worth of doubt compressed into a fat second.

"Helder sent you," Martine said. He hoped he was keeping his voice even. "All right. Do you know why? You saw my letter?"

"Letter? Yes. *No.* Brother Helder got it—he said something about a letter, it was hard to follow him, he was very upset. I know he got it. He had it in his hand when he called me in." He stopped and stared at Martine, eyes begging for the alms of reassurance. "Oh, dear God, it is possible. I wouldn't say for sure, still. Of course there would be *some* changes, eighteen years, but there's something, even with the beard. . . ." His lips continued to move but no more sounds came.

"Did Helder tell you to get *more* proof?" Martine was incredulous.

"He said there was one other thing that would clinch it. He said—he told me to ask you about another day. A day at Coney Island? Something that happened in Coney Island?"

Please, the friendly boyish hazel eyes said. For the love of Allah.

"Coney Island?"

"Yes. About the afternoon you and he went to Coney Island? During vacation, you had a couple of girls with you, their names were Rosemary and Irene? You'd all been drinking gin-and-tonics at Rosemary's apartment, then you went out to Coney Island and somewhere, somewhere on the boardwalk, you passed this place?"

"Wait a minute," Martine said. "All of a sudden—sure! I'll be goddamned!" He began to laugh. "Sure! That's it, exactly! I'm an idiot not to have thought of it myself—that's the real proof, of course." His left hand went up, clapped his right shoulder resoundingly several times.

"You remember?" There was no pleading in Theo's voice now, just terror.

"Every last pin prick! Sure! This is how it was—we were pretty drunk, parading down the boardwalk we passed this tattoo artist's place. Sure! We stopped there, just for the hell of it I dared Helder to get something written on him and he dared *me* to. After a minute or two the thing got out of hand, it was serious, we were too drunk to control it, see—there was no backing down on either side. So we blustered it through. I said a tattoo was a damned good thing to have—suppose you dropped dead of heart failure on the street or got killed in an auto accident, all they'd find on you would be your name and your name doesn't tell a thing about you—what a man needs is something emblematic inscribed on his hide, one pithy thing that sums up his whole life, everything he's been up to. A slogan, maybe, something. That was it exactly, Helder said, but there was a problem: a man doesn't know himself, it's only others who see him as he really is, therefore the emblematic slogan that sums him up ought to be picked by another person. That was fine by me, I said, I'd be happy to let him pick my slogan if he would let me pick his. He agreed and we stepped into the place, the girls thought we were crazy and tried to stop us but the thing had gone too far. So the tattoo man wrote Helder's slogan for me on my arm, and my slogan for him on *his*. . . . Did he show you his arm?"

"Yes. Yes, he did. You—"

"Sure, I'll tell you exactly what it says on his arm. It says, in fine sweeping Spencerian script—'Onward and Upward!' Right?"

"Small letters. Blue, with a double underlining in red. . . ."

Releasing the gun in his pocket, Martine slipped out of his jacket, rolled up the shirt sleeve on his right arm. High up, just over the vaccination mark, the lettering came into sight, faded but still legible: "$2 \times 2 = 5$." Blue, double underlining in red.

"Of course," Martine said, "the references are pretty obscure. It's a pretty obscure joke, like masochism, the references to masochism."

"Dear God."

Theo spoke the words tonelessly. With a peculiar dipping motion, bent as though he had a stomach ache, he dropped to his knees, reached out for Martine's hand and pressed his lips to it.

Martine shuddered. This was the first time he had actually felt a pro, its texture was utterly and abdominably unexpected: the outer layer was soft, soft as skin and flesh, a sheath of softness, it had a yielding rubbery quality but about a quarter inch down the resiliency stopped and it was

324

bone hard. Salt Lake, foam rubber, gangster-baby breast. Still shuddering, he snatched his hand away.

"Get up, get up."

For all his disgust he said it so gently that he surprised himself. There was something about this boy, this perennial boy, something naïve and open in his face, that called out an unthinking kindliness in him, it was the same reaction he'd always had to trusting old Ubu. Now, too, there was a feeling of pity: touching those cadaver-cold plastic hands, he felt a deep wave of sorrow for the owner.

But he immediately caught himself. Sorry—sorry for this eraser of Parises, this sly mineralogist? "Get up off your knees, you idiot," he said harshly, almost barking.

"It's you, it's you!" Theo babbled. "You've come back to save us, always in the hour of need—" Somehow he got the words out—he was sobbing now, his broad football shoulders bobbing like waterwings.

"I haven't come back to save anybody!" Martine shouted. "Any more than I went away to save anybody! Get that through your thick tantalum skull!" There it was, he had only to reach out to touch it—the long jagged scar, under it the tantalum cup he had installed with such loving care. "Although I must say, if I'd known what you were going to be up to I'd have given you one of columbium instead."

Theo heard nothing, his gleaming hands were pressed over his face and he kept muttering, weaving from side to side, "You've come back, you've come back. . . ."

Martine took hold of Theo's lapels and jerked him to his feet. He pointed to a chair. "Now listen to me," he said. "Stop blubbering and act your age. I'm going to acquaint you with the facts of life. Sit—*down!*"

Bewildered, Theo dropped into the chair.

"All right. Now listen. First, we're going to get you straight about my comings and going on behalf of humanity. These comings and goings are and always have been on behalf of only one very minute segment of humanity, namely, me. Get it? Are you letting it sink in? Eighteen years ago, when I got into that plane and took off from our encampment in the Congo—"

"It's a miracle," Theo said, the stupefied look still on his face. "You went up to fight all those planes. And you came through it. There must be a reason, there was some hand—"

"You fool! If you've got a brain left in that tantalum cage of yours, use it man, use it for once in your life! Listen. You know that I took off in a plane, and you have before you now the living evidence that I got away safely. I was safe, I was in a plane. I could have gone anywhere I wanted, couldn't I? How come, then, that I never came back? Huh? Doesn't that bird brain of yours begin to understand that if I didn't come back for eighteen years, that must say something about why I went away? Think for a minute! *Think!*"

"Yes, you got away," Theo said dully, backward child counting his sums on his fingers. "Miracle, it was a miracle. With a plane. Then—safe, with a plane—eighteen years. . . . But it doesn't make sense! *Where were you?*"

Theo tried to smile, it was like a man gaping his mouth for the dentist.

"That's easy," Martine said. "Do you remember the Mandunji island?"

"Mandunji island?"

"Yes—as you put it so succinctly, the Mandunji island. You remember being there with the Olympic team last, let's see, last May, late in May?"

"Why—yes, I was. Yes, they have some remarkable Lepidoptera there. I caught some lovely specimens, an unusual *Argynnis leto,* that's the Fritillary type, you know, and a really incredible *Aglais j-album,* that's the Tortoise Shell. I remember the place well."

"You damned well should. That's where you went butterfly hunting with drills and pickaxes."

"Brother Martine!" Theo cried. "Please don't say those things! You talk just like Vishinu, surely *you* can't believe those rotten things about me?"

It was the same Theo who had appeared on the television over three months ago, on the night of his return, July 3, to make his tearful denial of Vishinu's charges—lips quivering, hazel eyes two transparent puddles of hurt, voice choked with earnestness. Then Martine had been on the verge of being taken in, had positively wanted to be taken in: how was it possible for this babyface, this congenital boy scout, this beamish sonny boy, to lie about anything? And now, to his infinite disgust, Martine found himself wavering again, it was simply impossible to ferret out anything of the scoundrelly in this wide-eyed do-gooder. One wanted to reach out and pat him gently on the head, as one would a loyal cocker spaniel, but—there were the ineluctable facts.

"I don't have to *believe* anything," Martine said. "I *know.* You were seen digging. Not you yourself, actually, but quite a few of your friends."

"Seen?" There was nothing but bewilderment on Theo's

face now. "How? We trained, we collected butterflies and orchids, we visited with the natives. That's all we did. For the love of Marti—for the love of heaven, how could we have been seen doing anything else?"

"Don't pull that big innocent act with me," Martine said. "You were seen. Do you remember the native boy who came to your camp the first night with a basket of cassava from Ubu? On his way to the camp he saw quite a few members of your party in the jungle with all kinds of fancy drilling and assaying equipment, examining specimens of rock. Not butterflies, rocks. I got a full report about the operation."

"But—some of the boys weren't with me in the camp, it's true—but those boys *couldn't* have been drilling that night! They weren't even on shore! They were—the captain told me they were staying on board ship to practice their d-and-d's, I remember distinctly. . . ." He was a bundle of outrage and hurt.

"Maybe that's what they told you. Maybe. I can't prove you're lying so O.K., I'll give you the benefit of the doubt. But if they told you that, *they* were lying. They were in the jungle, they were digging."

"How can you *know* that?"

"The young man who reported it to me, the one who brought you to the tapioca—you remember him?"

"Very well. I had several nice chats with him."

"I've had lots of nice chats with him. He's my son."

Theo's head snapped back, he looked as though he had been struck. "Oh, really," he said softly. "I don't see how—"

He shook his head slightly, a faint sickly smile frozen on his lips. Then he gripped the chair, the tubes in his plastic arms flickered, he bolted to his feet. "Oh," he said, face very serious now. "I *do* remember something. Mr. Ubu—he said in his tribe it was common for people to have some kind of sickness in the head. He explained that they had a certain kind of operation for this sickness, Mandunga it was called, a lot of people were operated on."

"The gossipy old bastard," Martine muttered. "I told him, I warned him to keep his trap shut."

"He said many people were trained to perform this operation," Theo went on mechanically, toneless as an electrovox. "He said for many years it had been done very scientifically, with asepsis and power-driven trepans and everything. He said that was because for many years a remarkable scientist had been living with them and teaching them how to do it scientifically. He said—this man, he'd had to leave not long before—he was a skilled scientist, he knew an awful lot about the brain. . . ."

Theo ran his plastic fingers through his close-cropped blond hair, blinked, swallowed hard. "Oh, no," he said. "Oh *no*. . . . But still. Ubu said. He said this man was white. *You're* white. You—you're a brain surgeon, a highly skilled brain surgeon. Oh, dear God."

Theo was beginning to cry again, a teardrop welled up in one large innocent hazel eye and flowed down his cheek. "Eighteen years?" he said shakily. "It's crazy, it doesn't make sense."

"How many times do I have to tell you?" Martine said. In exasperation he thumped the desk top with his fist. "I was a deserter. I was hiding. Not saving humanity, not dreaming up harebrained messianic stunts. Hiding! Hiding! Deserters hide, I was hiding!" He glared at Theo—the man was beseeching him with his eyes to ease his torment somehow.

"One thing," Theo whispered.

"Shoot."

"The notebook. You did *write* it. You did *leave* it."

"All right. I'll have to take the responsibility for writing it—and for leaving it around where somebody else could read it. But, you see, *you* never took the responsibility for *reading* it."

"Helder was wrong?"

"It's high time you found this out: the Helders are *always* wrong. They're always annotating the facts of history and personality out of existence, whenever those facts mess up their neat ideological packages. And shoving their footnotes, dressed up as facts, down the gullible throats of suckers like you."

Theo sat down again, transparent elbows on transparent knees, and regarded his dangling transparent hands. "Helder was *very* convincing," he said.

"Because you wanted to be convinced—you couldn't bring yourself to look the stark facts in the eye, you begged Helder to dress them up with his footnotes. One fact in particular you could never assess coolly—the fact of Helder himself. You think you know Helder?"

Martine explained what had happened to Rosemary. "I know the whole story, you see. That, dear Brother Theo, was the story I reminded him of in my letter this morning. You see, you really didn't have to go to the trouble of checking the tattoo on my arm. The son-of-a-bitch *knew* from my letter that it was really me. . . ."

Theo was silent, turning his hands forward and back, examining them as though they were prize specimens of *Aglais j-album*. Finally he said, without looking up, "Then you didn't mean all that about Immob either."

"I was warning against Immob—warning myself. I meant only one thing. I meant what I said about masochism—the one subject in my notes that Helder chose to overlook. I meant only that the human race was so goddamned masochistic it might very well, given an exalted programmatic cover by some bumblehead messiah like Helder, an excuse for self-maiming dressed up as a shining ideology, come to some ultimate sacrificial monstrosity like Immob—tear itself limb from limb, literally, and call the result salvation—create for itself the last word in limbos and consider that it had been jet-propelled straight through the pearly gates. . . . Only it was just an ironic figure of speech, you see, an elaborate pun. I didn't mean it literally. I thought I was just joking. . . ."

Theo held his fingers before his face and bent the knuckles, absorbedly watching the gleaming tubes. "The Theo part, that was a joke. You were *joking* about calling me Theo."

"The glossy theological sheen, and under it a savage plunging of the scalpel into oneself—that's the anatomy of all great political crusades, all messianic perfectionist and salvationist mass movements, from Cro-Magnon man to Cyber-Cyto man! Naturally, such movements must be led by men who are pacifists on the surface and raping babies at heart—only a leader with such raging ambivalence in himself can exert such a charismatic spell over the rest of humanity, the rank-and-file ambivaleers, the ambivaliants, as to mobilize them for anything and everything. . . ."

Theo raised his fingers still higher, studying their outlines against the background of the lumi-ceiling like a bacteriologist eyeing a rack of test tubes. "For nothing," he said. "The whole thing was a mistake."

There was no hysteria in his face now, the eyes were quite dry, steady. Something that ran deeper than tears, excluded tears, had taken hold of him now—he was lost in a dead emotional space in which the unspeakable facts gleamed, sputtered, beat like ramrods against the eyballs. It was a fact-ridden, fact-drenched becalmment in which he floated now, corpse riding on a Sargasso Sea of facts, enormities brushing against him like putrescent orange peels and stinking dead cats. He looked exactly as he had looked eighteen years ago on the operating table, eyes open and glassy and staring. But this time he saw.

But now that Theo was far beyond the paltry histrionics of grief, Martine himself felt moved to weep. It was absurd—what was there to weep for in this wretch? But there it was, Martine felt a prickling in his eyes as he watched Theo turn his gleaming plastic hands back and forth against the light, over and back; he began to blink rapidly.

"I'm no better than you," he said. "Worse, maybe. I didn't even believe. . . . All this talk, what good does it do? Are you going to take me to Helder?"

"You knew about Coney Island. He said if you knew, if the tattoo was there, I was to take you to him."

"Poor little Theo." Martine had intended to make it sound mocking, but there was instead a real sadness in his voice. "Poor little self-made ambulatory basket case. For centuries now you've been devotedly tailing your glorious martyrs—never suspecting that if you ever caught up with them they'd turn out to have feet of clay, and tattoos on their arms informing you that twice-two equals five. . . . Come on, let's get going. I've got a couple of footnotes I want to add to Helder's footnotes."

Martine rolled down his shirtsleeve and slipped into his jacket. He went to the door and opened it, waited for Theo to pass through. He followed.

"Don't feel too sorry for yourself," he said as the car swung into the highway. "Helder taught you the neat mathematical approach to things, the twice-two pitch, use it now. How many people did you eliminate in the war, twenty million, thirty million? How many did you disfigure or clip, hundreds and hundreds of thousands?" His voice grew harsh as he spoke, it satisfied him that his toughness was returning; sentimentality had no place in his plans at the moment. "The mathematics is all in your favor, you see—two legs ripped from you and two arms willingly given, twice-two equals four exactly. It's not a very stiff price to pay, you got off pretty damned easy."

To himself he added, "How many people did I eliminate in the cave? How stiff a price will I have to pay for *that?*"

Theo drove for a long time without saying anything; he left the highway and picked a devious route over bumpy back roads, concentrating on the wheel. Finally, as the buildings of Los Alamos loomed up in the distance, wavering a little in the rolling heat currents of the desert, he said very softly, "Why did you come back?"

Martine made a face, as though he had tasted something unpleasant. "Oh," he said. "To take responsibility for my notebook, I guess. To find out why I wrote it. To write an ending for it, maybe."

His thumb played with the safety catch of the automatic in his pocket. He studied Theo's large, frank, innocent, too steady hazel eye, eagle-scout eye, peace-on-earth eye. If he killed Helder, obviously he also had to kill Theo—matter of consistency, you can't kill just *one* Siamese twin. He did not know whether he could do it.

Ahead there was a long low concrete structure, one story high, with garage-like driveways between its thick columns; across the roof was a sign reading, DROP NUMBER SEVEN: LOS ALAMOS INDUSTRIAL SLOT. Theo took the cutoff leading to this building and drove through one of the entrances, stopping before a pair of wide doors and flicking his headlights on and off several times.

"We'll go the rest of the way underground," he said without expression. "Safer. Might run into some of Vishinu's men going through the streets."

In response to the signal from his headlights the doors slid open. Theo drove into the elevator, flashed his lights twice more, the doors closed and the elevator began to drop.

chapter twenty-two

FOR A MINUTE, close to a minute, they streaked downward. Then a slackening of speed, the elevator braked to a smooth halt, doors ground open again and Theo drove out into a narrow low-ceilinged corridor chipped through solid rock and whitewashed to a gleam. The car nosed into another such slot, then a third. More twistings and weavings, it was a trellis of underground speedways, a two-laned honeycomb, hospital-clean and morgue-still—then without warning they zoomed clear of imminent walls, shot from cramping confinement into the open as in some explosive chthonian birth.

Martine looked about him in dumb astonishment. They were now traveling at a hundred miles an hour along the rim of a chasm as wide across as the Grand Canyon or the Grand Coulee and seemingly without beginning or end.

The road they were speeding over was actually a sort of platform stretched in space only thirty feet or so from the roof

of this enormous pit, a catwalk arrangement supported by
cantilevers which jutted out from the sheer perpendicular
wall on the left: a spacious highway, wide enough for six
traffic lanes and edged with a raised ramp for pedestrians.
And below, to the right, fizzing and yammering all through
the incredible man-made gash, was a whole subterranean
supercity—a composite of many Pittsburghs and Detroits
buried under the desert sands. At some points the earth had
been hollowed out to greater depths than at others: the
topmost levels seemed to be hardly more than two or three
hundred feet below the overhanging road, the bottommost
levels a thousand feet down or even more. And the entire
floor of the hollow, at all levels, was strewn with machines
and manufacturing equipment, the litter of a miraculous
century which wrote its fables in steel and underscored them
in molybdenum: the squat metallic humps of atomic breeder
reactors, big around as a city block, and hovering over
them, traveling on suspended tracks, the delicate spidery
filigreed arms of cranes with magnetized fingers at their
restless lips; flame-geysering blast furnaces and sparkshow-
ering open hearths and incandescent kilns, close by them
many thin-lipped mouths from whose spinning cylindrical
dentures spewed flat sheets of steel and aluminum, and, just
beyond, to mold these metals, row upon row of planers and
shapers and drillers and bevelers and stampers and buffers
and riveters and welders; all the sleek devices invented by
men to supplement their own puny fingers and teeth, and to
muscle these super-biters and super-hammerers, to supply the
super-biceps, atomic power plants everywhere. It was Wil-
low Run and Oak Ridge and Hanford rolled up in one. And
besides the magnetized fingers and the giant hooks, belt lines
ran everywhere, conveyor bands and escalators: mechanized
carrier pigeons and St. Bernard dogs which loped dutifully
about feeding the raw materials of metal and plastic into the
processors and the finished parts into sub-assembly lines and
the sub-assemblies into final assembly, then herded the
finished products to the paint-sprayers and plastic-coaters and
after that to the packaging and loading platforms.

Straining to fix his eye on discrete objects as the fantastic
blur sped by, Martine could make out here and there
squadrons of manufactured items riding out on the conveyors
to the shipping departments: refrigerators, bicycles, uphol-
stered armchairs, prefabricated cottages, electric toasters,
automobiles, passenger planes, tractors, television sets, typewriters, adding machines, books, bathtubs, flags. And artificial

limbs: at one point Martine was sure he spotted a line of gleaming plastic legs traveling along.

Visually the scene was like carnival fireworks, some amuck Mardi Gras, the whole pit danced with sparks and flares and gleams and licking flames, interspersed with puffs of steam and spurts of dust and spray—and the sound was an infernal hubbub of clangings and crunchings, whines and burrs, cracklings and hissings. But, curiously, there was an impersonal cast to the whole picture, the machines gave the impression of being on their own, impervious, self-contained. Here and there Martine could make out the dwarfed, irrelevant figure of a man—most of the workers seemed to be Negroes, he couldn't be sure because of the distance and the speed at which the car was traveling—dressed in overalls, they all seemed to be puttering impotently, applying oil cans, sweeping up refuse, wiping away smudges of oil, wheeling carts of waste, while the machines, smug, indifferent, aloof, growled and thumped.

Martine pointed down at another belt line loaded with artificial limbs. "More legs," he said. "To genuflect before the machines that make legs."

His eyes hurt, it was too much. He looked away. For the first time he noticed that on their left, at eye level, carved into the face of the great cavern close to the ceiling, were many deep cubicles, separated from the elevated speedway by walls of glass and filled, lined on all sides, with more equipment: panel upon panel of levers and dials and switches and calibrated indicators and fluttering needles, batteries of electronic controls. It was easy to see what these instruments were for—up above the control boards loomed racks of flickering electronic tubes and a fantastic hodge-podge of multicolored wires running in a diabolic tangle from wall to wall, like neurone foliations seen through an electron microscope. Here was the reason why the few workmen below looked like such surplus commodities; these were the robot engineers which ran the sunken factories, caches of brains to ride herd on the brawn below. It was uncanny: as though the calculating machines up in their supervisory crannies were actually looking down upon their metallic slaves in the pit, literally overseeing them, eyes tyrannizing hands and feet, barking silent orders and blowing unheard whistles. Even before the war Martine had visited whole factories that were robotized from end to end all along the flow-chart, from the feed-in of ores and crude rubbers to the trundling out of neatly packaged jeeps and anti-aircraft

333

guns; but he had never seen anything on this scale, whole cities run together and put under the surveillance of the *machina ratiocinatrix.* The most disconcerting thing about it was that he had a feeling *he* was being watched—as all the cogs in all the machines were watched. The atmosphere was one of peeping Toms everywhere, snoops and hawk-shaws swarming over the white aseptic-looking walls.

"I don't mean to be nosy," Martine said, "but when a guy wants a raise around here, or would like to ask for the day off, who does he see—the third knob on the right?"

The strained joke didn't relieve his nervousness, Theo seemed not to notice it. They drove in silence for a time, then Theo slowed down and took a left turn into a narrow tunnel. More zagging through the maze; then a pause before another elevator and a greased ascent, Martine relieved now to be back in cramped quarters after the agoraphobic wildness of the last few minutes.

When they emerged from the elevator this time there were lavish sweeps of window all about them and a downpour of sunlight—they were, Martine could see as soon as his eyes adjusted themselves to the glare, somewhere in the upper reaches of a skyscraper, some thirty-five or forty stories up, and the ramp they were traveling on mounted further still, curling wormlike around on the outside of the building and then shooting indoors again with each full circle, completing one loop per floor.

On the topmost floor, which was domed with solid glass, Theo drove off the ramp into a parking space and came to a halt. He climbed out—there was an absent look about him, he seemed to be moving as though drugged—and Martine followed him.

"This is it," Theo said. "I'd better call before we go in."

He walked over to a switchboard set in the wall, pressed one of the plastic knobs several times. A light flashed on the board.

"We're here," he said tensely after a moment, speaking into the board. "I've got him with me."

A silence; then a clipped "O.K." Theo signaled to Martine to follow him.

Through corridors again, spacious ones this time, with bouncy soft-plasticized floors and much window and walls of soothing pastel shades, azure and magenta. They passed many doors on which there were neat little signs: BUREAU OF LABOR STATISTICS, BUREAU OF THE CENSUS, BUREAU OF NEURO-LOCO EDUCATION, BUREAU OF PRICE CONTROL—through the glass Martine could see that the offices within were inhabited not by people but by machines, more robot brains: panels of controls and circuits of tubes and transistors everywhere. Vishinu could mow down all the bureaucrats in the Strip and business would go on much as usual for a long time—*these* were the real bureaucrats, no migraine, the human ones were by far the most expendable. Shades of Wiener.

He stopped before the door marked BUREAU OF PRICE CONTROL and peered in. Directly before him was a huge panel running from floor to ceiling, labeled "Official Wholesale Price of Eggs Per Gross"; in the slot for the date were the figures "10/20/90" and in the slot which indicated the price per gross the figures changed, as Martine watched, from "$8.273" to "$8.274."

"Very neat," he said. "Just too, too twice-two."

Theo stood by his side without saying anything, waiting for him.

"What price glory?" Martine said. "You got a calculator for that? I don't know what that's got to do with the price of eggs."

They went on into another wing, passed through a door marked OFFICE OF THE PRESIDENT. An anteroom, several outer offices—then another door on which Theo knocked.

"Come in," a voice called.

Theo stepped to one side to let Martine go first. It was a very large room, heavily carpeted with a deep-tufted rug of maroon, at the far end was a long low semicircular desk. Behind the desk, fingers on his temples, sat Helder, sniffing.

"Marty?" Helder made as if to get up, rose halfway, then sank back in his chair. His hands, on a bureaucratic parade of their own, some parodying desk maneuver, transferred a stack of documents from the left side of the table to the right, then shifted them back again. "You?"

The man's face was ashen pale and yet there was a suggestion of some mottled darkness in it, like much-trampled slush, like rocquefort. He sniffed.

Martine went over to the desk, saluted with a mock flourish. "It's me," he said. "Hail the prodigal steamroller."

"It's really you."

Helder's hands went up in mute protest, palms pushing away from him, it looked as though he was holding some round fat mucky thing and couldn't find a place to throw it.

"Oh no," he whispered, his hands emphatically echoing the words. "It couldn't be."

"Brother Helder," Martine said, "I want to congratulate you on your twice-two-equals-foresight. It was the intuition of a natural-born bureaucrat that led you to keep your hands on. All God's bureaucrats got hands."

"Impossible," Helder said.

Martine pointed a pedantic finger at Theo. "Observe, Brother Tambo," he said. "Get this picture—martyr returns to gang up on his annotator, text rebelling against the footnotes. First time it's ever happened—when did a Bible, a Bhagavad-Gita, a Koran, a *Wealth of Nations,* a *Das Kapital,* a *Mein Kampf* ever rear up and lunge at its Number One disciple? The word turning on the wordy! It's an occasion, history's being made before your eyes! Leave us all up-ass and cakewalk for joy and jubilee!"

"Marty, Marty," Helder said, sniffing heavily. "This is no time for jokes. I know you, you pretend to be cynical and wisecracking on the surface but underneath there's a concern for the things that count—"

"Not things that count like you," Martine said. "On your fingers, always coming out with the logical right score. You swine."

"Marty! Marty! For once, don't pretend to be so tough and calloused! You're the only one who can help us now—"

"I'm going to help you, all right." Martine got up and walked over to Helder's chair. "Get up," he said. Helder stared at him for a moment, then got to his feet. "I am going to help you," Martine repeated. He took hold of Helder's tie just under the knot, gripping it with such force that Helder's head was thrown back. "I'm going to kill you."

"Brother Martine!" Theo said suddenly, leaping to his feet. "What have you got in your pocket?"

"You stay out of this," Martine said. "Keep your babyface out of men's affairs—it wasn't *your* notebook that was made the human race's epitaph, don't interfere, I'm warning you. . . ."

He let go of Helder and signaled abruptly with his free hand to Theo, ordering him away. Theo backed off to the window. Martine took a tight grip on the gun in his pocket, slipped the safety catch down.

"I'm through giving you alibis, you swine, do you hear! I'm going to put an end to the bloody farce and to you too—it's only fitting that I should be the one who finally invokes the Assassination Clause against you. And if your little stooge there tries to stop me, I'll plug him too. Gladly. It'll help clear the air."

Helder's shoulders sagged, he seemed to age ten years as he stood there looking at Martine and not believing what he saw. "You can't," he said, almost sadly. "You can't do it, Marty."

"*You're* telling *me* what I can and can't do? Pig! I'll—"

"No, no, Marty. You don't understand. Harm me, do so much as take that gun out of your pocket, and you'll never get out of here. There are men watching, Marty, twelve of them. . . ."

"Twelve?" Martine said. "Oh, I see—the apostles." He stepped back to the window seat and studied the two men, hand still in his pocket.

But now Helder was not concerned with Martine: he was looking at Theo thoughtfully. "This does complicate matters a bit," Martine said; nobody paid any attention to him.

"Twelve men watching?" Theo said incredulously. "*Guards?*"

"Oh, for Christ's *sake*, Theo!" Helder burst out. "I'm sorry you've got to find out about it like this, but—put yourself in *my* place, man! Matter of fact, though, you *are* in my place— how do you think you've been getting around so easily when there're people all over the place just dying to take a pot shot at you! You lead a charmed life, sure, but not *that* charmed, it takes some arranging. . . ."

"I'm guarded too?" Theo said.

"For months. All right! Sure, it's defensism, it violates the Assassination Clause, I know that. But what's the alternative? It's a matter of simple logic—a leader's function is to lead, that's his responsibility, and he can't do much leading if he's full of bullet holes, can he? Never mind whether or not *you* think a leader's got a responsibility to stay alive—our followers *do* think so, and they're determined to guard us whether we like it or not. What would you have me do, guard myself against these guards? But, according to the letter of the law, *that's* illegal too. . . . Call it defensism, call it anything you want, they won't let you take a step without protection. They argue that the Assassination Clause is abrogated for the duration of the crisis, and I don't think even you could give them a good argument to the contrary. Not after yesterday."

Yesterday. Four hundred plastic arms outstretched: Vishinu's arm dropping: flashes, explosions: the officials crumpling, but Helder and Theo—

"Ho," Martine said. The two men turned to him in surprise. "I begin to smell something. Tell me one thing, Helder. Some fifty or sixty men got it yesterday, they stayed there like sitting ducks when Vishinu's men took aim, but you, you knew enough to take a dive and pull Theo down with you. Tell me, please, *how did you know when to take a dive?*"

Helder studied the floor for a long moment, looked up at Theo, then dropped his eyes again. He shrugged, sniffled. "All right," he said. "That's very smart of you, Marty—sure, I knew their arms were rifles. At least, I guessed they might be." He turned away to avoid Theo's eyes. "I mean, I knew they had these things. It occurred to me just in time, when they seemed to be taking aim so carefully, that that was what their pros might be. . . ."

"I see," Martine said. "While you're at it you might as well complete Theo's postgraduate course in Realpolitik. Tell us how, exactly, you knew about their arms being firearms."

"Isn't it obvious?" Helder sounded peevish; he seemed suddenly tired too, he spoke with great effort. "They have spies. They've had spies for a long time. So we've been forced to use spies too—I fought it at first but the others prevailed, they argued that we had to be practical and in the face of the evidence I didn't know any answer to that. We just spared Theo and others like him the full ugly knowledge of the situation, we knew they couldn't take it: some of us were meant for responsible office and others for the much softer job of charismatic inspiration."

There was bitterness in his voice.

"They always had better pros than they admitted, we knew that. So, for that matter, did we. They developed super flame-throwers, super rotary saws, super everything, while they kept on playing it humble and backward and losing the Games year after year. And we developed some pretty super models too, we could have won the Games this year if we'd thought it was good strategy to trot them out. Our timing was off. . . . Anyhow, we knew they'd developed the rifle arm. We got hold of a couple samples, we studied them carefully. As it happened, we already had one of our own in the works. Right this minute we've got them in mass production just as the Union has, although it's all a super-secret. So it occurred to me yesterday, after Vishinu's threatening speech, that what his athletes had up their sleeves—oh, excuse me, I'm a little upset—I got the idea that it might be wiser to duck, just in case. . . ."

There was no gratitude in Theo's eyes. "I see," he said. "I am beginning to see. There are some footnotes you haven't written yet."

Martine was grinning now. He was beginning to feel very good. "Say, I'm enjoying this," he said. "The Hyphen between the Siamese twins is getting a bit frayed. Let's kick it around a little more. . . . Are you going to pretend that you never took a so-called defensive step until you found out the Union had taken it first?"

"Stop it, Marty!" Helder cried. "I've had about enough. . . . As it happened, we got a head start on one thing, they did on another; either way, the other side soon found out about the new development and caught up. . . . Oh, it's a vicious, vicious circle, the whole thing. It's even hard to remember exactly how it started, a half-dozen years ago, I've forgotten who started what. Something bigger than all of us was involved, pushing us, it ran away with us before we knew it. . . ."

"Excellent," Martine said. "You are aware, of course, that your pretty little speech could have been delivered by Vishinu, word for word? Undoubtedly has been?"

"Don't misunderstand," Helder said. "Oh, he'd say those things, all right, but. . . . I don't want to give you the wrong impression—he started it, the Union started it! At least I'm pretty sure. . . . It's just that—once it got rolling everything moved so fast. . . ."

"Our platform," Theo said, "was commitment. Irrevocable commitment. But you didn't mean it that way. You meant, if the others don't play fair we take our irrevocable commitment back? It was irrevocable with strings, conditions?"

Martine clapped his hands and did a few steps of a soft-shoe shuffle. "Mistuh Interlocutuh!" he shouted. "Brother Tambo done gone an' fo'git his lines! He done throw de script away! He really ad-libbin' some now! Wheah it say twice-two equal fo' he fo'git de arit'metic an' come sashayin' an' hifalutin all lickity-split an' kerplunk down to de footnotes, Ah mean de footlights, an' he say uppity as ole Brer Rabbit dat de multiplacatin' tables done been abrogationed—"

But he got no further. There was a blinding flash outside, the whole ozone turned incandescent: the atmosphere shimmied, space caught on fire. Then the dancing lights, shifting like anti-aircraft searchlights, like the Aurora Borealis, went off. Then danced again, the ether doing a hula. Subsided for a moment. Flared up still another time. And while the air ignited, was snuffed out, flamed again, there was an incredible booming explosion outside, some ultimate noise-maker at work, the earth heaving up a belching basso from its bowels—then another, then a third, then another. The building quaked, moving what seemed to be inches at a time: floor shuddered, walls seemed to jiggle.

It went on for fully a minute. Air sporadically blazing. Staccato rumblings beating on the eardrums. The whole structure stricken with palsy. And they all stood, all three of them, rooted to their places, arms akimbo and mouths ludicrously frozen open.

Then it stopped. For a moment longer they stood where they were, animated as scarecrows. Then Helder, first to snap out of it, rushed to the window; a second later he was joined by Theo and Martine.

It was something to see: at several points around the city dense white mushrooms seething above the highest sky-scrapers, symmetrical top-heavy alps sculpted of fleece and cotton batting, sprouting on the double like buds in a speeded-up zoological film. And in their wake, licking up around their bases, were sheets of flame—fires everywhere, giving off swirling clouds of black smoke.

"Oh, no," Helder said. "Oh, no." It sounded as though he were saying a prayer.

"Atom bombs," Theo said.

"Lots of atom bombs," Martine said.

He suppressed an impulse to giggle; something was breaking loose in him, he was on the edge of hysteria. They were, he thought, like three little boys way back at the dawn of television, sitting on the edges of their seats in the parlor and exchanging awed whispers about Hopalong Cassidy's dead-eye marksmanship.

"They're using small ones," Helder said. "Very small. Implosive type. Subcritical amounts of plutonium, probably." He pressed his palms against the window. "It's really fine glass," he said irrelevantly. "They tell me it'll stand up against almost anything. Keeps out the gamma rays, that's one thing, besides it's damn near shatterproof, they do something to the silica. Of course, we're pretty high up too, the blast couldn't be very strong this high up, that's to be considered. . . ." He made a sniffing noise. "My sinus is bad today."

"People who live in glass defenses," Martine said.

"Glass? Defensism?" It was Theo speaking, he sounded remote, sleepy, almost.

"Glass defense mechanism," Martine said. "Not shatterproof. You know, I was born on the day of the *first* mushroom."

A sound came up from his throat: maybe a giggle, maybe a hiccup, he wasn't sure.

A buzzing noise from the desk. Helder ran over and snapped a switch on the intercom box. "Yes?" he said.

A clipped metallic voice: "Anderson calling in, sir."

"Anderson! What's going on out there? Have you got anything on this?"

"We're getting a preliminary picture. It's a systematic fifth-column operation—not many Unioneers actively involved, as we make it out, mostly Strip agents. They planned to blow up the capitol building too, they were setting a bomb on one of the lower stories but their man was nabbed before he could get it rigged up—a Strip citizen, one of the staff janitors, Negro, he's talking now. . . . At least twelve limited-action bombs planted in L.A. All at key spots: the Neuro-Loco Institute, the Institute for Advanced Cyber-Cyto Studies, the Olympic Training Clubs headquarters, several prosthetics warehouses. They did quite a job downstairs too—three or four bombs were set in the power plants and whatnot, the Slot's a mess. The pattern seems to be a concerted attack on all plants and research centers concerned with pros. No delayed-action radiation, our disaster crews can be mobilized without anti-gamma-ray gear. At least for above-ground operations."

"All right," Helder said. "I see. Keep me posted."

"Yes, sir. . . . Just a minute, sir! Something more's coming in now. . . . Yes. The ticker from New Jamestown says the same thing's going on there. . . . And here's one from Martinesburg, same story—they also got the Radiation Research Labs up there. . . . Oh, something else. It's not just bombings. Uh, uh. There've been atacks on individuals too. On amps, wherever they could be found. Let's see. . . . Yes. Amps have been attacked on the streets, in classrooms, in rest homes, even in their own houses. Pretty damned systematic. In these individual attacks the men aren't injured, just their pros smashed. It seems to be directed against pros, no casualties except in the bombings. They've located some of our stock piles of pros too, they've been blown up too. . . ."

"All right," saig Helder. "They're trying to immobilize us. Of course. Prepare a list of the installations and stock piles that've been hit as soon as you can. I want to get a full picture of the extent of the damage. At once. What about the fires?"

"The boys think they'll be able to get them under control, here in L.A. anyway, haven't heard from the other cities yet. The disaster crews are out already."

"Keep me posted."

Helder switched off the intercom, sat down at his desk. He seemed to be lost in thought, fingers drumming on the blotter. Finally he nodded his head vehemently, three times, then reached for the intercom and pressed one of the buttons on its control board.

"Yes, sir?" the machine barked.

"Riley?" Helder said. "Now listen carefully, Riley. We can't have any slip-ups. This is it. As of this moment we're abandoning Plan A. Plan B goes into operation immediately. You know what to do. Send out the emergency B flash to all Olympic Training Clubs. Mobilization at the convergence points. Distribution of flame-arms, rotor-arms, heli-arms, rifle-arms from the secret stock piles, as per schedule. Designated shock units advance to meet the Union forces. Only the designated ones, understand—this slow pincers movement from the coasts looks like a maneuver to draw our defense units away from home base to make things easy for the fifth column. Designated anti-fifth-column units begin their security patrols. Atom bombs supplied the demolition squads in no case to exceed the size and strength of those employed by the Union agents. The hundred thousand kiloton bombs to be kept in reserve for Plan D, check on this. All units in Union territory to be given the B flash, they're to begin operations immediately. . . ."

"Got it, sir."

"Get going, Riley. Report back. . . . Oh, one more thing. Recall all personnel from the Victoria Dredging Project immediately. To be reassigned to fire-fighting and anti-fifth-column operations."

Theo had been listening to this conversation. He left the window now and approached Helder. "You even have plans?" he said.

"Grow up, Theo!" Helder grunted. "Of course—they've got plans, we've got plans, it's been that way for years."

"You even—have agents in the Union?"

"We'd be in a hell of a fix now if we didn't," Helder said. "A lot of Strippers, even underprivileged Negroes, are surprisingly loyal to their country, Theo. To Immob, that is. Many of them living around the Union at strategic points this very minute. They'll prove their loyalty pretty damned convincingly before the afternoon's over, take my word for it. . . ."

"You could have given them some reason for their loyalty," Theo said. "All the discrimination—I tried to tell you, it was making a very bad impression in the East. . . ."

"What could I have suggested—a few more anti-discrimination and fair-employment-practice laws? I did, but I got voted down. A lot of good all that crap does anyway—remember the old South, did the law ever do anything about lynchings there? . . . No, no, Theo, it wasn't anything to be solved by decree. I'd hoped that with time, by patient education—it was a transitional period, people had to be changed slowly. . . ."

"Amputation isn't slow," Theo said, hands raised. "It only takes an hour." He sat down across from Helder and fell into what seemed to be his chief pastime this afternoon: he stared at his hands in a sort of reverie. "So we take everything back," he said. "It's a transitional period, we can't be irrevocable overnight." He held his hands up. "We take everything back. But suppose I want to take my hands back?" For the first time his voice lost its soft, pleasant modulations, rose almost to a scream. "*Who will give me back my hands? Who will give back my hands?*"

"Don't get so dramatic," Helder said with disgust. "Remember, I gave my legs too."

Martine came over and stood between the two. "I didn't give anything," he said, twirling around like a mannikin. "Not so much as a callus or a hangnail. I ask you both to note this carefully, in case anybody's ever in a position to write any more disarming footnotes." But then disgust came into his face, a wave of dyspepsia. He looked at his hands as though they were enemies, and said, "But I did give my hands—to the cave. Who will give the lobotomist back his hands?"

Helder's face was grim. "I'm not going to be in a position to do much of anything," he said. "I'm going to be dead."

"Dead?" Martine echoed.

"Sure. Oh, I'm being guarded, all right, but sooner or later, tomorrow, next week, somebody will get to thinking about the Assassination Clause and decide to get me. It would probably have happened years ago, if my colleagues hadn't taken steps. They'll get Vishinu too, sooner or later, and a lot of his pals along with him. They'll keep knocking off the leaders on both sides, one after the other. The war will go on—we'll win in the end, of course, justice is on our side, but a lot of leaders will fall by the way. It only takes one man, slipping by the guards. . . ."

"Or maybe one guard," Martine said. "You've got twelve guards. Twelve apostles. There's usually at least one Judas in every twelve apostles, that's about the ratio. The figure ought to interest a neat mathematician like you."

But Helder seemed bored by the discussion of his own fate. He was absorbed in his own thoughts again, lips pressed tightly together and eyes far away, nose twitching as he sniffed. "The transition is tougher than we'd anticipated," he said dreamily. "There's much trouble ahead still—but we're moving, we'll get there. We must believe that." He cocked his head and looked at Martine. "If this didn't work, even this—then good God, what will? What could? It'll work, it's got to."

"What else'll work?" Martine felt the hysteria stirring in him again. "I'll tell you what else'll work—I've spent nearly eighteen years studing the question! You haven't asked me where I've been all these years, Helder, you've been distracted. I'll tell you what I've been up to for over seventeen years! I've been on a little island in the Indian Ocean, that's where, cutting open heads and tracing the aggressions in them. Sitting in a little cave, the Mandunga cave, performing Mandunga lobotomies, Christ only knows how many thousands of skulls I've pried open trying to get at the secret of aggression—how many hundreds of thousands of pages I've filled with data on where aggressiveness is rooted in the human cortex and how it can be sliced and scissored out—there's more information on the aggression areas of the human cortex back in that cave, probably, than anybody ever dreamed about. Oh, I've become an expert on the subject, I can tell you a thing or two about lobotomizing little rapists down to good little pacifists, I've turned out more and better pacifists with my trepans than all your Immob surgeons ever did. . . ."

When Martine spat the word "Mandunga" at him, Helder stiffened, looked quickly at Theo, then back again. He was suddenly alert and concentrating.

"I'll tell you what *won't* work!" Martine babbled. "Attacking the human organism with a scalpel won't work, that's sure! I can slice up the worst homicidal maniac's prefrontal lobes and give you a real lamb of a pacifist, sure, the best little basket case you ever saw—but he's not a human being any more, just a lump! Just like an amp! Ambulatory basket case! For good! No, no, the knife won't work, you shit, you swine! Look at yourself this moment—the pacifist's flown out the window, the rapist's back in action with emergency flashes and Plan B's! More Rosemarys, eh, you love it! I could have done a hell of a lot better job on you with *my* scalpel, back in the Mandunga cave. I'd have made your commitment irrevocable, all right—only you'd have become an irrevocable vegetable too! You know what's wrong with the butcher-boy approach to the problem? I'll tell you—it just says aggression wherever there's any sign of violence and goes after it with a knife, not bothering to determine whether the thing's real or phony. It attacks the pretense as though it were the real thing—so the essential psychological problem's untouched, the phony rapist's phony premises become the premises of the psycho-surgeon's science, he's operating on the basis of a gigantic lie! There's only one thing that'll work, you pig, that has any chance of saving man before he's annihilated through his own masochism, it's to get behind his shows of violence and pound it home to him that 99 per cent of them are phony, masochistic in inception and masochistic in aim, born of death and striving for death. That'll work, only that, all the rest is suicide disguised as science and humanitarianism, you swine, you dirty swine. . . ."

"Marty!" Helder had risen again, he was looking at Martine in utter disbelief. "Mandunga—why, when Theo came back from Africa he told me about this island and a white man. . . . Marty! This Mandunga thing! *You* were the white man—*you* performed all those operations—we haven't done too much with lobotomy and things like that, of course, the cyber-cyto emphasis is a little different—*you've* been at it for eighteen years, you kept records. . . ." As he talked his eyes narrowed.

Martine shook his head, trying to get control of himself. "You're getting that programmatic look," he said. "Skip it— I've talked too goddamned much already. . . ."

"Marty," Helder said. "Look, it's not accidental, your returning like this. The timing's too neat, there *must* be a reason. . . . Listen, this thing could still work, there's time. Even if you pretend not to believe in Immob, hell, you wrote it, it came from you—sometimes a man is picked to convey more than he knows, he's a vehicle for something bigger than himself. . . ."

"I've been a vehicle," Martine said slowly, "for something smaller than myself. Smaller, and deader. That was my sin."

"It could still work!" Helder insisted, his eyes shining.

"*You* could make it work! Listen, all you've got to do is—become a vol-amp! A quadro! We could arrange it in no time. Then right after the surgery we'll announce your return, it'll be the most magical charismatic thing that ever happened—it'll shock people back to their senses, even Vishinu'll be stopped in his tracks. . . . You can do it, Marty! You could save humanity!"

Martine glared at Helder. He clamped his palms to his temples as though he had to exert pressure to keep his skull from flying off. And he began to laugh. "Say," he said, "that *would* be a pretty good punch line for the joke." He began to laugh harder. "No, thanks just the same. Maybe I'm one of you in my heart—but all the same, I'll keep my amble."

"Think, Marty!" Helder shouted. "You could save the human race! It would be like the Second Coming!"

"I'm going to leave now. I don't think you'll do anything about it—you know I could spill some pretty unsavory beans. No, I think you're going to let me walk out of here."

"Don't do it, Marty," Helder pleaded. "The fate of the world is in your hands."

"The fate of your hands is in your hands," Theo said. He was regarding his own again, bending the fingers slowly.

"Speaking of ambivalence," Martine said, "I'd like to make one final point. You've both got quite a taste for twice-two's, this should warm the cockles of your Euclidean hearts. I've just figured out another ratio—I'm twice the man either of you is! You know why? Because I'm *two* men! I'm *both* of you, both of you rolled up in one, the neatest little packaging job in history! Yes, I'm Helder, and I'm Theo too—the gangster and the baby, the demon activist and the cherubic passivist, the leader and the follower, the martyrizer and the martyrized, the doer and the done-to, the megalomaniacal 'T'-pusher and the self-annihilating 'It'-seeker, messiah and apostle, eye-plucker and cheek-turner, ganja and rota, never mind what that means, Dog and God. Only—I'm both of them, every minute and all day long and far into the night! Never one without the other, you see, I never quite get to the point where my left hand doesn't know what my right one's doing, I've got the most exquisitely shaky balance. The Hyphen's snapping between you two, the Hyphen's still somehow holding within me. Which only means that I'm life's delicate child, that hypertonic hyphenated wonder of the anthropoid ages, the half-man, half-woman, the ambulatory basket case. But you two, you're *less* than human. Because each of you has denied his doubleness. In only one

346

respect are you human—each of you, each in his own way, is the goddamnedest little old masochist the world's ever seen, the one with the phony aggression of the rapist, the other with the phony mildness and meekness and beatitude of the willingly raped. You two, together, you're the living example of how all messianic movements got organized. The chunk of full human ambivalence is falsely split down the middle and the two halves become runaways—out of the apparently ambulatory side come the leaders and out of the basket-case side the followers. The real sin is the split. . . . Between the two of you you'd make a human being. You two ought to get together. And have a good long talk. I suggest you get together and have a good long talk about columbium, for instance. . . ."

He clicked his heels and bowed deeply to Helder. "*Mi*stuh Interlocutuh," he said. "I hope your sinus is better—you'll have to do a lot of deep breathing." He repeated the movement. "*Brud*der Tambo. May the scalpel stay on the other side of the river—you haven't got many spare parts left." He straightened up and waved his hand. "It's been a real nice fish fry." He opened the door and went out.

His face was drenched, his hands fluttering, but he felt an intense exhilaration. Going down the corridor, he skipped once or twice. When he came to the door marked OFFICE OF PRICE CONTROL he stopped and looked through the glass panel again. "What price migraine." The wholesale price of eggs per gross was now up to $8.276. "What price mushrooms." To the tune of an old song he sang,

Too-too-twosie, good-bye,
Too-too-twosie, don't cry. . . .

At the elevator he had to make a decision: go back to the underground cavern or get out at street level? He had to sneak away from the city—he couldn't think beyond that. Which would be the safer way? Underground he might get lost; and there had been bombs set off in the Industrial Slot, the way might be blocked; all in all, it would be wiser to take his chances in the street, out in the open— there were fires, things must be a mess out there, but he might be able to pick his way through. At least, there was no danger of radiation.

When he got into the elevator he pressed the button marked "Main Floor." He hummed to himself, a strain from the Mandunji work song.

347

Smoke everywhere, churning black balls ricocheting from the roof tops; the sun was screened off as in an eclipse. Sirens whinnying; shouts; feet slapping excited paradiddles on pavements; growl of trucks in side streets—he heard more than he could see; his eyes smarted from the smoke, he held his hand over them and went along stumbling. At the corner a motorcade of ambulances raced past with a cacophony of moans; a moment later, down the cross street, a clanging fire truck thundered by, some kind of hook-and-ladder affair with men clinging to its sides—quadros, wearing heli-arms in place of the orthodox left ones.

Rush of scorching wind, some agitated eddying of heat-currents—suddenly the soupy haze cleared away in the area to his right, he could see down the street for three or four blocks. Fire down there, huge flames were licking from a tall building and smoke poured from it as from a giant smokestack. Clutter of fire-fighting apparatus in the street. Up above, all along the face of the building, buglike figures hovering in the air—men, quadros, equipped with umbrella-like heli-arms, bodies and heads swathed in puffy sacks, asbestos probably. Each one with a long thick nozzle tucked under the right arm, and a hose trailing to the ground from it, and a spray of water or some fire-extinguishing chemical flaring from the nozzle's mouth.

Fire-fighting—Martine remembered the lectures at the M. E. University—was one of the Immob attacks on the elements, one of the four prime Moral Equivalents for war. Interesting twist: practicing a Moral Equivalent for war in the midst of war. Most peculiar limbo, this, in which all the sizzling Limbodians, hallucinated, imagined that they were in paradise—a paradise with hook-and-ladders and asbestos suits. Angels in asbestos suits.

Oversight: in this non-Aristotelian paradise the angels had been so busy with their fire-fighting drills, they'd forgotten to invent any cybernetic wings. The cyberneticists could have cooked up some dillies—ram-jet wings, atom-powered wings all fluffy and alabaster and supersonic. But their imaginations had faltered, they'd stopped at heli-arms. For especially high-temperature paradises they might have concocted some asbestos wings—better yet, some columbium-alloy wings, they'd stand up in a real inferno of a paradise. . . .

People darted here and there, flitted across the street and then back again, chattering, grunting, hallooing. He paid no attention to them—the smoke was swirling down on him again, he groped his way along as best he could, coughing and dabbing at his inflamed eyes with a handkerchief.

Entering one of the target areas now, apparently: buildings pretty badly wrecked, wisps of smoke curling from windows, streets cracked and buckled. A shattered store front, jumble of wares in it—something moving in the debris, some tiny glistening thing. He stopped and peered in F. A. O. SCHWAB, a sagging sign said—branch of the toy shop he'd seen in New Jamestown.

Some small bright thing moving. He recognized it: a miniature quadro cut-up, strutting absurdly on its tiny transparent legs and swinging its tiny transparent arms—tripping, rolling over, springing to its feet, marching, tripping again, scattering broken dolls' heads and torsos before it as it made its slapstick stumblebum way back and forth. Nobody laughing now. Playing to an empty house. More spectacular pratfalls on view elsewhere. . . .

Diagonally across the street, a building with half its face blasted away. Strands of smoke streaming lazily from some of the windows, here and there a flick of flame. Something sticking from one of the windows, burning with a wavery orgonotic blue glow—pair of cybernetic arms, firearms, burning, blue flames sprouting from the fingers, no telling if a body was attached to them.

The Greeks, good Apollonians, had had the right idea about the plastic arts: eventually they had to set the world on Dionysian fire. But there were no eyes on these fingers, they blazed in blindness.

These paradisiac limbs needed more columbium, they weren't designed to withstand the heat of limbo. The fingers drooped like melting candles, droplets fell from their burning tips, plastic, dripping tears, weeping for their absent eyes. . . .

Choking, acrid fumes in his mouth, he turned a corner and proceeded down the block. There on the sidewalk, suddenly, slivers of glass all around, was a face staring up at him—Helder's face. Martine blinked. It was a cheap print, reproduction of a painting: Helder full-face, thin straight lips boldly set and gray eyes hypnotically fixed; on each side of the painting a towering thick-leaved giant sequoia, only the trunk was in the shape of a plastic limb, transparent—pillars of strength echoing the sculpted strength of Helder's long jutting columnar nose; behind the head and extending beyond it, wings splendidly spread, a regal American bald eagle, the old national symbol reincarnated—and just behind

349

it and not quite overlaid by it another eagle, and behind that a third, a long line of triumphant eagles overlapping like clouded mountains in an old Japanese print. So they *had*, in a sense, invented wings for their hero.

"Parakeets and raffias," Martine said aloud in disgust.

He had thought that by taking this course he would skirt the damaged area to the right, but after walking a short distance he saw that he was heading into another one—more fire, smoke, wreckage in the street. Here the streets and sidewalks seemed to have erupted: they had not only buckled, here and there almost impassable holes gaped in the concrete, maybe the effect of an underground explosion. Martine picked his way carefully around these pits; as he was passing a half-toppled store, he froze, there seemed to be human sounds coming from the crumbled and littered window. "Oh!" somebody said obliquely.

A gurgling sound, something percolating deep in the throat. Another: some incredible smothered hee-heeing, titter or hysterical quaver or cry that went beyond fright, one of them or all three. Somebody saying, without emotion, "Aaaiiiiiiiiiii," voweling some obscure and drawn-out comment on the unutterable.

Silence for a moment. Then the first voice croaking: "Oh! Oh! Oh!"

Hard to tell where the sounds were coming from: beams had crashed down into the window, there was nothing but a welter of mangled steel. But—there *was* something else. Here and there, hidden under the tangled girders, some small yellow thing—a series of yellow objects, small, compact, yellow baskets. Yellow, dripping red.

Baskets. Blood trickling from them into the street.

This is the way a world ends, this is the way a world ends, this is the way a notebook ends: with a bang, a mushroom, and a whimper.

"Oh. Oh. Oh." Quietly, no dramatics. Just an observation, neutral.

Betewen two large holes in the pavement there was a narrow stretch, more or less intact, that led to the window: delicately, testing before each step, Martine made his way across it as he had to—no chocolate layer cakes with him, no glasses of milk, too late for that. There was room for him to stand outside the window, a ledge of solid pavement, was left there, spattered with coagulating blood, was left there.

Most of the amps were dead: one had been run through the gut by a girder, another's skull was squashed flat by the broad side of a beam, a third had had his neck neatly slit from ear to ear, apparently by flying glass—blood everywhere, trickling, forming in pools, dripping down into the street like plastic, running fingers.

Three or four were still alive. A head squirmed: eyes bulged at Martine, "Aaaaiiiiiiii" bansheed the ambulatory lips. Sobbing laughter from another head three baskets away: "Heeheeheehee."

He went on to the end, as he had to. Past the miniatured groaner, the stunted titterer, the shrunken gurgler, stepping over the puddles of blood—to the yellow basket in the corner, as he had to. Basket neatly trapped in a mesh of girders, caged with ribbons of steel, blood oozing from it over the window's edge and down to the sidewalk.

Stood there looking down at the blood at his feet, his blood. Raised his eyes and looked at the face in the basket, his face. Lids of the face that was his face closed and fluttering, peevish mouth erupting soft noncommittal oh's, blood-flecked foam churning at the corners of the lips—his lips.

Baby-blue blanket still draped over the body that was his body yet less than his body—gashed in the middle now, blood surging through the rip, great blot of blood at the middle. Ripped by glass, probably: glass all about.

Itching in his throat, coughed.

Twitching eyelids snapped open. Blood-caked lips clamped on an "oh."

Reached between two beams, caressed the clammy forehead. Found the handkerchief in his pocket, brought it out and wiped the lips clean, mopped the forehead.

Question in the wide-open eyes that were his eyes: enormous unspeakable question, the ultimate interrogation which takes place in an echo chamber.

"Why?"

"I don't know, son. Something went wrong. We'll have to find out."

"Something went wrong we. Something. We."

"No, no, son, you mustn't blame yourself. It wasn't your fault—you did everything you could. Maybe people weren't ready yet."

Talking softly, all the while reaching for the lower edge of the blanket, lifting it gently.

"You have nothing to reproach yourself for. You went all the way. Others fell behind, not you."

Lifting gently, the wound coming into view. The whole

351

belly ripped open, hole big enough for two fists, lacerated guts hanging out.

Patting the head that was his head, soothing the feverish brow that was his brow, crooning yeses for noes, as he had to.

Eyes caught by something else: strange emptiness between the legs, what was left of the legs, the stumps. Where the genitals should be, something missing. Phallus lying unpropped. No testicles. Of course. Castrated. Programmatically.

Shock: of recognition; dream backfiring. Icy prickling at the nape of the neck, along the spine. Blanket back in place, mouth that was his mouth absent-mindedly going "Oh, oh, oh."

"You did everything you could."

"Maybe we were wrong!" Head raised from pillow now, jerking from side to side, eyes wild and rolling. "Everybody! They and we too and on all the sides! War—there was an explosion, outside people standing listening I was telling them the right and then explosion they disappeared sank down into the ground I was talking telling them they weren't there. . . . If! The slightest in the world! Understand! Then if we were wrong the arms the legs everything. . . . Do you hear me! Stay there, don't sink! Then in that case. Oh. Oh. Oh. Oh. But they never bring the milk."

Martine reached all the way between the beams, slid his arm under the boy's shoulder, cradling him, trying not to feel the stumps of the vanished arms that had been his arms.

"I want my arms I want my legs. You do that. And the milk. Like a piece of chocolate cake too, please. Hungry, feel empty."

"Listen to me, son! You were right! Never doubt it for a minute. The world will thank you for all this one day—you'll see, it will work yet. Don't lose your faith! You did not make your sacrifice for nothing—you are the true son of Martine, your father would be proud of you, you are flesh of his flesh. . . ."

Trying to keep the nausea from his voice. Rocking back and forth gently, rocking his son.

Body that was his body tense and trembling in his arm, relaxing slowly as he spoke the noes as yeses. Eyes that were his eyes looking up at him with diminishing fright, trust growing in them.

"All right then? You say of course? No war?"

"There will be peace. Close your eyes and breathe deeply. Don't be afraid, son."

Breathing regular now, languid. Martine put his free hand into his jacket pocket, as he had to, took out the automatic. He reached in until the mouth of the gun was an inch away from the boy's right temple, rocking softly, crooning, "Sleep, son, sleep." Aimed directly at young Tom's prefrontal lobes, as he had to, at the prefrontal lobes that were his prefrontal lobes, as he had to, pulled the trigger, as he had to.

Spasm: body arched, he cradled it around the shoulders, poor maimed truncated shoulders, gripped it tight. "Son, son," he said. Then the body shivered cruelly, fell limp. Mouth closed in a pout. But the eyes never opened.

Tonus gone.

First successful lobotomy he had ever performed. As he had to. Last he would ever perform. As he had to.

Close notebook.

Way a notebook ends: with whimper for milk and chocolate cake. And the chamber of the cave echoing unspeakably.

"Aaaaiiiiiiiii," from down the window.

"Sleep, son," he said.

Question: Would he have pulled the trigger if Tom Martine, sin of his sin, had not been mortally wounded? Unspeakable question, answer in the echo cave.

He rose to his feet, made his way back across the pavement, stepping over the pools of blood. At the curb, what was left of the curb, he sat down, hands spotted with blood of his blood. Hid face in his hands, and sobbed.

For a long time he sat there. When he rose he dried his eyes on his sleeve and began to grope his way through the smoking city again, heading north, northwest.

"Ee-ee-ee-ee-ee," behind him, blubbering, sniggering.

chapter twenty-three

IT TOOK almost an hour of maneuvering through the streets, detouring tediously around the trouble spots, before he reached the outskirts. His sense of direction hadn't failed him: signs began to appear, indicating the route to DROP NUMBER SEVEN. Ten minutes more and he sighted the low concrete building which housed the elevator entrances—and from this orientation point it was easy to find the highway which ran northwest.

He began to walk along the highway, stirring up puffs of chalky dust along the soft sandy shoulder. His mind was empty; the automatic in his pocket bumped against his side as he went, he did not notice it. He was numbed, couldn't think. First to the motel, to sleep.

A vehicle came up from behind him and wheezed to a halt—battered hulk of a touring car, in its open window the friendly tanned face of a man perhaps forty, rawboned, eyes green and direct. His arms, lean and muscular, extending from the rolled sleeves of a blue denim shirt, were his own; Martine could see that he was wearing long trousers, faded dungarees, instead of the shorts worn by amps.

"Where you headed?"

"Sviridoff's—motel about twenty miles down the—"

"Hop in, if you want a lift. I'm going right past there."

The man's voice was deep and pleasant, neither unctuous nor gruff, just straightforward—the twang Martine recognized as Western, his father had had it too.

Martine climbed in, the car started off. They drove for a minute or two in silence.

"Bad back there," the driver said.

"Yes." A twitch of suspicion: "What made you pick me up?"

"Oh. . . ." The driver kept his eyes on the road. "I don't know—wanted company, I guess. Saw some bad things back there."

"I didn't ask you for a ride."

"Don't get me wrong." The man rubbed one palm against the side of his face. "I'm not posing as the good-Samaritan type. Good Samaritans give me the bellyache. I was just lonely, I reckon."

That was all he chose to say: he fished a cigarette out of his shirt pocket, offered one to Martine, lit one for himself. Then he gave Martine a quizzical sidelong glance, rubbed his tongue slowly over his lips, and added,

"Well, I'll give it to you straight. You interested me. I notice it when a man's got his own arms and legs."

"You don't disapprove of backward elements like me? Of course, you look pretty backward yourself."

The man didn't reply: he simply reached out and switched on the radio. A tense announcer's voice faded in: ". . . . bulletin received at our news desk just five minutes ago. Omaha, Des Moines, Theo City and Helderfort have been hit badly too, at key surface installations as well as underground, but the news is not all bad. Hundreds of fifth columnists have already been rounded up around the Strip and the number is growing by the minute. More reassuring yet, it seems that in many places the boys of the Olympic training clubs have spontaneously organized and equipped themselves with special-function arms and are now marching out to meet the invading Union forces—skirmishes have already been reported in several areas, the Union casualties are reported to be heavy. President Helder, ladies and gentlemen, is safe at the capitol, he has just issued an urgent appeal to all true Immobs in the Union, calling on them to throw off their imperialist oppressors and—"

The man snapped the radio off. "Backward?" he drawled. "Hard to tell just what's backward and what's forward any more."

"Yes. . . . Where *you* headed for?"

"Bar Limbo."

"*What?*" Martine jerked, grunted, began to shake his hand violently. He'd been reaching for the cigarette between his lips when the man answered, his fingers had suddenly clamped together directly over the lighted tip. He sucked at the burned knuckles.

"Oh—that's my ranch, it's up in the foothills about three hundred miles north of here. . . . That name, it's just a joke."

"What the hell kind of a joke is that?" Martine's voice was rough.

"Well, you know, there are those references to Limbo in Martine's notebook. That's how we hit on the name—we just like the way it sounds."

"Listen!" Martine sat up straight and turned toward the driver. "What are you trying to say, man? Give it to me straight, I've got to know! Is it—do you mean you've held out, never became an amp, because you're sick of the whole thing—all this shit—you've kept your arms and legs because—"

The man held up an admonishing hand. "Don't get the wrong idea about me," he said. "I'm not as well-preserved as I look."

He reached down with his free hand and tugged at one trouser leg, then the other: his legs were exposed to the knees. Martine blinked: both legs were plastic.

"Oh. . . . But I don't get it, you hide them. . . ."

"Sure I hide them!" the man said violently. "I'm no goddamned vol-amp! I didn't turn in my legs, I lost them—same way Theo lost his—in the Third, during the hell-bombing of Moscow. Is that something to be proud of, that a burst of ack-ack plowed off your legs eighty thousand feet over Moscow? So proud that you go and do more of the same to yourself?" He pushed his trouser legs down again. "They gave me a medal for it," he went on more calmly. "I don't display that either."

"I don't understand your bitterness." Martine found it had to keep the excitement out of his voice.

"That's what it's come to," the man said, his lips curled. "A man who's bitter about being cut down to something less than a man is considered—peculiar. Twisted. Off the beam, somehow. . . . Theo says his glorification of amputeeism, his sawing off his arms to complete the job—in a revelation he saw that this was what Martine called upon him to do in the Notebook. You know what I answer to that? Theo can't read! There're lots of things in that book I don't understand—"

"Me too," Martine said. His throat muscles were so tight he could hardly get the words out, they came in a whisper.

"—but I understand this much. Whatever confusion there was in this guy Martine's mind—even if he finally went up and got himself killed for no earthly reason—and to the extent that it makes any goddamned difference at all *what* he thought and did—in the end he was saying that anybody who's half a man has got to feel bitter about being cut down to less than human size. Got to stand up, even on his miserable little stumps or whatever's left of his standing-up apparatus, and yell no to all steamrollers. . . . Remember that last speech in the Notebook, in the dialogue part, where Martine has Theo, Babyface he calls him, speak his piece for a couple of pages? That comes *after* all the fine talk about immobilization and passivity and all that muck, all the stuff Helder and Theo took seriously. And *after* all of that, what does Martine have Theo say? Only the fuck you. Only: you've got your legs and I haven't got mine—you talk about fine humanitarian programs, I lie here and massage my stumps. That's the *last* thing in the Notebook. What's it mean, except that immobilization and passivity are one big dirty joke, not the way out of war but the logical end-result of war, the thing behind war, the thing war disguises. . . ."

Martine turned his head away; his lips were trembling, he did not want the man to see how moved he was. "You— figured all that out for youreelf?"

"Doesn't take much figuring. Just some plain simple feeling. . . . Look at it this way. In past centuries people had some pretty gaudy ideas about human integrity: it was knightly chivalry in the Middle Ages, being well-rounded and versatile in the Renaissance, the full use of your rational powers in the Enlightenment, the right to be 'natural' and all that for Rousseau, the right to 'pursue happiness' for Tom Paine, the freedom to buy and sell in the nineteenth century. Lots of things. But in the twentieth century all the fancy definitions of integrity are thrown away. It becomes a simple matter of life and death—integrity is staying alive, just simply staying alive, and the lack of integrity is looking for death. By the end of the century integrity is simply a matter of keeping—not body and soul together—just body together. Of keeping yourself in one piece. That's progress, I guess—from galloping out on a white charger to joust against infidels and dragons for some lady fair, to just simply trying to keep your arms and legs, trying to establish that it's bad to surrender them willingly, the worst thing. Our century's made everything very simple. . . ."

"Yes," Martine echoed, "that's the sin. To allow that a man can live as sheer basket case, with no face-saving amble. . . ."

The driver thumped on one plastic thigh with his knuckles. "They want me to believe I'm better off!" he said. "In place of my frail, stumbling old flesh-and-blood legs I've got infinitely superior ones—superstrong, supersensitive, superdexterous, and all. No, I'm not better off. Because, no matter how cleverly these plastic legs are made, they're still plastic. They're dead. Part of me is dead. It's sinful to be dead. A man's not a man unless he's got all his parts and is alive in all of them, uses them. . . . I miss my own legs. I know these artificial ones will do the job better—they'll never buckle, ache, get shinned, fracture, develop charley horses or sunburn or arteriosclerosis or frostbite, never sweat in the summer and knock at the knees in the winter, never quake. And if they do go wrong I can always get replacements. But a man should be able to stand on his *own* two legs, his own. With all their frailties. I want legs that are less perfect but more alive. Even if they stumble a little, and quake. A man should stumble and quake a little. Only robots never stumble and quake. . . . You know why people laugh so hard when they see an amp trip or take a dive? Because the horror in a human being is perfection, infallibility—that's inhuman, and the idea that you can get it, short of death—that's a laugh. The stumble, the fall, it reminds people of the frail humanity behind all the mechanical perfection, the *life*—it's a hell of a relief to see it pop up. If men were meant to be perfect, they'd be hatched somewhere up in those fleecy clouds, where the angels hang out, not down here on earth and earthbound, a damned sight closer to hell, to limbo anyhow, than to heaven. Not that it's not human to *want* to be perfect—but the deeper part of humanity is wanting it and never getting it, knowing damned well it's a mirage. . . . I'm scared of the perfectionist who takes himself seriously. What happened just now back there in Los Alamos—that was the work of perfectionists, every war is. Looks like the only really perfect thing they'll be able to boast about is a perfect war. . . ."

Martine rubbed his hands over his knees: his palms were soaking wet. "There's a lot I don't know," he finally managed to say. "I'm a parasitologist—I've been away for a long time, doing research. . . . Let me ask you: are there many people who feel the way you do?"

"Quite a few," the man answered. "A pretty fair number. You don't see them around much."

"I know, you're the first one I've met. . . . Why should that be?"

Now it was the driver's turn to study Martine. He looked directly at his passenger, green eyes suddenly narrow and cautious, appraising. For a long moment Martine stared back, waiting for him to break the silence.

The man shifted his eyes back to the road. He seemed lost in thought. Then he took a deep breath, pressed his lips together and bit them—it was clear that he was trying to make some difficult decision.

Finally he spoke: "I'm probably shooting my mouth off more than I should. But you look O.K., I'll take a chance. . . . You really a stranger around here?"

"That's on the level. I've been in Africa studying tropical diseases. The little I've seen of Immob makes me sick to my stomach."

"All right. Here's the picture. . . ."

As the rancher told it, a lot of people were pretty badly banged up in the Third—lots of amputees, as well as paraplegics and other kinds of cripples. Even more civilians wounded than vets. All right. Then the pacifist movement took over the government, there was a lot of fancy talk about Martine's Notebook, the international situation got bad again, there was more talk about the Notebook—then, pop, there was Immob. Suddenly able-bodied kids all over the place were rushing to recruiting offices to sign up for ampism, holy gleam in their eyes. Some people, a lot of people, were horrified. In their own simple-minded way, the war wounded had been thinking that what had happened to them was a dirty rotten kind of deprivement; now here were all these

358

fanatical kids fighting for a place in line so they could acquire the same damage *voluntarily*.

Of course, the Theos couldn't wait to cripple themselves still further. Others, though, couldn't see making a horror into something holy. . . . Not that the rancher wanted to exaggerate. Not all the anti-Immobs had noble motives; none did, probably. Some, in fact, were moved by pretty low considerations: they'd come by their wounds the hard way, and as a result were the first heroes of the postwar period; now here were all these Johnny-Come-Latelys getting crippled painlessly and threatening to take over the whole hero business. Naturally, some of the vets had a gripe. . . . But, no matter what moved this or that particular guy, a lot of guys objected. Pretty soon they were joined by others with less embattled motives. Young fellows who were just too attached to their limbs to part with them on any basis: the rancher's eighteen-year-old son was one of them. Mothers and fathers who had sweated to get their sons out of the baby carriage and didn't care to see them installed there again. Girls—some who were against this thing simply because they weren't allowed to join themselves; others, not for feminist reasons but just because they didn't want their men less than men. (The rancher's wife was one such, his twenty-year-old daughter another.) Minority peoples, Negroes and such; like a lot of women, they saw that the old status system was only taking on a new and more spectacular form in Immob and that they'd be as carefully discriminated against in the new order as in the old. . . . All sorts of people. With all sorts of motives. But with the same urge—to scream no to this final cuddling up to the steamroller. . . .

They screamed in lots of places. In the Union as well as the Strip. It was bad, they were squelched in more effective ways than by a policeman's club. The irate citizens mobbed them. First the parents and wives and girl friends of the new heroes: after their darling boys had sliced off their legs they didn't want anybody going through the streets yelling that it was all a dirty mistake. There were some pretty bloody skirmishes, people were killed. Then it got worse. After a while the cyberneticists invented their new pros and the young heroes were fitted out with super-arms and super-legs. They began to get around. And they attacked the anti-Immob meetings; lots more people killed. In the Union as well as the Strip. In the Union they even began to accuse the oppositionists of sabotage and terrorism, they staged spectacular mass trials, everybody confessing to everything. . . .

The anti-Immobs went underground, in a way. That is, clammed up. They began to meet among themselves, in little informal study circles, and the circles kept in touch with each other. The Immob world stopped hearing about the opposition. . . . Well, the opposition was still there. In both the Union and the Strip. With their own ideas about what Martine was really getting at; they'd had a lot of years in which to talk it over. They didn't have any elaborate program to save humanity. Except one thing, maybe: never, in politics, to make anything irrevocable. . . . It was just that they had some notion about integrity. Which, maybe, was a lot closer to what Martine had been driving at than the filthy farce of Immob. . . .

"That's about it," the rancher said. "This afternoon I was at a meeting at L.A. when the attack came. All us vet-amps got away safely because we were in disguise, you see. Reckon modesty does pay. . . . I don't know. Maybe, when the war's far enough along, there'll be a chance for us to do something. We're discussing it now. We're waiting to hear from our friends in the Union about it. . . . Of course, we don't have any big gaudy program to offer people, no sensations. Maybe those of us who don't buddy up to the steamroller will always be the outcasts, maybe we'll always have to go around with our eyes cast down and our lips buttoned up. If the war doesn't eliminate everybody. We'll see. . . ."

Several minutes passed by while Martine sat without moving a muscle, concentrating on the shimmer of the desert landscape. His heart was hammering, his throat was parched, his fingers trembled. Twice he opened his mouth as though to speak, then thought better of it—once he even shook his head emphatically. The driver glanced over at him from time to time, curious.

At last Martine came to life and said, "Thanks." He thought for a moment, then added: "I want to thank you for trusting me. I think the most important single thing that ever happened to me was meeting up with you today."

Another silence, his lips working.

"You see, I had a son back there—one of the Anti-Pro leaders. He was killed in one of the bombings. I despised everything he represented, but until this moment I never suspected there was anything else left. It's a good thing to know somebody like you exists—whether you have any impact on events or not. . . ."

360

The picture was complete at last. There had been one ingredient missing until now: the opposition. Now he saw the whole thing—the horror, and the opposition to the horror. Of course. He'd been an idiot not to suspect that there must be an opposition. Of coure there was an opposition, the seed of opposition, the potentiality of opposition. Just as, on the island, there were the young people of the cave—beginning to laugh. Just as, in him, some dank cave was opening up, and in it a ghastly laughter was beginning to echo. . . . Life had not yet turned into a stone, even under Immob. It had gone on seething a bit, under the surface of bland benignity. . . . There was opposition. With a program: integrity as intactness, as all-at-onceness: the acceptance of the human condition. Which might, just barely might, be the beginning of a turn, however belated, against the masochistic tide. Out of Immob came anti-Immob: maybe the spiral was whirling downward, but there was still a dynamic and a history. Martine's Notebook was too confusedly human to be a stone, an epitaph. . . .

"Thanks," he said again. "Now there's something I'd like to tell you. You're interested in Martine?"

"Well—sure. Not as an authority—we've had a bellyfull of authorities—just as a man. I've got a feeling he and I might have had something in common. . . ."

"You would have. That's not just a guess—I used to know him, there were periods when we were very close."

The green eyes when they turned to Martine were bright, startled, brimming with questions. "What was he like?"

"Confused! Let's establish that first—no angel, no messiah, no savior, just stumbling and quaking and confused as hell! Whatever he was, he wasn't a perfectionist. He had too much of a sense of humor for that."

"Still, the Notebook, parts of it. . . ."

"Confused too, like it's author. Sure! But it didn't have any of the meanings Helder read into it—Martine wasn't confused about Helder's meanings, at least. . . . No. You see, he'd been stunned by the line he'd once come across in Rimbaud: *To every creature several other lives were due*—which suggested to him that, just as his analysis indicated, he was a hell of a lot more than what he appeared to be on the surface, he was filled with smothered personalities, everybody was. But he'd also been hit hard by that other line of Rimbaud's: *Don't be a victim*. That meant, as he saw it, that you mustn't victimize one part of you in favor of another, sacrifice one of your potential lives to another. In

361

other words, he had your idea: integrity, intactness—living with the whole being, trying to bring it all to the surface, never truncating any dimension of personality. He was afraid that pacifism, which no doubt originated in the decent and civilized impulses of mankind, would never get anywhere at all, only become a partner to catastrophe after catastrophe, so long as it persisted in seeing man as a truncated monolithic thing, all potential goodness. That if the do-gooders saw man as truncated, they'd wind up truncating him—theories have a habit of proving themselves that way."

"Funny you never reported that to anybody."

"I've been away. I didn't even know—"

The driver pointed at something up ahead. "There's the motel," he said, his voice almost inaudible. He slowed up and turned into the drive, parked the car on the gravel stretch in front of the cottages. He took his hands from the wheel and raised them part way toward Martine, palms up, as though begging for something—it was the Mandunji gesture of greeting, parodied.

"But then," he said. "His taking off that way?"

"Ah!" Martine said. "But how, exactly, *did* he go? That's the whole question! Do you really believe that, after writing what he did about masochism, he could have stepped out and taken that plane up to what was certain death—in a silly suicidal gesture that served no sensible purpose at all? You believe that?"

"But in that case—"

"Yes, he may have gotten away. There's a chance he's still alive, somewhere. If he could get back here and stay, if it were possible for him to come back, I believe he'd be with you and your friends. One way or another. Provided you didn't go too messianic and programmatic on him."

The man stared at him, mouth open. He was breathing hard.

"What's your name?" Martine said.

"Don Thurman."

"I'm Dr. Lazarus. Lazare, for short. Nice name for a parasitologist, don't you think? The leprous victim of the pest, student of pestilences. . . . Look, I've got something I want to give you. Wait here a minute, will you?"

Martine got out of the car and went off to his cabin. He was in a sweat, he sat down and tried to think. Thurman was certainly beginning to suspect. Why not spill everything to him? But there was a danger—if Thurman and his friends knew for sure who he was they might, conceivably, try to keep him in the Strip. There was a choice to be made: do everything to get back to Ooda and Rambo, or tie up with the Strip opposition and very possibly end his life here. For the messiah in him the answer was clear; but not for the man. Was he man or messiah? . . . No, he had to get back to the island, too much unfinished business there, he must not do anything that would interfere. On the other hand, he had a certain obligation: he *had* written the Notebook, he must do everything possible to undo the damage it had caused. That meant revealing the truth about himself, somehow or other. In some way that would not suck him back into messiahdom. He was coming to know the anatomy of this salvationist bent as he knew the bone structure of his own hand: a technique for self-extinction under the banner of saving others from extinction, for throwing yourself under the steamroller while pretending *you* were the steamroller. Even when it was entered into queasily and with qualms—when you "went along" with this or that Mandunga "only" to save lives and add to the fund of human knowledge. No more messiahdoms for him: he could no longer be an addict of the glossier "Its," that range of incognitos, at least, had been snatched from him. . . . Well, he would have to take a chance on Thurman. . . .

He searched through his valise until he found his worn copy of *Dodge the Steamroller;* the margins were filled with annotations. He sat down at the desk and opened the book to the first blank page after Helder's postcript. He took a pen and wrote another entry there:

OCTOBER 20, 1990.
Sviridoff's Motel, Outside Los Alamos
L.A. bombed couple hours ago. Got away all right. Found Tom in a window, guts ripped to bits by glass: he was castrated: real meaning of Immob. Picked up on the highway by a rancher named Don Thurman. Long talk with him.

Wish I could stay in the Strip. For one reason: to get to know Thurman better, maybe work with him and his friends. Because they're the only ones who understand this notebook. But I wouldn't be true to myself if I stayed here. I am involved in another life, in another part of the world; my job is to return and encourage the opposition there—a job I should have started eighteen years ago. Meeting Thurman has made that clear to me. Every man has some no to say in

363

some place—and some yes too. Unmessianically. My place is not here any more.

This book should be dedicated to Don Thurman, his wife, his son, his daughter, and his friends. Because if its author could, he would want to live in Bar Limbo with them. Because they are human beings. But I must go to the place that is my home and try to create my own Bar Limbo there. Not for humanity's salvation. For mine.

This notebook is now ended.

Dr. "Lazarus"

That should do it, Martine thought. To clinch the thing, there were facsimiles of several original manuscript pages in the Notebook; sooner or later it would occur to Thurman to compare them with this last notation. . . .

Martine stepped into the office and asked the clerk if he had a large envelope. The man was so distraught that he hardly heard the question: he had the radio on, the newscaster was talking: "Late flash. Discontent is growing in the cities of the Union, there are signs that it may result in outbursts against the treacherous Union leadership at any moment. . . ." Martine repeated his question, the envelope was produced, he stuck the book inside and sealed the flap. He returned to the car, stood outside the driver's window.

"Here's a book I want you to have," he said. "It's a copy of Martine's Notebook—I've filled the margins with comments containing everything I could remember about Martine, to correct the lies in Helder's footnotes. You'll learn quite a bit from it—so long as you hold to your idea that essentially *all* appeals to authority are a lot of shit. . . . Just promise me two things. Don't open the book until tomorrow. That's important. When you do get into it, make sure to read every page. Every one."

"O.K." A long pause, the green eyes searching. "I'm glad to have it. Maybe—" The eyes lit up, lips curved in a smile. "Yes?"

"Maybe—if any of us come out of this alive—maybe we'll put out another edition of the thing. With *your* footnotes correcting Helder's footnotes—they should be *very* pertinent. . . ."

And the man began to laugh—his mouth was open wide now, he was panting, the gales of convulsive laughter making his throat quiver, they roared out in a rush of wild sounds. Going beyond gall, spleen, nausea, the trivial titters of mere sardonic disenchantment—a cosmic laughter, big and round, all-embracing: oceanic laughter, the ultimate Om.

It was infectious. Watching the man shake, Martine found himself caught up in the wave of immense merriment. He began to laugh too—snickered at first, then abandoned himself to it and bent over with the delightful hurt, holding his sides, tears pouring down his cheeks.

It went on for a long time: the motel clerk came to the door of the office, stuck his frightened drawn face out and stared at the two men. Finally Thurman regained control of himself, wiped his eyes with his arm. Martine followed suit, patting his wet face with his handkerchief.

"If I could stay here," Martine said, "we might be friends. We've got a lot in common. I feel that."

"You're going away?"

"If I can manage it—I must go back to Africa. That's where my home is. I've got a wife and son there—without them I'm not alive. Although often, when I *was* with them. . . . I've got to go back."

"I'm sorry. We might have worked together."

"If there were any way for me to stay," Martine said simply, "I would work with you. I would try."

Thurman held his lean brown hand out and Martine took it. "Good luck to you and your family," Thurman said. "I hope you get where you want to go. I've got to get back to my family too—there's a lot to do."

"Thanks," Martine said. "Thanks for the lift—it was quite a lift. Good luck to you and your family too."

Thurman started up the car.

"You'll be interested in this," Martine said. "I've really got a hunch that Martine's still alive."

The steady green eyes widened, searched.

"So have I," Thurman said.

"When I get back home," Martine said, "I'm going to look for him. I've got an idea where to look for him now."

"I think," Thurman said, "that the most important single thing that ever happened to me was meeting you." He waved. The car rolled off to the highway, stopped for a moment, turned and sped away to the north.

Martine stood in the driveway for a moment, watching until the touring car disappeared. Then he went back to his cabin, stripped and sank into bed. He had never been so tired in his life, he was asleep almost before his head hit the pillow. . . .

Much later—many hours later, he'd slept through the evening, according to the wall clock it was almost one in the morning—he was awakened by a rapping at the door. He bolted out of bed, groped for the gun in his jacket. He went to the door and opened it cautiously.

Theo stood on the step, swaying like a drunken man. He was dressed in greasy long-legged trousers and a work shirt with the sleeves rolled down, there was a stained felt hat on his head. His face was chalky white.

"Please," he whispered.

He came blindly into the room and sank into a chair. For several minutes he sat there, frozen. Then, at Martine's urging, he began to speak.

chapter twenty-four

IT HAD been hectic after Martine left. Helder, it was clear, was getting ready to put into effect the next phase of his operational scheme, what he had referred to as "Plan C"— a step which, it quickly dawned on Theo, meant a bold swinging over from defense to offense at the psychological moment. Helder himself made it plain: in between conversations with his agents in the field he explained impatiently, as though spelling out the bald verities for a retarded child, that it would be suicidally naïve to stick to purely defensive measures out of some soupy programmatic sentimentality— the best and only really effective defense was offense. . . . So, in the course of one brief afternoon, Helder's metamorphosis was completed—from irrevocable pacifist to reluctant defensist to a whirlwind generalissimo of the classic combative mold who reminded Theo far more of Hannibal and Napoleon than of the dedicated man who had launched Immob. Helder had become EMSIAC.

During momentary lulls, they talked. At cross purposes. Theo, his mind full of Martine's last mocking words, had been concerned with columbium—Helder, for some reason, had stuck doggedly to one subject: Mandunga. He indicated an extraordinary interest in Martine's references to Mandunga.

Martine, Helder suggested, had been a remarkably gifted lobotomist—if he had spent twenty years at that kind of research, he must have come up with some incredible discoveries. Martine himself had hinted as much: he claimed that he had hit upon an infallible surgical procedure for

366

removing the aggressive centers from the prefrontal areas and destroying all the tonus which is mobilized in aggression. That would be exciting to know about. There were many volumes of technical information back there on the island, according to Martine. What did Theo know about this fantastic cache of scientific literature? What did he know about this whole Mandunga thing—he had had many friendly and informative talks with that old chief—what was his name?— Ubu. On and on.

Theo did not answer. Not simply because he did not care to: he had no more answers. Over and over again he parried Helder's questions with one of his own: What about columbium? At first Helder was indifferent; then annoyed; then so exasperated that he turned to Theo furiously and told him the whole story, bluntly.

Of course there was a race for the limited sources of columbium, it had been going on for years. Never mind who started it—Vishinu's men had taken the first sly steps, no time to go into the proofs now. The race had gotten under way very soon after the invention of the atom-powered pro. Actually it had been borne home to Helder and a few of his most intimate advisers—Theo didn't have to bother with these vexing details of running a government, oh, no, he was a full-time hero—that it might be a good idea, operating in an entirely confidential way, to place some expert metallurgists on the Olympic Team. Just to pick up a little helpful data on their travels: it would hurt nobody and it would allow the Strip to bargain more intelligently at international conferences. The move had been extremely wise. For soon, at the conferences, it became clear that the Union had at its fingertips far more information than it was conceivable for anybody to have without some very elaborate undercover exploration.

Helder's agents checked. They learned that for some time the Union had been staffing *its* Olympic Team almost exclusively with metallurgists and mining engineers, and sending the Team on systematic expeditions disguised as training cruises. The race was intensified. In the last couple of years it had reached the point where hardly any traveler of any description whatsoever, whether Unioneer or Stripper, was concerned with anything but columbium—*everybody* was looking for columbium. . . . Now, what was Theo's question: Had any members of this year's Team been looking for columbium around the Indian Ocean?

The answer was very simple: practically *all* the members of this year's Team had been looking for columbium in the Indian Ocean. Except Theo, of course. There had been no reason to bother his inspirational, glowing mind about such mundane matters—might dim his charisma. So the captain of the cruising yacht, and a few key members of the Team, had been instructed to keep the charismatic Theo charismatically occupied while the metallurgists went about their job. Did that answer Theo's question?

It did. It told him all he wanted to know: that he had been used. But by this time Helder was so overwrought and bitter that he proceeded to give Theo the answers to a few other questions he had *not* asked, questions he didn't even know existed. The members of the Olympic Team hadn't only been looking for columbium. They had also been planting stores of weapons everywhere they went, weapons flown in quietly from the hush-hush armories of the Strip. Because the Union Team was doing precisely the same thing, and the Strip could not ignore it.

This was the point: if another war did break out over the question of columbium, it would hardly be an all-out H-bomb and RW dust war. No, after the holocaust of the Third, nobody would dare to initiate full-scale atomic warfare again—because both sides had about equal atomic-pile and breeder-reactor facilities, and each knew that if it started any real area-wide hell-bombing and dusting the other could promptly retaliate with at least equal effectiveness. Whatever atomic bombing might be done would be limited in character, confined to specific targets, and neither side would dare to go very far beyond the limits which the other imposed on itself. So it was entirely likely that there would be other types of combat, with less deadly and more primitive weapons. The war could be pretty well visualized: for the most part individual combatants, rigged up as human helicopters, would come flying at each other in a kind of aerial joust, hurling flame or bullets from their arms or trying to carve each other up with their rotary saws and drills. . . . It might interest Theo to know that quite impressive quantites of arms had been deposited in a few safe places on the Mandunji island too. Against the day when Strip soldiers might be stranded in that area, cut off from home bases. This, Helder trusted, would drive home to Theo the very uncharismatic facts of political life. Helder was exceedingly sorry that he had to force a hero like Theo to grow up in such a rush—but there it was. Tough titty, he knew. Nothing to be done. And now, please—what about this Mandunga?

"I'm glad I had this talk with you," Theo said. "It's opened my eyes. . . . Look, if this information about Mandunga is so important I think I know how to get it."

"How?"

"From Martine himself. Whether he wants to talk or not. He's got volumes of information on the thing with him, I saw them myself when I went out to the motel to get him."

Helder jumped up. "Well!" he said. "Fine! Fine! I'll send some of the boys out right now. Nothing to it if he's still there, and if he's not, a general alarm—"

"That won't do," Theo said as Helder was reaching for the intercom. "The books aren't there now and Martine hasn't got them with him no matter where he is. He packed a valise and brought it along when I took him into town. All the volumes are in the valise."

"Well? Where's the valise?"

"He hid it down in the Slot. He insisted. He told me he wouldn't come any farther unless I stopped and let him get out and hide the valise—without following him. I drove off to a parking strip, at a place where the Slot seemed to be completely deserted. I showed him where the elevator was and he went down. He was gone for about twenty minutes—he couldn't have gone very far from the elevator, we can cover the area in no time. When he came back he didn't have the suitcase."

"But that's no good," Helder said, frowning. "Good God, man, he's been gone for hours. He's had time to pick up the suitcase and get hundreds of miles from L.A."

"Wrong," Theo said. "He may be hundreds of miles from L.A., but he hasn't got the suitcase with him."

"How the hell do you know that?"

"Well, while you've been busy on the intercom I've been reading the details of the bombings as they came in over the ticker tape. Here's one tape I saved." He handed the crumpled ribbon to Helder. "You see. Passage through the Slot's been blocked off in several places—he couldn't have gotten through. The alternative, of course, is that he went straight down in the capitol building, all the way down on Drop Number One, got his suitcase, then came back up the same way. Well, that's out too. There's considerable damage close by the Number One elevator entrances below—the way from the elevators to the Slot itself has collapsed. There's just one chance—the emergency footpaths may still be open—we could investigate—but you know how tough they are to find, even for people familiar with the layout. No. He may still be down there, but it's practically impossible that he's found it and gotten away. . . ."

"What do you propose?"

"I'll go down and look for it. If you'll come with me."

Helder looked at Theo queerly. "Why me?"

"There's been too much already that you've had to shoulder without me—I see that now and I'm sorry. It's time we acted as a team again, especially in something as important as this."

Helder paced up and down the room a couple of times, rubbing his forefinger down his long majestic nose, sniffing. Theo guessed what he was thinking: it would be safe, so long as the men watching him knew where he was going and could follow. Finally he sat down at his desk, looking at Theo with a friendly smile: slouched elaborately.

"All right, Theo," he said. "I'm glad you feel that way about it. Sure, let's go and grab a Slot elevator right now. We'll take the elevator down to the Slot."

"Wait—the Geiger count might be pretty high down there. We'd better not go in unprotected."

"Right." Helder went to a closet door and opened it. "All the gear we need's in here." He took out two plastic anti-radiation suits and two pairs of goggles. Then he opened a can of anti-gamma skin protectant, motioned to Theo to help himself, applied the bright blue grease liberally to his hands, his face, his scalp and neck. In three or four minutes they were ready.

They left the office, went through the outer rooms, emerged on the corridor and headed for the elevators. Nobody in sight yet: good. Theo had a pretty good idea of what Helder had done. Sitting down at his desk that way, he must have pressed a switch with his knee or his foot that turned on the audio circuits for his bodyguards. He was going to chance a trip down in the elevator alone with Theo because he knew his bodyguards would be covering him at both ends, up here and down below too—and he knew Theo knew it. So the point was not to take the passenger elevator. Now—if only the passenger elevator wasn't there.

It wasn't. No doubt there was a lot of traffic in the building as a result of the bombings: Theo had been counting on it.

"Oh, the hell with it," Theo said, after they'd waited for a minute. "The passenger elevators are probably all tied up. Let's take my car, it's right here—we'll have better luck getting one of the freight elevators on a lower floor."

He made the suggestion casually, trying to conceal his tension. Maybe, because he was so used to being chauffeured about, Helder wouldn't remember one all-important fact: that down below, the freight cars and the passenger cars opened up on opposite sides of the great elevator shaft. If Helder's guards had heard him and were down there, they would expect him to come out on the passenger side.

"Well. . . ." Helder said. "That makes sense. . . . Oh, all right."

They got into Theo's car and started down the motor ramp which snaked in and out of the building, spiraling downward a floor at a time. Some fifteen floors below, Theo drove off the ramp, stopped in front of a freight elevator, and flashed his headlights three times. In a matter of seconds the doors yawned open.

"Just as I thought," Theo said carelessly. "Not many people using their cars now."

"Right," Helder said.

In less than a minute they were down to the Slot exit. The elevator ground to a smooth halt. Now: if only none of the guards had wandered over to this side. . . .

The doors sprang open. Theo took a deep breath. There was nobody in sight.

Helder peered out on both sides as they drove off, puzzled. After a couple of minutes of winding through the maze, Theo stopped the car: there was a cave-in some fifty yards ahead.

"Good," he said. "That block's some distance beyond the footpath. Here's a clear entrance, let's try it."

They got out and approached the doorway—hardly noticeable, covered with a sheet of steel that ran flush with the wall. Helder looked up and down uneasily: nobody in sight.

"Come on," Theo said, opening the door. "No sense wasting time—he *did* have a big head start, there's just an outside chance he may have found a way through."

Helder followed him into the low arched tunnel. They went a long distance, descended by a flight of stairs; then more turns, two more stairways, footsteps echoing in the cramped cavern. Finally they passed through another door and were out in the Slot's great hollow, down on its floor.

"Just look at that," Helder whispered.

They had entered the Slot at a point almost midway between two power-plant bombings; to the right was the smoking ruin of one breeder reactor, a tremendous hole blasted in the floor, machinery lying in melted and twisted heaps for hundreds of feet around—to the left, where another explosion had occurred, there was a mountainous rock pile reaching up some two or three hundred feet, composed of boulders and rubble which had been blasted loose from the walls and from the roof far above. The area in which they were standing had contained an enormous prosthetics manufacturing plant: on all sides were furnaces and cauldrons, plastic mixers, some of them still steaming; extruders with their nozzles still dripping gooey plastic; machines for stamping out and winding and assembling the solenoid coils and cores; on a belt line nearby, not moving now, a long row of hollow plastic fingers ready for final assembly.

"It's not far from here," Theo said. "To the right—this way."

They set off, picking their way between the silent, steaming machines.

"Here," Theo said. "Right about here, I'd say."

Directly in front of them, at their feet, was a round hole some ten feet across. Thick yellowish vapors were rising from the hole, the odor sharp and noxious.

"What?" Helder said. "You're—that's crazy, man, this is a vat. There's nothing down there but plastic—look at that steam, it's still cooking."

They looked around carefully: still no sign of another human being. "Weren't you looking for the rest of Martine?" he said: his voice was hollow and choked. "There's the rest of him. He is not dead, he has but become an ocean of plastic. Now you're going to drink. Humbly. This is *your* Lake Victoria."

There was incredulity in Helder's eyes, burning bright now. "Listen here," he said, sniffing rapidly. "You're mad. . . ."

He stepped back, Theo reached out and took hold of his neck with both hands.

"Don't struggle," Theo said. "You know, I'm quite an athlete, I haven't spent the last fifteen years going soft at a desk. I co-ordinate beautifully."

"Theo!" Helder cried. "What are you thinking of! Let go before—"

"Besides," Theo said, "you've only got super-legs. I've got

372

super-arms as well, thanks to you. You can't get away from these hands. They were made to fit around your neck—I could snap it like a toothpick right now, without even trying. Thank you for these wonderful hands. They're about to send you onward and upward."

Helder was fighting desperately, making strangled sounds; Theo stood there quietly, holding him in the vise like a boy holding a caterpillar gingerly in a pair of tweezers.

"I'd like to tell you why," he said. "In the name of the Twenty-third Amendment. For the hands you took from me. For Rosemary. To make sure you stay immobilized this time. To teach you how to be irrevocable. You shit. Fuck you, fuck you, fuck you."

He heaved, the bulbs in his arms jittered. "Aaaaaaahhhhh," Helder said—his legs flew up over his head. With a quick fling Theo catapulted him into the cauldron, head first. . . .

"That's all," Theo said. "Nobody saw. I stood there for a while—the steam changed from pale yellow to a bright orange, there were puffs of bright orange and it smelled bad. He went down slowly, his legs were half melted before they went under the surface, they started to droop. For a long time after he disappeared there were lots of bubbles on the surface. I watched them." A shudder ran through him. "Then I found these workmen's clothes. I put them on and got out on the streets and came here. By the back roads. Walked all the way." He shuddered again.

"Don't take on so," Martine said. "How many people did you kill in the last war: twenty million? This only makes twenty million and one. Of course, it's not such a neat figure."

"What am I to do now." It was constructed as a question, sounded like a statement of irreparable fact.

"You ask *me* that?" Martine brandished the tutorial forefinger again, furiously. "What the hell did you come here for, anyway? Now that you've run out of limbs to offer to the Helders, run out of Helders too, you come knocking on *my* door—what for? Maybe you want me to gouge out your prefrontal lobes, since that's about all you can spare?"

"I came. . . . I had no place else to go."

"You came because you want approval for what you've done, isn't that so? That's another form of lobotomy. Sorry, Brother Theo, I won't be your conscience. Look behind your eyeballs for the answer. Where it aches the most."

"I did right. I'm sure I did right."

"I won't tell you whether it was right or wrong!" Martine exploded.

"Tell me where to go now." Theo was back to his old game: wiggling his fingers in slow motion, watching them intently.

"I do know one place you could go," Martine said. "There's a ranch up north a ways. . . . Wait a minute. There's one thing you didn't tell me: Why was Helder so interested in finding out about Mandunga?"

"He didn't say."

"Of course, he *would* be interested. He was such an inveterate whittler—he'd perk up at the first sign of any new whittling technique. But he must have had something in mind. . . ."

"I don't know. I pretended I understood just to get him down to the Slot."

Martine crossed the room and planted himself in front of Theo. "Look—maybe it *was* a good idea, your coming here. You might be able to help me. I've got to go home."

"Home?"

"To the Mandunji island. I *must* get there, right away. Can you help me?"

Theo was stunned: he began to think: his eyes opened wide with excitement. "Sure!" he said. "Of course I can—at least I think so. Out at Helder's ranch, just thirty miles north of here—there's an airfield on the grounds, there're always ten or twelve fast planes there. Maybe I could get you into one. . . ." He rose to his feet, raised his hands prayerfully toward Martine. "Take me with you, Martine! These new planes are pretty damned complicated, I'm still one of the best pilots in the Strip. Take me with you!"

"No! Christ, you think I need leeches? I'm not the sort of devoted parasitologist who attaches parasites to his own hide!" Martine backed away, an expression of disgust creasing his face. But then he began to look puzzled. "Of course, it's true, I probably couldn't even get one of these new jobs off the ground, I haven't flown a plane in sixteen years. . . . I'd have to have *somebody* along to run it. . . ."

"Let me do it," Theo pleaded. "I'll get you there."

Martine began to see the amusing side of the idea: "It *would* be an interesting experiment. The world's greatest mass murderer applying for Mandunji citizenship! . . . I warn you, though: if you want to complete your birth and become a man, you may have to come back here, back to the scene of the crime. You've got a big debt to work off, just as I have. . . . All right, it's settled. How do we proceed?"

Theo could hardly contain his joy. "Well, we'll have to be careful. There's no telling what the situation is over at Helder's place. I'd better go on ahead. I'll need about an hour—suppose you meet me in about an hour, in back of the hangar. I'll draw a map for you." He went to the desk, took a pencil, and began to trace the route on a piece of stationery.

"I'm glad to see," Martine said, "that even plastic fingers can develop a tremor."

"I'll need a car."

"You can take mine. I'll scare up another one."

Two minutes later Theo was in Martine's car, the motor running.

"See you in an hour," he said.

"One hour."

A two-thousand-dollar deposit mightily impressed the motel clerk, even in his panicky state: he promptly turned over the keys of his car and no questions asked. Martine ordered ten sandwiches, wrapped and packaged, plus two containers of coffee.

Back in his cabin, fretting over the insufferable slowness with which his watch ticked away the minutes, he tried to order his scampering thoughts. There was a danger: Theo might now become addicted to him, faltering enemy of addicts. Bah. Grimaces. Would have to limber up his kicking leg—the Zen Buddhist monks used to give their disciples a swift one in the slats when they learned their lessons too well. And what did Helder have in mind about Mandunga?

But why honor the integrity of an "instrument" as lame and fumbling as the brain? Because that's where all the secrets are. Men had looked everywhere else, in the heavens, the stars, Nature, beyond the Styx, the entrails of animals, trees and stones, geometric forms, the soul, dreams, genes, and found nothing: the search now centered on the onion. Hard for the brain to dig out its own secrets. Never know itself until it became as smooth and infallible as a calculating machine. Price of perfection is perfect robotization. But: no secrets in a robot brain worth knowing. . . . And, after all, is the perfect brain the most desirable one? It's the infirm one, full of migraine, anticipatory and anxious, riddled with ambivalence, stuffed with memories forever lost to recall but echoing hauntingly through the circuits, caught up in a welter of conflicting tropisms, a-tremble always because the feedbacks never fully work, producing tonus and more tonus throughout the uneasy body, fluttery, sabotaged constantly by the fifth-column prefrontal lobes, hacked, slashed, as fragmented as the disorderly spattered multiverse it finds itself in and with which it must constantly cope somehow—it is this fantastically sick instrument, a blob of 10,000 million neurones torn from each other and trying desperately to get together, which in its never ceasing turmoil has produced all the arts and games and enthusiasms and ecstasies man has known—along with the migraine, to ease the migraine: produced them, and maintained the quivering consciousness, and the still more quivering unconsciousness, with which to enjoy them. Perfect it? The price would be the esthetic quality in life. For the esthetic is the crumb this aching old onion tosses itself in the morass of anticipatory anxiety; and to eliminate it would mean to eliminate all the uneasy sense and savor of life. No more neurosis, maybe. But something else is amputated too, humanness. And, with it, laughter. Laughter: the psychic snake oil which keeps the all too human brain from grinding itself to bits. The esthetic: a form of laughter, designed to take the sting out of ineradicable pain. Masochism, on the other hand, is a humorless reveling in the pain. . . . The robot never laughs at itself. Who can giggle at perfection? Which is why Hell, in the theological literature, always in the end sounds more inviting—as well as more painful—than any serene, vapid, machine-perfect Heaven. No wonder Mann always had his artist-heroes making pacts with the Devil, then agonizing through to a twisted-lips sort of wry holy laughter. Better to have one's heaven and hell right here on earth: the human condition in all its ambivalence, its ingredients not divided neatly into good and bad and then projected out of time and humanity, the one into the skies and the other into the bowels of the earth—better that than to become the infallible know-it-all-and-titter-at-nothing robot. The great lesson of cybernetics: the perfect machine never has the jitters—and never laughs. Cost of perfection would be superboredom. Worst of all, the perfect robot wouldn't even know it was bored. . . . But Theo, the perfect God, was now becoming perfectionistically absorbed in Martine. And Helder, perfect Dog, was becoming perfectionistically interested in Mandunga. Why? Leg needed limbering. . . .

According to his watch he had twelve minutes to get to the airport: just about what he needed. He slipped on his jacket—the gun was still in the pocket—gathered up his valise, his notebook, the carton of sandwiches, and went out to the clerk's car. Great pall of smoke over the horizon to the south. When he got on the highway he did not even think of using the robo-drive.

The field was almost a mile from the cluster of ranch houses, it seemed quite deserted. Seven silvery jets of various sizes were lined up on the concrete apron in front of the hangar, upended, ready for vertical take-off; like a row of stubby cigars wrapped in tin foil, gleaming in the moonlight. Martine parked his car behind a small water-pump shed, walked over to the grassy strip at the rear of the hangar. Nobody there.

He strained to hear: a chilling, muffled sound. Choked, panting—the sort of moan one would expect from an animal, but undoubtedly coming from a human throat: not a sound that antedates words, like an animal cry, but one which, like Oedipus's shriek, has gone far beyond the paltry Apollonian syllables of known words to the expression of ultimate Dionysian wordless pain. "Uh-uh-uh-uh-uh"—in broken rhythm, syncopated by torment.

It stopped: a sudden piercing scream, swallowed abruptly at the soaring end. Then the chesty chugging sound again.

Martine ran toward the front of the hangar, in the direction of the sound. When he rounded the corner he saw Theo, stretched out on the concrete.

Something grotesque about the way he was lying—limbs twisted and curled, bent at points where there were no joints: a thigh changing direction midway between hip and knee, a foot veering off almost at right angles to its leg. Here and there in the mauled limbs bulbs were flickering fitfully although Theo was not moving, apparently could not move. Intense yellow fumes rising from the pros; a sizzling sound, they were cooking in their own heat. Theo's sleeves and trouser legs had been burned away—the thumb and forefinger of the left hand had melted off, they lay on the concrete, smoking.

"Uh," Theo barked through his teeth. "Uh. Uh. Uh." He

seemed to be grinning like a movie star—teeth clamped together, lips curled back. His wild eyes darted to Martine, bulged. "Help me!" he screamed. "Take them off!"

Martine bent over. "All right, just—"

"I can't stand it, I can't stand it! Please take them off!"

"All right, I'm going to— Ow!"

Martine jumped back, shaking his hand. The limbs were scorching hot, he'd burned his fingers merely by bringing them close. He saw that the surface of the arm, the one he'd started to reach for, was bubbling.

"Take them off. Take them off or shoot me. Please. Shoot me. I'm not a coward but I can't stand it you must shoot me please. . . ."

"Wait," Martine said. "Just a minute."

He ran into the hangar, looked around wildly, spotted a tool bench over in the corner. On the bench several heavy blocks of wood. He snatched up two of these blocks and ran back to Theo. Holding the blocks in both hands, using them as a pincers, he got a firm grip on the upper part of Theo's left arm and twisted as hard as he could, the wood crackling as it burned—the arm came off, he threw it on the grass. Three more wrenches and the other limbs were off too.

Gasping sound, a weird hilarity.

"Water," Theo gasped.

Martine found a tin cup inside, filled it at a spigot, brought it back and fed some of the water in little sips to Theo, holding his head up. With what was left he soaked his handkerchief and wiped Theo's cheeks and forehead.

The four pros lay on the grass, fizzing. Yellow vapors streaming from them.

"What happened?"

"Uh. Uh. . . . I was attacked."

"Vishinu's men?"

"No. Uh. Helder's."

"Helder's? How the hell—?"

"About fifteen. Knew several, Olympic athletes, on training cruise with me. Arrived few minutes after I got here. They didn't know about Helder being dead, acted friendly. Uh. Uh." Theo stopped talking for a few seconds, panted, sucking in air like a greedy child lapping at an ice cream cone.

"What were they doing here?"

"I asked where they were going. They were in a great

hurry. Said they were on a confidential mission for Helder. Going to the Mandunji island. To the Mandunji island to get important documents."

"But Helder's dead! How could he—"

"Think I know. While I was in his office yesterday, after you left, he kept writing memos and dropping them into the suction-tube slot. One of them must have had the orders for this mission."

"Theo!" Martine stood up, panicky, pressed his hands together and rocked them back and forth in dismay. "Oh, God, they're after the Mandunga files. . . . But why? What would Helder have wanted them for?"

"They hinted at that too. From Helder's instructions they got the idea this information was about a revolutionary technique for cutting aggression out of the brain. Helder thought that if he could get the dope fast enough he might be able to use it in the war. On captured Unioneers. He has his agents planted everywhere in the Union—figured he might be able to capture some of their key men, maybe even Vishinu. Then carry out this operation on them and produce them in public, put them on the television or something, and have them talk about the terrible aggressive things they did. . . . These men even talked about a plan for setting up flying surgery units that would roam up and down just behind the front, operating on all captured military personnel. New humane pacifist way of ending a war, no more killing the enemy, just what Immob needed. . . ."

"So." Martine closed his eyes and rubbed the lids with his fingers; he felt dizzy. "He wanted to make a weapon out of lobotomy too. Let children play with knives. . . . They mustn't get my documents! What about these men—did they leave?"

"About fifteen minutes ago. I pleaded with them not to go. Tried to stop them—that's when they attacked me. They knew exactly how to cripple a pro. I think they must have been trained. . . ."

Martine looked down at the absurdly small figure on the concrete. He pointed toward the planes squatting on their tails on the launching ramp. "We've got to get moving. Can we take one of these ships?"

"The end one, on the far left. It's the latest model, fastest supersonic job we have."

"But I can't fly it! And you—without arms and legs. . . ."

"That's easily fixed. There are always spare pros stocked in

379

every plane's equipment, in case of emergency. Carry me to the plane, we'll find them."

Martine stooped, slipped his arms under Theo's body, one under the buttocks, the other under the neck. Cradling Theo as he would a baby, he lifted. He swayed, almost fainted: he was back eighteen years, back in the Congo encampment, lifting this body from the operating table—light as a sack of potatoes, it sent a spurt of nausea all through him. Theo was even lighter now. . . .

He shook his head clear, hurried to the plane. There he had to sling Theo over his shoulder in order to climb the ladder which ran from the entry hatch straight up through the ship. Grunting, he reached the cockpit, eased Theo down in one of the swivel chairs. As soon as he caught his breath he hurried down and sprinted to the car to get his luggage, returned in a couple of minutes.

"Where are the spare pros?" he asked.

"The storeroom, just below. Go down the ladder about five steps, you'll see the door."

Martine found the door, yanked it open, inside there were some twenty arms and legs of various sizes, neatly racked. He pulled down two of the largest arms and two of the largest legs—making a face when he touched them: the rubbery softness outside, the suggestion of steel under the give—and brought them to Theo. He had to fumble with the first arm until he had it fitted into the socket of Theo's right stump; then, using this hand, Theo expertly attached the other three limbs himself. His face was twisted in pain: beads of sweat on his forehead.

"Are you all right?"

"I ache all over, even the plate in my skull feels hot. When pro cooling units break down it really messes up the nervous system some. I'll be all right. The shock generally wears off in a few days."

"Take this," Martine said. "It'll kill the pain." He slipped one of the pencils from his pocket, drew out the eraser, handed it over; Theo swallowed the liquid.

"All set?" Theo said.

Martine nodded. Theo pressed a button on the instrument board: the ship shuddered, roared, reluctantly rose a few feet in the air—then began with incredible acceleration to bullet up. The ground fell away, suddenly the hangar was a toy block below them.

"Think we'll make it?" Martine said.

"There are some things in our favor," Theo said. "They've

380

got about a thirty-minute head start. All right. But they had to take a bigger plane to accommodate their party, it's an older job. Then, too, we've got a much lighter load. Besides, I know some special tricks with the atom power plant—I've kept up with things. . . . I can't promise anything, but we've got a chance."

Theo gradually eased off from vertical to horizontal flight, their chairs swiveling smoothly as the angle changed. There was a weird whistling, the whole atmosphere suddenly seemed to have the jumps, a fluttering, a groaning—then they were through the sonic barrier and gliding like silk on silk.

"Is there a radio?" Martine said. "Let's find out what's happening."

Theo fiddled with a couple of dials. A voice boomed out: ". . . where he is. There has been no communiqué from Brother Helder for almost twelve hours. Brother Theo has not been heard from either. Efforts to reach them at the capitol have proved useless. . . . But the news elsewhere is encouraging. Reports from the fronts indicate that the enemy advance has been halted in many places, the Union forces are beginning to fall back. . . . And the long-awaited crisis in the Union has been reached! Ladies and gentlemen, according to word received just a few minutes ago, the loyal Immobs in the Union are on the march—key installations have been destroyed in New Surabaya and New Pyongyang, New Saigon is reported to be badly hit, many sections of New Tolstoygrad are in flames. . . ."

"Plan C," Martine said. "And twenty-three letters to go."

"Here's a flash!" the announcer shouted. "Oh, this is spectacular! Ladies and gentlemen—Vishinu is dead! He was killed just forty minutes ago, in his office in New Tolstoygrad! It looks like the tide is beginning to turn—Vishinu was shot with a rifle-arm by one of the members of his own Olympic Team—the winner of the d-and-d's in the recent Olympic Games, a Negro émigré from the Strip who remained true to Immob and decided to invoke the Assassination Clause against his false leader. . . .

"But wait! Something's happening!" The announcer's voice veered from joy to horror. "I can't tell—there's a peculiar rumbling—from our studios here in L.A. I can see out across the city—my God, everything's shaking, I just saw a ten-story tower fall over, just like that! Oh—there goes the capitol building! Everything's shaking—why, ladies and gentlemen, the whole town's shaking—there goes another building, I don't understand it—the rumble—*oh*—"

They could hear it over the loud-speaker: an incredible groan from somewhere at the profound heart of things, a stretching of cosmic vocal cords, the earth itself yawning. Louder; louder still, mounting to a roar—and then nothing. Silence. The radio gone dead. And—

It was as though a giant hand suddenly caught up their plane from underneath and tossed it into the troposphere—they zoomed straight up for a distance of several hundred feet, bobbling crazily. Then dropped. The plane continued its forward rush but with jerks and flutters now: the silken atmosphere was suddenly hammered into a corrugated sheet, creased with invisible buttes and coulees across which they lurched drunkenly.

"It's Los Alamos!" Theo shouted, pointing down. "Something—look!"

Los Alamos was stretched out directly below them. It seemed to be seething, writhing, through its whole length; a convulsive boil ran through the toy city, the building blocks jiggled.

Then—the whole city disappeared.

Fell in on itself. Collapsed into the earth from which it had sprung. One minute a city—the next, nothing but a tremendous fissure, a trench cutting across the moon-bathed desert, and in that great slit a city swallowed. Only the suburbs remained, landscaped leftovers.

The plane was still bobbing. Theo worked feverishly at the controls.

"Currents!" he yelled. "Did you see—gone! It's gone!"

Martine was pressing his hands with all his might against the ceiling of the Plexiglas bubble, trying to protect his head. "Maybe the whole Slot collapsed by itself!" he yelled back. "Or maybe—Vishinu's men might have moved up to *their* Plan D. . . ."

Another moment and they were beyond the turbulence. Martine fell back in his seat, gasping.

"I just thought of something," Theo said. "Now nobody'll ever know what happened to Helder. Or me either. They'll just assume we were swallowed up with the city."

"That's how martyrs are born," Martine said. He looked closely at Theo. "They'll never know the real story—unless you come back and tell them."

"That's true," Theo said quietly. "I would never have known about you if you hadn't come back."

Martine turned and looked down. The slit-trench was a tiny scratch in the barren sands now; great columns of dust and smoke fanning up into the skies from the little vent.

"You see," he said. "You needn't ever have bothered erasing cities. Cities sometimes fall of their own weight." He shook his head. "As Brother Lenin said to Brother Trotsky the night Moscow fell to the Bolsheviks—*Es schwindelt.*"

He pointed his finger at Theo.

"Never mind what I did," he said. "To hell with the precedents. If you decide to pull a Lazarus and want it to have some human meaning, better find the precedents in yourself. Under that tantalum plate are the only precedents that count."

Miami, no giraffes now. He would see no more giraffes.

"Suppose we do get there first" Martine said. "Suppose we have enough time to find the hidden arms—what then? You're the only one who can use them."

"Anybody can use them. They've got special controls for manual operation. That's so monos and duos can work them."

"Good." A little later: "You don't have any regrets about taking off this way? Didn't you have a wife or a girl somewhere?"

"Nobody in particular."

"You're—not castrated?"

"No, it's not that. I thought a lot about it, sometimes I thought the more extreme Anti-Pros had some pretty convincing arguments for it, but the idea made me sick too. No—I've had girls now and then, but I just never got too involved. I was always too much on the go, I guess. I'm a little uncomfortable with women."

"The shy charismaticist. . . . What about Helder?"

"Oh, he wasn't the shy type. He had lots of women. Never got married, though—funny, lots of amps never got married, come to think of it. . . . He never seemed to get along with his women, he was pretty brutal with them. It used to bother me."

"Not half as much as it bothered him, I'll bet. Strange thing about professional humanists, the ones I've known anyway—they manage to stir up mighty little brotherly love, or any other kind of love, in the bedroom."

Martine began to whistle, then broke off, sickened, when he realized what the song was: "I'm Putting All My Eggs in One Basket." He studied the glassy view below. The Bahamas were floating by, puny patches of white against a background of undulant blue-black mica. Sun just beginning to heave up ahead, red as shame, granddaddy of all electonic tubes; strands of cloud twisting here and there, scribblings of an illiterate skywriter. . . . When he turned again to Theo he was surprised to see that there were tears in his eyes: he sat stiffly in his seat, looking straight ahead, trying to blink away the tears.

"Oh, Theo," Martine said. "In any case, don't cry."

Don Thurman had roared with laughter: Theo was crying, audibly now: the sounds were disconcertingly alike.

"I don't know if this'll help," Martine said, "but listen. I've just made a discovery: those whom the gods would destroy they first make solemn. . . . Look, Immob aimed to raise man from the animal to the truly human; the great humanist project. But what distinguishes man from animal? Not hands, not superego, not logic, not the ability to abstract and make instruments, not his myths and dreams and nightmares—the beginnings of all these things are there in the higher animals, it's just a matter of man having more of the same. There's only one thing man can do that's beyond all other animals on earth: he can laugh. . . ."

Theo's whimpering was louder now, his whole body was beginning to shake.

"Listen to me, Theo. Don't you see? Laughter, nothing but laughter, is the final answer to the steamroller. Yesterday I met a man who laughed. Even yesterday. . . . Don't cry, Theo. . . ."

"Why," Theo said chokingly, "why did he laugh?"

"Oh—because there's something else that distinguishes man from animal: he's secretly in cahoots with the steamroller and secretly knows it—it's from the cave of this secret knowledge, maybe, that most anxiously anticipatory human laughter comes. Laughter is a sort of short-circuited sob—maybe that's why it brings tears to the eyes."

"Is that—is that the way you were laughing in your notebook?"

"Yes," Martine said. "I guess I was."

He felt in his pocket, took out his notebook. He opened it to the last entry and added some lines:

OCTOBER 21, 1990
Somewhere southeast of Bermuda
Correction. *Two* things that distinguish man from the

384

animal. He laughs—uses throat and vocal cords in a most unfunctional manner. Also cries—first time in the animal kingdom the tear ducts were ever put to such fantastic unfunctional use. And performs both unfunctional activities as one function, when he's fully human. Homo Dei, the weepy titterer: laughs till the tears come.

Both Immob and Mandunga are subtractions, when what's called for is a radical addition.

The addition? Merely a Hyphen—between Dog and God.

Vow: never to contemplate my divinity without seeing its hilarious canine underside.

But there's no peace to be found at either extreme, at the pole of godhead or the pole of doghead: only spuriously neat incognitos.

My sin? It was to make those jokes about the steamroller and immobilization. Because to joke about such things is a way of thrusting them aside—and you wouldn't thrust so hard if they weren't so close to you—if you weren't already "one of them" in your heart. The laughter hides the tears.

Neen was right, under my hyper-amble was the basket case. I refused to recognize it, dropped it like a hot potato after my analysis—dropped my analysis so I could drop the potato. But it was there, in all its mewling glory. . . .

Spent a good part of my life in a mythic world stuffed with fists. I was an overly cerebrotone, hunched-up, in-dwelling sort of guy, suspicious, sensing—while I secretly sponsored—unfriendly plots against me. Stand-offish; with women too. Even Ooda. The Dark Lady, Ominous Mom, Mominous Om, everywhere. . . .

Said no to all that once, October 19, 1972, immediately thereafter let myself be overcome by the pressure of Mandunga, a new EMSIAC. All because I shied away from the insights I began to get in my analysis: that at the core of *my* characterological onion were two festering seeds, a myth of victimization and a need for such victimization. From which came my "jokes."

But the immobilization joke gave away the steamroller joke. If I ironically proposed that in future the mutilation be voluntary, it was a furtive admission that with everybody, me included, it always *is*, in the deepest sense, voluntary.

Masochism: an inner need to objectivize and dramatize and perpetuate the myth of the steamroller, under the pretense that one has had nothing whatever to do with planting it in the environment and can therefore feel innocently abused and righteously indignant over its presence. Man: only animal that can convert pain into pleasure—and not even know he's doing it!

That kind of humor is gallows humor, under the shadow of a self-constructed gallows. Very sour, very wilted.

I will take responsbility for my jokes too. . . .

Some notebook: turns out to be the record of the Dog-God, whose name is legion. As in the old English ballad *Turpin Hero*—as in *Stephen Hero*—the thing "begins in the first person and ends in the third person." Which is one way to achieve the oceanic.

Everybody has his own built-in steamroller. Not everybody has an *idea* of the steamroller, a blueprint of it, a genealogy of it. The man who could photograph it and dissect it would be really unique. If he simply *wanted* to photograph and dissect it, he would be unique. That way, maybe, lies a new kind of identity. . . .

There is something I *can* accept. The picture of man—me—as the incipiently introspective Dog-God. Curious to distinguish between the 1 per cent of aggressiveness in him which is a response to reality and the 99 per cent which is phony, designed to make the God look like the Dog and cheek-turning like tooth-for-toothing. Who begins to see, dimly, that the real target for most of his vicious blows is himself, via others. That most of his blows are all boomerang and backfire. And therefore begins to investigate the steamroller behind the eyeballs, sadly and merrily. In order that his story, which began in the third person, can turn, belatedly, into the first. O pioneer!

To this hyphenated *Wunderkind* I can say yes. To his caceptance of the Hyphen, and his curiosity about it. And his hyphenated tearful-laughing reaction to it. And his awakening thirst for first-personality.

To this I say yes.

I say *yes*.

YES.

I say

Funny. Wrote a big NO in my notebook eighteen years ago. Now, at last, a big YES. Another hyphen, I'm the original no-yesman. Name should have been NOYES. . . .

Good Christ. Been staring at that last entry for five minutes, stupefied. Noyes *is* my name, in a way. It's my mother's maiden name, haven't thought of it in years. Oh, blessed mother of myth, fount of multiness, source of all twos! . . .

This notebook, too, is now ended. My messianic addiction to notebooks is now ended. I want no more to make a mark: those who set out to make their mark usually wind up leaving mutilations. From now on I want to have an impact on *myself*. If I now set out to create an opposition on the island of coma, it is not for my third-person incognito, my "race"—it is for myself. I need this opposition in order to live as something other than a cripple. Messiah's in the cold cold ground!

Once you go into the cave, you've got to grope along to the bitter end: no exit. And no end. Each man his own speliologist. We're in for an indefinite turbulence in human affairs: Man's not only the animal who makes words, he's the animal who's eternally obliged to eat his own words.

Now and forever it's a tough transitional period for all of us anxious c-and-c systems, for all our d-and-d's.

Old myth-mother, old artificialer, stand me now and forever in not too bad stead!

Signed (without incognito)
Dr. Lazarus (his own best parasite)

Theo was biting his lower lip, tears were streaming down his face. Martine looked away. Below, the Atlantic, lapping, rippling, like molten plastic.

"What's that thing back in the belly of the plane?" Martine said. "Some sort of bomb bay?"

"No. It's for dropping supplies to men doing their M.E.'s in inaccessible places—at the South Pole, in forests and jungles."

"Are there controls for the inner doors?"

"Yes. Sure."

"Well, open them, will you? I'll tell you why in a minute."

Theo leaned forward and made some adjustments on the instrument panel.

"I'll be right back," Martine said.

He slipped out of the cockpit and made his way back to the boxlike installation set into the plane's underside. The inside doors were pulled back. He dropped his notebook into the hollow, returned to his seat.

"All right," he said. "You're the world's greatest bombardier—this is your last bombing run! When I give you the signal, open the outer doors. . . . Ready! Set! Go! Om—bomb away!"

Theo squeezed another button. Martine craned his neck: there was the notebook, leaves flapping, dropping end over end through the vapid blue like a lackadaisical tern—it plummeted and was gone.

"There are all sorts of ways to achieve the oceanic," Martine said. "Helder did it one way, very meltingly. I think I prefer my way. Om! Enough of notebooks. My God, I hope I didn't leave any more of the damned things around."

Theo was silent, his cheeks still wet. Martine felt the tears welling up in his own eyes.

. . . . Maybe the bruise to the infant ego is irreparable: once it's pounded home to the budding "I" that it's not kingpin of the whole cosmic shebang, it's saddled permanently with a sickening sense of an indifferent, even hostile Outside, an overriding and ego-humiliating "It." Myth of the steamroller begins there. Forever after, a yearning for reunion with the Other—as in hypnosis, politics—an aching need to recapture the uterine warmth, the nursery's sense of lush intimate catering surround. Forever after, a sense of alienation, fostered by the machine and machined living, the man-made juggernauts. But for all the lure of the One, the romantic-poetic cry for the oceanic is only a thirst for oblivion: when a grown man yearns for the megalomaniacal grandeur of the nursery, for the delusions of omnipotence of the breast-feeding infant, it can have only one meaning—he wants to truncate himself, whittle down his humanness, die. Call his mirage the ecstasy of sainthood, Brahman, Yoga, Vedanta, Tao, Immob, what you will: it's still the same old wearisome death instinct. And so is the communist yearning for the oblivion of the proletarian herd or the American yearning for the oblivion of the Jonesian herd, and for the same reasons. All ways of evading the alienating sheath of skin by signing the "I's" death warrant. People afraid of standing on their own two feet, of living with the impossible anguished tension of humanness.

"Of course," Martine said. "A grown man simply won't fit into a perambulator. Of course he has to cut off his arms and legs."

. . . . But there *was* a way to pierce one's personal iron

389

curtains—fleetingly, through heartbreakingly tiny, all too self-sealing rents: to love another person, genuinely to feel love, with its full burden of ambiguities and ironies. Slim Hyphen, but the only one.

"I must get back to Ooda. I'll be better to her."

. . . . He saw them clearly, his mother and Irene, bending over the carriage. Distraught, harried, faces etched with pain. Oh, they had their crosses, these women, no doubt about it: a lot of them self-created. But not all. One thing they couldn't be blamed for—they hadn't delimbed and desexed the man lying in the basket. Yet, from the beginning of things, men had acted toward them as though they were attacking the whole male world with scalpels, or wanted to, anyhow. That had certainly been the premise of all his, Martine's, dealings with these two niggling, hopeless women. And what if, in a revolutionary moment, he had reared up on his own two feet, flung aside the whole petulant male myth of amputeeism and threats of amputeeism, and approached these two without fear and therefore without anxious, anticipatory rage? Had, for once, stopped amputating himself in order to blame them for it? Well, if it was suffering they had needed most, they would still have had to get it—but somewhere else. Not from him any more. Between him and them, the air would at least have been cleared. He would probably, in that case, never have looked twice at Irene—there would have been no Bitch in his mother that he needed to reincarnate in his wife—but between him and both these women there might at least have been room for something other than tension. A bit of warmth. Even a certain tenderness. They were human beings too, maimed in human ways. He might even have brought some good things into their lives, and into his own. . . . He was weeping now, thinking of their lined, hopeless faces. So many things he would like to make up to them, so little he could do about it now.

He remembered Ooda's words: "With you it is very low one moment, very high the next." That was something he *could* do something about. There were more plateaus possible than he had allowed for: meandering stretches of placidity, ease. Maybe he could do something to cushion the drops—if he could cut down his need to punish her, and through her, himself. Maybe she would still need her quota of hurts; no doubt she was that normal, that much like himself. But they need not come from him so lavishly: he need not be such a good provider of hurts. Love did not have to be a continuation of politics by other means. For him, that game

had been about played out. He would try. . . . If he
stopped going away from her a bit at a time. Was the best
you could hope for a merger across barricades? Maybe.
But there were barricades and barricades: some stout as
fortress walls, others that could be stormed at an easy
saunter. They could be whittled down, the mergement could
be encouraged. If the worst tonus-making devils in the head
were brought under control a little. . . .

The sun was dazzling, ferocious, all pure unperspectived
light. Smashing through a skylight in his skull, to dispel the
fetid fumes of the temple-cave and illuminate at last its
cocooned secret—the ultimate joke: the cave was empty! No
cackling dug-dragging witches there, tearing the helpless
infant limb from limb, feasting on its mauled dripping
flesh: the cave was empty! Pandora's box meticulously looted
before the grand opening. Except—in the reechy corner
there, over 'where the petulant whine was coming from, in
the basket—a man-baby, pouting. Delimbed: by himself.
Desexed: by himself. Fuming forever about the cannibalistic
hags, mapping humanistic campaigns against the steamroller.
And outside, in the sun, the dancers with their soured smiles
and wilted glidings—nobody guessed. Who is empiric about
myths, who checks up on nightmares? What Jo-Jo clears
his own clogged feedbacks? The temple-cave was empty.
It existed, this Limbo with its foul blood-dripping dankness,
its souring and wilting hermeticism, only in the echo
chamber behind the apprehensive eyeballs, the Hallucinator
under the skull. This was *not* the City of God. It was the
City of the Dog-God not yet turned introspective, no skylight
in the skull. . . .

"Goddamn that sun," Theo said, squinting. "Can't see a
thing."

"I can," Martine said. "Too much."

The sun was in his head, a boil of incandescence. Light
poured from his eyes—into another shadowy cubicle, a
thatched hut. There in the darkness, surrounded by paintings of writhing mountains and mahogany figures with
fanged genitals, on a foam rubber mattress, a man was
making love to a woman. And it was good—but the man did
not know how good it was. For he was sunk in a miasma
of words, between him and the woman there was a smokescreen of words. Generated in his own uneasy head, a
noxious literary fog to pollute the experience. Words about
the act of love which transmuted it from experience into maneuver—words about the passage from Itness to I-ness, from

391

drift to drive, from the done-to to the doing—sick, ego-
pushing words which the man would one day have to eat:
which Martine, seeing now for the first time in his life, in the
most terrible moment of his life, was now eating. For all
the words, and all the feeble images bobbing through them,
were born of an exaggerated sense of otherness and the
menace of otherness: of the need to conquer everything
outside one's own skin, bring the not-I to its knees. And
this belligerence was what poisoned sex with aggression,
turned the caressing hand into a clenched fist—and without
it, yes, without it, it was possible, just barely possible, that
love-making, instead of being deed, performance, act, force,
striving, driving, could be just the opposite—sheer egoless
feeling, abandonment, the one great chance to move *from*
drive *to* drift—the one supreme giving over. Orgasm, somehow, could go beyond triumphant doing: become yielding,
an immersion. If selfness, the Eros without Agape, could be
for the moment eluded—the selfness that makes of the bel-
loved an object, a thing, "a soft merchandise." It was impossible all the way, maybe. The full immobilization of the
basket case, that was death. But it was a thing to want,
to grope toward—all the rest was a game of charades with
this or that Neen, the jockeying of two frantic egos for
position—not sex, not love, but war by other means. The
inescapable tragedy of skin, of boundaries, remained—no
need to make it worse with insipid words, it was enough
to experience directly, wordlessly. . . .

"Lot to do," he went on. "Lots of caves to let a little sun
into. . . . Only way to cut down your tonus a little. Relax. A
little tapioca isn't so bad, really. . . ."

He had meant to say it jokingly, in good humor, but he
was crying unashamedly now, unhyphenatedly. Thinking of
the great coruscating merriment in the sunlight, the laughter
that illumination brings—thinking too that tears are always
the camouflage of the vol-amp, part of the masochist's blind
of self-pity—and weeping furiously all the while.

"My sin," he said, "was that I carried Tom in my head
before I sired him in the flesh." Added, "But also Rambo—
there was Rambo."

Eyes filmed, he turned to Theo once more, saw him as
through the window of a bathysphere. He remembered what
somebody—Malraux—had written long ago: The nineteenth
century faced the question, Is God dead?—the twentieth
century was facing the question, Is man dead?

Was the answer in himself? He had carried death in

himself, in a cave with no skylights. But not only death. Was the answer in Theo? He was half-dead, undoubtedly: legs dead, arms dead, plate the prefrontal lobes, bulging with miracles; and in the eyeballs, tear ducts—he could cry. He was crying now. Could enough light be let into that seething temple-cave—not with a scalpel: that destroyed the cave without illuminating it, leaving everybody as much in the dark as ever—to temper the tears a bit, relax the tense lips into a flickering smile, purge the smile bit by bit of its grave shadows. . . .

"Can't we go faster?"

"We're making pretty good time."

"We've *got* to make it."

Sobbing hilariously, yes and no, Martine leaned forward, trying not to hear the agonized choked sniffling from the seat next to him, knowing that it came from his own seat as well. Peering into the nauseating blue vacuum ahead, into the sun, the glare of the sun, straining with anxious anticipation to catch a glimpse of that cave-ridden ocean-lapped island which, miraculously, or maybe just because maps so rarely catch up with territories, had never been charted on any map by any cartographer.

Part Seven

THE MANDUNJI, MEANWHILE. . . .

chapter twenty-five

ABOVE, IN the raffia trees, animals made a sound like laughing, but down in the clearing it was quiet, gravely quiet, quiet as the grave. To one side of the sputtering fire sat the elders on stools of cane and braided bamboo, Ubu at their head; across from them the villagers, squatting in awed expectancy.

Rambo rose from his cross-legged position and advanced toward the old men. His intelligent dark face was drawn and strained, he walked as though he wished not to but were being shoved from behind. In his hand a small volume, grease-stained.

He stopped a few steps from Ubu, coughed. He opened the book and began to read in a tight quavering voice, stumbling now and then over an unfamiliar word: " 'This village is built on a lie. The lie is that the healthy ones are without aggression. They cut off many of their human qualities, to pretend that they are not men but gods. Gods stuffed with tapioca.' "

Ubu leaned forward, face knitted in a scowl. From somewhere in the rustling raffia trees behind the clustered huts a tarsier made a throaty noise, chortled, chuckled.

" 'But there is a worse lie yet,' " Rambo continued. His voice was a little stronger now; he pointed an index finger at Ubu. " 'Despite all the precautions taken by the normal ones, all their aggression is not stilled. Some comes out even so, in a disguised form. The one great disguised aggression of our normal ones is known by a very polite name—Mandunga. It means, to drive the devils from the skull. But with the devils go the men.' "

Ubu jerked at the word, rose to his feet. He was trembling. But Rambo would not stop, his finger rose and fell.

" 'Mandunga is the aggression of self-crippled men disguised as gods against those who cannot cripple themselves the same way: of the paralyzed against the berserk. It is a punishment, not a help—it calls itself therapy but it is inspired by murderous venom. The venom of the less-than-human, pretending to be more-than-human, for the all-too-human—' "

"Stop!"

Ubu's eyes widened in astonishment: it was the loudest sound he had ever uttered in his life. It took a second before he could calm himself enough to go on: "Young man, you go too far. . . . For months we allowed you and the young ones of the cave to add your figures and make your studies. We of the council did not interfere. Tonight when you asked for a special council meeting, and for permission to address it, we gave you your way too. But you go too far, the elders and your fellow villagers did not come here to listen to you and be insulted. . . . Why do you say these bad things in English? These obscenities? From what bad book do you read these obscenities to us?"

"This bad book," Rambo said proudly, standing very straight, "was written by Dr. Martine, my father. It is a very old notebook, almost empty. Before he left, my father instructed us to study much, to read many books in the cave. On one of the shelves, hidden behind some of these books, we found this volume. The dates are very old, the notes were made only during the first year after he came to the island, then they stop. . . ."

"Martine? Martine?" the old man stuttered. There was dread in his tired troubled eyes. "He would not say such things—he would not say them now. No, not now! Earlier, it is possible—when he first came to the island, he did not understand. . . ."

"The night he left," Rambo said loudly, "he said the same thing to us in the cave. More. He told us that we must not do any more Mandunga, we must only study Mandunga, all the statistics from all the case histories. We have finished the studies now, we have all the statistics. They are here."

From the leaves of the notebook he withdrew a sheet of paper, unfolded it and began to read. Total number of Mandungabas, so-and-so many. Number of recidivists, so-and-so many. Cases in which new symptoms or debilities developed postoperatively, so-and-so many. Percentage of cases which, because no relapses occurred *and* no other symptoms developed, could be considered successful without serious qualification—such-and-such. Rambo broke the figures down relapse by relapse, symptom by symptom, reciting them like a prosecuting attorney, vigorously, with exaggeratedly correct precision; at the end his voice rose and began to tremble.

"These are the figures!" he cried, his finger rigid with indignation. "The picture is—negative, all negative! We are trying to do a job with magic, not logic! We have not learned yet the way of science!"

"Young man," Ubu thundered, shocked at the sound of his own voice, "you must not talk this way! Everything that is sacred—"

"Nothing is sacred if it does not work! Mandunga does not work!"

Ubu drew himself up to his full majestic height, pulled his chieftain's robe, studded with drawings of parakeets, tighter about his frail body. "You young scientists of the cave," he said ironically, "you are very, very good with figures. Do your figures tell you some other way? You have something else to offer instead of the Mandunga of your forefathers?"

"Yes!" Rambo shouted. "*My* forefather has something else to offer." He opened the notebook and began excitedly to read again:

" 'We must recognize that aggression exists in all men. But then we must go further: we must learn, and teach other people, that 99 per cent of all the aggression in this world is not genuine aggression but pseudo-aggression. That those who attack others generally do it only to conceal something about their own innermost natures—that their most secret wish is to attack themselves, that behind the sadist is the masochist: that under the pretense of hurting others is the deepest desire to be hurt, to hurt oneself. This is equally true of the aggression of man against wife and wife against man, of soldier against soldier (especially in modern war), of friend against friend, of the troubled against the normal but also of the normal against the troubled. The study must begin by dragging the secret pseudo part of the aggressiveness out of the cave of the mind and into the full light of analytic day. Then the difference between true and false aggression can be pondered clinically. We might begin with a sort of rule-of-thumb chart. . . .'"

Rambo signaled to the young men sitting behind him, they jumped to their feet and came forward carrying a tripod constructed of canes lashed together. They set the frame down next to Rambo and handed him a long roll of pounded bark; he let the roll drop open and hung it from a notch on the stand.

"Here is the table my father put down in his notebook," he said. "It is in English—I was unable to change it into our language because for many of these things we have no words." He turned to the words he had painstakingly printed on the bark and began to read, falteringly, line by line:

Aggression: True and False

Normal Aggression	Neurotic Aggression (Pseudo-Aggression)
1. Used only in self-defense.	1. Used indiscriminately when an infantile pattern is repeated with an innocent bystander.
2. Object of aggression is a "real" enemy.	2. Object of aggression is a "fantasied" or artificially created enemy.
3. No accompanying unconscious feeling of guilt.	3. Feeling of guilt always present.
4. Dosis: Amount of aggression discharged corresponds to provocation.	4. Dosis: Slightest provocation —greatest aggression.
5. Aggression always used to harm enemy.	5. Pseudo-aggression often used to provoke "masochistic pleasure" expected from enemy's retaliation.
6. Timing: Ability to wait until enemy is vulnerable.	6. Timing: Inability to wait, since pseudo-aggression used as defense mechanism against inner reproach of psychic masochism.
7. Not easily provoked.	7. Easily provoked.
8. Element of infantile game absent; no combination with masochistic-sadistic tendencies; feeling that a necessary though disagreeable job has to be done.	8. Element of infantile game present, combined with masochistic-sadistic excitement, usually repressed.
9. Success expected.	9. Defeat unconsciously expected.

"This is as my father wrote it," Rambo said, his face lit with great pride, "word for word. After there is one more note: 'Learned this table years ago, during my analysis. This is the truth which all Mandungas try to hide. (Did I become a lobotomist instead of a psychoanalyst in order to hide from it?) Sometime I must try to explain all this to my students in the cave—must think about it more myself, much more. If there only were time. We are all so busy with our scalpels, our surgical pseudo-aggressions, there is no time. . . .' After this my father wrote no more."

"Many words," Ubu said, pointing to the table. "No meaning. Long before these words without meaning, our fore-fathers—"

"They *have* meaning!" Rambo shouted. "You do not understand them—I do not either, entirely, many of them I do not know, but I shall study more—they mean much! My father perhaps will not return, but in these words is his heritage to our village. Study them!"

"Perhaps you do not understand these words of your father. There is in them a kind of joke, what he used to call a joke. He says in this table that there are some types of, ah, aggressions which are good and normal and healthy—surely this he meant to be a joke. . . ."

"*You* do not understand!" Rambo said with considerable heat. "He meant that the joke is in those who pretend they are gods and not men—their aggressions are hidden and false, like Mandunga, they cripple themselves and the whole village. That is one joke. Also, to beat up your wife or your mother-in-law, that is no good either, naturally—this is a joke too, because the aggression is a lie. But some aggressions *are* good. Those which are not lies. Those truly for defense. I will show you."

He waved again: several youths came around from the other side of the fire, bearing long narrow boxes of metal. They set their packages down on the ground at Rambo's feet, removed their lids. From the elders, from all the hushed villagers gathered around, a long terrified "oh": inside the cases were various sorts of plastic arms and legs—fire-arms, rotor-arms flame-arms, drill-arms.

"You see?" Rambo shouted. "You were very nice and friendly with the queer-limbs when they were here, but we, we young people of the cave, we were suspicious, as my father was. We spied on them and we saw them bury many of these terrible machines in the jungle. When they were gone we dug them up and studied them."

He picked up a rotor-arm and opened it out until it stretched some twenty feet before him; he pressed some buttons near the shoulder and—the circular saw began to whir. Rambo maneuvered the cutting end until it came into contact with the trunk of a slender raffia sapling which stood near the maize grinder: a quick metallic ringing sound, zip, zing, as of some soprano wind instrument, and the top half of the tree crashed to the ground. The villagers gasped. The next moment Rambo had a fully extended flame-arm in his hands. Again he pressed the controls: a tongue of fire snaked out from its funnel-like mouth, growling like a bassoon, and what remained of the raffia tree was gone in one garish puff.

The villagers sighed, in the intense harsh light thrown off by the flame their faces stood out sweaty and knotted in fright. Rambo snapped the fire off.

"We have practiced much," Rambo said. "We have acquired much skill with these arms that cut and burn. Now we are armed—we have better bolos and poison darts than were ever manufactured secretly by our troubled ones. We have no wish to use these terrible weapons, but we will, if we are forced to. Only to defend ourselves."

"Against what?" Ubu said harshly. "On this peaceful island there is no need to defend."

"There is! Much! It is not by an accident that the queer-limbs left these machines hidden here. It is a bad sign—if they buried such things they mean to return, and for no good. My father was right, there is some evil in these people, we must not trust them. If they come we will not hold out empty hands and say peace to all. We will say peace to all—but in our outstretched hands will be flames and saws, run by atoms. This kind of aggression is good and healthy, according to my father's table which I have studied much. This is normal! It is a new kind of health, dy, dynamic, that comes now to our village. . . ."

"Health!" Ubu's face was twisted in disgust, there was so much tension in his muscles that it hurt. "This is a kind of madness you bring. Health comes only through Mandunga."

"There will be no more Mandunga," Rambo said, his voice quiet. "We have decided on this in the cave."

"*You* have decided? *You*? It is the elders who decide."

"No," Rambo said. "This the elders will not decide—they are not fit to decide, they are not trained in the ways of—of logic and science."

There was a long tense moment in which no one said anything: the old man glowered at the boy in speechless dismay, the boy stared back with a look which was more than juvenile impudence—in it too was some newly found conviction, some granite sturdiness, whose appearance startled even its possessor into silence.

Then Ubu spoke, unsteadily: "You—would stop us?"

Another vibrant pause.

"Yes."

Many of the villagers, the older ones, turned their eyes to the ground—they were embarrased to watch this scene of shame. It was a bad sight, like discovering a man secretly carving a bolo, like watching one man hit another.

"Do not misunderstand," Rambo pleaded. "It is not to be important and humiliate you that I speak this way. We need now a real therapy. We must learn now to be psychiatrists, and use our knowledge to help the sick to know themselves so they will no longer be so sick. Also, to decide what is health—how much sickness a healthy village can allow, what is sickness and what is only being different. This means: the knives of knowledge, not the knives of the butcher. That is why we make up our minds there will be no more Mandunga. If you agree, all will be peaceful, but if you insist on this ceremony which is a lie we shall oppose you. And if you try to do this thing against our wishes, with force, and if we cannot stop you another way, then we shall use these weapons against you too—with great weeping in our hearts. Only if we have to. Only because we cannot come to truth in our village, and learn to live with truth, unless you stop this great lie with the knives. This is not sick aggression. This is the beginning of our health."

There was agitated whispering among the elders. Ubu raised his bony emaciated hand, let it fall to his side again; he sank back weakly into his chair, shaking his head. He pointed to the motor which was attached to the maize grinder.

"So," he said. "Ah, so then. It has come. The bad things from the machines. I told him many times that they thought too much about machines in the cave—it is not good to let machines do everything, it breaks the habits of work and the young have too much time to dream what should not be dreamed. Men should grind their own corn and catch their own fish, it is better so. The machines have destroyed our peaceful village."

"No," Rambo said, "not the machine. My father was aware

400

of this danger too, he wrote some lines about it." Again he flipped the notebook open and read: " 'March 7, 1973. Hopped over to Johannesburg today with Ubu, picked up some motors for the fishing boats in the village. The first step toward mechanization: it's a responsibility, thought about it a lot before I decided to do it against Ubu's wishes. Who was the early analyst—Hanns Sachs?—who wrote that excellent essay about man's fear of mechanization? Point was that man hesitated to mechanize his work processes for many hundreds of years, until the eighteenth century, because of narcissism and because he was afraid of his machine turning into a juggernaut. (Because he was afraid of what he might do—to himself—with reinforced hands and feet?) Until then the machine was a thing of magic—as with the Greeks' *deus ex machina*, the Romans' automatic marionette theater, the holy-water slot machine in Egyptian temples— a worker of playful miracles, a thing to wonder at, a sideshow exhibit, a laughable toy, a creator of merriment. After the First Industrial Revolution, a steamroller. But the robot laborer is not in itself a steamroller: it becomes one only because men need the steamroller so much that they make it into one. Men shrink from the machine only at the expense of full humanness: until they free themselves from the backbreaking drudgery of primitive labor they have no time to carve skylights in the skull, only then can they begin to join history—without supplementary arms and legs, no budding prefrontal lobes, no anxiety, no anticipation. . . . In any case, we must not produce more Ford plants on this island. Nothing is worth *that*. But there are two ways to escape being steamrollered by the machine, granted the will to escape is there. One is to limit mechanization to the absolute minimum. The other: to make the machine laughable, as the Greeks and ancients did, to take the threat out of it. It is not so threatening when I can laugh at it, because the machine can't laugh back. A hierarchy is established: "I" over "It." What's needed is a new mythology in which the machine, until now a bugaboo, becomes a buffoon. Not impossible to arrange. For there is something hilariously, outrageously funny about the machine. It's a perfect man. . . ."

Rambo stopped. A remarkable change had come over him in the course of the council meeting: he had begun with much stammering, his voice small and tight with immaturity; toward the end he had lost his trepidation, had shouted— too loudly, at times—his shyness yielding bit by bit to a forcefulness which lent new depth to his voice and incipient

401

dignity to his intent adolescent features. Toward the end his finger, rigid with newly acquired pedagogic thrust, had tilted with quite impressive authority—almost charismatic and yet a little shy—at the circle of elders.

But now he seemed to hestiate once more; his voice grew soft and unsure again, the forefinger drooped in a curl of diffidence, a puzzled look came over his bronzed face. He stooped and picked up the flame-arm he had demonstrated.

"I do not know what these words mean," he said quite without bombast, humble now. "My father saw there was danger in the machine—he also saw a way to lessen this danger. Laugh at the machine, he said. I do not understand about the laughter."

He held the flame-arm up—absurd object, limb of transparent plastic with things that lit up inside like fireflies, shaped like a human arm from shoulder down through elbow and almost to wrist, but then continuing much farther than a human arm does, out far beyond the hand, to flare up at its end into a mouth which belched fire for fifty feet because things nobody had ever seen, rumors called atoms, were breaking up somewhere inside. He looked at this arm that was not an arm, this machine shaped like an arm and also like a mouth, this fire-arm, and there was bewilderment on his solemn face. His lips curled at the corners—he was trying to smile, experimenting with a smile, but there was a tremendous gravity holding the smile back. He stood there gravely smiling, more grave than smiling but trying very hard, and he said, his voice very solemn, "Perhaps the machine is very funny. There must be some joke in the machine that we do not understand. I do not know. We must study more—the jokes too. Especially the jokes. History—"

His lips twitched, searching for the joke: shy rehearsal of a smile. From a branch over the thatched roof of Dr. Martine's hut a tarsier chattered, it sounded like a chuckle.

Beyond the fire, on the outermost ring of the villagers, Ooda sat with her hands folded on her belly. She listened to Rambo's voice. In one hand she clutched a wrinkled piece of paper, as she listened she pressed her belly with her fingers. The sound of Rambo's voice as he talked about history, always about history, hypnotized her: it had started as a child's shaky voice, suddenly it sounded exactly like his father's only without the laughing—Martine without the laughing.

Where was Martine now? Into what ears talking his talk about history and cerebrotone and jealousy and love and orgasm? She rubbed a finger over the piece of paper. She did not have to unfold it to see the words, she knew them by heart; every day since she had found the paper on his desk, right after he left, she had studied the words, the words he had written with his own hand, trying to find some answer in them to a question she did not know how to put.

She knew the words by heart now: "Guess I'll never be entirely without ambivalence in my feelings toward Ooda: there'll always be a bit of a cuff in each caress, the genitals are never altogether without fangs. But she loves me, at bottom it's good. She's warm, she gives—too often I forget that. With enough to build on, with that much, a man's gratitude might in the long run outweigh his savage resentment of his woman simply because she is a woman and therefore the mythic denying mother and therefore to be scorned and mistreated—to conceal the fact that secretly what he really wants is to be scorned and mistreated by her, to bolster his myth. (Haven't thought in those terms for a long time: well over twenty years.) I haven't been good enough to Ooda, been too much by myself. If I get back I must make things better for her. I must get back to her, because then. . . ."

That was all. She knew all the words, down to the last "because then." She did not know what they meant. She knew only one thing: he wanted to get back to her. No matter what thing had made him go away, he wanted to get back—to her. This was enough. It meant, to use the word from his peculiar language, that he "loved" her. From the time she had found the piece of paper and read the words and known, even without understanding all the words, that he "loved" her, that with her he was made "happy," used himself up, was not "bored," wanted to come back to her— from that time she had not smoked one cigarette of ganja. It was his wish. She was already too—somatotone, he had said. Then she would be less somatotone, try to be. If he wanted to come back, she wanted to be the way he liked. He had to come back. She wanted to lie down again with him. She would lie down with no other man, the thought sickened her.

She listened to Rambo's voice as it gathered strength, Martine's voice. She pressed her belly, ran her fingers over the beginning bulge. When had he left? In May, the time he called May. Five months ago. When would the child be born? Four months more—what he called February. If he did not come back, some part of him was in her. Would it be a son?

In seventeen years the son would look like Rambo, with the growing Martine voice. What would the village be like in seventeen years? in forty-five years he would look like Martine. Very cerebrotone, like Martine.

What would the village be like in forty-five years? Now with history working in it? Whose voices would ring out at the council meetings around the fire? What would they say?

She tightened her hold on the paper, fingering the scrap of the past that ended in mid-sentence, rubbed the bulge of the future in her belly.

The sun was sinking now, a bowl of blood: it looked like the cup of a Mandungaba's skull, brimming with blood. Ubu still felt cold, he pulled his bark robe tighter around him. All night long, and all the following day, he had sat in the clearing on the mountain top, at the center of the doomed Mandunga Circle, the Circle that had become a noose, too upset by the council meeting to sleep. Here he had first met Martine, eighteen years ago: Martine had dropped from the sun directly into the cave, like a bolt of light. Now there was nothing but a vacuum stretching before him. Beyond the carpet of raffia leaves, beyond the saw-tooth cliffs, a cobalt vacuum with no hope in it; empty, and blue—as a baboon's ass.

He was tired, there was a pain in his chest. He should not have climbed the mountain, of course—without much care, prognosis unfavorable. But why take care? Everything he knew and believed in was going now, the machines were destroying the village, the cave was destroying the village, the village was toppling like Johannesburg, there was nothing left to live for. Martine had dropped into the cave like a bolt from the sun, and from the cave had come all the bad things—machines, science, logic, statistics, books, dreams, jokes; now psychiatry. And dy, dynamism. These things were good, Martine said. They meant that the Mandunji were joining history. But this joining history was not good: it made a man feel uncomfortable, people stopped eating tapioca and began to smoke ganja. When you joined this history each day was unlike the other days and there was no more soothing sameness—you did not know what to expect. Soon he would die, he could feel the prognosis in his chest. What would come after him? Only trouble. Dizziness. Shouting. People were beginning to shout: last night he too

404

had shouted. He wished Martine had not gone away. Martine was good in time of trouble.

The old man scrubbed his thatch of bristly white hair, searching for an itch that eluded fingers, bent down with a sigh and rubbed his aching feet through the cricket sneakers which had once belonged to the British naval attaché at Johannesburg. He listened to the hypertense sounds of the jungle, scowling. With envy he looked down at the untonused old ocean: good to be like the ocean, placid as tapioca. He wished he had some tapioca now.

Then he gave a start: over to the west there, where the sun was collapsing in the smear of flame-tinged blue emptiness above the horizon, over in the direction of Mauritius and Réunion and Madagascar and all the toppled African cities, coming from the lands of cummerbunds and electroencephalographs, the source of history—something moving.

He stood up, shielding his terrified-hopeful old eyes with a bony tremorous hand. A dark speck there, in the sky. Moving east, southeast. Not a bird: it glinted in the sun, this bird had aluminum feathers. He was sure it was moving this way, as eighteen years ago Martine's metal bird had moved—heading unerringly from the sun like a poison dart from a blowgun, straight for the island that had never been charted on any map by any cartographer.

"May war always stay on other side of river," the old man whispered in English, without conviction. Immediately he corrected himself: "May *the* war always stay on *the* other side of *the* river."

What prognoses this day?

THE END

The activity of these people interested me only as an illustration of the law of predetermination which in my opinion guides history, and of that psychological law which compels a man who commits actions under the greatest compulsion, to supply in his imagination a whole series of retrospective reflections to prove his freedom to himself.

—TOLSTOY

Author's Notes and Warnings

A word about Mandunga. Over the centuries men have hit upon all sorts of ingenious ways to disfigure, or at least discomfort, themselves: bound their feet, stretched their lips into saucers, pierced their nostrils and cheeks and ears, filed their teeth, used swathings to taper their skulls into pyramids, circumcised themselves, castrated themselves to become choirboys or harem eunuchs, cut off fingers and toes and tore out hair in rituals of grief, branded and tattooed their hides, crushed their abdomens with corsets, gormandized themselves senile, grown gaunt and "furry as a hedgehog" crouching on flagpoles, poisoned themselves with nicotine and alcohol and other drugs, found a sartorial use for hairshirts and even sackcloth and ashes; the Amazons, determined to get into the self-lacerating act (equal rights forever!), lopped off their right breasts to make room for the bow. An endless fitful hacking away at the body. You don't have to dig into the military record to prove that man, whatever else he may be, is certainly the self-maiming animal. In a sense, a voluntary amp.

Lobotomy is presented in this story as yet another technique for destructive self-tinkering. (Not true unless it's voluntary? But it often *is* voluntary. "The Operation of Last Resort," in the *Saturday Evening Post* for October 20, 1951, gruesomely details how one man solicited such surgery. And the *New York Herald Tribune* for January 16, 1952, tells the story of Frank di Cicco, embezzler and forger, who, while serving time in an Ohio penitentiary, arranged to have a lobotomy "in an effort to rid himself of criminal traits.") I had thought, however, that the primitive version of lobotomy here called "Mandunga" was only a convenient storyteller's fiction. No such thing: in these literally hair-raising fields the imagination is reality's straggler. In April of 1951 a Peruvian surgeon named Dr. Francisco Grana announced before the Italian chapter of the International College of Surgeons (*New York Times*, April 30, 1951) that "he had examined 200 [American Indian] skulls in tombs and ruins, and found evidence of excellent brain surgery. The death rate from Indian surgery was about 30 per cent of all brain operations, the same as the present rate, he declared." One skull which Dr. Grana placed on display, from the Fourth Century, A.D., had two perfect surgical perforations.

This book is a grab bag of ideas that were more or less around at the mid-century mark. I would like here to list those writings from which I borrowed ideological materials with a free hand: often mauling them badly in the process: sometimes unintentionally.

My debt to Norbert Wiener throughout is obvious. The concept of "charisma" is developed in the sociological works of Max Weber. The Mandunji tribe is patterned in part after the mild-tempered American Zuñi Indians, as described by Ruth Benedict in her *Patterns of Culture;* and, of course, her terminology of the "Apollonian" as against the "Dionysian" is straight out of Nietzsche's *The Birth of Tragedy from the Spirit of Music* (the only book I know which says something about bebop).

The writings consulted on neuro-surgery are too numerous to itemize; I should mention, though, that the fine quotation on page 48, from R. W. Gerard, is reproduced by Dr. Mary A. B. Brazier in her paper, "Neural Nets and the Integration of Behaviour," in *Perspectives in Neuropsychiatry.* The novelistic possibilities of a non-Aristotelian society were suggested to me by a clever work of science fiction, A. A. van Vogt's *The World of $\overline{A}$.*

A sickly shadow is cast over many of these pages by the first portion of Dostoevsky's *Notes from Underground,* that appalling anti-rationalist fulmination which has been called the great pathological document of the nineteenth century. But the sickness of this outrageous work goes beyond morbidity; Thomas Mann considers it "holy disease." Of this section of *Notes from Underground* Mann has written (in his introduction to *The Short Novels of Dostoevsky*):

> Granted. . . . that it is hazardous talk in the strongest sense of the word, dangerously likely to confuse naïve minds, because it stresses skepticism against faith, and because it heretically attacks civilization and democracy and the humanitarians and the meliorists who believe that man strives for happiness and advancement while he is actually thirsting just as much for suffering, the only source of knowledge, that he really does not want the crystal palace and the anthill of social consumma-

tion, and that he will never renounce his predilection for destruction and chaos. All that sounds like reactionary wickedness and may worry well-meaning minds who believe that the most important thing today is the bridging of the chasm that yawns between intellectual realization and scandalously retarded social and economic reality. It *is* the most important thing—and yet those heresies are the truth: the dark side of truth, away from the sun, which no one dares to neglect who is interested in the truth, the whole truth, truth about man. The tortured paradoxes which Dostoevsky's 'hero' hurls at his positivistic adversaries, antihuman as they sound, are spoken in the name of and out of love for humanity: on behalf of a new, deeper, and unrhetorical humanity that has passed through all the hells of suffering and of understanding.

That is the only justification I can think of for Martine's sickly, tortured paradoxes à la Dostoevsky. But, to be sure, he is damned rhetorical about them—which may be the special pathology of the *twentieth* century.

This book could hardly have been written, obviously, without the body of psychoanalytic literature now generally available. I have leaned especially heavily on Freud; for example, on his discussion of the "oceanic" in *Civilization and Its Discontents* and of the struggle between the forces of Eros and Thanatos in *Beyond the Pleasure Principle*. Indeed, this novel might be taken as the result of a too literal reading of Freud's remarks, in the first-mentioned volume, about man and his machines: "Man has become a god by means of artificial limbs, so to speak, quite magnificent when equipped with all his accessory organs; but they do not grow on him and they still give him trouble at times. However, he is entitled to console himself with the thought that this evolution will not come to an end in A.D. 1930. Future ages will produce further great advances in this realm of culture. . . ."

The idea of the "It" comes from Georg Groddeck's *The Book of the It* and *The Unknown Self*. On the self-damaging tendency I found some useful speculation in Theodor Reik's *Masochism in Modern Man;* but here, as in so many other connections, far and away my greatest debt is to Dr. Edmund Bergler's jolting analysis of aggression and pseudo-aggression in his *The Battle of the Conscience, The Basic Neurosis: Oral Regression and Psychic Masochism,* and *Neurotic Counterfeit-Sex.* Starting from Freudian premises,

411

but with enough openness of mind to expand or revise them as new clinical data appeared, Dr. Bergler has, in his many books and technical papers, made an immensely valuable contribution to psychiatry by developing the view that the "basic neurosis" is "psychic masochism," which he traces to the drives and thwartings of the oral phase; and his analysis sheds much new light on man as an "injustice-collecting" animal. For purposes of this book I have assumed that, by the mid-sixties, analytic thought has pretty much come around to the ideas and emphases worked out by Dr. Bergler. The table entitled "Aggression: True and False" (page 424) is from *The Battle of the Conscience,* and is reproduced here with the kind permission of the author.

The sketches on pages 294 and 299 were done by Fred Segal, the one on page 292 by Nanno DeGroot; for the expert draftsmanship on page 292 the author himself is responsible. The doodles on pages 291 and 300 are from *Tristram Shandy.*

Limbo makes it sufficiently clear, I think, that many of the things it satirizes are, in the opinion of its author, to be found in even more obnoxious abundance in Soviet culture than in American; but those who specialize in the fine fabulist's art of quoting-out-of-context overlook such details. I want, therefore, to make this point:

After writing a book that deals pretty harshly with my own country I found no difficulty whatever in getting it published—exactly as I wrote it. The book is now in circulation, and so am I; nothing worse has come my way than a royalty (*not* loyalty) check. What would happen to a novelist anywhere behind the Iron Curtain who conceived such a book about his own world and offered it for sale, or was discovered scribbling it simply for his own amusement on the backs of menus? He would, it hardly needs saying, promptly find himself shorter by a career and a head.

Anybody who "paints a picture" of some coming year is kidding—he's only fancying up something in the present or past, not blueprinting the future. All such writing is essentially satiric (today-centered), not utopic (tomorrow-centered). This book, then, is a rather bilious rib on 1950— on what 1950 might have been like if it had been allowed to fulfill itself, if it had gone on being 1950, only more and more so, for four more decades. But no year ever fulfills itself: the cowpath of History is littered with the corpses of years, their silly throats slit from ear to ear by the improbable.

I am writing about the overtone and undertow of *now*—in the guise of 1990 because it would take decades for a year like 1950 to be milked of its implications. What 1990 will really look like I haven't the slightest idea. Nobody can train his mind to think effectively, without vertigo, in terms of accelerations and accelerated accelerations—and nobody can foretell Clio's pratfalls. On the spurious map of the future presented herein, on the far side of the pinpoint of now, I have to inscribe, as did the medieval cartographers over all the the terrifying areas outside their ken: HERE LIVE LIONS. They could, of course, be unicorns, or hippographs, or even giraffes. I don't even know if there's going to *be* a 1990. Neither does ENIAC—I keep telling myself.

Bernard Wolfe (1915–1985) was born in New Haven, Connecticut. He worked as a military correspondent for a number of science magazines during the Second World War, and began to write fiction in 1946. He became best known for his 1952 SF novel *Limbo*.

BEYOND
SPACE AND TIME

ESSENTIAL
CONTEMPORARY
CLASSICS

ABOUT GOLLANCZ

Gollancz is the oldest SF publishing imprint in the world. Since being founded in 1927 Gollancz has continued to publish a focused selection of bestselling and award-winning authors. The front-list includes **Ben Aaronovitch**, **Joe Abercrombie**, **Charlaine Harris**, **Joanne Harris**, **Joe Hill**, **Alastair Reynolds**, **Patrick Rothfus**s, **Nalini Singh** and **Brandon Sanderson**.

As one of the largest Science Fiction and Fantasy imprints in the UK it is no surprise we have one of the most extensive backlists in the world. Find high quality SF on Gateway written by such authors as **Philip K. Dick**, **Ursula Le Guin**, **Connie Willis**, **Sir Arthur C. Clarke**, **Pat Cadigan**, **Michael Moorcock** and **George R.R. Martin**.

We also have a strand of publishing in translation, which includes French, Polish and Russian authors. Gollancz is home to more award-winning authors than any other imprint, with names including **Aliette de Bodard**, **M. John Harrison**, **Paul McAuley**, **Sarah Pinborough**, **Pierre Pevel**, **Justina Robson** and many more.

The SF Gateway
More than 3,000 classic, rare and previously out-of-print SF novels at your fingertips.
www.sfgateway.com

The Gollancz Blog
Bringing you news from our worlds to yours. Stories, interviews, articles and exclusive extracts just for you!
www.gollancz.co.uk

GOLLANCZ
LONDON